ANIMALIA

Jean-Baptiste Del Amo, born in 1981, is one of France's most exciting and ambitious young writers. *Animalia*, his fourth novel, is his first to appear in English.

Frank Wynne is a literary translator. He has translated works by Francophone authors including Michel Houellebecq, Patrick Modiano, Pierre Lemaitre, Ahmadou Kourouma and Virginie Despentes. Having spent almost a decade living in Latin America he began translating from Spanish in 2010, with authors including Tómas Eloy Martínez, Javier Cercas and Almudena Grandes. His work has earned various awards, including the IMPAC Prize (2002), the Independent Foreign Fiction Prize (2005), the Scott Moncrieff Prize (2008, 2016) and the Premio Valle Inclán (2012, 2014).

'*Animalia* is a book about sex and violence, but it has unusual sobriety, and a story with a deep pull. The way it senses the natural world, in seed, vein, hair, grain, pore, bud, fluid, is like nothing I've read.'
— Daisy Hildyard, author of *The Second Body*

'Jean-Baptiste Del Amo's talent is impressive, his writing bountiful and explicit, sinuous and sharp, sensual and surgical.'
— Bernard Pivot, *Le Journal du Dimanche*

'Reminiscent of *The Sound and the Fury* by Faulker.'
— Patrick Grainville, *Le Figaro*

'Brutal, violent, raw, harrowing. Here, the smell of manure, blood, piss and viscera permeates every chapter; madness, sex, alcohol and death ooze out of every page.
— Thierry Gandillat, *Les Echos*

'A tour de force.'
— Eric Naulleau, *Le Point*

'An epic book on family and the savagery of humanity. An astonishing novel.'
— Baptiste Liger, *L'Express*

'Radical and brutal to the point of unease.'
— Michel Abescat, *Télérama*

Fitzcarraldo Editions

ANIMALIA

JEAN-BAPTISTE DEL AMO

Translated by

FRANK WYNNE

For Sébastien,
For my parents and my sister.

CONTENTS

I. THIS FILTHY EARTH (1898-1914) 11

II. POST-TENEBRAS LUX (1914–1917) 109

III. THE HERD (1981) 209

IV. THE COLLAPSE (1981) 305

From the first evening in spring to the last vigils of autumn, he sits on the little worm-eaten hobnailed bench, his body hunched, beneath the window set into the stone wall that frames a theatre of shadows. Inside, a spluttering oil lamp on the oak table and the fire in the hearth project the bustling shadow of his wife onto walls mottled with saltpetre, shooting it up towards the rafters or breaking it on a corner, and this hesitant, yellow light swells the room then pierces the darkness of the farmyard, leaving the father motionless, silhouetted against a semblance of sunlight. Regardless of the season, he waits for night here, on the wooden bench where he saw his father sit before him, its moss-covered legs buckled by the years now beginning to give way. When he sits on this bench, his knees come a quarter-way up his belly and he has trouble getting to his feet, yet he has never considered replacing it, not if there were nothing left but a plank lying on the ground. He believes that things should remain as he has always known them for as long as possible, as others before him believed they should be, or as custom and wear has made them.

Coming home from the fields, he leans against the door frame and removes his boots, carefully scraping the mud off the soles, then stops on the threshold and inhales the damp air, the breath of the animals, the unpleasant smells of the ragout and the soup that mist the windows, just as he stood as a child, waiting for his mother to beckon him to the table, or for his father to come and hurry him along with a dig in the shoulder. At the nape of his neck, his long, lean body curves and takes a curious angle. A neck so bronzed that even in winter it does not pale, but looks as though it is covered by grimy, cracked leather and seems broken. The first vertebra protrudes from

12

between the shoulder blades like a bony cyst. He takes off his shapeless hat, revealing a pate already bald and freckled by the sun, holds it in his hands for a moment, perhaps trying to remember what he should do next, perhaps waiting for a command from that same mother, long since dead, swallowed and consumed by the earth. Faced with the wife's determined silence, he finally decides to step inside, trailing his own stench and the stench of the animals as far as the box-bed, and pulls the door open. Sitting on the edge of the mattress, or leaning against the carved wood, he unbuttons his rancid shirt between fits of coughing. At day's end, what he cannot bear is not the weight of a body which disease has painstakingly stripped of fat and muscle, but his own verticality; at any moment it looks as though he might collapse, might fall like a leaf, fluttering in the musty air of the room, right to left, left to right, before settling on the floor or sliding under the bed.

On the fire, in a cast-iron cauldron, the water has finally begun to boil and the genetrix hands Éléonore the pitcher of cold water. The child takes slow steps, fearful of tilting the jug which, despite her intense concentration on her hands and forearms, splashes, soaks the rolled-up sleeves of her blouse, as she ceremoniously advances towards the father. She feels a shiver run down her spine beneath the reproachful gaze of the genetrix who is following close on her heels, threatening to spill the basin of boiling water over her if she does not hurry. Framed in the half-light like a great brig, elbows on his knees, hands hanging limply before him, the father is lost in contemplation of the knotted wood of the wardrobe, or the taper burning on the washstand whose flames struggle against the shadows. The oval of the mirror nailed to the wall offers a distorted, barely visible

13

reflection of the room. Two cows, chewing the cud, poke their heads through an opening cut into the cob wall at waist-height. The heat from their stationary bodies and their excreta warm the people. The little scenes played out in the glow of the hearth are reflected in their bluish pupils. At the sight of the wife and the child, the father seems to return from some vague daydream to this puny, deep-veined body. Despite himself, he summons the strength to move, stretches his pale back, straightens the torso where grey hairs sprout like rye grass in the furrows of ribs and collarbones. His belly is gaunt, yellow in the candlelight. He extends the arms with their calloused elbows and sometimes gives a faint smile.

The genetrix pours hot water into the bowl set on the washstand. She takes the pitcher from Éléonore and sets it on the shelf before returning to her kitchen without so much as looking at the father, keen to avoid the sight of this man, bare-chested and raw-boned as the Christ nailed to the wall at the foot of the bed. From high on the cross, He watches over her as she sleeps and appears to her in her late, drowsy prayers, the crucified, funereal effigy of the father sleeping next to her, outlined by a glimmer of moonlight or the guttering stub of a candle whose glow slips through a chink in the door of the box-bed, the man she carefully keeps at arm's length, since she cannot bear his sweat, his sharp bones, his ragged breathing. But at times she thinks that, in turning away from this man who married her and made her pregnant, she is betraying her faith and turning away from the Son, and from God Himself. At such times, moved by guilt, she turns to this man, the husband, with a half-look, a faint, grudging gesture of compassion, and gets up to empty the basin of blood-mottled gobs of spittle he hawks up during the night, prepares a poultice of

14

beyond the ridges of the fingers and their bony knuckles, the grubby fingernails. He says grace in a voice made deeper by his cough and finally they eat, with no sound but their mastication, the grating of cutlery against the bottom of their plates and the buzzing of the flies they no longer shoo from the corners of their lips, the genetrix swallowing hard to choke down the stone lodged against her glottis, the irritation caused by the slavering grunts and grinding of molars that escape the husband's lips.

Of all bodily functions, ingestion is the one the genetrix truly abhors. And yet this woman has no qualms about hiking up her skirt and petticoats and spreading her legs to relieve herself wherever she might find herself – in the middle of a field, over the gutter in a village street, even the dungheap that dominates the farmyard, her urine streaming along the ground, mingling with that of the animals – or, when the call of nature is different, scarcely ducks behind a bush to hunker down and defecate. She consumes only meagre rations, niggardly mouthfuls that she swallows reluctantly, with a pout of disgust or immediate satiation. She finds the appetite of others more abhorrent still. She chastises the child and the man who have learned to eat with their heads bowed, and whenever the father piteously pleads for another glass of wine she reminds him – glancing warily at the girl – how Noah when in drink revealed his nakedness before his sons, or how Lot committed incest. She practises self-imposed fasts that last for days, for weeks, allowing herself only a few sips of water when racked with thirst. In summer, she vows to economize and eat only blackberries or fruits from the orchard. When she finds a worm buried in the heart of a plum, an apple, she looks at it, shows it, then eats it. She finds in it the taste of sacrifice. She has shrivelled until she is no more than a sheath of bloodless skin stretched taut over knotty muscles and jagged bones. Only during the Eucharist, at Sunday mass, when she receives communion at the altar rail, does Éléonore see the genetrix take pleasure in eating. She rapturously sucks the Body of Christ, then walks back to her pew with a haughty air, greedily eyeing the pyx in which Father Antoine jealously guards the consecrated hosts. As she leaves the church, she pauses on the square, imperious, while people around her chatter, as though she needs to rouse herself from a daydream in which the communion, received by all but only truly by her, conferred on her a singular importance, marking her out from the throng of villagers. With her tongue, she detaches the last crumbs of unleavened bread from the roof of her mouth, then sets off along the path into the hills without exchanging a word with anyone, dragging the girl by the arm while the father, profiting from the rare hours of freedom she allows, goes off to drink in the company of other men. Once a year, she feels the need to make a pilgrimage to Cahuzac, in Gimoès, where she prays to Our Lady of the Seven Sorrows, *Beata Maria Virgo Perdolens*, whose statue, discovered by a farmer in the middle ages, is said to work miracles, and to which she feels connected by some mystery. But when, in Advent, young men come to her door to sing *l'Aiguillonné*, which promises health and happiness, she is reluctant to open the door, complaining at having to squander a little eau-de-vie or a few eggs in exchange. She alone knows what distinguishes faith from superstition. At market, she sometimes encounters fortune tellers: on such occasions she jerks the child away with such force she might dislocate her shoulder, while over her own shoulder she shoots the soothsayer a look of mingled envy, anger and regret.

Once the meal is over, the father pushes back his chair, gets up with a heavy sigh, pulls on his wool coat again and finally goes to sit on the bench where he fills and lights his clay pipe, which quickly begins to glow, reddening the sharp bridge of his nose and accentuating the dark recesses of his eye sockets. At this point, Éléonore brings him mulled wine spiced with cloves, a glass of eau-de-vie, or Armagnac, then she sits next to him on the little worm-eaten hobnailed bench, breathing in the bitter smell of tobacco that rises into the twilight or into the pitch darkness and mingles with the perfumes of damp clay sodden by the rains or, on torrid evenings, the smell of baked earth and sun-scorched thickets. In the distance, a herd of sheep moves slowly through the gathering dusk in a tintinnabulation of bells. The genetrix remains by her hearth, winding flax thread onto a distaff. Although the father does not speak, he accepts the slight, delicate presence of Éléonore, her arm brushing against his. She strives to share his contemplation, to scrutinize the darkness and the silence of the farmyard, the purple backcloth of the sky, cerulean, beyond the black line of the ridge tiles on the outhouses, the tops of the towering oaks and the chestnut trees, then the muffled sound of the animals, the meagre livestock dozing behind the doors of the henhouse or the byres, the grunting of the pig in the sty and the clucking of the hens. On cool nights in late summer, when the cloudless sky forms a majestic, constellated vault, she shivers and slips her feet under the quivering flank of the dog lying in front of them, presses herself against the father, and sometimes he lifts his arm so that she can bury her head in the hollow of his armpit.

This body is as alien to her as the being it incarnates, this sickly, taciturn father with whom she has not exchanged more than a hundred words since she came into the world, this wretched peasant farmer who is working himself to death or hastening his end, as though eager to be done with it, but only after the harvest, after the sowing, after the labouring, after... The genetrix shrugs and sighs. She says, 'We'll see,' 'God willing,' 'From your lips to God's ears, may He take pity on us.' She is consumed by the fear that he may not be with them indefinitely, for what will she do then, orphaned of mother and father, and with a child to feed? She also talks of the agonies of childbirth and the misfortune of giving birth too late, already old at twenty-eight. And not even a son who, when he reached adolescence, might help the father, this brave, stubborn man who lacked ambition and will leave nothing behind but a patch of hard and stony ground, one of those small family farms that yield little. Time was, the husband's family owned a vineyard, but the plague of phylloxera did not spare their few scant acres and the forbear, the father's father, passed away from one day to the next without a word. Dropped dead beside his ox, which was found grazing in the ditch where it had dragged the cart, while he lay sprawled between the furrows, dried and shrivelled as a withered vine stock. Nothing, or almost nothing, seems to have survived the agricultural crisis and the plummeting wheat prices. Fallow land has increased, young people are leaving the land, the girls to seek positions as wet nurses or maidservants for middle-class families in the town. The boys can parlay the muscular arms made strong through working in the fields for greater reward in the quarries or the building trade. She sometimes says that soon they will be the only people left on this hostile, implacable land, tilling the intractable earth that will one day be the death of them.

Éléonore sits motionless, enveloped in the smell of the father, his breath that stinks of tobacco smoke, the camphor and the tinctures he inhales and sprinkles on the kerchief he slips up his sleeve all day. She feels the hard swelling of his ribs beneath his shirt whenever he inhales deeply, or when he is taken by a coughing fit and hacks gobs of spit onto the floor. The child droops a little, half-dozing. One by one the stone outhouses in the farmyard sink into darkness, then the ground beneath them, and all that remains is the girl, the father, and the invisible dog at their feet in the thick, aqueous darkness that seeps into her nostrils and fills her lungs. They alone, suspended in a hieratic space-time in which the calls of the insects and the raptors seem to come from a distant bygone era, like the glow of the long-dead stars above. Finally, when his clay pipe has gone out, the father draws on his last reserves of strength to lift his own weight and that of Éléonore, whose legs immediately encircle his waist, his arms, his neck, and her chin rests on his shoulder. He lays her on a small bed like a trunk next to that of her parents. He tucks her in with such care that she never remembers coming back into the house and wakes the following morning unsure whether she shared these moments with him.

The genetrix, a lean, cold woman, with a ruddy neck and hands that are ever busy, affords the child scant attention. She is content merely to instruct her, to pass on the skills for those chores that are the preserve of their sex, and the child quickly learns to emulate her in her tasks, to mimic her gestures and her bearing. At five years old, she holds herself stiff and staid as a farmer's wife, feet planted firmly on the ground, clenched fists resting on her narrow hips. She beats the laundry, churns the butter and draws water from the well or the spring without expecting affection or gratitude in return. Before Éléonore was born, the father twice impregnated the genetrix, but her menses are light, irregular, and continued to flow during the months when, in hindsight, she realizes that she was pregnant, though her belly had barely begun to swell. Although scrawny, she had a pot-belly as a child, her organs strained and bloated from parasitic infections contracted through playing in dirt and dungheaps, or eating infected meat, a condition her mother vainly attempted to treat with decoctions of garlic.

One October morning, alone in the sty, tending to the sow about to farrow, the genetrix is felled by a pain and, without even a cry, falls to her knees on the freshly scattered straw whose pale, perfumed dust is still rising in whorls. Her breaking waters drench her undergarments and her thighs. The sow, also in the throes of labour, trots in circles, making high whining sounds, her huge belly jiggling, her teats already swollen with milk, her swollen vulva dilated; and it is here, on her knees, and later on her side, that the genetrix gives birth, like a bitch, like a sow, panting, red-faced, her forehead bathed with sweat. Slipping a hand between her thighs, she feel the viscid mass tearing her apart. She buries her fingers in the fontanelle, rips out the stillborn foetus and flings it far from her. She grips the bluish umbilical cord attached to it and from her belly pulls the placenta which falls to the ground with a spongy sound. She stares at the tiny body covered in vernix caseosa, it looks like a yellowish worm, like the grey and golden larva of a potato beetle ripped from the rich soil and the roots on which it feeds. Daylight filters between loose boards, streaking the sour, dusty air, the bleak half-light that reeks of a knacker's yard, and falls on the lifeless form lying on the straw. The genetrix gets to her feet, split in two, one hand under her skirt touching the swollen lips of her sex. She steps back, horrified, and leaves the sty, careful to latch the door, leaving to the sow the afterbirth and its fruit. For a long time she leans against the wall of the sty, motionless, gasping for breath. Bright blurred shapes float in her field of vision. Then she leaves the farm and takes the road towards Puy-Larroque, limping through a heavy drizzle that washes her face and the skirt stained brown with lochia. Without a glance at anyone, she crosses the village square. Those who see her notice the soiled skirt she is gripping in one fist, the pallid face, the lips pressed so tightly that the mouth is white as an old scar. Her brown hair has escaped her scarf and is plastered to her face and neck. She pushes open the church door and falls to her knees before the crucifix.

She walks back to the farm through the lashing rain, following the ditches, under the stoic gaze of cattle that stand unmoving in the downpour, her clenched fists pulling her cardigan over her flat chest. Head sunk between her shoulders, she drags her muddy clogs along the road, droning an *Ave Maria* to the rhythm of her breath and the sucking of the wooden soles in the soft ground. As she crosses the farmyard, she sees the figures of two men standing at the gate of the sty. She stops, checked by a primitive fear. Her heart, having faltered, is now pounding in her throat. The driving rain streaks a sky of slate; the air seems filled with a million needles. The figures seem to dissolve, to merge with the brown expanse of the sty wall, so that, at first, she cannot tell whether the men are turned towards her or away. Finally she makes out the gesticulating hands, the clouds of vaporous breath, the fitful snatches of raised voices. She

22

risks a step, a movement of the leg, but it is involuntary, or ordered by some unconscious impulse, before racing into the farmhouse, where she quickly undresses, throws her underclothes and skirt onto the fire, where they hiss like a nest of vipers before bursting into flame under the indifferent eyes of the two cows. She sluices herself with dishwater, wipes herself with a rag she slips between her legs, before putting on clean, dry clothes.

She sits on the bench at the table. She stares out the window, at the torrential rain outside, splashing on the muddy farmyard. She sees the figures of the men appear in the frame and recognizes the hobbling gait of Albert Brisard, a local man with a club foot who works as a day-labourer. She does not move as they approach. In her lap, her white knuckles grip a rosary and she intones in Latin:

'...Thou who takest away the sins of the world, have mercy upon us, Thou who takest away the sins of the world, hear my prayer, Thou who art seated at the right hand of the Father, have mercy upon us...'

When they push open the door, she quickly gets to her feet and stands stiffly by the table. A gust of wind sweeps through the farmyard and into the room, bringing with it the drizzle and the smell of the men as they take off their gabardines, catch their breath and mop their faces. The husband says:

'So there you are.'

They stand for a moment in the damp, smoky half-light, then the husband gestures for Brisard to pull up a chair and they sit down at the table. She walks over to the dresser, on which she places the rosary, and takes the bottle of Armagnac and two glasses that she sets before the men and fills to the brim. The neck of the bottle is clinking so loudly against the rim of the glasses that she has to steady her forearm with her other hand.

'Where did you get to?' the husband asks.

'I went into the village,' she says.

'With the gilt there about to farrow?'

'I strawed down the sty, but there was no sign it was coming any time soon.'

'She ate the litter, and there's nothing now can be saved,' he adds.

'Fraid not,' says Brisard, plunging his thick moustache into the brandy.

The men drain their glasses, she pours again, they drink again and then she pours two more glasses, corks the bottle and puts it back in the dresser. She sits off to one side on the wooden flour chest.

'Not even that sow of yours,' Albert Brisard says, his cheeks flushed from a belch. 'You can be sure she'll do it again... She's got the taste for it, as they say... It's in her blood now. If you spare her and mate her again, even if you hobble her so she can't get at the litter, they'll be infected and the sows in the litter will eat their young the same way. It's like a weakness, a vice... I've seen it with my own two eyes. There's nothing to be done but slaughter her.'

He nods and snuffles, wipes his nose with the back of his hand, leaving a streak of snot, and brings the empty glass to his lips, lifting it high, tipping his head back in the hope of savouring a last drop of Armagnac.

He says:

'Fraid so.'

'I wouldn't mind but we feed 'em well, our beasts,' the husband says.

Brisard shrugs.

'Maybe it's to make up for the blood she lost. Or maybe it's the pain as does it... Best to pick up the afterbirth and change the straw when it's soiled. Once as the litter have suckled the sow of her first milk, there's not much to fear.'

Then he glances over his shoulder and gets to his feet:

'Well, the rains seems to have eased off. We'll talk soon.'

The husband nods, gets up in turn and walks Brisard to the doorstep. They watch as he puts on his coat, wrings out his beret, which sprays brown liquid onto the gleaming grey flagstones of the farmyard, puts it on, and walks off after addressing them a curt nod. Surly, the husband pulls on a leather jerkin, a pair of fed boots and heads out to the sty. The genetrix closes the door. She watches the broad back of this man she must think of as her own, his long, slow gait beneath a sky now smudged with black ravelled clouds, then turns away, goes to the bed and lies down, trembling from head to toe, and immediately sinks into sleep.

By evening, the happening feels remote. All that remains is a vague recollection, an impression of the kind left by a dream that flares after waking and is all the more confusing; a nebulous feeling rekindled by some chance detail that contains the dream or the memory of the dream, a thread that snaps when one tries to draw it towards consciousness and, though for a time she recalls a particular physical sensation, a bottomless void, it fades with each passing day until it effaces everything, or almost everything, about this parturition on the floor of the sty. The infanticidal sow is fattened for slaughter and a boar is brought from a neighbouring farm to service the other sow, who farrows down three months, three weeks and three days later. On the advice of Albert Brisard, as a precaution, the newborn piglets are smeared with a bitter concoction of sour apple and juniper. The incident is forgotten.

At the end of every week, after he has smoked his pipe and drunk his glass of eau-de-vie or mulled wine on the little worm-eaten hobnailed bench while watching the day wane behind the mossy rooftops of the farm buildings, on which pairs of woodpigeons doze, the husband goes back to the conjugal bed. In the glow of the lamp, he undresses, slips on a nightshirt, slides under the sheet, closes the door of the box-bed, and tries to embrace the body of the wife, who is lying on her side or on her stomach, feigning sleep or unreceptive oblivion. There is nothing to suggest that she participates in these couplings beyond stoically enduring the clumsy gestures with which he feverishly rumples their nightclothes, grabs her small breasts or encircles her shoulders, fumbles between her legs with scant ceremony and slips in a penis that is long, hard and gnarled as a bone or the beef tendon men dry in the sun to make whips. Eyes closed, mute, she listens to the grotesque creaking of the box-bed, whose walls seem about to split. She is aware of the weight of this body, the contact of this skin, the pungent smell of rancid sweat, of soil and dung, the fierce, repeated intrusions of this excrescence into her, the musty stench as he lifts the sheet and spits in his hand to lubricate the knotty penis, the rancid breath from the mouth as he moans into her ear, rubs his soft moustache against her cheek before burying his face in the bolster with the guttural wail of a gutshot animal dragging itself through the brush, in a final shudder that could be a death spasm, then rolls onto his side. She waits until he is asleep before she gets up and washes, hunkered over a basin of water, her crotch smeared with cold semen, then she kneels down at the foot of the bed, calloused knees pressed into the beaten earth, hands joined high on her forehead, and murmurs a prayer.

Whenever she comes upon two rutting dogs, she rushes at them with a broom, a pitchfork, a cudgel. She furiously beats the male with the handle and the dog, at first unable to detach himself, takes the blows, yelping, while the bitch struggles to break free, sometimes fracturing the penile bone. Then she stands there, panting, foaming at the mouth, and wipes her forehead with the back of her hand. She despises all animals, or almost all, and if, by chance, she seems to soften at the sight of a child, it is only because he is dragging a stunted, muddy, half-dead puppy by a length of string attached to its paw, or tossing a pigeon held captive by the same string into the air. Alphonse, whose spirit she has broken, avoids her like the plague. She has a soft spot for the cows, however, because she milks them, squeezing the teats with dry hands she smears in butter. The end justifies the means, and she attaches little importance to the sexual appetites of animals destined for fattening or breeding. When the gilt, the cow or the filly is brought to be serviced, she assesses the colour, dilation, the swelling of the vulva, stimulates the sire if necessary, retracting the sheath, masturbating the corkscrewed, lanceolate or sigmoid penis and guiding it towards its destination, restrains the balking female and the reluctant sire, then wipes the thick semen coating her hand on the animal's croup, into her skirts or onto a handful of straw. All around, animals fornicate and copulate: the ducks with their coiled penises frantically mount the females with their tortuous vaginas, ganders ejaculate into the spiral folds of geese, the peacock spreads its tail and covers the alarmed peahen with its weight, sperm pearls, drips, oozes, explodes and spurts between hair and feathers, bringing forth cries and clucks of a brief or enviable climax. While a handful of men watch a boar mount a sow, Albert Brisard, who knows his subject, remarks in Gascon:

'The spasms in them bastards can go on for half an hour.'

Then, to himself, in a low voice:

'Half an hour...'

And the men, engrossed in their thoughts, slowly shake their heads, never taking their eyes off the rutting animal.

The year following the incident with the sow, in the crushing heat of a summer night, heavy with the scent of broom and wool in the grease, the wife is wakened by an ominous feeling. She sits on the edge of the bed, lays a hand on her belly, her eyes feverish but unseeing, sounding the strangeness of her flesh, the subterranean river that seems to spring from this alien body and spill onto the mattress, streaming down her calves and dripping onto the floor. She gets up, crosses the room unsteadily, goes into the scullery, closes the door behind her and gives birth in the same basin where, every week, she washes away the opalescent semen of the husband while he snores behind the walls of the box-bed, in the next room. The thing is quick and there is almost no pain, only a single excruciating spasm as though she – her body – were relieving herself of a weight, ridding herself of the mute, motionless encumbrance she now contemplates, gripped by a terror that annihilates all thought, before she drapes a shawl around her shoulders, grabs the basin and crosses the farmyard to the sty, where the pigs are sleeping under the piles of straw and twigs with which they furnish their nests.

The following morning, just as, in the distance, dawn rends the sky with a slash of ultramarine blue that delineates the distant black line of the Pyrenees, she takes the bicycle, rides into the village and crosses the quiet square where tall chestnut trees, their topmost branches invisible, form hulking shadows. She throws wide the doors of the church, which exhales a breath of cold stone, of myrrh and frankincense. She moves pews and prie-dieux, sweeps and, on her knees, scrubs the floor of the nave with black soap. She polishes the confessional, the retable and the woodwork, dusts the candles and the iridescent body of Christ. She rubs the scarlet wound in his right side. When finally she sits down on the church steps, bathed in sweat, day is breaking over the chestnut trees, inscribing the crenelated outline of the leaves. Three Charolaise cows with disproportionate hindquarters, with faltering calves clamped to their udders, are grazing on the square, their flanks beaded with dew, their grinding jaws and the gentle tinkle of cowbells punctuating the chirruping of the sparrows. Their misty breath carries to the genetrix the smell of the cud and the methane they belch and fart at regular intervals into the pale air, and these mingle with the smells of dough and of bread baking in the boulangerie. She gets to her feet, ignoring the cracking of her joints, walks across the square to the lavoir, where she splashes her perspiring face with water from the huge pool. She dries herself on her blouse and, from her cupped hands, drinks the cloudy water as one of the cows listlessly wanders over to slake its thirst, steam rising from its flanks and bony rump. Between its legs, a trembling calf that smells of whey observes the farmwoman with a dull, feverish eye, in whose pupil she contemplates the convex reflection of herself and the square behind, where the remainder of the herd is still calmly grazing.

When the husband falls ill for the first time, she hopes for some reprieve. But like those ephemeral insects whose sole purpose, once they have metamorphosed, is to procreate and lay their eggs in fresh or stagnant waters, the frequency and violence of his desires intensifies. Perhaps he senses the seriousness of his illness and is instinctively trying to pass on the defects of his stock and of his blood. When he impregnates her again, in the spring of the following year, she believes that her self-abnegation and her countless acts of contrition have found higher grace because her menses stop. Her belly swells, though not much: what she is carrying must therefore be a human child and not one of those creatures expelled from her flesh, one of the Devil's runts she can hardly believe were ever real. And yet it is with a certain detachment, with that now familiar sense of alienation, that she watches herself transformed into a gravid, doleful creature, carrying her pregnancy as though it were the weight of the world.

By the time Éléonore is born, the black fields have hardened, it is cold enough to split the stones and the animals wander, lost souls, over the hostile moors in search of tufts of grass frozen by the wintry weather. A fire is burning in the hearth, but the father is waiting outside in the cold, on the little worm-eaten wooden bench, draped in blankets. He keeps a firm distance from the midwives bustling from scullery to bed, from bed to scullery, brewing infusions of cloves and raspberry leaves that scent the rooms, rinsing the bedlinen, pouring hot water into copper basins, raising their voices to encourage the parturient woman to push harder or to bite down on a strip of leather slipped between her teeth. With their expert hands they knead the swollen belly, pushing the flesh with each contraction of the womb. Éléonore is born, blue and silent, with the cord around her neck, and the women cut it with a knife, shake the baby by her feet until they extract a howl, then wash her before laying her on the stomach of the genetrix, who is still as a gallows, watching her newborn reach towards the breast. One of the midwives goes out to the farmyard and speaks to the father, who gravely gets to his feet and stands in the doorway, not daring to cross the threshold. Tiny flecks of frost turn to liquid on his shoulders and are instantly absorbed by the fleecy wool of the blankets. He looks at the wife and the ruddy child.

'It's a girl,' she says.

He nods and replies:

'I'll go feed the animals,' then goes out into the darkness to piss.

The midwives hang the sheets to dry in front of the fire. They rearrange their shawls and their faces, and, one hand clutching the knotted fabric under their chins, they head back to Puy-Larroque. The parturient is left alone with the infant, so puny it can fit in the hollow of one hand, but driven by a form of prescience, balled fists struggling with the breast to extract the colostrum, suddenly eager to exist. For weeks, the baby languishes in her swaddling clothes, now and then managing to shake herself from an anaemic torpor to pose her grey, seemingly sightless eyes on the forbidding face of the genetrix, who vainly tries to slip a brown nipple between the small, pale lips.

They hasten to baptize the baby whose days, they say, are numbered. Made unclean by childbirth, the genetrix refuses to leave the house and makes a point of honour of no longer preparing the soup or drawing water from the well. She simply sits, dazed and sombre, with Éléonore on her lap or in the wickerwork crib next to her while the father stirs a pot-au-feu or cornmeal porridge prepared according to her instructions. When neighbours from the surrounding farms come to visit, she disapproves of the gifts they bring to celebrate the child's birth. Under the eye of the painstakingly polished Christ, swaddled in a crocheted white cotton gown trimmed with lace, Éléonore is presented before God in the presence of the reticent father dressed in his Sunday best. He is contemptuous of religious sentiment and silently disavows the wife's sanctimony. Like sailors, farm folk are superstitious and attend church out of a sense of propriety. But he finds a mysterious beauty in the act of worship, in the gestures repeated since times long forgotten. He stands next to the baptismal font and responds to the exhortations of Father Antoine, the wheezing priest, who blows his nose on his alb and preaches in the Gascon tongue so he will be understood by his flock:

'Do you reject sin?'

'I do reject it.'

'Do you reject the path which leads to evil?'

'I do reject it.'

'Do you renounce Satan, father of sin?'

'I do renounce him.'

'Do you believe in God, the Father almighty, creator of heaven and earth?'

'I do believe.'

The villagers, sitting in rows, squeezed into darned or threadbare suits, and dowdy dresses with pockets bloated by mothballs whose smell overpowers that of the candles and the incense, intone in unison:

32

'This is our faith. This is the faith of the Church. We are proud to profess it, in Christ Jesus our Lord.'

Care of the animals falls to the genetrix, just as, since time immemorial, tilling the land and slaughtering the cattle has fallen to the men. She crosses the farmyard as the flagstones are beginning to blue, the wicker basket in which Éléonore is sleeping hangs from the crook of one elbow, carrying a pail of grain and stale bread in her other hand. The baby emerges from her night to the smell of poultry litter, dust from the hay, the powdery heat wafted by the chickens' wings, as the genetrix sets the warm, perfumed eggs at her feet, in the folds of the blanket, then goes to the sty, padding over the soft ground, one hand hiking up her skirt, toes gripping the broken wooden clogs. In the sty, a sow lying on her side in the straw is peacefully suckling a drift of piglets that scrabbled for one of the bristly teats, a privilege acquired only after an initial battle, and are squealing contentedly, eyes closed. Their greedy snouts spew a white foam. The genetrix watches them for a long moment, then remembers an old wives' tales that is still told around the fireside. She picks up one of the piglets, which wriggles in her hand and lets out shrill squeals, and she lays it in the wicker basket on the blankets warmed by Éléonore's body, where it rummages for a moment and falls asleep. She takes her daughter and lays her on the straw against the belly of the sow and, with two fingers, brings the sow's teat to the mouth of the baby, who immediately starts to suckle greedily. Her hands knead the milk sac, swelling the teat that she is sucking, and the piglets warm her pink, hairless body. The genetrix slips a hand into the wicker basket, grips the neck of the sleeping piglet and twists violently until she hears a sharp crack. As she re-crosses the farmyard, she makes a hole in the dung-heap with the tip of her shoe, pushes the body inside and covers it over.

They rear only one or two pigs, since they can not afford to feed more. The first they keep, the second is reared to be sold. Every year, for the *Marché au Gras*, they take a wooden crate and load the pig they have been carefully force-feeding for several days, and take it to market in a cart. Sitting next to the crate on the slatted trailer, the genetrix feeds boiled potatoes between the planks that serve as bars so that the pig will remain calm and not lose weight by defecating as they ride along the bumpy road. If the animal is of sound constitution and they take good care of it, it can weigh two hundred kilos, sometimes more, and they can make a thousand or even fifteen hundred francs, with which they buy two young porkers from a rubicund pigman who wears a thick cardigan, velvet breeches and a pair of leather boots. The man makes a fortune from pigs bought elsewhere, often in Ariège, that he transports and resells. If it is a bad year and the farm is not producing enough cereals and tubers, they fatten only one pig and pay the pigman in ham the following year. Then they choose one of the piglets the merchant has rubbed with vinegar and red ochre to make them look handsome and gorged with blood. And thus, no sooner has it died than the pig – a vulgar phoenix – is endlessly reborn from its ashes; there are only a few scant days in which the sty is not occupied. In prosperous years, they have a sow and manage to get it serviced. The litter is sold off as soon as they are weaned so they do not have to feed them. The pigman comes and collects them.

Then comes the day of the churching ceremony. The genetrix gets up before dawn and ceremoniously performs her ablutions in the light of a candle. She brushes her hair and pins it at the back of her head. She pours a few drops of oil into her palm and carefully smooths it. She places a white cotton scarf high on her forehead and ties it at the throat. She slips on a blouse and a wool dress, then looks into the mirror at the reflection of her face drawn tight by the scarf. Over the years, the mouth has been reduced to a line of lip, the cheeks have atrophied against the zygomatic bones, the skin has thickened and is covered with translucent down. It looks as though she is wearing the death mask of her poor mother, whose bones lie in the graveyard of a neighbouring village mixed with others' bones that are not hers, with slivers of wood and rotted taffeta. She turns away. From the wooden flour bin, she chooses the largest cob loaf and wraps it in a cloth, then leans over the crib, picks up the babe in swaddling clothes and lays her next to the loaf in the wicker basket. As the genetrix passes the little wooden bridge on the road to Puy-Larroque, Venus is still pulsing, a blade of daylight pierces the sky and carves out the confines of the world. Coypus disappear between clumps of bulrushes and the razor-sharp sedge leaves. The humidity of night, transferred by the grass, darkens her skirt and her heart grows lighter as she moves farther from the farm. In the basket, Éléonore has woken but says nothing; her misty eyes are fixed on the blurred, oblong face seen from below, and the leafy branches that extend beyond in dark veins. When she begins to cry with hunger, the genetrix walks over to the roadside crucifix, whose plinth is covered with silvery lichen. She sets down the wicker basket, unfastens the buttons of her blouse and offers her scrawny breast to

'You came on your own?'

His breath reeks of communion wine and poor sleep. She looks up and nods and the priest says:

'Where is she, t'other one, the woman that was meant to come with you?'

'There's no-one with me,' says the genetrix, painfully getting to her feet.

Father Antoine irritably whistles through his teeth, then, noticing a chubby, pale young woman passing, calls to her:

'Suzanne, come here to me for a minute.'

The girl comes over and mounts the three steps to the porch. She looks at the genetrix, the sleeping baby in the basket and finally the priest.

'Go on in,' says the man of the cloth, 'and bring her out the Holy Water.'

The young woman goes into the church after Father Antoine, who strides down the nave, his alb rustling, then she re-emerges and holds out her cupped hands in which the holy water pools between folds of calloused skin, the lifelines short and deep as crevasses. The genetrix sets the basket on the ground, dips her index and middle fingers into the leathery font, crosses herself twice. Then the young woman opens her hands and the rest of the water drips onto her clogs and the dull flagstones of the porch. She crosses herself in turn, wipes her palms on her skirts and goes into the church. Her forehead gleams and the sanctified water trickles along the curve of her snub nose. Father Antoine is waiting beside the side chapel, a stole embroidered with gold thread draped over his shoulders. A thin, pasty altar boy, stiff as a church candle, is standing next to him. The priest holds out one end of his stole to the genetrix.

'Enter thou into the temple of God, adore the Son of

the Blessed Virgin Mary, who giveth thee fruitfulness of offspring.'

She hurries now and kneels at the foot of the altar, hands clasped at her forehead, and recites the act of thanksgiving, her exhortations mingling with those of the priest, who declaims:

'Lord, have mercy. Christ, have mercy. Lord, have mercy... And lead us not into temptation. But deliver us from evil. O Lord, save Thy handmaiden. O my God who putteth her trust in Thee. Send her help, O Lord, from Thy holy place...'

They pray together, Suzanne mumbling in turn, and he blesses the genetrix, who quivers beneath the holy water he sprinkles on her.

'Pax et benedictio Dei Omnipotentis, Patris et Filii et Spiritus Sancti, descendat super te, et maneat semper. Amen.'

Then he blesses the bread and the genetrix stands up, sorrowful, exalted. She blows out the candle she has been holding. She tears the loaf and gives a piece to the altar boy. Overcome by a wave of gratitude, she reaches out to tousle his hair, but the boy shies away.

With a walnut cane in one hand, and Alphonse following behind, Éléonore leads the two pigs down the dirt track to the grove of pubescent oaks. She sits among the mossy roots or the bare branches of a fallen tree while the pigs gorge themselves on acorns, chestnuts they extract from their burrs and snails. Shimmering blue dung beetles crawl up her wool stockings and jackdaws spread their iridescent wings to keep their balance in the treetops. They give a cry and once again take wing into the steel-grey sky. Éléonore lies on a bed of leaves that smells of rotting vegetation, burst puffballs and worm casts. She finds a moment of respite, far from the farm and the presence of the genetrix. As a light drizzle begins to fall, she remains motionless, staring at the branches from which whirling russet leaves fall. She allows the tiny droplets to bead on her face and the fabric of her dress and imagines disappearing, little by little, covered over by lichen, the insects and the invertebrates that would bore galleries through which she could continue to breathe, to drink and to perceive the world from her mineral stillness. The old pointer keeps watch for her, circling the pigs and keeping them in line with a yap. His halting, arthritic gait stirs up the leaves, from which, as from an ossuary, branches emerge, split or burned by time, and the first January snowdrops. On the coldest days, she feels a numbness in her fingers, in her nose, a stabbing pain in the cartilage of her ears, but she does not allow herself to move and would not go back early for anything in the world. She loves the calm of the oak grove, the feeling of profound solitude, the presence of the pigs, their grunts of satisfaction, the calls and the rustling wings of invisible birds, the outline of the chapel she can just glimpse through the ferns and the trees, a wall covered in thick creepers and fringed with ivy. When the rain is heavy, she walks up the old path now overgrown with brambles, through which she has cut a path. With the animals trotting on ahead, she enters through the gothic portico, the rotting wooden doors, one of which has fallen from its hinges and now lies on the cracked flagstones, where tufts of grass sprout in spring from seeds blown in by the flurries of wind that fill the chancel with drifts of dead leaves in which farandoles of shrews nest. The pigs forage for larvae in the debris where generations of pigeons and raptors have defecated, covering the broken timbers of the ancient pews with guano then taking off, with a coo and a rustle of wings, to perch among the pitted rafters slowly eaten away by weevils that send a shower of sawdust swirling through the light cast by the remaining stained-glass windows, encrusted with dust, with sap and pollen. The ancient chapel smells like an open wound in the earth: the musty odour of a cave, of quartz and clay and silt. Flares of shifting colour glide over the rubble whenever the sun manages to pierce the tangle of branches. From the floor, Éléonore picks up the regurgitated pellets left by barn owls, which she will later soak in warm water so that she can extract the white, delicate bones of rodents, and slips them into the pockets of her dress, then, finally, she heads back to the farm, reluctantly followed by the gorged pigs. On fine days, using a billhook, she cuts roadside nettles for them, thistles and wild spinach in the fallow fields, the stalks and bulbs of onions, dandelions and sorrel, sprigs of sagebrush and the poppy flowers that thin and invigorate the blood of animals. Éléonore carries the foraged plants in the fold of her raised skirt and the genetrix chops them on the kitchen table before cooking them with the slop intended for the pigs.

The first years pass between caring for the animals and days of boredom spent in the classroom of the local school adjoining the town hall, heated by a wood-burning stove, its windows overlooking a dirt playground that turns into a mire with the first rains. When the local distiller sets up his still on the village square, alcohol fumes fill the schoolyard and intoxicate the pupils' playtime. Though barely six years old, the skin on her hands and her feet is grey and scored with deep fissures from which, using a needle in the candlelight, she extracts the small pebbles and blades of grass that sometimes cause her to bleed. Her thumbs are also cracked and just stunned with a sharp blow to the back of the neck, its pulse still beating, and hangs it from a hook on the wall above a bowl of hammered copper. As its dying spasms set the rabbit spinning, the brown eye with its dilated pupil alternately reflects the farmyard, where large puddles of water shimmer, then the lowering autumn sky, and then the face of the genetrix as she busies herself whetting the blade of a knife on the barrel of a rifle before using the point to remove the eyes with a sharp jerk of the wrist so as not to damage the fur, before tossing the little eyeballs into the dust, and the rabbit bleeds out from the cerebral haemorrhage through the empty sockets, the black, clotted blood dripping into the copper bowl with a regular plop-plop-plop, and when she removes the receptacle in which the black pool quivers, the blood continues to drip onto a block of granite as burnished as a sacrificial altar. The genetrix cuts the fur around the hock joints and skins the rabbit with a quick jerk, as though undressing it. She sets the pelts out in the sun to dry, with the tails that bring good luck whose cartilaginous vertebrae glisten between the tufts of hair and are sometimes carried off by the cats, who chew them in some dark corner away from prying human eyes. The genetrix has her own beliefs: whenever she comes across a garden spider, its back marked with the sign of the cross, the blesses herself. She hangs dried pigs' bladders from the kitchen rafters to protect the family from the evil eye. Some she will use as flasks. On stormy days, fearful of the lightning bolts that people say can decimate a clutch of chickens, she slips old horseshoes under the laying hens. During the storms, the chickens take refuge in a cage made of interwoven branches covered with broom, as the lightning bolts freeze the landscape in flashes of white. In the August heat, the animals seek

4 2

out the shade of the trees, lazily shooing swarms of gnats and horseflies. The father has built a small pen attached to the sty. A young piglet is pressed against the cool water trough from which it is drinking. A sow is preparing to farrow down in the shade of a wall. During a trip to find acorns she mated with a wild boar and her litter is born covered with velvety striped hair. When a sow is suckling, Éléonore still takes a secret pleasure in lying in the straw, pressed against her flank and sucking a little of her milk, her forehead pressed against the soft, warm, delicate scented skin of the udder. When they sell the piglets, it is the responsibility of the *langueyeur* – the tongue inspector – to examine them for *taenia solium*, that strange illness that afflicts pigs, though few people could say exactly what it is. Ringed by children and onlookers, under the watchful eye of both breeder and buyer, in a corral teeming with piglets, the inspector picks up each shoat by the hind leg and holds it still in his lap. The animal squeals, struggles, then surrenders. Then the *langueyeur* forces its mouth open with much earnest shouting and swearing. Using pliers, he extracts the needle teeth from the gums, then pulls out the tongue, twists it, looking for the mucus and the white spots that indicate the presence of the parasite. Sometimes he lingers a little, hesitant, exasperated. He scrapes the tongue, applies himself diligently, but always gets up and says:

'No sign of tapeworm.'

At which point the animal, unsullied and restored to life, gambols off to join his siblings. The deal is done.

Around the fire, on winter evenings, when the puddles of mud have frozen in the farmyard, which they have to cross with care, scattering coarse salt in front of them, Éléonore sits next to the gaunt-faced father, who turns the crackling logs with the aid of a wrought-iron poker. He plunges his hand into the embers, grabs one with an abstracted air, bounces it in the palm, then replaces it in the hearth. From the perforated pan, he takes and peels for her the scalding chestnuts, whose wrinkled flesh gives off a subtle aroma. The genetrix prepares inhalations for the father and he disappears under a sheet as the vapour of herbs and roots perfumes the whole room. The doctor comes and sets down on the table the leather bag which exhales a smell of ether; then the father unbuttons his shirt and sits, bent as a reed, tensing his back as the doctor moves the stethoscope over his milky skin, and breathing painfully when asked. A wheezing sound comes from his trachea, as though some parasitic animal were living in his ribcage and breathing in his stead. Then the doctor digs into his bag and takes out a reflex hammer, which he uses to tap the knotty joints, occasionally triggering an involuntary jerk, then slips a tongue-depressor into the father's mouth. Sitting at the table, a scarf around her head, her hair parted in the middle and plastered to her forehead, her hands folded around a rosary as she tells her beads, the genetrix observes the doctor's every gesture and searches for meaning in his murmurs of approbation, his sighs, the glances he directs at the floor or at the hollow stone sink as he listens through the stethoscope. Insistently, she interrogates him, comments, offers answers to questions the doctor has not asked. She says:

'He coughs all night, can't get a wink of sleep, and in the morning too, and his spits, yellow it is, and sometimes green. He's bound to have an infection. He complains about aches, show the doctor where, in his chest and his back, his legs are all swollen, see that?, like varicose veins. Ah, and he's running a fever, night and day...'

44

The father sits motionless, paralyzed, as though each of the genetrix's words is raining on his back, forcing him to bend ever further to ward off the blows. The doctor gets to his feet, puts away his instruments, and the father slips on his shirt, his cardigan and the work trousers he holds up with baling twine. The genetrix takes the bottle of plum brandy from the dresser and pours a single glass.

'He needs a change of air,' the doctor says, draining the glass, 'a trip to the mountains.'

The genetrix and the father sit frozen, silent.

'At the very least, he needs rest,' the doctor adds, setting down the glass and donning a felt hat.

The couple are speechless.

'Try not to exert yourself too much,' he goes on. 'Take on a farmhand.'

When he puts on his coat, the genetrix disappears into the scullery and comes back a moment later and offers the doctor a handful of small change that she can hardly bring herself to let go. No sooner has the door closed than the father once more takes his place in front of the fire and the genetrix watches, fuming, as the doctor's carriage moves off, drawn by a bay gelding, jolting over the potholes and disappearing behind the pigsty.

When people in the village suggest she send for a healer, she becomes indignant and quotes Leviticus:

'Regard not them that have familiar spirits, neither seek after wizards, to be defiled by them.'

She suggests a pilgrimage to Lourdes, but the father refuses, muttering – who would look after the farm and the animals in their absence? Every night, she enjoins Éléonore to pray for his recovery, giving her a detailed litany of the misfortunes, the privations and the sufferings to which his death would condemn them, and the child falls to her knees next to the genetrix at the foot of the cross, imploring God's mercy, then nestles even closer to the father on the little worm-eaten hobnailed bench as nightjars claw the air and swoop on moths.

Éléonore sticks her thumb between the lips, into the warm, acrid saliva, the breath steaming in the chill dawn, and slides the bit into the horse's mouth and the animal bites, its eyes half-closed, lying on its left flank, then she passes the bridle and adjusts the blinkers while the father fits and adjusts the harness by the light of a lantern set on one of the guard stones of the well, whose glow deepens the mare's saltcellars and gilds her neck. Snowflakes fall heavily into this halo of light, landing on the black mane, lingering on the leather, and melting on the blue lips of Éléonore, whose numbed, purple fingers bury themselves for warmth in the animal's winter coat. Their wooden clogs smeared with pine tar crunch across the snow fallen during the night. The pointer frisks through the snow, tracing wide circles around them, and when the father, wrapped in a twill cloak, climbs into the dogcart, whips the mare's hindquarters, and as horse and cart move off down the stony track, with the dog bounding ahead, the little girl races along the ruts left in the snow and the mud by the metal cartwheels, shouting the father's name as the cart fades into the distance, and she finally stops, panting for breath, her throat burning, her hands pressed to her thighs, her angular face upturned, her teeth and her eyes made grey by the night as it pales to a deep blue, restoring to the hills their materiality.

As she retraces her steps, their sinusoidal curves appear, arcs of amplitude, while motionless, insubstantial layers of mist appear in the depths of the valleys. The horizon breaks free of the snow-covered earth, as though the former brusquely gives birth to its converse, shaking off its muddy taint, then swells with an expectation that bows the sky with a purple halo, with a ribbed vault in which the stars still shimmer. Each lungful of icy air she inhales stings her sinuses and her chest. Alphonse bounds from one side to the other of ditches iced over with hoarfrost, slips his leash and races after a hare that disappears in the middle of a field, then trots back and jumps up to lick her snotty face. As she reaches the farmyard, now lit by the pale, grey dawn, Éléonore grasps the dog's collar. Through the frosted windows of the house she can see lamps burning and the shadow of the genetrix moving over the limewashed walls. She leads Alphonse to his kennel and persuades him to lie down amid the straw and the burlap sacks, then, casting worried glances over her shoulder, she climbs the ladder to the hayloft, her clogs slipping on rungs jagged with icy stalactites.

Hanging from the beams of the hayloft, pipistrelles shiver, shrouded in their delicate wings. Tegenaria spiders have woven and rewoven dense funnel webs, frozen by the sediment of time, swollen and made heavy as oriental hangings by dirt, sawdust, the husks of insects and the translucent chitin moulted by distant generations of arachnids. In a corner of the loft, between two piles of hay, a feral cat has produced a late litter. Éléonore is feeding it, unbeknownst to the genetrix, taking bones from Alphonse's bowl or stealing a little buttermilk from the scullery. As the little girl approaches, taking care to avoid the loose and broken boards beneath which the cattle are beginning to wake, to stir, to piss and makes them flout rules without seeming to. Excepting the leftovers they feed to Alphonse, nothing can afford to be wasted that might provide sustenance for their meagre livestock and can thereby be immediately transmuted into meat in a cycle of constant renewal. She is as loath to throw out radish tops or beet greens as she is to think that a ladle of buttermilk has gone to feed stray cats rather than to fatten pigs, she who every morning carries out the chamber pots and empties them onto the manure heap, since nothing is too vile for the nourishing earth. And besides, she thinks as she walks back to the farmhouse, that way Éléonore has of trying to cosy up to the father, and of giving her a wide berth whenever he is around, of perceptibly shifting and favouring the closeness of the farmer, as though anticipating some protection, some respite from him. As she has grown, Éléonore has ceased to seem a stranger to her – she has become accustomed to the existence of the child, even to the idea that they are bound by blood ties – and while she is polishing the pots or scrubbing the flagstones, washing the bedsheets with the other women in the village washhouse or feeding slops to the chickens and plucking them, Éléonore is constantly avoiding her and taking advantage of the slightest inattention, the slightest slackening of her authority, like the young of carnivores, whose instinct prompts them to steal food from their parents and to anticipate their moods and fits of temper so that they can slip away.

And so, those periods when the father is absent – a few days that seem to her like weeks – take place in a climate of mutual defiance, a stilted atmosphere, a habitual silence, broken only by the sound of the wind, the cries of the animals and the remonstrations of the genetrix, who notices Éléonore hovering around the scullery where she churns butter every day, and, as soon as she turns her back, quickly taking a ladle of cream from the churn and disappearing up to the hayloft at the first opportunity. Every evening, she insists that Éléonore read aloud from the Holy Scriptures, because it is important to her that her daughter be pious and literate, and Éléonore applies herself to the task, one finger on the page, following the sentence, stumbling over syllables and words as the genetrix listens to her laboured pronunciation, eyes closed, hands joined, as though her interminable labour added to the mystery of the Book. And yet the genetrix never goes to confession, nor does she send her daughter; the very idea of confiding her most inoffensive thoughts, her most venial sins, to Father Antoine, that discreditable priestling who is not even sober for All Saints' Day, is repellent to her. There is no intermediary between her and God, and she considers herself the best channel between Éléonore's words and the Lord's mercy. So she persuades Éléonore to confess to her, to make her act of contrition, recount all her most shameful thoughts, and the little girl, feeling she must satisfy the genetrix's curiosity if it is to be done with as quickly as possible, babbles childish sins, swearing, covetousness, trivial lies, which delight and scandalize the genetrix, who then compels her to recite:

'Have mercy upon me, O God, according to thy loving kindness: according unto the multitude of thy tender mercies blot out my transgressions. Wash me thoroughly from mine iniquity, and cleanse me from my sin. For I acknowledge my transgressions: and my sin is ever before me. Against thee, thee only, have I sinned, and done this evil in thy sight.'

One snowy morning, taking advantage of the fact that her mother is at her toilette, Éléonore takes a bowl of food to the kittens. She finds them lying stiffly in their nest, the mother a few steps away, next to another bowl that still contains a few balls of poisoned bacon fat. Blood has trickled from her mouth, her nose, her anus, and darkens on the floor. Her teats, still sticky with saliva, are stiff and purple. Éléonore picks the kittens up one by one, slips them under her dress and holds them against her belly for a long time, hoping she might bring them back to life, then she lays them on top of the body of the cat in a burlap sack she ties with a length of string. She climbs down the ladder, walks far away from the farm to the outskirts of the forest and, with her bare hands, digs a hole, throws in the canvas bag, and fills the hole, stopping now and then to blow on her aching, blackened hands. Alphonse appears as she is covering the burial mound with smooth stones and holly branches to serve as a wreath, then he looks up, sniffs the icy air and races down the road that leads to the village.

Éléonore is watching him run off, yapping, when in the distance she sees the mare and the cart appear, and she rubs the palms of her filthy hands on her dress. She raises her arms to wave, then changes her mind. She has just spotted a figure whom she first thought was the father, since he is holding the reins, and a quivering bundle next to him, but as the cart approaches, she realizes that the figure is a stranger and what she took to be a bundle of old rags bumped about by the potholes is the father. As they pass close to her, he does not even seem to notice her and she sees his gaunt, grey face turning slowly in her direction. She stands for a moment without moving before following the cart into the farmyard. The stranger has stepped down and she keeps her distance as the father painfully clambers down in turn, shattered from the journey, accepting the support of the sturdy arm the boy offers him, before the boy unharnesses the mare and leads her to the stable the father signals with a weary gesture. She can see the boy's face now, red with cold, still babyish, the cheeks invaded by patches of downy, red beard, the bulging muscles in his jaw and his forearms as he tows the cart into the shade, the small piercing eyes beneath his eyebrows, brown irises so dark that it is almost impossible to distinguish the green pupils, ringed with pale circles, that contrast with the shock of his filthy hair. When he sees Éléonore, the father gestures for her to come to him and the stranger stares at the child's calloused, muddy hands, impassive. The father lays an icy hand on Éléonore's head in a vague caress.

'This is Marcel, the cousin,' he says. 'He'll be living with us from now on. You'll show him where to find hay and twigs. Tomorrow, I'll go fetch a mattress.'

Behind them, the kitchen door has opened and the genetrix is standing on the threshold, pulling her shawl up over her throat and the lower part of her face. The father walks over and she stands aside to let him in without saying a word, then she scornfully weighs up the young man exhaling plumes of thick breath, and the child next to him hiding her dirty hands behind her back. Marcel follows Éléonore into the kitchen, where the father has taken a seat by the fire. With a jerk of her chin, the genetrix indicates the former scullery, and Marcel, his burlap sack over one shoulder, bows his head to step through the doorway. The room is a square of beaten earth into which the grey day interferes through holes in the knots of wood and gaps in the joists. The floor is littered with rusted scythes, a cartwheel, a few

52

sacks of charcoal and basins of stagnant water. Opposite the fireplace, its hearth an ogre's mouth, a narrow sash window peers out onto the yard. The room smells of rat urine, worm-eaten timber, the slurry that trickles down the wall from the adjoining stable. Marcel looks at the scrawny, grubby child, whose breath as she exhales creates fleecy clouds around her nostrils. He follows her up to the hayloft, carries down armfuls of dry hay, which he scatters to create a thick, compact mattress, then he unties his pack, spreads out the burlap sacking, stands up and looks around the room with a satisfied air. He says:

'Go fetch me some water, I need to hose myself down.'

When Éléonore reappears, carrying a pitcher of hot water, there is a fire crackling in the grate and Marcel has taken off his shirt and his vest. She stops and watches, just as she watches the father wash when he comes in from the fields, but this body is sturdy, the skin, puckered by the cold, hugs ligneous muscles, the knot in the navel is the globe of a small, perfectly round eye beneath a delicately rimmed lid of flesh with a line of red hairs running down the lower abdomen and disappearing beneath the worn leather belt. Freckles cover his back, his neck and his cheeks. He plunges the washcloth into the basin, wrings it out into the hollow of his hand. Streams of water trickle along his forearm and drip onto the floor from his elbow. He vigorously scrubs his face, his torso and his armpits, leaving large red blotches on the back of his neck and his sides, then drops the cloth into the basin of water, which is now grey and soapy. Éléonore steps forward to take the basin and their eyes meet. She blushes, turns away, and rushes out of the room.

Marcel wakes before dawn in the cold room where his breath condenses. He stretches his numbed limbs, then blindly gropes at the foot of the bed for the coarse patched trousers, the vest, the cotton shirt, the thick-knit sweater and pulls them on, his eyes open yet sightless. A shudder runs along his skin. Arms outstretched, barefoot on the icy floor, he walks as far as the fireplace. He stirs the black coals in the hearth, roots through the ashes for a still-glowing ember, blows on it and sets a handful of dried twigs on top. As the flame catches, hesitates, then flares, his face appears, blazing in the flickering light, hollowed by the shifting shadows, and he makes out his hands, grey with ash. In the main room, where Éléonore and her parents are still sleeping, the flyspecked glass shade of the oil lamp casts a dappled yellow light on the walls. Several weeks have passed since he arrived at the farm. As usual, he gulps down a bowl of groat gruel, and a hunk of bread dipped in wine or simply a bowl of reheated coffee. He runs his tongue along the uneven line of his teeth, dislodging coffee grounds from between the gaps, from the rim of his gums, using the tip of his tongue to push the saliva onto the edge of his lips and wiping it away with the back of his hand, leaving a trail of grounds through the thick blond hairs. As he steps through the door, he peers into the darkness but can see nothing. Night rests, unfathomable, coal-black, reducing everything to silence, and for a moment it seems to him that he can make out a breath, the panting of an animal hidden in the darkness; it is his pulse beating in his ear or the flame of the lantern he is holding, the wick hissing softly. He can sense that it is going to snow, there are no stars to be seen, the bracing air bites into his face and at his sinuses when he inhales. He rubs his palms together, then brings his fists up to his face to warm them with his breath.

Alphonse appears and sniffs him, tail whipping his trousers. Marcel catches the smell of the dog's damp coat mingled with that of the night. He follows the dog as he trots ahead, leading him towards the still sleeping animals. He lifts the wooden latch of the stable door and, with his foot, rolls away the stone that keeps it closed. Rats scurry away from the feeding troughs as the halo of light from the lantern Marcel hangs on a nail casts concentric circles on the joists and the laths. The mare is dozing, standing on her left diagonal, neck lowered, mouth slack. Marcel runs a hand over the round, warm muscle of the croup, strokes the flank and feels the veiny skin quiver beneath his palm. Two cows with pearl-grey coats are munching fodder in their stalls; on the wooden bars marked by the ruminants' incisors, a few chickens have found a temporary perch for the night and are wrapped up warmly in their feathers. Marcel takes a deep breath of the smell of the animals that permeates the shed, his arm resting on the mare's croup. He savours this magnetic presence, preferable to that of the creatures of his own species, then goes out into the yard and walks over to the well, now silhouetted in the wispy grey dawn light, this well which men to whom he is linked by obscure ties of blood dug with their bare hands at a precise spot designated by the twitch of the forked hazel twig of a local dowser, digging with pickaxes for sixty days, slicing through labyrinthine galleries fashioned by blind animals and shattering shadows of glittering quartz. As he grabs the bucket of coopered wood and tosses it into the silent maw of the well, which explodes with the sound of water, an image surfaces from some ancestral memory: the head of a pickaxe ripping a lump from the muliebral earth and the wound filling with water, then a human face raised towards the animal's throat and force-feeds it grain. Her dress hiked up over her knees reveals the varicose veins just beneath the skin that seems to twine around her tibias like the serpent around the caduceus. When her legs ache, she compresses them with strips of fabric cut from old bedsheets. When Éléonore complains of toothache, the genetrix takes her to the market to the tooth-puller, who extracts the toothy-peg and leaves the child in tears, her mouth bleeding, feeling the tip of her tongue probing the soft, metallic hole in her gum. At the end of Lent, they go to the village to watch the magnificent bulls, to be sacrificed on the eve of Good Friday, being proudly paraded by the farmers. Life carries on.

By spring, the father no longer goes to sit on the little worm-eaten hobnailed bench. Shut up in the box-bed that he leaves only at mealtimes, spectral and emaciated, he has to support his elbow to lift the trembling soup spoon to his lips. Lumps as hard as stones are caught in his beard. His shirts are spattered with dried food. Every Monday, the doctor comes and listens to his chest in silence under the watchful eye of the genetrix, who has also fallen silent, disbelieving, weary of the list of symptoms, and together they sit at the table while the father offers his scrawny body to be examined, opening the black hole of his mouth, extending his knotted joints, coughing and spluttering when requested. Eventually, the doctor sets his battered leather bag on the table, packs away his instruments as usual, says the same words, gives the same advice, sometimes recommends some variant of the ineffectual treatment, drinks the glass of brandy or *vin de noix* set out for him, pockets the handful of grubby coins, then stops in the doorway and bids the assembled company goodbye, touching the

57

brim of his hat.

'See you Monday, then,' he says.

They do not say a word until the carriage has left the yard and the clatter of hooves has faded, then they all get to their feet and return to their occupations. The genetrix resigns herself: Father Louis, a healer from the neighbouring village, well-known for resetting dislocated limbs, conjuring away burns and treating warts, comes and lays hands on the father's chest at length. He mutters prayers and traces the sign of the cross with his thumb, leaving an imprint on the skin from his long, dirt-black nail. Finally, he turns to the genetrix and gently shakes his head. Since she has heard that a child can be cured of fever by applying an eviscerated dove to the forehead, she wrings the neck of a white pigeon, thinking it will serve her purpose, slices open the body, parting the immaculate plumage to reveal the warm, bluish entrails, which leave a viscid red stain on the father's brow. But the father protests, pushing away the tiny carcass, whose head droops, beak open, against his head, then tumbles among the pillows.

One September morning, Marcel takes Éléonore with him. For a long time, they walk through meadows, past a quarry of dressed stone and aggregate, cross fallow fields, skirt around a small valley overgrown with brambles, from which rises the dilapidated shell of an old barn. As every morning, the diadem spider destroys its web and patiently weaves it anew. The sky is clear, limewashed, the air still hums with swarms of bees heavy with pollen. The earth is round and dappled as the croup of a Percheron. From time to time they stop, look up, shield their eyes with one hand to watch the stately flight of an airship and the aeroplanes passing over the landscape, buys *La Croix du Gers*, or *La Semaine religieuse*, whereas the father reads *La République des travailleurs*, *Le Réveil des communes* or *L'Indépendance gasconne*. From almanacs and newspapers she clips illustrations, reproductions of sacred pictures, religious paintings that buckle and yellow on the walls. She comments on the articles and news stories that reinforce her longstanding and definitive idea of the dereliction of the world. She is fascinated by the 'African project', the French army's advance through hostile terrain brought to her in harrowing retouched photographs, portraits of savages and hellish beasts. She is excited by the Balkan war, the tales of battles, the images of infantrymen, their bodies littering the trenches, or piled at the feet of a chaplain praying over a mass grave. As the father's eyes become blurred, she is moved by the testimony of those who have witnessed the bronze statues of Pope Martin V in the church of Saint-Jean-de-Latran weeping, thereby portending the imminent death of Pius X. From an issue of *L'Illustration* she picked up at the market, she reads aloud the horrors suffered by a Bulgarian garrison on an island in the Tundzha, where soldiers are dying in the shade of trees from which they have stripped and eaten the bark: 'Oh, the torment! A constant hum of moans, of gasps and wails pierces your ears and makes your hair stand on end. Men on fatigue duty and prisoners come and go carrying stretchers bearing corpses, pale skin stretched taut over bones as though mummified, others black, bloated by contagion. Here men are dying everywhere in the open air beneath the glorious spring sunshine, at the foot of budding trees on the sodden shore, by fast-flowing waters that sweep the contagion even farther, everywhere and in the most ignoble positions, wretched beasts with little respect for man, excrete the pestilential evil from every orifice.

And yet some use their hands or feet to crawl to the dark hole at the foot of the crumbling tower and creep into the shadows, there to die in peace: every morning, this cesspit is filled with contorted bodies.' She nods slowly, thereby signifying that she has had her fill, and that this should be seen as the fulfilment of one of her many prognostications about man's propensity for evil and the inevitable consequences.

The father's authority once ranged and resonated through his customary toil and labours outside in the fields, in the proximity of the animals. Now it is condensed to the point of nausea in the only room in the house, where it pervades and saturates the dark hours, the furniture, the saltpetre on the walls, and as the father gradually withdraws into himself, so the authority of Marcel flourishes and becomes indispensable, since he now performs the tasks that once fell to the father, that justified his existence, and from which illness has utterly excluded him. The genetrix has complete power over this last agony. No-one but she is authorized to watch over the father, not even his daughter. She who, since their bleak wedding day, has seemed able to bear the presence of the husband only with great difficulty, she who was constantly exasperated and responded to the first signs of illness with revulsion, now cannot bring herself to leave his bedside, redoubling her attentions, her prayers and her care. She is not distraught at the probable death of the father – she recognizes the banality of death and has too much faith in her superstitions – but as she feels her universe gradually teeter, then crumble, she clings to it with the obstinacy of despair, as though it were enough to keep the father alive to safeguard their reality, however impoverished, and preserve it from the inevitable cataclysm. She believes that the father can vegetate like this until the end of time, that he will never actually die if she cares for him with sufficient persistence and conviction, and can thereby maintain the tenuous equilibrium of the farm and of their lives, which the arrival of Marcel has shattered into pieces. She had been opposed to this intrusion, believing that they had no need for a farmhand, even if he was obscurely related to them, of another mouth to feed, and that the father could assume the burden while the last of his strength was not yet completely exhausted. Then, faced with the evidence, she had had to reconcile herself, but the boy's arrival had coincided with the father's decline and she believes that this parasitic male presence feeds on the old man's life force, the latter wasting away to the benefit of the one making himself at home as he becomes accustomed to the farm, the land and the animals. So she can muster no fondness for Marcel, only defiance. Their relationship has no need of words. The genetrix contents herself with simply dishing out his food, heating water for his ablutions, watching him out of the corner of her eye without ever looking at him directly. She has no thoughts of extending her influence over Marcel. She knows instinctively that he is beyond her control, immured in his stubborn silence, his dogged passion for the job at hand. She fears that there is something suspect, something intransigent about him that she cannot name. Time was, when a piglet was born with red hair, it was drowned; its coat indicated an abnormality, a vicious temperament. She sees an omen in Marcel's flaming shock of hair, his too-pale skin. But he will soon be nineteen, and when he is, she will meekly contribute to the purchase of his leather work boots, in the event that the medical board and military service should pass him fit for service.

his lower lip. Hands spread on the mattress, head bowed, eyes closed, he savours the dark, unpleasant saliva, then spits into the palm Éléonore is holding out for him. The child throws the quid into the fire, where it sizzles and shrivels among the logs. As she patiently turns her back, the father relieves himself in the chamber pot beside him. Finally, she helps him back to bed, tucks him in and lies next to him, pressed against this long, frail, shivering body that looks at her through eyes that are bigger than they were, and roiled by dark currents. By the time the genetrix reappears, Éléonore is sitting at the table, engrossed in reading a missal. The peasant woman silently loosens her shawl, eyes the room with a suspicious glance, lays a hand on the brow of the father, who is now dozing, asks whether he 'moved his bowels' and examines the colour and fluidity of the contents of the chamber pot – sometimes she takes a long stick and probes the pale or bloody stool, jabbing or splitting it as though she might read some augury there – then sends Éléonore outside at the first opportunity. The child goes to find Marcel, whose presence is a substitute for the father, and who demonstrates a genuine affection for her. She follows him when he goes to the fields, sometimes lends a hand. She often stays and plays a few metres from him, without their exchanging a word. She scrapes the ground to root out earthworms that she feeds to the hens, or throws a stick for Alphonse. The looks Marcel gives her and his faint smile are a balm to her melancholy soul. She enjoys watching him work, trails in his wake to catch the smell of his body when he pants from the effort, the odour that his thick sweater gives off when he bends down next to her, which must be the strange and exhilarating smells of his milky skin, the hidden folds of his body. In spring, she saw a pair of asps mating

6 4

in the crevice of the flat, foliated rocks, the pulsing knot of their sinuous curves, and she feels as though there is a similar knot within her, an unknown force emerging, quivering deep in her belly.

In the evening, Marcel drags over the bench, sits close to the father and gives a detailed account of his day in a low, deeply respectful tone that he does not use at any other time. The father listens to him talk about the importance of developing the livestock, which now brings in much more than the arable and is less labour-intensive. The father sometimes nods but does not say anything, as though the business of the farm is now so remote that it is beyond his reach. Since the patriarch is no longer able to wash himself, it is Marcel who takes care of his ablutions. The women keep their distance from this ritual, where, in the privacy of their sex and their contemplation, the young man undresses the farmer, settles him on a stool in the inglenook next to the fire, plunges a washcloth into a basin of hot water then carefully soaps the pale, sickly skin, one hand massaging the atrophied muscles, the bloodless flesh, the other gripping the acute angle of a shoulder, an arm, an ankle. His shirtsleeves are rolled up to his elbows, the grey foam that wrung from the washing mitt trickles heavily over the translucent skin of his wrists, and the father surrenders, feeling no shame that his ravaged body is given over to the care of the boy. Of these moments that are shielded from her view, Éléonore conjures up ceremonial after-images whose aura envelopes and crowns Marcel. As the father declines, this body, like a ghost ship inhabited only by a faltering breath, seems hallowed. Their every gesture, their grave, solemn movements, serve only to sanctify it, bringing a flood of liturgical images, and when, to relieve his numbness, the genetrix washes the father's feet, for an instant she embodies the sinful woman who, in the Pharisee's house, washed the Son of God's feet with her tears and anointed them with oil. Then the Gospels become confused in her memory, and Éléonore imagines the words of Christ in the father's closed mouth: 'She hath done what she could: she is come aforehand to anoint my body to the burying.'

In a corner of the pigsty, four dry-stone walls form a cramped pen for fattening animals, where no daylight ever enters. A low door of thick oak planks allows access to a trough, into which every morning Éléonore, who is charged with the task, pours the brown water from the boiled dirt-caked potatoes mixed with flour and kitchen scraps. The animal is fattened behind the low door in almost total darkness. A slit between the timbers sometimes lets in a streak of light that slashes the inky darkness, but the pig, accustomed to the darkness, flees the light, scurrying into the farthest corner of its universe. When Éléonore lifts the latch and opens the half-door, she sees through the warm, acrid cloud a flickering, feverish eye, a flecked snout, a patch of grubby skin where the bristles are caked in crusted slops. She hastily pours the contents of the bucket into the trough and shuts the door and the latch while the animal greedily gobbles the swill with loud sucking and swallowing noises. She is intimately acquainted with the pig – no animal is more familiar to her, from some remote time on the fringes of memory, she feels a sense of comforting closeness – but she also knows she should be wary of their cunning, their insatiable appetite and extraordinary strength. And yet the pig sent for fattening, screened from the eyes of men, seems to her shrouded in mystery, a rampant, nameless beast, sprung from legend

66

or mythology, that never truly dies, even when its blood is shed, but endlessly reappears, as though born of the shadows of the sty. When it is time to scrub out the pen, where layers of excrement quickly build up, the animal is evicted by force, jabbed in the flanks or beaten with a switch until it appears, like the meadow crickets that Éléonore flushes out on long, hot summer days, poking long twigs into their burrow, hiking her skirts and dousing it in urine until she sees the insect hop out, dazed and vulnerable, exposed to the dazzling light of the world. The pig is like other animals, but wilder, more unpredictable, almost savage, and Éléonore prudently seeks out the protection of the men who control it with cries and jabs.

To neuter a sow that is to be fattened, the father sends for Albert Brisard, because, left to her cycle, the animal turns nasty, no longer fattens, and 'in a week loses all the weight she's gained in a month'. The man introduces the tip of a metal cone into the animal's vulva, and into the flared end pours some of the lead shot used for hunting. The metal pellets become embedded in the uterus and the ovaries, and the sow no longer goes into heat. Only Brisard can determine the best method of neutering a particular animal, and sometimes he decides to 'open up'. In such cases, the sow is restrained in a wooden cage with gaps between the slats large enough to introduce a hand. Brisard sets a leather case next to him and takes out a blade, then makes an incision in the flank as the animal squeals and struggles vainly, confined by the walls of the crate. The man with the club foot pushes his forefinger into the wound, runs it along the peritoneum until he feels the swollen surface of the ovaries, which he pulls towards the incision, pressing his thumb against the flank for leverage. Then he takes a bobbin of thread from his leather case, snaps off a length, and ties off the ovarian vein and artery before excising the organs, pushing the stumps into the abdominal cavity and suturing the belly of the sow.

Each year, a few days before All Saints' Day, the animal is slaughtered. In the early morning, there is a great commotion. Mother and daughter, joined by women from the neighbouring farms – old mother Fabre and her daughter-in-law, Madame Roque, and her brood of children – set to boiling large quantities of water, and ready the basins and a large barrel of tarred wooden staves. Brisard, summoned for the occasion, sharpens the blade of his knife on an oiled whetstone. With a new lease of life, the father demands that they get him up and dress him, and the protestations of the genetrix do not succeed in dissuading him. The shirt they dress him in is baggy now, and the trousers are held up by a length of twine threaded through the belt loops. Like a tattered, jerky puppet, he manages to walk, with Éléonore's hand supporting his elbow. Once on the doorstep, he stands for a long moment without moving, his face bathing in the cold sunlight. He breathes deeply, inhaling the comforting smells of the manure heap, of the dead leaves beginning their slow decomposition beneath the black, bare trees that ring the farm, and his daughter feels the life-giving shudder that courses through his body. Dragging his feet, he reaches the little worm-eaten hobnailed bench with its warped seat and sits on it one last time, while the genetrix drapes two thick blankets and his cloak over his shoulders.

'You can't say I didn't warn you,' she says.

The father does not seem to hear her and turns towards Alphonse, who comes over to sniff him. He reaches out a hand to stroke the greying head, but the dog scurries away, his tail between his legs, under the misted eyes of the father. Soon, shrieks can be heard from the sty. Alphonse stands in the middle of the yard barking and Brisard gets to his feet, running the sharpened blade of his knife against the pad of his thumb, leaving a shallow gash in the hard skin. Marcel suddenly appears, dragging behind him, into the daylight, and using every ounce of strength, the pig he has hog-tied and muzzled with a length of rope. He drags the still struggling animal on its side, as a long guttural squeal comes from its snout in a spray of white spittle. The mother brings over a basin and, in the instant when the 'sticker' approaches and the sun reflected on the knife's blade casts a fleeting flicker onto Marcel's face, the pig surrenders and freezes in the vice of hands restraining it. Its eye fixes on the blue of the sky streaked with wisps of low fog. Its breath condenses, its bladder empties onto its hind hocks. From the bench, the father approvingly gauges the size of the pig. Albert Brisard plunges the blade into the throat up to the hilt, severs the artery in a trice, withdraws the spotless blade as the animal's heart pulses fitful spurts of blood into the bucket pressed to the lips of the wound, and the stern face of the genetrix and the top of her white blouse are spotted with a fine mist that splashes from the bucket. Éléonore slips between the adults and lays a hand on the animal's back as its breathing diminishes and dies. When the genetrix straightens up and hands the bucket to the neighbours who carry it away, she does not bother to wipe away the drops caught in her eyebrows and the downy hair on her cheeks. The men grab the now pliable carcass and lift it up so that the last of the fluid can drain out. They lift it into the vat and the women bring the pans of boiling washes and boils the sheets as quickly as she can. On the wool-stuffed mattress, after the father has died, a large stain of uncertain colour will remain and, prudently, the farmwoman will turn it over to sleep on the other side. The air is fouled by the unbearable excremental stench. Feeling nauseous, they sit down to eat in the acidic miasma given off each time the father moves or opens his mouth to gasp something, his breath betraying the alchemy already at work inside him. It is no longer possible to get him out of bed to wash for fear of breaking him. Marcel sponges him as best he can, eliciting howls of pain despite his carefully controlled movements and, if the mother and the daughter continue to avert their gaze, the father no longer has any modesty and kicks off sheets and blankets with his bandaged feet, the spindly, yellow legs, unable to bear the weight, the feel of them, exposing a body like a daddy-longlegs, his limp penis in the thatch of still-black pubic hair. The mother no longer leaves his bedside. She talks of maledictions that have surely struck them and curses the faith healer for failing to lift them and turn them against those who, somewhere and without a shadow of doubt, are casting them.

The dog no longer runs on ahead of Éléonore, no longer splashes in the ditches, but walks to heel, his coat prickling with drizzle, and they walk the ravaged fields bristling with clumps of brown, broken stalks from last year's crop, while harriers glide far-off in the bloated grey sky, then swoop on a young rabbit or a shrew and carry it off with a cry. Tufts of wool and horsehair quiver on the barbed-wire fences, and rain-sodden sheep watch her from afar. When she reaches the village, Éléonore raps on the door of the presbytery, but the only response is the muffled echo of her knocking. So she sits on the step, pulls the shawl down over her forehead, beaded with raindrops, while Alphonse presses himself against her. She puts an arm around the dog, buries her hand in the warm, damp hair of his belly and feels the animal's heart beating behind his ribs. The rain, the trudging men and animals have turned the village square into a mire. The cuffs of trousers and the hems of dresses have hardened into a black crust. The passing dogs have knots in their fur as hard and heavy as stones. Cartwheels and hooves spatter faces with a foul sludge like that which the father's belly seems to produce inexhaustibly. Villagers approach Éléonore, question her: she tells them she has come on the mother's orders to fetch the priest. They realize that her father is going to 'pass' and that soon the bell will sound the knell. But Father Antoine is in the neighbouring village for a service; he will certainly not have passed up a tour of the cafés and is not due back for several hours. Éléonore declines the offer of taking shelter in a kitchen to wait for him, even though she would have a view of the presbytery and the main road leading to the church. They give up trying to persuade her, bring her a bowl of scalding milk, and though she has no appetite, she eats the cream, then gives the rest to the dog, who burns his lips. The hours pass, the day wanes, painting the façades of the houses a livid blue. The tops of the chestnut trees have been swallowed by the twilight by the time Father Antoine finally appears, juddering along on the back of a little donkey led by the last of a long line of altar boys, who looks as though he too has survived the flood, a boy whose name the priest cannot for the life of him remember, just as he could not remember the names of those who came before him, carefully avoiding addressing them as anything other than 'my son' or 'my child', while fond of constantly stroking their soft nape, bristling with downy hair. Éléonore watches priest lights an oil lamp, then pokes the fire in the cast-iron stove. He rummages in the cupboard, brings out a bottle of alcohol, pours a glass and sits down on the trunk next to the stove, elbows resting on his knees, face bowed over the glass he is holding in both hands. Éléonore stands mute and motionless by the door with Alphonse lying at her feet, and at first she thinks the priest has dozed off again, but he sighs and gives a little cough, then brings the glass to his lips and sits up.

'Well, sit down, girl!' he says.

Éléonore remains standing and he studies her, before asking in a laboured voice:

'Were you very fond of your papa?'

Then, since Éléonore does not respond, he adds: 'That's good, you're a good child, a good child, good child,' before lapsing back into contemplation, then he sits up again, brings the glass to his lips and declares:

'Honour thy father and thy mother: that thy days may be long upon the land which the Lord thy God giveth thee.'

They are silent for a long time, the only sound the crackling of logs in the stove and the rain pattering on the sloping roof of the presbytery. At length, there comes a knock at the door. It is Raymond Carrère, the verger, who stands on the threshold, wrapped in an oil-skin cloak.

'The boy's not with you?' says the priest as the man steps inside and looks at Éléonore.

'His mother says it's not fit weather for a dog to be out abroad, says he's already caught his death tramping out in the rain,' the man says.

The clergyman dismisses the response with a scowl and an irritated flick of his wrist. Carrère removes his beret and greets Éléonore with an affected nod of the head, while Father Antoine drags himself as far as the sacristy door, which he unlocks, and disappears behind. He rummages for a moment, then reappears, tangled in his surplice and a purple stole, the parish cross tucked under one arm, the sacramental oils slipped into a fabric bag and a brass bell in one hand.

'Let's go, let's go,' he says, pushing them towards the door.

The procession sets off. Éléonore leads the way, lighting the road as best she can, holding before her the oil lamp whose light fractures and fades in the ruts. With the other hand she shakes the little bell, muffled by the rain. Alphonse walks on ahead of them, skirting the puddles. Raymond Carrère carries the parish cross, the base tucked into the crook of his left elbow, the body leaning against his shoulder and resting against his cheek. The rain plasters the mourning veil that surmounts the cross against the wood and the gaunt, dripping face of Christ so that the radiant visage lifted towards the night becomes that of a corpse in a winding shroud. As they cross the square, the villagers gather at their windows in a halo of candlelight and make the sign of the cross. The women they encounter lift their muddy skirts and, unable to kneel, bend their legs and bow their heads. Since they pass by the smithy, where the furnace is blazing, the blacksmith stops beating the anvil and quickly blesses himself. In the embers, a horseshoe glimmers lazily beneath the lava. From the shelter of barns and storehouses, dogs bark and tug at their leashes as Alphonse passes. From doorsteps, children watch the black, silent procession as it moves away from the village beneath the ragged sky, stinging their cheeks with driving rain. Soon, the barking of the dogs dies away, Puy-Larroque disappears behind them and there remains only the deep, electric twilight, the grey-green recesses in the hollows of the hills whose curves their eyes can barely make out. Convulsive thunderbolts, silent and simmering, light up the higher strata, illuminated domes. Hen pheasants run through the brambles; small game, blue, furtive, soundless, scurry around the edges of the fields. A gust of wind lifts the black veil from the mourning face of Christ, then, with a crack, whips it away and the procession pauses for a moment, helpless and shivering, and watches the funeral veil fly off into the chilly night, scamper along the lane, caught up in the eddies of dead leaves, rise into the air and then disappear, as lithe and capricious as a noctule bat. They resume their laborious march. Father Antoine staggers along the side of the road in the tufts of springy grass, trying his best to lift the soutane trampled by his muddy clogs. He is shouting words at them which reach them only in snatches. The purple stole slaps his face and he pushes it down, then stops, half-bent, his hands resting on his thighs. They are coming to the roadside cross at the foot of which they agree to stop for a moment, and the priest sits down, breathlessly muttering:

'Oh, Lord, oh, Lord, oh, Lord!'

He rummages in the bag containing the sacramental oils, takes out a flask of eau-de-vie and brings it to his lips while Éléonore and the verger wait, she still tinkling the bell, he struggling against the wind blustering around the parish cross, whose weight is digging into his shoulder, and taking one step forward and two steps back trying to keep his balance. The night is coal-black now, pierced only by the turbulent flame of the lamp being held by the frozen little girl. A sudden lightning flash reveals them, fixing them like dazed fallow deer before returning them to the darkness, leaving on the disc of the sightless pupils a negative afterimage of the roadside cross and their outlined silhouettes. Father Antoine carefully packs away his flask and they help him up, each pulling on one arm with all their might, then they set off once more. In an enclosed field, forgotten, invisible cattle stand in the shelter of the trees, and all that is visible are the pale eyes reflecting the glow of the lamp. As they near the farm, which is still only a vague shadow, a deep rumbling rips the heavens and, despite Éléonore's calls, Alphonse bolts straight ahead and disappears. The lightning strikes close by, hitting the topmost branches of the hundred-year-old cedar and, from behind her, Éléonore hears the asthmatic voice of the priest:

'Yea... though I walk... through the valley... of the... shadow... of death, I will fear no... evil: for Thou art... Thou art with me; Thy rod... and Thy staff... they comfort me...'

A fresh gust of wind sweeps along the road, lifting the parish cross, which escapes the slippery hands of Raymond Carrère; the verger tries to regain his footing, racing behind the cross as it lifts itself upright for a moment, as though raised into the night by some higher power, then it bends, dragging him through the ditch, where he falls, sprawling, in a fallow field. Father Antoine and Éléonore watch dumbfounded as Raymond Carrère, his mouth filled with dirt, painfully tries to get up, slips, falls again, struggles and finally manages to get to his feet, spits and wipes his muddy face with his hand. The verger looks at the priest, the child looks at the priest, the priest looks from one to the other and says nothing, then the verger pulls the parish cross from the mud, heaves it onto his shoulder and steps across the ditch. By the time they arrive at the farm, the rain has sheets in the half-light of the room and painstakingly smooths them out over the mattress with the flat of her hand. They dress the father's body in his formal suit, the one he wore for his wedding and for Éléonore's baptism and which now makes him look like a scarecrow. Marcel forces the arms; the joints crack and break. He folds them over the shroud in which they have wrapped him, and the widow kneads and with great difficulty entwines the fingers around her rosary, brushes the father's hair and his beard, which will continue to grow even in the grave. With the aid of a sewing needle, she cleans the father's fingernails, removing the remnants of soil and dried excrement, then delicately pushes back the cuticles. Sitting next to the bed, she pats the worn cover of her little missal and, in a low voice, murmurs indistinct litanies, vague psalms. Soon, the barbarous horde of villagers arrives on foot, by bicycle or cart, and crowds into the room. The widow now affects a tearful expression. They approach the body, bless it, shaking the sprig of boxtree over the forehead. The beads of water lie, motionless, on the sagging skin of the face. They sit on the benches lined up along the walls and, not knowing what to do with their coarse hands, place them on the angles carved out by their knees beneath the fabric of the trousers or their mourning dresses. In the little hillside cemetery, beneath the first spring sunshine, a gravedigger buries the blade of a shovel between two graves and lifts out a clod of soft earth veined with rootlets. Farther off, the carpenter Jocelyn Lagarde planes timbers and crudely assembles the coffin in which the father will lie, and the hammer falling on the heads of the nails echoes through the streets of Puy-Larroque and far beyond. So, the widow thinks, he's gone now, gone for good. The proof, if it were needed, is that people

In a corner of the hayloft, Éléonore hugs her knees, draped in her little mourning dress. A black cat that has found shelter here rubs its lice-infested fur against her. Back arched, tail erect, it lets out a guttural purr. From the yard, she can hear voices, the snuffling of the horses and the clink of the harness when they snort. Her hands are numb with cold and she slips her fingers between her thighs. She thinks about the father's body, on display for all to see. Although something inside her throbs and threatens, for a long time she sits stock-still, staring at the floor, where silverfish race in the dust. The cat continues to come and go, rubbing itself against her leg, pushing its nose into the folds of her mourning dress, and at first she does not move. Then she directs her gaze to the scrawny, friendly animal, whose pale green eyes are ringed with sleep. Éléonore reaches out her right hand and the cat rises up on its hind paws to press its head against the outstretched palm. From the lips raised by two worn incisors, a drop of saliva pearls and falls onto the wooden floorboards. As it soaks in, it leaves a tiny brown halo. Éléonore grabs the cat by the scruff of the neck and gently pulls it towards her. She extends her other arm, grips the throat of the animal, which at first continues to purr, half-closing its eyes, then swallows with difficulty and sticks out the tip of its pink tongue. Éléonore tightens the vice and the cat begins to struggle to escape her, shows its claws and tries to push away her hands, scratching her skin so that she has to pin the animal down on the ground between her legs and crush its head against the floor using her whole weight. The cat bristles, convulses, lets out a frantic mewling, then she lets go and it scampers to the far end of the hayloft, where it coughs, mouth open, as though about to vomit, then is still. Éléonore's wrists and the backs of her hands are covered with thin slashes that pearl with drops of heavy blood, which merge and slide over her pale skin. She watches as they trickle the length of her forearms, then she brings them to her lips. She licks the blood and sucks the painless scratches, staring at the cat which has also begun to carefully wash itself, still keeping a wary eye on her. Eventually it stops, eyes half-closed. Éléonore calls to it. She gently drums her fingers on her legs. The cat freezes. It hesitates, crosses the hayloft with slow, loping strides, recoils when she extends her hand again, then accepts the caress and makes its irrepressible purring heard. Éléonore picks it up, sets it on her lap, where, after turning around a few times, it curls up, and before long Éléonore too is dozing, one injured hand resting against the warm, vibrant body of the animal.

All day the body lies, august and imperious, between the panels of the box-bed. Beneath the immaculate shroud, beneath the sheet smoothed by the widow's calloused hands, inside the formal suit fitted over the limbs purpled with lividity, secretly, yet in full view of everyone, the ruins of the father roil and begin their metamorphosis. In the faecal magma of the abdomen, a silent army emerges. The commensal bacteria toil, proliferate and transform the guts into a primordial sludge. Discreetly, the corpse egests into the flannels with which the undergarments have been carefully stuffed. A greenish discoloration has appeared on the epidermis, in the region of the iliac fossa, above the already putrefying maggot of the caecum. The pancreas is already reduced to a formless slick that leaches between the other organs. Cells break down and self-digest. The now permeable linings make all barriers obsolete. The remains are nothing more than a Great Whole in which bacteria flourish and course through the maze of atrophied vessels. The father is beginning to smell. Not that pungent stench that poured from his every orifice in the last throes of death, but the sickly, nauseating perfume of swamps in whose stagnant waters floats the bloated carcass of some barely recognizable animal, of the pungent black humus teeming with larvae at the roots of huge rotting trees. The widow, the villagers and Marcel say nothing. From time to time, they burn small bunches of dried sage while they cough politely. The room is cold as a crypt. Now and then a sound rises from the deathbed, a rumbling noise softly escapes the closed lips, a fetid gas is released into the sheets and spreads through the room in the awkward silence. The glow of the candles casts a sickly yellow fresco on the walls, the faces and the shadowy corners. The wooden table gradually piles up with earthenware cups stained black with coffee grounds, plates of biscuits and balls of wool as the women continue to knit to kill time and relieve the torpor of the wake. Mourners whose tears have long since run dry, elderly women worn out by life, by childbirth and tilling the land talk in low voices, get up to offer their seat to some woman who is older, more broken, or to bustle about the scullery, tramping their muddy clogs across the floor, their legs blotchy with varicose veins and swollen from standing around.

The sound of her name reaches her from some far-off place and Éléonore wakes, numb with cold, in the hayloft. Only a few hours have passed, but the day is already waning over the land, the low-angled sun sets the hills ablaze and the rooks, perhaps attracted by the smell of death, perch in the trees all around, smoothing their purple-tinged feathers and calling to each other. Their cries ring out in the pure air. The gravedigger has long since completed his task. Now the grave is an unfathomable chasm into which the shadows of the crosses fall. Earthworms and lucifugous insects emerge from the mound of earth, slither back to the grave and let themselves fall. In the quiet of the now empty workshop, the crude coffin of rickety planed planks exhales its sweet smell of sawdust and the veins of the wood ooze a little sap. A small cross carrying the Christ is screwed to the coffin lid. Again, a voice from the farmyard calls Éléonore's name. The cat left the hayloft while she was asleep, and if her dress did not bear the imprint of its body and her hands the coagulated traces of its scratches, she would doubt it had ever existed, for she has only a dazed memory of the past hours. She gets up and leans against a beam until the feeling returns to her algid limbs, then she climbs down the ladder. Marcel spots her, runs to her, wraps his arms around her shoulders and cries:

'Hours we've been looking for you!'

He lays a hand on her face, on the nape of her neck, then grabs her wrists and see the scratches on her hands and her forearms. Surely this is the first time he touches her in this way, lavishes on her the care she longed for from the father?

'What happened here?' he asks.

Éléonore cannot answer and Marcel slips an arm around her shoulders to lead her back to the farmhouse. The father's face is a death mask draped over the contours of the skull. The room reeks of decay and sour sweat, of the fumes of hooch and of soup served to warm people up, of the breath that mouths of rotting teeth and ulcerous stomachs have been spewing all day, endlessly rebreathing the same musty air that mists the windowpanes. When they see Éléonore finally come through the door, everyone falls silent. The child is inert, dishevelled, her little mourning dress rumpled and smudged with dust, wisps of hay and tufts of shed hair; her arms scratched.

'She fell asleep up in the hayloft,' Marcel says.

The assembled company lets out a murmur of relief. Dumbfounded at first, the widow stares at her daughter for a moment, then gets up with a crack of vertebrae. She carefully sets the missal with the worn cover on her chair, crosses the room so slowly that everyone has time to follow her progress and wonder what her intentions are, then she slaps Éléonore with all her strength. The little girl staggers and falls against the wall, knocking over a chair whose back shatters on the floor before Marcel has the time to catch her. The child gets to her feet, stunned, falls and gets up again. The widow grabs her by the hair and drags her to the father's bedside, where, twisting her neck, she forces her to sit on the bench. Then she goes back to her chair, picks up the missal with the worn cover and sits down. In the embarrassed silence, someone picks up and tries to mend the chair. Hands gripping her knees to hide their trembling, her eyes clouded with tears, Éléonore stares at the floor. She has bitten her tongue and can feel the wound throb against the roof of her mouth to the rhythm of the muffled beating of her heart. She swallows mouthfuls of blood, thick and metallic as black bile, as poison, determined to hold it all in. Soon, willingly or reluctantly, conversations resume and dispel the awkward atmosphere. Éléonore senses the presence of Marcel at the far end of the room, his eyes on her, but she does not dare look up for fear of meeting the triumphant gaze of the widow and allowing her to gloat at her humiliation. When, stiff-necked, she finally decides to lift her face, the black cat has cut a path through the room and is looking at her with pale, indifferent eyes from under the box-bed, phlegmatic psychopomp or a sombre omen visible only to her.

By late afternoon, the men are lingering on the steps, exchanging a few words in listless tones about the state of the harvest or the livestock, plans for the future, fears of blackthorn winter adversely affecting the sowing, or of summer heat and drought. The clatter of cartwheels echoes around the yard and the women who have been forewarned get to their feet, rousing the children who are sleeping in their laps and drooling on their skirts. Accompanied by the local gendarme and by Father Antoine, still hungover from the hooch the night before and cradling his aching head in his hands, Jocelyn Lagarde steps down. Three boys go over to the haycart, talk among themselves for a moment, then pull the coffin towards them, lift it and carry it into the house. The rest of the men stand aside to let them pass, then greet the gendarme with a hearty handshake. The coffin is set on two trestles next to the bed, and the carpenter and the gendarme offer their condolences to the widow and then to Marcel. The open coffin exhales a smell of sanded softwood. For want of padding and silks, the widow lines the bottom with sheets, which she rumples and pleats to give them volume, so that the formal suit will not be worn and the bony elbows and heels of the mortal remains will not knock and rub against the timber, or pick up splinters. The mourners pay their last respects to the deceased, bid farewell to the kinfolk and head home along the byway in the twilight, filling their lungs with the fresh spring air. Only Marcel, the gendarme, the carpenter, the widow, the priest and the child now remain.

With the greatest care the shroud covering the mortal remains is removed, then Marcel and Jocelyn Lagarde take the body by the shoulders and the heels and lower it into the coffin. A brown liquid drips from the corpse onto the edge of the box-bed, the beaten-earth floor and the wrist of Jocelyn Lagarde, who stifles a dry heave and wipes himself on the trousers of the dead man, while the widow hastily pulls the sheet over the obscene stain on the mattress. She carefully places the embroidered shroud in the coffin as she might tuck a child into her cradle, and replaces the cushion under the head of the deceased to raise it up. They all step forward together, surrounding the coffin, and for the last time they look at the grey, waxy simulacrum of the farmer, whom the widow now wants gone as soon as possible.

'After the suffering and the tears that have veiled his eyes,' the priest intones, 'grant, O Lord, that he might see Thy face.'

They make the sign of the cross. The carpenter puts the lid on the coffin, waits for a nod from the gendarme, then seals the lid with flat-headed nails he carefully grips between the thick pads of his fingers, using a sidelong blow to drive home those that buckle against the edge, splitting the timber and sending up splinters of wood. They watch in silence, flinching at each impact, until the final nail has sealed the coffin and the mortal remains repose in complete darkness. All through the night, a candle burns in a small dish on top of the coffin and the wax spills over, trickles away and congeals around the little effigy of Christ screwed to the wood before the wick gutters out in a clear pool at first light. A wisp of smoke, translucent as semen, shielded by sleep from the eyes of the living, then rises in the cold room.

The following day, they set out early. The widow and the child follow the cart pulled by the drowsy mare, stumbling now and then, led by Marcel, next to whom they have hoisted and settled an old woman wrapped in a grey woollen shawl. On the road, the wheels of the cart screech and throw up jets of mud. The dawn glistens in the beads of dew caught in the curves of the blades of grass. The bell tolls and the wave ripples out in concentric circles through the quivering air, faintly echoing from the still waters of the ponds and the drinking troughs. The crows fall silent and study the funeral cortège. On the village square, Father Antoine opens wide the church doors before which the villagers have gathered. Éléonore walks next to the widow, her face haggard beneath a mourning veil like a mantilla, her narrow, piteous shoulders draped in the black shawl, her firm calf muscles beneath the black woollen stockings moving like stones along the scrawny legs. Éléonore is careful that her swinging arm does not brush against the widow's. As a sharp pain suddenly claws at her belly, she silently resolves to reduce the widow to nothing, vows that soon she will walk behind the widow's coffin just as today she is walking behind the father's. As the cortège advances and passes the neighbouring farms, a few silent, sullen farmers join them, stepping over tracks and ditches to fall into step behind, their eyes following the coffin as it clatters on the cart, whose rattling planks sporadically send up showers of twigs and manure dust.

In the very centre of a plot of land grows a centennial oak whose morning shadow darkens the outer walls of the cemetery. At the foot of the tree, thick roots plunge down and, in negative, map out a maze that mirrors the

89

branches above. The roots reach down towards the mineral strata, towards the water table from which the tree drinks, towards telluric landscapes unknown to man, retracing ages long since past. The trunk of the oak tree is so thick that children from every generation in Puy-Larroque have circled it, hands clasped in strange ring dances, never passed on and yet ever repeated, pressing their pale, veined cheeks against the bark; in doing so, their arms embrace a whole universe, that of the world buried beneath their bare feet and under the armour of the tree at whose heart wells and rises the majestic sap, the world of microscopic fauna unceasingly coursing between the stones lodged in the roots, the silvery lichens and the patches of bark, but also the world of the branches into which the children heave themselves by the strength of their arms to rest in the cool of the leaves, the shimmering daylight dappled by the topmost branches swaying in the breeze. The oak reigns, indifferent to the destiny of men, to their pitiful lives and deaths. Lovers have spilled their seeds at its base, proud drunken lads have pissed on its trunk, lips have whispered secrets and promises into the hollows in its bark. Tree houses have been built in its branches and crumbled to dust, abandoned by playing children. Nails have been planted that have rusted and disappeared. Old men still walk from the village to this little meadow, following the track made by endless passing feet, to shelter in the shadow of the oak. If they have always known this tree, the tree has always known them, and their forebears who laid their hands on the very same spot, stroking the trunk with the same caress their gnarled hands now trace, the hand of a child becoming that of an old man, then the hand of a child once more.

Father Antoine swings the aspergillum over the coffin, showering drops of holy water on the wood. When the widow steps forward to bid farewell to the mortal remains before they are carried from the church to Puy-Larroque cemetery she bows low, in a surge of grief, and kisses the foot of the coffin. When she goes back to the pew, Éléonore quickly turns her face away so she does not have to see, glistening on her lips, the drop of holy water picked up by her kiss, the only kiss she will ever see her give, the sight of which seems so obscene that her stomach churns with shame. Next to the grave, the downpour has melted away the mound of earth like sugar. The men have hoisted the coffin onto their shoulders, crossed the village square and passed through the gates of the cemetery built on the south-facing slope of the hill, now bathed in light from a sky wrung dry. The funeral procession has descended the steps, as Father Antoine walked on ahead, leaning on the puny shoulder of the altar boy. Anxious not to be too quick to join their kinfolk already at rest beneath their faltering steps, the villagers take care not to slip on the slippery stone and the mounds of soil washed down by the torrent. They gather around and stand gloomily next to the pit dug by the gravedigger, some in the blazing sun, others in the perfumed shade of cypresses heavy with rain. The pall-bearers set down the coffin, so light it looks as though it is empty, in a pool of warm sunlight, and soon wisps of steam begin to rise from the unseasoned wood and from the mosses gorged with water that edge the tombstones. Father Antoine stands stiffly next to the grave, his hands joined over his soutane and white surplice, draped with a black stole and a cope. He stares at the villagers who have not yet joined the cortège and are standing gossiping outside the gates. Marcel stands next to Éléonore

91

collecting the water from the natural streams whose narrow stony beds zigzag between the tombstones. There, a toad floats on the surface among the leaves and branches blown by the wind. Drawn by the downpour and racked with hunger, he has ventured from the winter hide created for him by a lifted gravestone and the abandoned burrow of a mole. Coppery eyes staring up at the mouth of the grave and the shadows of the men, the amphibian floats, hind legs extended, occasionally scratching at the dirt wall with its useless fingers. While the priest recites the Canticle of Zechariah, the toad swims a few strokes to the other side of the grave, tracing ripples on the surface of the water, and, in the silent interlude, lets out a loud croak.

'*Requiem æternam dona eis, Domine, et lux perpetua luceat eis. Kyrie eleison, Christe eleison, Kyrie eleison,*' Father Antoine continues, immediately followed by another croak, which brings a murmur from the congregation and sends a shudder through the crowd as though it were a voice from beyond the grave.

The mourners crowd closer to the pit so they can see the anura.

'Come now, come now!' Father Antoine protests, calling to order his flock as they jostle and trample the hem of his soutane.

He embarks on an Our Father and sprinkles the coffin with holy water:

'... And lead us not into temptation but deliver us from evil, from the gates of hell. Deliver his soul, O Lord. May he rest in peace. Amen. Lord, hear my prayer, and let my cry come to you. The Lord be with you. Let us pray.'

Roused from the prayerful contemplation imposed by the circumstances, the widow has opened her eyes under her mourning veil and, tight-lipped, she too steps towards the grave. From all around come comments, a few sniggers.

'What in God's name is that?'

'A toad?'

'Where, where?'

Children slip between the legs of the adults the better to peer into the hole, their hands buried in the mound of earth.

'Don't get yourself dirty, you little wretch!'

'Get out of there, Thérèse, for God's sake, you'll ruin your dress!'

'Let us pray!' the priest bellows and a few villagers half-heartedly respond:

'Grant to Thy servant departed, O Lord, we beseech Thee, Thy mercy, that he, who prayed that Thy will might be done, may not receive punishments for his misdeeds, but that even as here below the true Faith united him to the ranks of the faithful, so in heaven by Thy mercy he may have fellowship with the choirs of angels. Through Christ our Lord. Amen.'

'Eternal rest grant unto him, O Lord: and let perpetual light shine upon him. May he rest in peace. Amen.'

'Amen.'

'Anima eius et animae omnium fidelium defunctorum, per misericordiam Dei requiescant in pace. Amen.'

'Amen,' the villagers murmur, and the priest motions to the pallbearers, who slip the ropes under the coffin, lift it, then, keeping close together, walk to the graveside, where shingles are laid around the pit, and suspend the battered coffin above the abyss. Father Antoine makes sweeping gestures to the indifferent parishioners, who huddle together. Inadvertently, he knees a girl crawling in the mud on all fours, sending her scurrying back to her mother.

'Come on, step back! Step back!'

The ropes blanche the bronzed hands of the men and wind around their wrists as they slowly lower the coffin into the grave. The assembled company are now holding their breath because the toad has disappeared in the shadow cast by the coffin, which soon fills the hole as the pallbearers slide it down.

'Will he get squashed?' a little one asks shrilly and is quickly silenced by a clip around his blond head.

The assembled mourners step a little closer, if that were possible, craning their necks the better to see, and without a word they watch as the coffin makes contact with the muddy water, floats for an instant while the ropes, relieved of their burden, slacken and are hauled back to the surface. Then water begins to seep between the loose boards and the coffin sinks, foot first, the head rising, giving everyone the opportunity to imagine the dead man's shoes and the bottoms of his trousers being plunged up to the knee in cold mud. A silence descends and the blackbirds perched on the crosses of the graves sing. A few lazy bubbles break the surface of the water under the disconcerted eyes of the villagers, and the widow stifles a cry of dread with her veil. The toad everyone thought buried alive has resurfaced and calmly climbs the lid as far as the effigy of Christ. With its front leg it brushes away a twig stuck to its head, raising a snort of indignation from the crowd.

'We can't bury him like that,' someone cries.

''Tis an ill omen.'

'Proof that the beast had its eye on him, poor man.'

'Time was, they were crucified upside down, by all accounts.'

95

'It's the devil.'

'Balderdash, t'ain't but a dumb animal.'

Small groups form, there are whispered discussions, everyone has his say, his superstition, while the widow, whose head is spinning, is made to sit on a little gravestone. It is first agreed to lift the toad out with a branch, which needs to be forked at the end to support the weight. The children are sent off to search for the tool at the foot of the cypresses, outside the cemetery walls, under the oak and walnut trees. But none of the branches they bring back is long enough to reach the bottom of the grave. Someone suggests a pitchfork, a shovel. It might injure the animal, protests Jeanne Cadours – who owns the grocer's shop on the village square – surely they have to be careful not to spill blood into the grave? Father Antoine shrugs his shoulders, he does not know, and warns that if the villagers do not step back from the edge of the pit, whose walls are threatening to collapse, they will all be down there and will be spoiled for choice as to which of them fishes out the accursed animal. Everyone prudently takes a few steps back.

'I'll climb down and get it,' Marcel proposes.

'And get that good suit mucky?'

'Where the hell is Jocelyn? This coffin of his don't seem too solid to me, it's already soaked through...'

'Who said that? It's perfectly solid, my coffin. I suppose you'll be buried in a walnut casket, will you? You pinch pennies then you go complaining, well, you can sort out your own bloody mess.'

'For the love of God, stop arguing,' roars Father Antoine. 'This is a funeral and here you are blaspheming.'

'A coffin isn't made to take the weight of a man, that's all I'm saying,' adds Jocelyn Lagarde.

The villagers fall silent for a moment as the steeple

toes touch the lid of the coffin, which rocks under her weight, pitches, sinks and releases a revolting stench. At first she steadies herself against the clayey walls, and has just managed to lay her palms on the coffin, leaving handprints on the polished wood, when the piercing pain splits her again, making her groan and forcing her to release her grip and bring a hand to her belly. Then Éléonore feels something warm trickle down her thigh and her calf. She lifts the sodden hem of her dress and sees the blood stream, following a tortuous path through the downy hair that covers her pale skin, and then dripping onto the coffin lid; a single drop, a tiny crimson dome that gleams for a moment in the half-light before disappearing, soaking into a knot of wood. Éléonore has already seen her mother wash her brown napkins and tip the pinkish water out of the basin, but surreptitiously and as though mortified. Gripped by a dark feeling of shame, she hurriedly wipes herself with the damp material of her dress, then looks up. Still unmoving, the amphibian is sitting on the little effigy of Christ, its sides pulsing, pupils dilated, but so exhausted from hours of swimming that it does not even try to flee when Éléonore cups it in her trembling hands, lifts it up and brings it to her face. She looks at it for a moment, kneeling on the half-submerged coffin in the grave, and just as she sometimes dreams of being buried in the soft, sweet-smelling earth of the forest, it occurs to her that it would be possible for her to lie down on the coffin lid, parallel to the mortal remains of the father, cradling the toad in her hands, and wait, eyes fixed on the sky and the soaring seagulls, for the villagers to bury her alive on the orders of the widow. But Marcel, kneeling on the shingles, pulls the rope that still connects Éléonore to the world of the living and draws her towards him

9 8

until he can grasp her under the arms, then sets her down on the cemetery ground, in the blinding sunlight.

The villagers stare at her in silence for a long moment, the dazzled child whose dress, stockings and hair are soiled. She holds the toad before her in her mud-blackened fingers like an offering.

'Are we supposed to kill it?' someone finally ventures.

There come no answers, no-one being certain what to do in the circumstances. Already the countryfolk, weary and satisfied, are drifting away and heading back to the village, and the gravedigger buries the blade of his shovel in the trampled hillock and throws a first shovelful of mud into the grave, which lands on the coffin with a muffled thud. Éléonore takes advantage of the adults' newfound indifference to escape, pushing open the cemetery gates and following the wall until she comes to the thickets below where a small brook runs not far from the foot of the great oak. Here, the voices and the clang of the shovel reach her only distantly, softened by the rustling of the branches of the oak tree and the unbroken song of the birds nesting there. Éléonore crouches down and sits on a root. Pain radiates from the lower abdomen. She half-opens the hands holding the toad again and in its eyes seeks the gentle look of her father's eyes, because it does not seem to her impossible that something of him has survived and lived on in this creature, not the soul but a vestige, some faint echo. When she sets it on the ground, the toad at first squats on its stubby legs, then, convinced that the child does not represent a threat, calmly disappears into the grass. Éléonore watches it for a moment until she sees it disappear. She huddles against the trunk of the oak as she used to do against the father's body and lays a hand against the bark rubbed smooth by the rasp of clogs and of bare feet. She feels a great wave of tiredness. The seagulls have forsaken the sky. The branches of the great oak break up the light, scattering it in flashes over the trunk, the ground and Éléonore's face. Violets are growing in the short grass and in the moss, perfuming the sprawling shade of the tree. She picks one and eats it. A few squirrels, red, furtive shadows, skirt around the trunk, suddenly appearing and disappearing with little squeaks. The mud stains on her mourning dress have dried and exhaustion gradually overcomes the child, whose eyelids close in spite of her, so she can see only the tawny daylight, luminous, flickering lines between her eyelashes. Later, it is a hand that wakes her, then the face of Marcel bending over her. The funeral is over and the father now reposes in eternal darkness. Éléonore grasps the hand Marcel offers and he helps her to her feet.

'Let's go home,' he says.

The child nods and together they climb the slope to where the widow is waiting on the road that leads from the village to Puy-Larroque cemetery.

In the evening, as they are undressing to put on their nightclothes, the widow notices the brown stains on the girl's underclothes. Immediately, she grabs them, brings them to her nose and sniffs, inhaling in little gulps, savouring the smell of the first period, the irrefutable proof of her sexual maturity. Slowly, she lowers her arms. Her lips tremble and her eyes come to rest on Éléonore.

'You are unclean,' she says, in a toneless voice. 'You are sullied now. And you will sin.'

'No,' Éléonore says. 'No, I...'

'Shut up. Say what you like, you will sin. Oh, yes.

Remember how Eve allowed the serpent to beguile her. He will beguile you too. Don't forget that we are here on this earth through her fault. And the Lord said: "I will greatly multiply thy sorrow and thy conception; in sorrow thou shalt bring forth children; and thy desire shall be to thy husband, and he shall rule over thee." And to the man He said: "Cursed is the ground for thy sake; in sorrow shalt thou eat of it all the days of thy life; thorns also and thistles shall it bring forth to thee; and thou shalt eat the herb of the field; in the sweat of thy face shalt thou eat bread, till thou return unto the ground; for out of it wast thou taken: for dust thou art, and unto dust shalt thou return."'

The widow lays a hand on the girl's shoulders, pressing with all her weight until Éléonore's legs buckle and they both fall to their knees.

'Let us pray,' she says, 'for the salvation of your soul and your father's. *Miserere mei, Deus: secundum magnam misericordiam tuam.* And according to the multitude of Thy tender mercies blot out my iniquity. Wash me yet more from my iniquity, and cleanse me from my sin...'

In the days that follow the funeral, they wash the house with lye soap to clean away the smell, scrubbing the sheets and then the floors until the skin on their knees and their palms is blistered. The widow opens the old wardrobe fashioned by the father's father long ago, when she was trundling along in her wedding dress in a cart drawn by a Pyrenean donkey, then she takes out the clothes belonging to the dead husband who rattled along next to her, proud as a peacock, wearing the same suit in which he is now rotting in Puy-Larroque cemetery. She unfolds the shirts and the patched trousers, folds them again and lays them on the table in two piles. In his glory

101

days, the father was much the same build as Marcel, and the widow, who cannot abide waste, could offer the nephew enough to dress himself and supplement his meagre attire, two shirts and two sweaters he wears alternately, changing one when he stinks enough and it has become stiff as a board over his pale torso – it is considered appropriate for a man to smell, as it is from their smell that one can gauge their worth and their efforts – but she takes the old clothes to a corner of the yard, puts some dry branches in the bottom of a metal barrel and burns everything, standing guard in the black, acrid smoke, arms folded, staring straight ahead, until there is nothing left but an insubstantial pile of ash carried off by the first gust of wind. She sorts through her own clothes, and packs away the dresses, cardigans and stockings that are not black into a wicker basket. When she is not cleaning or tending to the animals, she sets a chair by the front door and waits, sitting in her widow's weeds, hands resting in her lap, rigid as a sphinx.

Several times a year, pedlars set up shop on the village square and, for a morning, offer more or less anything that can be bought in town at the ironmonger's, the haberdasher's and the dressmaker's, sharpening knives and buying up old clothes. The village women eagerly await the market, their meagre savings slipped next to their breast, then hurry to the cart, fighting over the merchandise, feeling the fabrics, engaging in protracted negotiations. The widow, who has no desire to be part of the profligate exhilaration of the other women, watches from her vantage point the road that leads to Puy-Larroque. A cart approaches drawn by a mangy, stubborn mule urged on by a pedlar who has whipped the animal so hard its croup is bald. Very soon, she will

102

die somewhere along the road, bowing her head with a heavy sigh, her body held upright by the shafts, the harness and the weight of the cart, and the pedlar will carry on roaring and thrashing the bare leather of its croup for a moment before climbing down to discover that the animal's tongue is lolling in the dust and its large, cloudy eye is half-closed. Her old heart will simply have given up after twenty years of drudgery and more lashes of the whip than any beast on earth could endure. Just now, the widow is gesturing to the pedlar, beckoning him over. The hawker lacerates the animal's mouth, leaning back on the reins with all his weight and brings the cart to a halt in the middle of the farmyard. The mule's shoes are thin and cracked, its hooves worn down, and she drinks thirstily from the bucket Éléonore has brought. The pedlar is so small he could be taken for a dwarf – he has the same plump hands, the same bandy legs, the same swagger to his gait – but his head is that of a man of normal constitution, so that it looks as though it has been screwed onto this squat body by mistake. As always he is elegantly dressed in a three-piece suit that, Éléonore assumes, was made for a city boy from a well-heeled family, a nine-year-old at most, with a bow tie tightly cinched into his fat red neck, about to garrotte him. Though he is the smallest creature that Éléonore has ever seen, the pedlar is also the fattest, with folds of skin at his wrists and at his elbows. Like those dolls of wood or porcelain she has dreamed about, where the parts are separate but held together by a metal wire, when she sees the pedlar twice or three times a year, she imagines his body is filled with pliable metal wires in place of bones, which – more than his weight – would explain the difficulty he has moving, his manner of turning his flushed, sweaty head without ever nodding to say yes or no as

103

the reflection she takes care not to look at in the mirror. She comforts herself with the thought that black better suits their ghostly complexion. The merchant examines each piece of clothing.

'I'll not get much for these, dear,' he says, turning his head.

Her pride wounded, the widow recoils slightly.

'I've always taken good care of them,' she says.

The dealer shrugs, then examines the clothes again and says,'I'll not get much for them.'

In the ensuing silence, the mule lifts its tail and defecates.

'What I want is material like that there,' the widow says, pointing to the cart.

The pedlar seems to think for a moment.

'Three, four lengths,' the widow adds. 'That's all I'm asking. After all, I have to dress appropriately now that my husband's dead.'

The merchant once more pretends to hesitate, then waves his arm to say, 'Go on, then,' and with a magnanimous swagger he steps towards his wares, picks up a pair of scissors, unrolls a bolt of black fabric, measuring it against the side of the cart, doubles it, then triples it before cutting under the watchful eye of the widow. He folds the fabric, proffers it to the customer and holds out his doll-like hand, the same hand that moments earlier was tugging his penis in front of the little child, and the widow takes it in her thin grey, masculine hand.

'There you go, m'dear! It's a deal, as they say.'

The pedlar gives Éléonore a wink and, touching the brim of his hat, jumps up onto the cart and whips the croup of the mule, who, roused from her doze, stifles a bray and sets in motion her old bones. The widow and the girl watch as the cart pulls out of the farmyard. Then the peasant woman heads back towards the house, running her hand over the fabric, from which she will painstakingly cut and sew the two dresses that she will wear from this day forward until she takes her last breath. She has always envied the solemnity of widows and mourning is a balm to her, like the pitiable expression that she already likes to affect, suggesting a suppressed, relentless pain, an open wound that both lifts and transcends her. These are the clothes, she thinks, that will safeguard her authority over the child and the nephew, to whose tender mercies she has been left by the husband's death. Éléonore remains in the yard, seized by a feeling that she has been sullied, a bitter aftertaste in her mouth. Alphonse is lying at her feet, in the dust raised by the pedlar's departure. For the first time since his passing, the father's death seems to her real, inevitable, and consigns her to an unbearable loneliness, confronted by the dark forces she cannot name but which are welling within her, stirring nefarious urges. In the pale sunlight that illuminates the farmyard, she shivers like a small prey animal.

The earth begins to murmur, the sap to well in the trees, rising slowly through the trunks, and buds swell beneath the bark along the bare branches. Opalescent larvae writhe beneath the layers of humus and in the rotting stumps, woken from their torpor by the thaw, and brown pupae begin to hatch. In the village cemetery, at first light, the grass snakes slither from a vault and rest on a gravestone half-hidden by ferns. The ice from the reservoir, which the more reckless village children cross in the dead of winter, has long since melted and water striders ripple the surface of the water as they scurry. In spring, the women of Puy-Larroque and the surrounding farms gather at dawn around the village wash-house. They come on foot, on carts, on mules, with a barrow or carrying large burlap sacks filled with the linens they wash only once a year, as though starched with sweat, mud, with the secretions of men and those of animals. All winter, they have collected the ashes from the hearth and protected it from inclement weather in these same burlap sacks. The washing is laid out on the cool, dew-damp grass, in the morning sun and the smell of hay. The washerwomen set out buckets of water drawn from the wash trough, and in them dissolve flakes of lye soap, which gradually scents the air. At the hour when the cocks are crowing and calling to one another, the men are sharpening scythes and setting off, donning their caps, beneath the deep blue sky in which a sliver of moon and a handful of stars still gleam, scythe handles resting on their shoulders, a few dogs trotting at their heels. Since the father's death, Alphonse will only go with Marcel, but he no longer runs ahead of him or of Éléonore, nor bounds across ditches. He simply walks alongside, head hanging low, and lies down as soon as possible to rest his hind legs, which have grown stiff.

His eyes are covered with a bluish pall and his coat has turned white. The washerwomen plunge the laundry into the soapy water, where it disgorges swirls of blackish fluid. In the quiet farms the chickens grow bolder and venture into the houses whose doors stand open to let in a little cool morning air; they peck about under the tables, perch on the backs of chairs, hop up on the beds, where sometimes they lay an egg which they sit on until they are chased off with a broom. Sitting on the grass, in the shade of fig trees heavy with sap, the washerwomen talk. Sometimes one of them will get up to stir the laundry, which is left to soak all day. The blades of the scythes blaze in the midday sun and white flashes course through the meadows. Wearing scarves and armed with washboards, the women trample the grass, which gives off a sweet perfume. The youngest children are sitting or lying at the foot of the trees, watched over by their sisters; from time to time, a young mother lies down, unbuttons her blouse to reveal a swollen breast and suckles a newborn. The air smells of the women's perspiration, of trampled grass and sweltering cattle. From field to meadow, the farmers call to one another in jubilant voices; the haymaking is good this year and will carry on into July for the late fields. They will have enough to feed the animals and face the harsh winter.

From the edge of the field where she stands, Éléonore looks at Marcel, his damp shirt clinging to the long, flat muscles of his back, his torso, the hay dust settling on his sunburned neck, the fringe of hair that falls over his forehead and which he sweeps away with the back of his hand, the assiduous gestures that are slower and less precise than those of the father. When he drinks from the flask she proffers, he lets the water trickle into his

111

cupped hands and vigorously rubs his face, blowing tiny droplets that land on Éléonore's forehead or at the corners of her mouth. The washerwomen place a sheet into one of the tubs of coopered wood, then, with the aid of small shovels, scoop the ashes into small cloth bags tied with fine string and place them into the tubs beneath the layers of laundry.

Every evening during haymaking season, Marcel draws water from the well and pours it into the tub used to scald the slaughtered pig before winter. He undresses, leaving his clothes on the coping of the well, and reveals the white skin that contrasts with his suntanned neck and forearms. The hair on his legs forms a pale, dense froth that suddenly trails off as it reaches his marbled ankles, with only a thin line of red hair following the arch of his foot as far as the big toe. In the other direction, at the groin, the foam breaks into a darker wave. Éléonore imagines that if she laid her hand flat against the thighs, the coarse hair would resist the pressure of her palms, then she would push her slim fingers through the thick tangle until she felt the hard, pale, naked flesh of Marcel. When he climbs into the tub, a shiver runs through his skin, he goes deeper and sits for a long time, his arms hugging his knees; the murky water traces a line on his upper lip and ripples each time he exhales.

On the edge of the fields, Éléonore gathers spring flowers, broom, daisies and cornflowers, which she lays on the mound beneath which lie the father's mortal remains. She pulls up the green shoots of grasses sown by the wind in the crevices of the ochre mound surmounted by a metal cross that is already tottering. The washerwomen pour boiling water into the tubs. The laundry slowly

112

becomes soaked with water and ash, a process the women repeat as many times as are necessary, until the water they expel is also boiling, at which point they plunge in sturdy wooden poles, with the tips of which they lift out the grey, steaming sheets before depositing them on an openwork cart. On the third day of spring laundry, the sheets are immersed in the huge wash trough, rinsed, soaped and vigorously beaten. Bare-armed, the women lay cloths on the edge of the trough, on which they kneel. Their heads are spinning when they sit back to wipe their brows with the backs of their arms, or tuck in locks of hair that have escaped from beneath their scarves. Their cheeks are red, and the thick white suds leave frothy trails clinging to their wrists, like the cuckoo spit left clinging to blades of grass by the froghopper larvae.

Soon, the young corvids still haloed in downy feathers begin to venture beyond their nests of twigs. Marcel rescues a young crow that has fallen from the top of a chestnut tree and is hopping around between the roots, trailing a bent, broken leg. Marcel sits in the shadow of the tree, which quivers with points of light. He unbuttons his shirt and nestles the fledgling against his damp belly, talking in a low whisper to calm it. He scans the surrounding patch of ground, running his fingers over the leaves and old burrs, chooses a greenwood sapling, and strips away the bark with his knife. Cradling the chick in the hollow of his hand, he unfurls its delicate wings, turns it over and lays it on his thigh, then attaches a splint to the leg. When he brings the bird back to the farmhouse and sets it next to his bed, in a little cage he has cobbled together, the widow blenches and says nothing, though she seethes to herself: have they not sorrows enough without sheltering one of these nasty, filthy, thieving carrion feeders under their roof? The father would never have allowed the nephew to do such a thing. He would have shown him the door, him and his bird of ill omen. She is already reinventing her memory of the father, rambling on about her grief, rewriting history, fashioning for him a retrospective dignity. She speaks regretfully of the memory of the man she so loved, the respect the patriarch inspired, the natural authority to which she willingly submitted, because the man was loving, and dignified, to his last breath.

The hay has dried in the sun and the farmers are now building tall hayricks, whose shadows, at twilight, are grave, gilded mounds.

'I confess to Almighty God, to blessed Mary ever Virgin, to blessed Michael the Archangel, to blessed John the Baptist, to the holy Apostles Peter and Paul, to all the Saints, and to You, my God, that I have sinned exceedingly in thought, word and deed: through my fault, through my fault, through my most grievous fault. Therefore I beseech blessed Mary ever Virgin, blessed Michael the Archangel, blessed John the Baptist, the holy Apostles Peter and Paul, all the Saints, and you, brethren, to pray for me to the Lord our God,' Éléonore recites.

The widow sits next to her, her mourning dress like the black soutane of the confessor, and says:

'Speak, child. I am listening.'

Left alone on the farm, Éléonore takes down the crucifix nailed at the foot of the box-bed, places it at the bottom of the chamber pot and, hiking up her dress, hunkers down and sprays long jets of urine over the face

114

of Christ. She stares at him for a moment, immersed in micturition, then plunges two fingers into the bucket, fishes out the crucifix and hangs it back on the nail, from where it trickles two or three translucent drops onto the widow's bed. Éléonore spends the following days in terror, fearing some retribution, some punishment, but nothing happens and the blued sheets dry on washing lines strung between the trees, and the menfolk bring the forage back to the farms and lay it in the sun to dry, while the baby crow hops onto the forefinger Marcel holds out, and, in little bounds, climbs onto his shoulder, where it perches and eats the balls of breadcrumbs the boy rolls between his fingertips. On the day of her First Communion, Éléonore secretly vows to expel from her heart all feeling, all religious tendencies, and this act of desertion leaves a small fracture in her, a hole, a painless but persistent wound. The sun dazzles the communicants, who stand, proud and solemn, on the steps of the church.

In the early hours of the first day of summer, Father Antoine brusquely awakens from a dream in which the altar boys in their white albs cover him with kisses and caresses, pressing their warm, lithe bodies against him. When he half-opens his eyes and looks at the peeling wall of his bedroom, it is an altar boy he sees crucified on the plaster cross nailed to the wall, the crown of thorns lacerating his pale, smooth forehead, the modest loincloth hanging from his narrow hips, the tilted face staring fixedly at him. Then the priest is jolted back to himself by a chasm deeper and more unfathomable even than sleep, a vertiginous fall into an endless night where there is no light.

The body of Father Antoine is carried on a cart to its final resting place, the family vault in which lie a father and a mother who died in childbirth, whose blind, comforting memory he invoked when he was mercilessly gripped by the terror of the Last Judgement and the deafening silence of God, and, as the assembled villagers look on, the coffin draped with his alb is borne away and disappears behind the old castle walls.

'*Ite, missa est*,' an insolent voice pipes up, and a few laughs can be heard among the offended sighs of the sempiternal mourners who head back to the fields in a clatter of clogs.

Summer definitively settles in. Not a drop of rain has fallen for several weeks. The tall wheat ripens and the ears rustle when the west wind blows. The earth cracks, the air quivers and shimmers above the ground, fragile, and tremulous mirages appear on roads and on bare farmland in the distance. Hens scratch at the dust in search of a little coolness and the pig lies in the evaporated puddles. At dawn, furtive game roam around the edges of the woods and the field crops, then spend all day hiding in burrows and in bramble thickets. In the muggy heat of the byre, one of the two cows is lying on the straw, about to calve. Éléonore sees the round, white amniotic sac appear. For a moment, it looks as though the cow is about to lay an egg, a giant pearl; then the thin membrane splits and spills translucent liquid over the udder, the hocks and the apron tied around the waist of the widow, who soaks cloths in hot water and applies them to the animal's back. She runs a hand over the cow's taut belly, over the damp spine. All the while, she talks to the animal in a low, soothing voice, and if Éléonore is standing off to one side in a corner of the byre, it is because the widow's tone of voice is so unfamiliar that it seems indecent, obscene. Dumbfounded, she watches the widow's gestures, the caresses merited by the heifer yet not by her, her daughter, and she listens to the soft, soothing words. The widow touches the folds of the vulva, slips in a hand greased with butter and feels the sticky hooves and the muzzle of the calf, then goes and sits in a corner of the barn, where she waits, shooing flies from her face, staring at the heifer, at the swollen udders, at its eyes that toll in the half-light as each spasm shudders through her. Finally, the white hooves and the slimy muzzle emerge, the cloudy eye appears from the uterine darkness, the calf is pushed from the womb by the contractions in the cow as the anus rhythmically discharges jets of green dung. The widow gets to her feet, grips the calf at the cannon bones and heaves with all her might, following the rhythm of the contractions, sweating like the cow every drop of water in her body. Once the calf is lying, motionless and steaming on the straw, the widow slips three fingers into its mouth and pulls out a fistful of mucus and wipes it on the apron smeared with blood, dung and amniotic fluid. Swarms of flies hover and the calf breathes and contemplates the closed, shadowy world of the byre, the face of the widow looming over it, then the head of the cow as she struggles to her feet and laps at its viscid coating. The placenta oozes out of the red, gaping vulva. The widow tosses it into a bucket and takes it away, hugging it to her belly. Alone, Éléonore picks up a handful of straw and rubs the calf, which suddenly gets up onto its unsteady legs and, taking the girl's fingers for its mother's udder, sucks at her hand. She feels the warm, undulating palate, the soft, greedy tongue against her palm.

117

Some days after Father Antoine's death, Jean Roujas, the last of the altar boys on whom the priest lavished his favours, leaves the family home on a balmy night; only a few dogs see him as he wanders through Puy-Larroque carrying a length of rope. The following morning, he is found wearing his nightshirt, damp with dew, hanging from the lowest branch of the old oak. His frail body spins in slow circles like a star, his face now bathed in the dawn light, now engulfed by the night that still clings to the tree. He is buried in a small coffin fashioned to his size, which his father, mad with rage and grief, insists on carrying alone, balanced on one shoulder. From the house where the child's remains were waked – his jaw is held in place by a cotton strip crocheted by his grieving mother and tied over his straw-blond hair – the father walks to the cemetery, swathed in clouds of ochre pollen, passes in front of the church whose doors are closed and deaf to his grief, his arms gripping the casket digging into the flesh of his neck.

Marcel rarely speaks about his family, about his parents, his brothers. On the last Sunday of each month, since the father's death, he harnesses the mare before daybreak and sets off to visit them, without ever proposing that Éléonore accompany him. By the time he comes back, she is already lying in the bed next to the widow's, and sees his sullen shadow pass close to her. The widow probably entertained thoughts of dismissing him, but the boy continues to prove himself a hard worker; he ploughs, he reaps, he digs, he hoes, then he collapses from exhaustion until dawn the following day. In the privacy of his room, he sometimes feels a tension, a frustration, and slips a hand beneath the sheet, but he does so only to assuage his body, and only vague images rise sensitive. He accepts her company, sometimes even her help whenever the widow gives her daughter a brief respite, because she is ever watchful, and gives Éléonore endless chores in an attempt to keep the girl away from him. The two children walk through the fields together, sleep at the foot of a tree in the afternoon heat, lead the cows and the mare out to the pasture to graze, talk about the animals, about the harvest, sometimes evoke memories of the father. The sun darkens their skin and brightens their eyes. They name the little crow Charbon, then set it free, but after clumsily taking wing, the bird follows them, cawing, flying close to the ground until one of them bends and stretches out a hand and it eagerly hops on. For the feast of Saint-Jean on Midsummer Day, Marcel joins a handful of villagers tasked with gathering branches in the woods and building a great bonfire on a peak overlooking a fallow valley, which they clear with scythes, cutting a path through the grasses and the poppies. A serene jubilation takes hold of Puy-Larroque and its inhabitants. Voices are raised, children run around, excited and boisterous. The smell of a sheep that has been spit-roasting since morning pervades the narrow streets and, in every house, cooks are busy at their ovens. At nightfall, a joyous procession leaves the village flanked by a pack of dogs, beneath swarms of mayflies that flutter around the torches they are holding. The menfolk carry the barrels of wine and the women the baskets of victuals. The glow of sunset turns the crops, the bramble thickets and the warm bark of the trees blood-red. The wilted petals of false acacia dance gently along the paths and get caught in the webs of wasp spiders. In a meadow, a foal being weaned kicks at the fences while his mother, her udder aching, whinnies from the stable. The fields still smell of hay, wild garlic, broom and warm stones.

120

As a torch sets the bonfire ablaze, the men gather round and watch the crackling flames, the burning ashes that rise and whirl and gutter out and disappear against the purple backcloth of the sky. They roast potatoes in the embers, tear open the charred crust and eat the steaming flesh from their hands, blowing between bites on fingers glistening with saliva and mutton fat. The wine from the barrels brings a flush to the brows, burns the stomachs and trickles down bare necks. A fiddler starts up a ritornel, which is immediately picked up by an accordion, and the men and women get to their feet and gather around the fire for a rondo, their faces crimson, sweating, smiling. Marcel has grabbed Éléonore's hand and is holding it tightly. She feels the vibrations of his dancing body and moves with them. She can smell his fitful breaths, heavy with alcohol. She can smell the odour of their bodies, united and frenzied, everyone here, all the farm folk, the smell of their lowly breed, of their aching, tired flesh, and suddenly they seem to her terribly old and fragile, on borrowed time at forty, their bodies battered, congenital, sagging from childbirth, goitrous, mutilated by blades, charred by the sun. No-one here will get through life without losing a limb, an eye, a child or a spouse, a piece of flesh, and Éléonore feels the thick, calloused skin of her knees, her elbows, brushing against the fabric of her dress, of her blouse. Even the children seem only to remain children for the blink of an eye. They come into the world like livestock, scrabble in the dust in search of meagre sustenance, and die in miserable solitude. They dance to the sound of a squeaky fiddle to forget that they were dead before they were born, and the alcohol, the music and the saraband lulls them into a gentle trance, the impression of life. When all that remains is a ring of embers where the

121

the mare, which takes a few steps forward each time
he taps her croup, then dozes again while the lanterns
gleam in the darkness like stars fallen from some distant
constellation. In the quiet of Puy-Larroque cemetery, a
will-o'-the-wisp flares, whirls and disappears, casting a
blue glow over the little patch of earth covering the coffin of the altar boy Jean Roujas.

They leave the swaths of wheat to dry in the sun, then
thresh them with a flail, and the frantic rhythm of the
blows echoes through the countryside. The widow then
sorts the grain from the chaff with a winnowing fan and
the sound of the wheel replaces that of the flail. Éléonore
pours the grain into the hopper. Soon the barn is filled
with dust, leaving on their tongues a taste of earth and
bran. Despite the rumblings – the assassination of the
Archduke in June, the mobilizing of the 9th, 88th and
288th regiments now camped in Agen and in Auch –
every now and then Marcel and Éléonore find moments
of calm freedom before they are brought back to earth by
the reality of the farm, and the great world beyond, about
which they know almost nothing, and whose upheavals
reach them as hushed quiverings, the last faint ripple of
a stone dropped into the middle of a vast lake on whose
shores they are standing. Since the father's death, the
widow no longer reads the newspapers, not even to clip
out sacred images or to revel in the depravity of man-
kind. The harvest affords little time for rest and summer
quickly sweeps away the ominous feelings that troubled
Éléonore's heart. Nothing can touch them, nothing can
possibly end at the height of summer and, like those mirages that tremble on the horizon, there hovers a feeling
of imaginable eternity; a serene happiness.

123

They are in the field on that first day of August beneath a perfect sky, an expanse of light, a crushing heat that seems about to set the earth ablaze, when they hear shouting in the distance. They straighten up, suspend their swinging scythes. An adolescent hurtles down the road on a bicycle. It is Octave, the son of the baker; he lets go of the handlebars and, cupping his hands into a loudhailer, yells something at them. From field to field, the farmers glance at each other.

'What did he say?' someone shouts.

Marcel shrugs. And yet he thinks he might have heard, and feels a prickling in his forearms that runs from his elbow, through his hands, his fingers, to the roots of his nails. He walks towards the edge of the field, his tread slow and heavy. He can feel the wooden handle of the scythe rub against his palm, the sweat that is trickling down his back and soaking the waistband of his trousers, he can smell the hot stones, the ripe wheat, the reek of the stables. He perceives with a new acuity the existence of each thing in itself, each detail that makes up the reality of this moment, and yet also their clandestine connection, their meshing into an indissoluble great whole: the white disc of the sun and the pulse of blood in his eardrums, the caw of a crow, the sound of his clogs on the dry ground, and Éléonore standing a few metres from him. Farther off, Octave has let his bicycle freewheel on and bury itself in a bramble thicket. The back wheel is spinning in the air as the boy carries on at a run, leaping the ditch that separates the road from the fields belonging to Georges Frejefond, to whom he is now talking, waving his arms and pointing towards the village. As Marcel approaches, he sees Frejefond nod his head, his expression grave, and lay a hand on the boy's shoulder.

124

'What's going on?' Marcel asks.

Octave turns to him, his eyes wild, and says breathlessly:

'It's war! Papa sent me to fetch you all. He says you have to come to the town hall! It's war!'

Then the church bells ring out, freezing them all to the spot. Drowning out the rustle of the fields, reducing it to a form of silence, because during the long minutes while the alarm is sounded, everything dissolves into the metallic undulations that spread in waves across a sky bereft of birds, piercing everything, echoing off everything: the valleys, the rocks, the dry-stone walls, the woods, the animals and the hearts of men.

The village is thronged. The farmers stream in from their fields, leave their houses, desert the café, the shopkeepers close up and hurry to the town hall to read, or have read to them, the general mobilization order. With Éléonore following behind, Marcel elbows his way closer to the steps of the town hall. An incredulous murmur ripples through the village square, where a few cows continue to graze. The villagers speak in hushed tones, as on the day of a funeral mass:

'... every man, from eighteen to forty...'

'But when?... and where will they go?...'

'... the harvest, who'll bring it in if our Paul isn't here?'

'Bloody nationalists, it's them as...'

'... you with your flat feet and your twisted spine, come off it...'

'They can't just leave like that, now...'

'How will they get there, the poor lads?'

'It's the Boches, didn't I say it?'

'... a good thrashing, that's what they need, sort their ideas out...'

'... they've already occupied Alsace-Lorraine...'

'And I suppose you know where that is, Alsace-Lorraine?'

'Well, I'll not go. Let them in Paris deal with it – what has it got to do with the rest of us...?'

'You'll see what it's got to do with you when they come for your livestock and your wife...'

'He'd be only too happy for some Boche to do his farm work for him, and take Louise off his hands!'

'... if it's like it was back in 1870, it'll be over before we know it...'

'... bring in the harvest, then there's the ploughing to think of. How am I supposed to cope, me and my three sons, if they're called up?'

'He's only a bit of a lad, he's never even held a rifle...'

The talk flourishes until Julien Beyries, the mayor, appears on the steps of the town hall, at which point mayhem ensues. The villagers clamour, pressing him for answers to their questions. He tries to calm them with a wave, then finally roars for them to shut up.

'It'll be over and done with in a few months, from what I've heard,' he says. 'Poincaré said there might not even be a war. But if there is, it'll be a short war.'

'So is there a war or isn't there?'

'And what the devil do you know, anyway, Beyries? There's no way of knowing how long a war will last.'

'We'll give them a good hiding and we'll be back by winter, it's obvious.'

'Calm down! The town hall will be open all night tonight. From eight o'clock, every man between eighteen and forty has to enlist. And I mean every man, no exceptions. You'll be given your papers, your posting orders, the name of the regiment or the corps you've been assigned to, and the departure time and number of the train you'll be taking in the next few days.'

'When exactly?'

'Me, I'm happy to leave right now if that's what it takes.'

'And I suppose you're going to come and harvest the rest of my wheat?'

'The first of you will leave the day after tomorrow. I've a son too, and he's the same age as your boy, Cazaux, so don't go thinking I'm happy about this.'

'So what happens if we don't go to war? What if we refuse the call-up?'

'Coward!'

'In that case you're refusing to serve, to defend your country. You'll be considered a deserter. You'll be court-martialled as a deserter and probably shot, that's what.'

A brief stunned silence falls over the village square as wild birds fly over, casting their shadows over the faces. The mayor is pale, his jaws clenched, his eyes glittering more than usual, and the telegrams he is clutching quivering in his hands.

'We have to hide our children,' says a woman in a strangled cry.

No-one responds at first, then Beyries says:

'We can't. They'll come for them. They'll find them.'

Then, squaring his shoulders:

'We will serve France with honour, Puy-Larroque will serve France with honour. For any of you who want to pray, the church will also be open all night. That's all.'

They applaud and for a moment they stand there, united in their bewilderment. To all but the few who remember 1870, war is an abstraction, an empty word, dizzying and exhilarating, the Germans are a barbarous, alien race, and the front a mysterious place somewhere in limbo, far beyond their horizon. The rash and patriotic among them say: 'We are going to war!', their eyes flickering from face to face like those of a young colt being broken, searching for the meaning of their own words. They will have to kill; they know this: it is an established fact, a certainty, a truth, the very purpose. In war, you kill, otherwise what would be the point? They have plunged knives into the throats of pigs and the eyes of rabbits. They have hunted deer and wild boar. They have drowned puppies and slit the throats of sheep. They have trapped foxes, poisoned rats, decapitated geese, ducks and chickens. Since birth, they have watched killings. They have watched their fathers and their mothers take the lives of animals. They learned the gestures and copied them. They in turn have killed hares, cocks, cattle, piglets, pigeons. They have shed blood, and sometimes drunk it. They know the smell, the taste. But a Boche? How do you kill a Boche? Surely that would make them murderers, even if this is a war? A few brawlers and braggarts are already boasting about the men they're going to kill, hurling themselves into the fray with bayonets drawn, but most of the men say nothing, reduced to silence. They quickly leave, head back to their houses and their farms to put together a makeshift kitbag, a few shirts, a few small tokens, to see the familiar faces, the familiar places that will soon be taken from them, or simply head back, dazed by the light, to work in the fields.

On the village square, Éléonore searches for Marcel among the berets, the hats, the identical faces, but he did not wait for the villagers to disperse and headed back without a word, picked up the scythe he abandoned in the middle of the field, the hot blade burning his fingers, and set to work again, urged on by rage and zeal. Éléonore leaves the square, races along the baked dirt road, one hand gripping the dusty fabric of her dress, and comes to the edge of the field, panting for breath. She catches sight of Marcel, who turns his back, busy swinging the scythe, and the wheat falls in large swaths, buzzing like a cicada. She walks over, catching her breath, her throat raw, then stands for a moment behind Marcel. He has not heard her, but when he sees Éléonore's skewed shadow bristling with wheat stubble, he pauses and brusquely turns.

'Can't you see I'm working?'

'You can't leave. You have to stay,' Éléonore says.

'And how, exactly? If you're not here to help, then don't just stand there. I can get this finished. By tomorrow. Maybe before midnight. I can... Go on, go, for God's sake! You think I need you getting under my feet? Go! Go! Go!'

He roars the words, brutally waving towards some distant horizon and putting to flight the flock of sparrows that has been pecking at the ground. Éléonore starts back, as though he has just slapped her, then she turns and runs off, tripping over the stones. Lips trembling, eyes blinking, Marcel watches the shadowy figure fade, pale, disappear. For a long moment, he does not move. The scythe shimmers, the sparrows grow bolder and once more land in the wheat stubble at his feet. Finally, he raises the handle.

The open doors of the church radiate the flickering glow of the votive candles that the sanctimonious snuff out every hour, since everyone feels some vestige of faith, some metaphysical need, and the stock of candles is beginning to run low. They stream past the crucifix, jostle each other on the pews and the prie-dieux, relight the candle, where nocturnal insects come to immolate themselves in the flames, slip a coin into the collection box and then leave, their souls troubled, their elbows and their knees caked in dust. The men emerge from the recruiting office clutching the promised military record and orders in hand, and gather in Puy-Larroque café to drown their sorrows, the older men gloomy as herd culls, the conscripts worried and restless. One climbs up on a stool and reads aloud an article from *La République des travailleurs*:

'In this solemn hour that has buried internecine strife for some time to come, there is but one party, the party of France, and but one rallying cry: "To the front!"'

A chorus of voices immediately takes up the cry, fists are raised, and they sing the Marseillaise to bolster their courage. Then they drink a last glass by the light of the paper lanterns beneath a low, frenzied flight of bats. They head home. They tuck in a sleeping child, lay a hand on his clammy forehead. They embrace their wife in the conjugal bed, or their lovers in a hayloft. They go into the byre, into the sheep pen, and stare at the sleeping animals. They savour the warm, acrid smell. They stroke the muzzles of the horses, the nourishing udders of the cows. They cradle a kid goat as it suckles on their fingers. They lie down in the straw against a filly's flank. They contemplate the calm, clear night, the cloudless sky of blazing constellations. They listen to the song of an owl, the shrill fight in the woods between two pine martens. They are overcome by a feeling, unfamiliar to them yet inevitable, of nostalgia. Some, with a heavy heart, remember the lines of Du Bellay they recited in school, whose meaning now pierces them to the quick:

When shall I see from my small hamlet-side
Once more the blue and curling smoke unrolled?
When the poor boundaries of my house behold,—
Poor, but to me as any province wide?

Early returned to the farm after roaming the byways,
Éléonore is sitting at the table staring at the woman
sitting facing her, to the right of the widow, and whose
curious face is lit by the glow of the lamp. She is an ugly
farmwoman of indeterminate age, though not as old as
she appears. She has a low forehead, lids that rest on
eyes that are bulging and swollen with tears. Her nose
has clearly been broken a long time ago and now points
towards one of her purple cheeks lined with angiomas,
small subcutaneous rivulets that rise and merge and
separate. Under her eyes, the skin hangs in pouches like
miniature game bags, as though she has not slept a wink
in her long, gruelling existence. The hair, which she
wears braided like a little girl's, was once white but has
yellowed with dirt and kitchen grease. The plait holds
together without need of a clip or a knot. Her body is
scrawny and wrung out, she wears a blouse speckled
with yellowish stains, a grimy black collar, and her
skirt looks as though it has been sewn together from old
rags. She would splinter underfoot as easily as a poultry
crate and catch fire as quickly as a pile of brambles. Her
hands are short, broad and traced with veins as thick as
slow worms. On her lap, pressed against her belly, she is
holding a wicker basket; her fingers, with their black tips
like fat cockchafer larvae that have just wriggled from
the soil, are entwined around the handle. She stares at
the table. She says nothing, and the widow says nothing.
From time to time, a thought seems to flicker through
her, a word that is an aside to herself, and at such times

she sadly shrugs her shoulders, murmurs something inaudible or rolls her eyeballs beneath the fringe of short, damp lashes. Sometimes she reaches out a hand and, with a lost, confused air, runs her fingertips over the wooden tabletop, following a vein or the groove of a knife. The widow eyes her with obvious scorn, almost a nauseated pout, because the woman is even more wretched than she, poorer, uglier, dragged from some hell crawling with tripe merchants, sharecroppers, whores, lunatics and beggars. And yet, *In the kingdom of the blind, the one-eyed man is king* is what the widow invariably says when she encounters someone from town, or someone of a vaguely superior status to her own, and feels that they are being arrogant or disdainful towards her. As to Christian charity, the widow's interpretation is highly personal, and her own penury exempts her from doing much.

'Well, now, I wouldn't mind a drink after such a long journey,' the woman says finally in a plaintive, rasping voice, but the widow does not move, as though she has not heard.

The visitor shrugs again and quickly resumes her contemplation of the table. She collects small breadcrumbs on the tip of her finger and abstractedly brings them to her lips. The soup on the fire gurgles, perfuming the room and bringing a constant rumbling from her belly that rises into her throat. On the far side of the hatch connected to the byre, the cows chew the cud and stare at these three motionless women, as ominous as the Fates. There comes a sound of cartwheels and a whinny from the mare, and the widow gets to her feet, the other woman likewise, still clutching the wicker basket covered with a cloth. The wick of the lamp goes black and the flame flickers. She leaves the kitchen and crosses the farmyard, walking towards her son, who is busy unharnessing the mare. Éléonore sees him break off and look at the little woman coming towards him, doubtless saying something, holding out the basket in which, by way of goodbye, she has brought a shirt, a hunk of saucisson and a few banknotes. Marcel takes the basket by the handle and accepts the hand his mother presses against his cheek for a moment.

'Don't delude yourself, my girl,' the widow says from behind Éléonore's back. 'He'll not be coming back. They'll send him to the front lines. He'll be sent into action, like all the lads who haven't done their military service.'

Éléonore tilts her head towards the widow.

'You think I haven't noticed you hanging around him like a bitch in heat?'

At that moment, Marcel pushes the door and bursts into the room.

'I'm going to take mother home,' he says.

His lips quiver a little. The widow does not respond.

'Right, then,' Marcel says, and he turns around and leaves, but Éléonore catches up with him in the yard and grabs his elbow.

'You'll come back,' she says.

'I won't be able to finish the harvest,' Marcel replies.

'Will you write?'

'Yeah, maybe,' he says, a little distraught. 'I'll write.'

He lowers his gaze to the hand gripping his elbow. He looks up at the widow standing in the doorway, black and grim as a bird of prey, a buzzard preparing to swoop, then at the fragile, pitiful mother waiting for him by the cart.

The gradual departure of the reservists who are to join the Régiment de Gascogne and the 288th Infantry

Regiment is accompanied by a general fervour. Surely they should be thrilled to experience something so exceptional, something that will transcend their ordinary lives? Every day, a group of them pile their kitbags – *two flannel shirts, one spare pair of underwear, two handkerchiefs, two jerseys, a sweater or a thick jumper, a flannel belt, two pairs of wool socks, a pair of wool gloves, a woollen blanket, to be reimbursed immediately after they arrive* – onto a cart driven by an old man, a father, a grandparent, who sometimes drives one or two or three of his own sons, and they wave goodbye to the sister, the mother, the lover sobbing on the square of Puy-Larroque, the villagers cheering them, the children and the dogs who run along behind in the cloud of dust raised by the wheels of the convoy, yelling and yapping, until they give up in exhaustion, then the shouts and the tears and the feverish, heart-rending goodbyes give way to the quiet of the countryside; the tranquil serenity of the uncaring, unchanging countryside, the chatter of magpies and crows, the stealthy race of a hare in the field, the cool shade of the trees and the smell of mignonettes that tugs at their brave patriotic hearts. Their elbows and their knees knock together, and they seek out the touch of a thigh, an arm, a familiar, reassuring body.

In Puy-Larroque, life is frozen in the bewilderment left by the departure of the men, their removal from the landscape, the palpable void felt everywhere that gives rise to new superstitions: the empty armchairs where they used to sit when they came home from the fields and where no-one now dares sit, the plates and the cutlery laid against all common sense to ward off evil, the closed door of the forge and the blacksmith's sign, where they bless themselves as they might when passing a roadside shrine, the suit of clothes that for a few hours, perhaps a few days, retains the smell of a body and becomes a shroud on which they sleep. In a lean-to shed, a clutch of chickens find a perch for the night atop a mechanical reaper. Bats wrap their young in their dry wings and the delicate silhouettes quiver in the warmth of the barn. The branches of the walnut trees rustle and a butcher-bird impales the remains of a silver-bellied shrew on a hawthorn bush. At nightfall, mothers step out onto their porches and call to their offspring. A gentle breeze blows over the land, carrying with it the braying of a forlorn donkey, the acrid smoke of brushwood fires, the smell of soup, the cry of a child. A sad, ineffectual old man roams the croplands, beating the verges with his cane, flushing hen pheasants from the ditches and dusty hedges. In the depths of the first nights that follow the soldiers' departure, lights roam about, flames quaver along the dark roads. These are women torn by doubt from restless sleep who reach out and touch the cold sheet, the empty side of the bed, then get up and wander about the countryside, lantern in hand, making sure that they did not forget to close the horse's paddock, flick the latch on the byre, or that the fields themselves have not gone, vanished, just like the men.

The charred skies of mournful evenings are followed by the steel-grey of listless mornings. The women wake and dress at the hour when the men used to wake and dress. They learn to whet the scythe blade, then head out into the fields wearing their grey dresses, scythe handle resting on their shoulders. They reap, they hoe, they dig, redoubling their strength and their determination. They drive the carts and the drays, lead the mules and the geldings. They tie up the swaths, haul up the bales of straw. They fall asleep at twilight over the piece of fabric they are darning, the needle whose eye they can no longer make out buried in a calloused thumb. On 20 August, Pope Pius X dies. The widow does not have time to get upset. The absence of men opens up a rift, another possible reality. The exhaustion brought on by the women's new tasks reveals a new image of the world, one in which they appear as free and responsible. For the moment, it is merely a sensation, a fleeting, indefinable impression which looms suddenly in the night. In their dreams the men come home from war, but nothing now is the same; an outmoded world seems to have disappeared with them.

The women look on those men who have stayed behind in the village, the old, the adolescents, the hunchback, the blind man, the simpleton. A time will come when they burn for them with a fierce desire, oblivious to their flaws, and to the fidelity they pledged at the altar. Some they will deflower, others they will reanimate in the corners of barns, in shady hedgerows, on beds of straw, hiking up their skirts to get it over quickly, kneeling on the ground and holding their hair up, hunkering in the tall grasses so they can keep an eye out. They will wrap their arms around old men, enfolding bellies as flabby and wrinkled as elbow skin. They will swallow semen, wipe it from their petticoats, let it trickle translucently down a thigh to the seam of a stocking, where it is soaked up. They will collect it in their hand, and throw it on the ground, with a quick disgusted flick, like snot. Much later, some will compress their swollen bellies beneath tight bandages and, in hushed rooms, give birth to tiny, misshapen bastards. They will drink potions by way of purges. They will visit 'women who know'. Many will remain chaste, faithful, cherishing a mental image of their husband long after those albumen print portraits have faded. According to the day, their mood, their forgetfulness, shifting memory will obscure and rearrange features, infinitesimal changes that will create a whole gallery of other faces, other bodies, other characters. Soon, even their personalities will no longer be fixed; drunkards will become *bons vivants*, brutes will be passionate and skinflints will seem thrifty. The women will speak reverentially to their children about their absent fathers, brothers, uncles; they will praise their courage and their self-sacrifice. In the gulf opened up by war, morality and common sense will undergo a shift. To kill and to die will be glorious and make heroes of ordinary men. Some credit is always accorded to the dead, all the more so if one dies on the front lines. War will carve their names in history long after they have faded from the stone monuments in Puy-Larroque cemetery. Their whole lives will be summed up by a single fact, 'He died a soldier,' and there will be nothing else to say.

The government, the Council of State and the Banque de France are relocated to Bordeaux. News from the front arrives via the press, and the women adapt to the vacuum left by the absence of the men. The widow once more reigns supreme on the farm. The morning after Marcel's departure, when Éléonore sets off to bake the bread in the communal oven, she goes into his room and grabs the little crow, its head tucked into its feathers, dozing on the handle of the wicker basket that serves as a perch. She goes out into the yard; she hesitates. She feels the fragile wings quiver in her hands, struggling to unfurl, feels the beak push between her fingers. She looks at the well, at the block on which the father and Marcel used to split wood. With a sudden movement, she tosses the bird into the air. It spreads its wings, glides in circles over the yard and then comes back and lands on the ground, a few metres from the widow. She bends down, picks up some pebbles, then throws them at the bird. The first misses its mark, and the little crow watches, head tilted to one side; a second pebble hits it on the beak and it flutters up onto the roof and totters along the ridge, cawing. The widow goes back into the farmhouse, into Marcel's bedroom. She throws the mattress onto the floor, tugs at the slats, raising the bed base and leaning it against the wall. She clears out the room, carrying the furniture out into the shed, then leans against the cob wall, panting for breath. When Éléonore returns, she finds the room bare, a simple square of beaten earth, and the sight is like a knife in her throat.

'What did you do?' she asks the widow, who is preparing the pigswill, her back pointedly turned.

'I need the space, I need it to stock firewood for the winter. What business is it of yours?'

Her tone is curt, rasping, exasperated.

'The crow, where's the little crow?' Éléonore says.

The widow spins around. Her daughter is standing before her in the middle of the room, pale but defiant, arms tense, fists clenched against her thighs. Something has changed, something they did not realize until now. At thirteen, Éléonore is now as tall as the widow. The mother no longer has any physical advantage over her daughter. But she slaps the girl, the tips of her fingers just grazing her chin, a formal, soundless slap that leaves Éléonore frozen, then she turns away again and says:

'How would I know where it is? And don't speak to me in that tone of voice.'

A thread of spittle sprays from her mouth. She is

138

aware of the controlled hostility of the girl standing behind her, of the precision of her own movements as she
stirs the pigswill. Éléonore steps forward, soundlessly,
just as she stole into the scullery as a child to take a ladle
of cream from the churn. She grabs the widow's left wrist
so tightly that she drops the wooden spoon, which clatters
to the ground, and stifles a cry, a barely audible moan.

'You listen to me,' Éléonore says, suddenly perfectly
calm. 'If you ever raise your hand to me again, I swear
I'll kill you. I'll kill you, do you understand?'

The widow studies the girl's impassive face. She tries
to move the wrist held in Éléonore's vice-like grip, then
says:

'Time you went out and fed the animals.'

Éléonore relaxes her fingers and the widow slowly
presses her forearm against her chest. She runs a thumb
over the tender skin on the inside of her wrist, where the
marks of the girl's fingers are still visible.

'It's late enough as it is,' she says.

Éléonore nods, takes the pot of pigswill and goes out.

The women continue with the harvest. The swaths stand
in sheaves along the windrows in the blazing afternoon
sun. Overhead, the buzzards trace wide circles in the
pale sky, watching for voles scampering away, then they
disappear, melting against the glare of the sun, only to reappear and swoop. The women and the children trample
the wheat stubble on the threshing floor, accompanied
by a little donkey, its hooves cracked. The war has taken
the blacksmith. The livestock begin to cast their shoes in
the meadows, to leave them embedded in the dirt. There
is no-one now to trim the hooves that crack and split.
Soon the fields are bare and reddish-brown. Clouds pile
up in layers in the dying day. Alphonse searches for a

quiet corner away from human sight. He finds one in a board leaning against a wall, scrabbles at the dust, turns around once or twice, then lies down with a groan. As Éléonore passes the fields on her way home, he recognizes her smell and wags his tail, but she does not see him and the dog dies alone, in his animal silence, as the girl's footsteps fade. Late that night, having called to the dog from the porch, she sets out with a lantern and finds him. His white eyes stare sightlessly into the night. Éléonore twines her fingers through the rough fur and pulls the already stiff corpse towards her. She sits on the bare ground and hugs the dead dog, her tears falling on his head, heavy as a stone, then she fetches the barrow, places the body on it, and pulls the funeral carriage while the widow watches from the doorway. Near the place where she buried the cat, she digs a grave for Alphonse in the stony ground. She rolls the corpse and it falls into the hole, then she tosses the first shovelful of earth over the dog's open eyes. The next day, she makes a small cross of wooden slats and plants it by the mound covered with smooth stones. Clouds accumulate to form a thick, ink-black mantle. Flashes of heat lightning illuminate them as they roll heavily over the countryside, plunging it into an electrical darkness. The air is heavy and muggy, cows stand motionless beneath the oaks and the chestnut trees. In a fallow field, split plum trees ooze sap. Suddenly, the rain begins to fall in torrents, bowing the branches of the trees, dislodging roof tiles, sending animals racing for their nests, their burrows, their lairs, causing brooks and water troughs to overflow, lashing the croups of the horses still out to pasture. Drenched children splash through vast puddles, their feet raising huge sprays of water. A willow sways its long tonsure in the twilight.

It is the oldest of the parish priests, Father Benoît, who now officiates at mass once a week, the other priests having quickly enlisted and gone to the front lines to serve in the ranks of porters or stretcher-bearers. Faced with a congregation of weary women and placid children, he gently preaches about the value of work, the riches of the earth, the omniscience of God:

'O, the depth of the riches both of the wisdom and knowledge of God! How unsearchable are His judgements, and His ways past finding out!'

The tragedy of her widowhood having been swept away and supplanted, the widow pretends to mourn the absence of Marcel and adds her voice to the chorus of those who plead, who worry and who pray. Soon, the first letters arrive from the front. They are read and re-read, carefully tucked into a bodice, sometimes until the ink leaches from the paper, imprinting itself on a clammy bosom. Every morning, Éléonore, like all the other women, races to the edge of the field as the old postman slowly makes his way from the village to deliver letters to the farms. But from Marcel there is nothing. She watches those who rush to tear open an envelope, unfold a letter and walk away, eagerly reading the lines traced by the hand of their man. Some sentences have been struck through by the *comité de contrôle* and are illegible, others have escaped the censor. The women whisper the words to themselves to make them more real, fragments of war that blossom into images – *the weather was fine yesterday... marched for so long some of the men's feet were bleeding... please don't worry about me... we leave Monday, though we don't know our destination... we cut a fine figure in our handsome uniforms... we will probably pass through Champagne and help out with the harvest... we have no choice but to sleep in the straw and the cold like pigs... ate our fill and drank good wine*

along the way... my darling wife... dear father... have you fin-
ished bringing in the wheat... how is my petite maman... things
we never imagined we would see that will probably haunt our
dreams to our dying day... my dear parents, I... the aeroplane
flew over us like a gigantic bird... give our son a kiss from his
father and tell him to be good and to be brave... I am writing to
you lying here in the grass in a clearing where I picked a little
bunch of flowers... sleep piled on top of each other... a few days in
the trenches, a few days in reserve... and transporting the crates
of supplies... impossible to sleep without suddenly jolting by the
fear of a bombing raid... before being sent to the front lines, I
wanted to send you my last wishes... I will soon have a furlough
and may come home... my darling Sylviane, never forget that
you and I are gazing at the same stars... that comforts me...
the rain is never-ending... fingers as pale and wrinkled as an
old man's... at least it washes our the clothes, which are caked
in mud ... pray for us... pray to God that He might deliver me
from this suffering... a sunny spell... silence over this unfamil-
iar, ravaged landscape... nothing else seems to exist... as though
peace were suddenly restored to the world... the long, long wait
for your letters... how many more months of days that never
seem to end... I think about you and I no longer write about
sad things that will serve only to rekindle bad memories later,
the hours of terror of physical and mental exhaustion of despair
followed by exhortations to yourself to react... farewell, my
dear parents... affectionately... your loving son – reciting the
words for those who received no letter that day, allowing
them to vicariously experience the anguish, the relief;
anything is better than the despair of silence. The first
death notices arrive from the regiment by courier or by
telegram, addressed to the mayor of Puy-Larroque, *I am*
writing to request that you notify the next of kin promptly in a
dignified and understanding manner appropriate to the circum-
stances, who solemnly sets about his duty, accompanied

142

by a member of the municipal council, walking through the village on a September day filled with birdsong and the scent of the trampled fruits at the foot of the fig trees, *of the death of soldier Lagrange, Jean-Philippe, regimental number 8656, 67th Infantry Division, 3rd Company, 288th Regiment, which occurred in the following circumstances*, stepping into a sunlit farmyard where a cock crows, removing their berets, knocking on a door that stands wide open, *most grateful if you would convey to the family the sincere condolences of Monsieur le Ministre de la Guerre and report back to me as to the date when this was done.*

Already, August is fast approaching its end. The school in Puy-Larroque will not reopen in September; everywhere, teachers have laced up their hobnailed boots; more than one hundred and thirty in the department have been called up. Children scratch their hands and arms on brambles heavy with blackberries, their fingers and their lips are purple. Carefree, they carry on with their games, and their shrill cries echo over the fields. Éléonore sometimes sees the little crow perched on the roof of the well, the edge of the cart, the branch of a tree. He calls to her, a single caw, in the early morning, but he no longer dares approach her and disappears as soon as the widow appears. Éléonore digs earthworms from the compost heap and leaves them in a clay pot for him. A scarecrow stands guard over the ripened grain, corncobs hanging from ochre, brittle stalks. Yapping dogs chase the wild boars that venture from the undergrowth to plunder the fields. The evenings are warm, later cool, always crimson, smouldering with the distant, hellish fire of war. After eating cornmeal porridge or fired offal with bread dipped in chicken broth, the women sit around the fire, in the inglenook, and Éléonore returns to her reading of the Scriptures. Nothing fascinates the widow more than the book of the Apocalypse. *And I looked, and behold a pale horse: and his name that sat on him was Death, and Hell followed with him. And power was given unto them over the fourth part of the earth, to kill with sword, and with hunger, and with death, and with the beasts of the earth.* At twilight, in the walkways of the cemetery, sparrows tremble on branches of blue cypress. In the father's grave, as in that of the altar boy Jean Roujas, nothing now remains but powdery, white bones held together by their formal suits.

They bring the cows from the byre and strap them into a head yoke. The widow grips the twin handles and guides the turn-plough. Éléonore leads the animals. They move the length of the field, shrouded in tatters of pale mist, beneath a leaden sky that seems to touch the earth. They can scarcely see more than a few metres ahead of them. All around, nature makes no sound – only the wheels juddering over the stones, the breath of the cows, and the ploughshare moving through the soil make a quivering that is deadened by the fog. The coulter slices through soil that is dry and thin from overcropping, the ploughshare cleaves the clods like the prow of a small ship, laboriously raising waves of black earth that are turned over by the mouldboard. The women do not talk. Their breath condenses in the chill air. It is just possible to make out the outline of a motionless form through the mist, a roe deer that snorts, then scampers off. In the first days, they manage to cover only a few acres with crude furrows. For many of the villagers, the land they farm lies on the valley slopes and they have to expend great effort to plough the hillsides. When it rains, they continue to advance along the furrows they news of the cataclysm, the order to retreat, the hail of fire and metal, the ruined bodies and the heaving earth, the names of the dead and of those taken prisoner. A wail goes up and echoes through the countryside; people appear on doorsteps and strain to hear, others rush towards the sound. The dogs bark in concert. It is a woman, a mother, a wife who has just learned that her man has died in battle; her legs cut from under her, she falls to her knees on the hard ground. Small children, many of whom have no memory of the soldier, stand sobbing next to her in unconscious imitation. The women now dread seeing Mayor Beyries emerge from the *mairie*. They curse him, him and his solemn mask of tragedy. But often a letter from a comrade-in-arms precedes the official death notice. The women stage wakes. They gather together a portrait, a shirt, a shepherd's crook or a sword, some beloved, neglected relic, to celebrate the memory of those now rotting on the fields of honour, broken, gnawed at by rats, pulverized by cannon fire or burned beneath a layer of quicklime in a rough-and-ready grave. Some fashion burial mounds and tombs, they worship at crosses planted over graves that contain only earth. The postman continues to tour the streets and the byways, a grim harbinger of doom. 'Nothing for you today, Miss Éléonore!' he calls as he passes the farm, then later: 'Still nothing!', then 'Nothing!' or 'Sorry!', and after a while he simply shrugs, turns away and Éléonore watches as he carries on, jolting along the path, then returns to her solitude filled with images. Marcel's silence makes his absence more poignant, more terrible. The memory of him is embedded in every object and she can see the world now only through the distorting prism of his parting, through a reality weighty with this monstrous fact that infects and unsettles her.

146

Every place, every detail reminds her of him: the paths he took, the words he spoke, the bucket from which he slaked his thirst, the mare whose mane he groomed. Éléonore thinks she hears his voice carried on a gust of wind; it is nothing but the sound of the wind, a branch breaking, an old farmer in the distance bringing in his flock. She thinks she can make out his smell beneath the smell of the animals, in their hair, the sickly sweat, their warm folds, their hooves. When she encounters a man, regardless of who he is, she closes her eyes and breathes in the air displaced by this body, a masculine smell that her memory probes in the hope of connecting it to a face that is already distant, vague, tenuous. She talks to the animals. Talks to the pigs, whose brown eyes and long lashes Marcel commented on. She creates a memory from scraps, breathes life into it with another's breath, the pale torso of a boy seen out in the fields, the distant solemn presence of a buzzard. In the little copse, she wraps her arms around a tree. She caresses the cold, damp trunk, the silken protuberance of a tinder fungus. She presses first her cheek, then her mouth against it and, eyes closed, parts her lips and darts out her tongue, licks the bark. On the roof of her mouth she has an after-taste of tannins and mosses; the taste of Marcel's breath. He had a sickle whose walnut handle he carved, sculpting the head of a horse, or the head of a bull, or the head of a pig. She finds the dusty tool in the shed. She slips it between the bed base and the wool mattress. At night, when the widow is asleep, Éléonore takes the sickle from its hiding place and lays it on her belly under the sheet. The cold metal of the blade takes her breath away. She feels the curve beneath the curve of her breast. She sees Marcel in his shirtsleeves, out in the fields, in the blazing sun, his hand holding the sickle as it cuts the swaths.

147

The trees blaze scarlet, then tan, leaves shrivel and fall to earth. Chestnut burrs strew layers of scarlet leaves, which now and then are whipped into eddies by the wind. Squirrels still scamper along the bare branches, brief explosions of red fur, searching for some last provision. Birds perch, windswept, in the grey, cold bushes. The fallow fields turn russet and, soon, the exposed game will make for the oak groves in search of brown acorns and chestnuts. Migratory birds choreograph their great ballet, come together to form a shifting, turbulent mass, tracing majestic curves, dark sinusoidal waves, only to scatter and fill the vast expanse of sky. They regroup and sit chirruping on the bare branches of trees, making it seem for a moment as though they have reclaimed their rustling foliage. Ultimately, they fly south to other latitudes, leaving the landscape taciturn and silent. Since Albert Brisard is now lying in a mass grave on the Marne battlefield, a black hole between the two eyes that have been plucked out by crows, his mouth filled with quicklime, it is left to the women to slaughter the pigs. With hesitant thrusts, they drive a blunt blade into the throats of fat beasts that are hog-tied and held fast by the strongest amongst them. November shrouds the land with early hoarfrost that glitters in the pale sunlight. Corvids peck at clods of earth as hard as stone, while wild boars rootle and forage in fields and ditches for tubers and shrivelled roots. As winter approaches, hope fades that the men will come home, that the war will be brief. In late September, ninety wounded soldiers were sent home to Auch and admitted to a makeshift hospital set up in the Hôtel-Dieu and Ancienne Préfecture, but still Éléonore has had no word of Marcel. The day before the homecoming, seventeen Gascon soldiers from the 23rd Company of the 288th Infantry Regiment, under the tubers, then the ground freezes. Deprived of shelter, the game seeks refuge in the brittle brown undergrowth. In the morning, a thick fog lies over the land, obliterating all perspective. The widow and her daughter go out now only to draw water from the well, to feed the livestock and bring in firewood. Cauldrons hanging from trammel hooks above open fires clatter all day long. Here, the women make soup of cabbage and lardons, ragouts and stews. Time and again, Éléonore imagines saddling the mare and setting off to see Marcel's mother, who may have received a letter, a notice; but she knows nothing of this woman, or of that sickly branch of the family tree with which her late father and the widow never kept in touch. Besides, there are times when not knowing seems preferable; Marcel's absence now plunges her into a sort of torpor, a numbness. She no longer speaks, not even in response to the widow's rare remarks. She eats little and loses weight, since she no longer feels hunger or thirst, only a joyless intoxication, a stupefaction. In the afternoon, she leaves the farm and walks the fields, following the paths, retracing her steps. She returns in the evening with no memory of the places she has been, the distance travelled, the hours spent, simply dazed with cold and exhaustion. Inanition makes her unsteady on her feet and creates blurred trails in her field of vision. The widow chides her for her behaviour, calls her mad, reminds her that she has a delicate constitution, that she almost died at birth, and how, believing her lost, they had hurriedly had her baptized. In fact, when Éléonore catches her face reflected in the mirror, she sees the widow's features beginning to appear beneath her own. Forsaking successive moults, she allows the widow's traits to resurface in her. Éléonore continues to tramp the fields, her face so muffled in shawls that only

152

her dark, expressionless eyes are visible. She inspects the graves, that of the father, those of the animals; she tends them with equal care. She no longer waits for the postman, who, though she does not seem to notice as he passes on the lane to Puy-Larroque, always dismounts his bicycle and turns to watch as she slowly walks away. She no longer listens to idle chatter, and while not spurning the company of women, she gladly avoids it. Soon, the days begin to blur, they are undifferentiated, a long scansion of dreary interchangeable hours varied only by the weather. The quince trees sag under the weight of fruit. Snow falls and lies heavily on the trees, branches break with a crack of gunfire that wakes the women with a start, bringing the phantom of war to their door. Over the fields, the snow drifts into banks, leaving the animals roaming, numb with cold and starvation. It buries the known world beneath flowing lines that glitter when there is a sunny spell. The cloudless nights offer a display of molten stars, electric constellations that shine dispassionately upon the hushed, white fields, and on the cesspit of the front lines, those trenches on the Marne where soldiers lie, sinking beneath the mortar shells in a predatory sleep, and the same moon shines down on both. Éléonore sometimes takes the old mare with her to stretch her legs, leading her with a halter, but the old nag lost her shoes in the autumn and is worn out, despite the oats she is fed and the blankets laid over her every night. Soon, it will be impossible for Éléonore to recall the things she has done, in what order, if not sequence, the weeks, the months. All that will remain is a sense of dense, static time. It feels as though the father died a lifetime since, as though Marcel left just yesterday and yet an eternity ago. Forgetfulness erodes their memory. Scenes and places fade and disappear. All that remain up and down the platform, sliding open doors, releasing clouds of pungent steam. They hose the beasts to cool them before loading more livestock into the wagons, more horses here, more pigs there, prompting a tumult of animal cries and hoof-kicks against wooden slats. Tongues lick at the water trickling down the planks and the necks. A young heifer kicked in the belly suffers a spontaneous miscarriage, delivering a half-formed calf, its bones still soft, which the cattle next to her trample to a pulp on the floorboards, through whose yawning gaps the railway sleepers flash past. Then darkness falls, leaving the beasts with only the whisper of the rails, the clack of piston rods and the whale-like breath of the engine. Some animals raise their heads to suck in a lungful of warm air, others briefly doze only to wake with a start, jolted by the train or gnawed at by hunger. In their singular temporality, the journey through the night and new day seems endless, until the animals are unloaded once more, reloaded once more, shipped through the cold, misty morning of northern France towards the cattle pens of an army corps stationed near a village on a desolate plain, where they are goaded one last time into the glare of daylight as the sun finally pierces the clouds. Under the orders of a quartermaster and several auxiliary officers, dozens of cowherds descend upon the cattle and drive them towards vast enclosures built a few kilometres from the front lines in open country that is eerily peaceful but for the infernal rumbling of that Gehenna, a cacophony of rumbling engines and the indistinguishable cries of men and beasts. The smell is bitter and metallic. The mingled stenches of an abattoir, a fetid byre and a charnel house. The number of beasts is unparalleled. The soil sodden with excrement and urine is trampled into mud by countless hooves. The slurry flows from the cattle pens in waves of faecal lava. The injuries suffered by the animals during transportation become infected and purulent. The air is dark with gnats and horseflies, which feverishly swarm over the livestock like the fourth plague of Egypt, clustering around eyes, around open wounds, gorging on sweat, on blood, on dung, as soon as the unloaded animals rush to the water troughs. The weakest animals struggle in vain to get a place at the troughs, and their eyes roll more wildly still. White flashes of sclera are visible everywhere. Long trails of saliva hang from their mouths and foam on flanks and hindquarters. Nostrils bleed. The horses' legs are ravaged by mud fever. Louse flies colonize their groins and even the men pick them from the folds of their flesh, from armpits, from buttocks, decapitating them with the swift flick of a fingernail. Crows in their hundreds wheel above the paddock. A veterinary surgeon fuddled by the constant din tours the barbed-wire fences, pointing out the beasts to be slaughtered; first and foremost those which can no longer stand. They survive for only a day or two here. The sole object of the cattle pens is to keep them alive as long as necessary. This herd is not intended to be fattened or bred. This farm is merely a stopping place, an assemblage of rickety fences driven into muddy fields and various tents to house the fifteen teams of butchers working long days to fulfil the orders of the supply officers. Often, more meat than is required is sent out. If it is returned in time, it is to be sent again with the proceeds of the next day's butchering. If not, it rots in the blazing midday sun. Stray dogs with blood-smeared muzzles fight over a pile of entrails until it is doused with petrol and torched, giving off the charred smell of a funeral pyre. Automobiles belch smoke as they become bogged down in the muddy goat he cut from its mother, which laid its head against his neck and suckled his earlobe as he carried it to the slaughtering tents. When darkness falls and they try to sleep, the night within them is red. Their ears ring with the phantom cries of beasts. Their mouths are filled with the taste of death. When reduced by half, the herd is relocated according to the troop movements. At such times, men and beasts leave behind a landscape of mud and desolation roamed by raw-boned dogs and carrion crows.

She has been sitting by the fire for an indeterminate period. Her face impassive, she is staring at the glistering coals beneath the ash when the sound of clogs rouses her from her daydream. Éléonore sees the widow get up and go to the window. 'Stay there,' she says, then wraps her shawl around her turkey neck and leaves the room.

Éléonore goes back to contemplating the fire. She does not blink and the heat dries out her eyes. She blinks, runs her hand over her face. She hears voices in the yard. She gets up to shake herself from her torpor; her legs are stiff and her hands cold. It must be late afternoon, she is not sure. The evenings are still cool and the light has waned. The empty byre is a cold, black chasm. She walks to the window and pushes back the crocheted curtain with the back of her hand. She sees a cart drawn by a small grey donkey led by a boy a little younger than she is. She has never seen him before, yet his features, though unclear, are not unfamiliar. The widow, her back turned, blocks the view of Éléonore. She supposes the widow is talking to a woman, though her voice and words are inaudible. The widow listens, nods occasionally. Éléonore can feel the hostility in her stiff back, the haughty tilt of her head. At length, she turns away and walks back to the farm, and in doing so reveals Marcel's mother, who stands motionless for a moment, wipes her eyes with a kerchief taken from the sleeve of her blouse, then takes the hand offered by the youngest of her sons, the only one who has remained at home with her, and climbs back into the cart. The crocheted curtain slips between her fingers as the widow comes through the door, taking off her shawl. She undoes the woollen knot, plasters her brittle hair against her head, wipes the bead of snot from her nose with the back of her hand, then simply goes back to her seat next to the fire, where she left a sheet she has been darning. Éléonore grabs the doorknob, pulls it towards her and goes out into the yard. The cart has already pulled away. She wants to run, but her legs give way and she grips the edge of the well to steady herself. When she goes back inside, the widow is busy darning. The flames yellow her cheeks; her profile is carved with a billhook. Éléonore says:

'That was his mother.'

The widow does not reply. She pushes the needle through the fabric and it clicks against the thimble.

'It was his mother,' Éléonore says again, and she sees the widow shrug imperceptibly.

Éléonore crosses the space that separates them, rips the needlework from her hands and tosses it onto the fire, where it blazes for a moment before shrivelling on the burning logs.

'Have you lost your wits?' the widow stammers, looking up, her face pale. 'He's dead, your precious Marcel. There! Happy now? And here I was trying to spare you.'

Éléonore's hip knocks against the table as she slumps onto a bench.

'Got himself killed just like all the rest. I warned you. And he never wrote, not once!' the widow shrieks at the

160

seem to see her. Dogs sniff at her bare, blackened feet.
The village continues to hum with its constant refrain.
Before long the chestnut trees will come into bud again,
their branches cast shadowy veins on the ground. Three
cows pad into a black, damp byre. The church tolls six
o'clock. Éléonore looks up at the steeple piercing a sky
empty of clouds, empty of stars, a deep cerulean blue,
and peers at it for a moment. She walks to the steps of
the church and slowly climbs them, leaving the imprint
of her feet on the stone. She steps into the cold half-light
and closes the door behind her, silencing the hum of
Puy-Larroque. The feeble flames of the few remaining candles are reflected in the grey stained glass. The
baptismal font is filled with a still pool of ink. Éléonore
bends over it. From between her lips she allows a thread
of saliva to trickle, extend and disappear, rippling the
surface of the water. She lays a hand on the back of one
of the front pews. She leans with all her weight and top-
ples it. She lifts the next pew and overturns it, sending
one end slamming into the wall. With her heel, she splits
the straw seats of the prie-dieu. She opens the missals
and rips out pages. She hurls the ciboria, the patens and
the candle spikes against the wall. A grimy tapestry de-
picting some obscure liturgical scene catches fire, and
the rising sparks eat away at the shadows in the hollows
of the vaulted arch. Éléonore unhooks the great crucifix
from the wall and it crashes to the floor, the face of Christ
scattering in a thousand plaster fragments. She has not
heard the great door open and the village women, drawn
by the commotion, rush towards her. The burning tapestry is pulled to the ground and trampled. The women
grab the heretic by the arms, the shoulders, the wrists,
struggling to restrain her. Even their voices and their
cries do not reach her. She hawks and spits on the floor,

162

onto the back of the fallen crucifix, while the women drag her out of the church, throw her to the bottom of the church steps and douse her with cold water drawn from the washhouse trough. Éléonore wraps her arms around her legs, presses her face against her knees and falls onto her side in a puddle of mud. The women gather in a circle around her. One lashes out with a vicious kick to the back. She lies there for a long time, drenched, numb with cold, until the widow, whom someone has gone to fetch, parts the silent throng of farmwomen. She sees her daughter huddled, filthy. A stone, a tree stump, a log. She looks at the flushed, forbidding faces of the women one by one. She hears the hateful words, the veiled threats, the accusations directed at her, her and her accursed daughter. She says nothing, kneels down next to Éléonore, slides a hand under her arm, sits her up, then hauls her to her feet. She walks away, bearing the weight of the body leaning against hers. The two women stagger down the road towards the farm with measured steps. Éléonore's wounds are raw now, her aching feet are black and blue from walking barefoot over the stones. Her every muscle is sapped. Soon, they are swallowed by the darkness. In front of the fire she has rekindled, the widow undresses Éléonore and lets her soiled clothes fall to the floor. She dips a cloth in a bucket of water and washes her, scouring the scratches and the bruises. She says:

'What on earth were you thinking getting yourself into such a state?'

Éléonore surrenders herself to the widow as she lifts an arm, stretches a limb. She watches the widow's brusque, assiduous movements.

'What you did, it was desecration. It was sacrilege.'

Her voice is low, but devoid of anger. From time to

time, she looks up at Éléonore, a look filled with terror and some form of respect. She patiently dries Éléonore's skin. She roughly combs her hair, pulling at the tangled knots until they give way, holding her head steady with the flat of her hand. Beneath the dry, caked mud the widow has brushed away, she sees that a lock of white hair has appeared over her forehead. Faced with the naked body of her daughter, she takes a step back, her eyes wide, and says:

'You must be possessed...'

She gathers up a nightshirt, slips Éléonore's head through the neck, her arms through the sleeves. She presses a rosary into her hands and winds the beads around her wrists.

'You'll do penance. Pray. Pray, now.'

She sits her in a chair by the fire, then kneels at her feet and, pressing Éléonore's hands in hers in her lap, recites an Our Father, nodding her head each time Éléonore vainly, atavistically tries to force the prayer from her bloodless lips.

'Forgive us our trespasses as we forgive those who trespass against us. And lead us not into temptation, but deliver us from Evil. Amen.'

Éléonore continues to allow herself to drift in a hazy languor. She no longer defies the widow, who gradually becomes accustomed to her asthenia. Since the livestock was commandeered, work on the farm is restricted to menial tasks. They watch the wheat crop grow and fear the blackthorn winter. The black earth has been fertilized by the snows and is covered with a soft velvet, and primroses are flowering along the edges of the fields. The widow and her daughter dig over and weed the kitchen garden. They plant, they sow, they transplant. Roused

As a child, she sometimes wondered about the nature of animal time, that of the tick on a blade of grass waiting for a host to pass, of the mayfly with its lacy wings, whose whole life is circumscribed by a few short hours, of the pond turtle, its shell green with mosses and algae, that the oldest villagers claim to have seen sunning itself in the roots of the willow tree on the banks of the reservoir. Éléonore no longer differentiates between months or the seasons. She continues to perform the chores allotted to her, with little enthusiasm or eagerness. She scatters feed for the chickens, fills the drinking troughs in the rabbit hutches. The widow no longer issues orders. She watches the ghost of her daughter come and go, dragging her clogs, performing the same weary, disembodied gestures. A changeable light moves over the farmyard, of dull, slate-grey days, of louring skies, of autumn fires, of bright mornings gilded with pollen. Some men come home, leaving behind at the front an arm or a leg, torn off by a shell or eaten away by gangrene. They go back to the fields and learn to use their tools with one hand. They can be seen limping across the nourishing earth at dawn and at dusk. The women gentle the stumps, the fingertips tracing the pale sutures, the swollen flesh. They overcome their disgust. Slugs have eaten away the little worm-eaten hobnailed bench where the father used to sit from the first evening in spring to the last vigils of autumn. It is now half-buried in the dirt, the nettles and the dandelions of the yard. One morning in 1917, at the end of May, Éléonore stops and contemplates what remains of the bench. It is a crumbling, pathetic ruin, with one blackened slat jutting above the clumps of grass. When she tries to lift it and rips it from the ground, the wood snaps. In the newly uncovered hollow that has served as their world, woodlice and centipedes slink

166

turned the corner and is walking back to the farmhouse when she sees a man standing stock-still. Dazzled by the sun, she brings a hand up to shield her eyes, the better to see the figure standing in the cloud of dust from the dirt road. He turns and seems to be looking at the quiet farmyard. He is wearing a pristine soldier's uniform, a blue woollen tunic buttoned over his jacket. At his feet, he has set a small kitbag. The eye of the crow perched on the ridge tiles offers a convex reflection of the figure. Neither the officer, nor Éléonore, nor anything around them moves. Time seems to have ceased to struggle and has finally stopped in the becalmed light of morning. Then it is he who steps forward, and his slow, loping gait makes Éléonore's heart burst in her breast. He reveals his horrid face to the light. How does she recognize him? How does she put a name on those ravaged features, this primitive, barbarous mask? Something spills out within her, heavy and cold as a haemorrhage. Marcel has grasped her arm and is holding her against him. His face had been that of a boy; now it is not even the face of a man. A red beard covers part of his cheeks, but the left side is a mass of scar tissue, smooth and livid in patches, withered and swollen in others. The ruined cheekbone has left a depression beneath the sightless eye, for there is nothing there now but an empty socket over which the eyelid has been sewn shut. The cheek is struck through by the line of a scar that runs over the chin and down the throat. He breathes hoarsely. The corners of his mouth twist as a cry comes from Éléonore, a guttural wail, a howl ripped from the depths of a mute grief. He lays a hand on the back of her head and presses her face into the collar of his tunic. The smell of straw, of animals and sweat has given way to that of alcohol and ether, of morphine and oil of camphor, of stale tobacco and hooch.

The widow has left the kitchen garden, dropped the knife and the carrot tops, which the wind blows across the flagstones of the yard. Marcel hugs the head that fits entirely within the span of his hand. He breathes in her hair. The white lock of hair runs between his fingers. He holds the motionless body in the light of the sun as it bursts from between two fugitive clouds. His profile is haunted by the solitary, black eye.

She does not ask a single question. She does not try to discover how he can have returned from among the dead, since she herself is restored to life the moment that his arms enfold her shoulders. His face is the most terrifying thing she has ever seen. His face, whose pre-cise features have blurred with time, leaving her with a memory of gentleness, even beauty, is now ruined, the wounds utterly obliterating the memory she thought she recollected.

'I don't want you to look at me,' Marcel says.

Éléonore turns away. From this moment, she will only ever look at him surreptitiously, a sidelong glance at the hideous eyelid that has been stitched over she knows not what – a void, a hole, a sightless, shrivelled eyeball – over something shocking, over the unspeak-able images that compel him to spring from his bed in the dead of night like a jack-in-the-box. She thinks she has found him again, but does not yet know what she has really lost. He is wearing a large hat with a wide brim, which shields his pale scars from the sun and hides his face from others when he bows his head. As they walk towards the farmhouse and he turns his face towards the widow, she sees that the skin on his mutilated face no longer moves in the same way, but forms folds and fault lines. Even his gait and the way he moves his whole body have changed. He adopts positions that hide him from prying eyes. He keeps to the shadows with which he has learned to blend. As soon as they cross the threshold, he takes a step to one side, out of the beam of light that spills into the room. He sets down his kitbag and goes to the former scullery, cleared out by the widow, and now filled with firewood for the winter. Éléonore stands behind him, stiff but unsteady. He takes off his jacket, rolls up his shirtsleeves, then gathers logs into his arms and begins to move the wood into the lean-to shed, crossing and recrossing the main room and the farmyard, where the widow is still standing by the kitchen garden, not daring to approach.

He puts the bed back in the place where it formerly stood. He lights the fire in the hearth, then goes to inspect the byre. Éléonore follows, urged on by the fear that he will disappear once more, step through a doorway never to re-emerge. She bites the inside of her cheek to make certain she is not dreaming, or that she has not gone completely mad. She talks to him to dispel her fear. She tells him how the livestock were commandeered, all except the mare, who died out in the pasture of old age; she tells him about the death of Alphonse, who has also passed away, and whom she buried over there. Marcel surveys the cold, gloomy byre, the silent, yawning pigsty. He follows her to the little mound of stones, already overgrown with brambles, beneath which Alphonse's bones have begun to poke through what remains of his tatty fur. He carries on walking towards the fields, like the men who came home before him, to go and see the land, and, as she walks beside him, Éléonore contemplates this landscape as though seeing it for the first time. There, where only death, tedium and despair were lodged in everything, she now sees life again: the flight of the birds, the quivering of the crops, the bray of a donkey, the smell of wet grass. She feels a warm breeze slip beneath her dress, across her bare legs, feels it swell her lungs, and she can smell Marcel as he rummages in his pocket for a pack of the cigarettes that the men learned to smoke while at war and lights one. He stops in front of the fields over which the widow and Éléonore have toiled to grow as much cereal as any man, and she thinks she sees his cyclopean eye glitter with a spark of jealousy or satisfaction. He brings the cigarette up to the right-hand side of his mouth, where his lips were spared, before exhaling pungent smoke.

'The harvest was good. The women of Puy-Larroque... We worked hard,' says Éléonore.

Marcel nods brusquely, then he crouches down at the edge of the field and scoops up a handful of soil, as she saw her father do long before him. He weighs it in the hollow of his hand, then crumbles it between his fingers, before saying:

'Everything is good.'

Only these words, barely whispered, addressed to himself. Then he gets to his feet, his knees cracking, and heads back towards the farm, his strange silhouette walking along the crest of the hill. Éléonore no longer walks behind him, but on his left. The back of her hand, as in the past, occasionally grazing the back of his.

The very next day, he starts back to work, more ardent-ly, more relentlessly, as though he feels the need to make up for lost time, or to win back an authority over the land. When Éléonore sees him toiling in the distance, in the middle of some field, unable to make out his face as it melts in the light, it feels as though he never went

171

away, that there never was a war, that all this has been an endless nightmare. She works in the kitchen. She throws open the windows and sweeps clouds of dust into the yard. She washes and hangs out the sheets. Alone in the scullery, she breathes in the smell of Marcel's clothes, to become accustomed to it, bringing his underclothes to her face before stuffing them into the turbid waters of a basin. She continues to work in the fields, like the other women. The demobilized men are astonished to see them carting tools, swinging a scythe or harnessing a donkey in no time at all. The women earn their respect. Marcel seems capable of anything. He works without fail from dawn to dusk, sweating out every drop of moisture in his body. He rebuilds a dry-stone wall that collapsed while he was away, seals up the hole in the main room where the wind was gusting in from the cold, empty byre, and even paves the floor. He replaces the tiles that have fallen from the roof and shattered in the yard. He mows the fallow land and clears the ditches overgrown with rushes and thorn bushes. In the autumn, he pulls the cart, taking the place of the lost oxen, roaring like an animal.

There is never a mention of the place where he convalesced, the name of any of his comrades-in-arms; never a detail, a memory, an allusion to the war, and Éléonore can only imagine the vast, bright wards that reek of ether, tobacco and necrosis, the windows overlooking gardens of shrubs and carefully ordered flowerbeds, the white metal bedsteads, the shutters and the white curtains drawn over all the red wounds, the holes in the bodies, spurting and oozing blood, pus and mucus, disinfected, packed and bandaged by nurses in white coats, the tender or harsh expressions these women have learned to mask the horror they feel at the sight of these human

172

wrecks. Work brings him back to his old self. His body is once more the rustic, nervous body she remembers, though driven by a new and mysterious force that both galvanizes and consumes him. The summer following his return, when Éléonore brings him a metal canteen to slake his thirst, he turns away and presses the flask to the more mobile part of his lips, already stained yellow with tobacco, as are the distal phalanges of his thumb and index finger. Often, a trickle of water escapes his lips, dribbles down his chin and into his neck, or drips onto the fabric of his shirt. In the evening, he refuses to eat with the women. He takes his plate into his room, closes the door and eats alone, sitting on the edge of his bed, ashamed of the painstaking way he must chew, the grimaces required by the stiffness in his jaws, the gobbets of food that fall from his mouth despite his efforts and are caught in the bushy red beard, already sprinkled with white hairs that glisten in the light, which he has grown to hide the glabrous ridges of his scars. Éléonore simply leaves a covered plate by the fire for him, waits for him to come home and watches as he carries it away, like an animal she is trying to tame, a feral cat one might give a saucer of milk, a wild dog that races away with a bone to gnaw on it out of sight. She sets a jug of water and a basket of bread on the chest of drawers next to his bed, then clears it away the following morning after he has left. One morning, she goes into the room while he is out. She studies the room: the chamber pot, the ashes quivering on the embers, the carefully made bed. She notices a bulge beneath one of the goose-feather pillows. Going over, she lifts it up and finds the jaw separator, not knowing what she is holding in her hand, this thing made from rubber, metal and springs that looks like a torture device, a tiny wolf trap. She sets it down again,

173

glasses from the dresser and sets them on the table, then she waits for Marcel to come through the door, watching at the window for him. When he finally comes in, she gets to her feet. Marcel sees the glasses and the bottle. He looks at her with such consternation that she is forced to avert her eyes, then he goes over to the table, picks up the bottle and goes out, leaving her with the ailing widow. For long hours he does not reappear while joy resounds in Puy-Larroque and over the countryside. When he comes home again, at dawn the following day, he slips into the house like a vanquished shadow, passing close to her without so much as a look, trailing in his wake the smell of tobacco, sweat and bile. He closes the door to his room and Éléonore hears the weight of his body collapse onto the bed.

Later, the granite slab of the war memorial carved with the names of the men from Puy-Larroque who fell at the front arrives on a cart drawn by two dray horses with foaming loins. With some difficulty, the villagers hoist it, bearing the weight on ropes coiled around their forearms, then set it down at the place designated by the local council during an extraordinary meeting. Marcel is chopping wood on a block in the lean-to when, dressed all in black, Éléonore and the widow leave the house. For a long moment they stop and watch Marcel swing the axe with the regularity of a metronome, ignoring their presence, then at last they set off along the road to the village, followed by the sound of splitting wood. He does not show his face at the memorial masses either. The villagers begin to gossip, offended by his indifference, his contempt, his selfishness: do his misfortunes mean more than theirs? Does his pain exempt him from showing solidarity?

In the year following Marcel's return, the widow declines markedly. At first she is quieter, then she says nothing, as though reduced to silence. She sits next to the fire or outside the door and spends hours staring at a fixed point in front of her, the beads of her rosary moving back and forth between her fingers. She continues to tend to the kitchen garden, to scatter grain for the chickens, to collect the eggs. Sometimes she stops in the middle of the farmyard and looks around, as though she does not know where she is nor which direction to take. She looks up at the sky, screwing her eyelids, lips parted to reveal her toothless gums. She observes the slow procession of the clouds, then bows her head, blinks, dazzled by the light, and, taking small steps, goes back inside. She mutters unintelligible words and, when Éléonore speaks to her, she cannot suppress a flinch. She thinks before she responds, and speaks in a voice that is restive, frail. Soon, she begins to neglect the vegetable garden and simply kneels in the dirt, the knees of her dress muddy, the sun burning the tanned skin of her neck, or she indiscriminately rips up weeds and vegetable shoots. Éléonore comes upon her one day when she has laid waste to a patch of lettuce. Until now, she has thought of the widow's errors and lapses as petty tricks, reprisals. She lets go the apron on which she was wiping her hands, rushes over to the old woman, grabs her by the arm and shakes her roughly.

'What the hell is your problem?' she screams. 'Are you planning to make my life a misery to the bitter end? Why can't you just get it over with and die?'

The widow falls on her backside and seems dazed. She looks at the upturned earth and stammers:

'I wanted... I wanted...' before dissolving into tears and burying her face in her blackened hands.

She forgets the eggs abandoned by the chickens and they rot. She wanders around with her wicker basket on her arm under the listless eye of the few remaining farm animals. When it comes time to wring the neck of a chicken, she botches it. The animal slips from her grasp and runs in circles, spraying the yard with blood, raising clouds of dry dirt and provoking shrieks from the rest of the flock. When she comes face to face with Marcel, her eyes grow wide and she lets out a terrified whimper.

'Crazy old bat,' he says.

The widow retreats to the inglenook, trembling and muttering snatches of prayers.

She grows even thinner. She is now no more than skin and bone. She confuses the days of the week, the months, the seasons, the years. Éléonore washes her, dresses her, brushes her hair, and the broken little creature accepts this without a word. The flame of the oil lamp is reflected in her balding scalp. Then, she recovers the power of speech; she no longer thinks of resisting, of remaining silent. She who was always so miserly with words now blathers all day long. She takes Éléonore's hand when she crosses the yard, then turns to her and says:

'Excuse me, I don't suppose you've seen my daughter? My little girl?'

'I'm your daughter,' Éléonore responds.

The widow shrugs her shoulders and giggles.

'Yes, yes, of course you are.'

When Marcel comes through the door, she sometimes mistakes him for her late husband and says:

'Oh, there you are. Where have you been? You need to look after that chest of yours in the cold weather.'

Then, when he takes off his hat, she shrieks:

'Oh, dear Lord, what have they done to you?' or, failing to recognize him, sighs, 'Poor devil...' before returning to her contemplation of the doily she is holding, unable to crochet a single stitch.

She gets lost in the countryside and they have to scour other farms in search of her. Or farmers bring her home and Éléonore finds her covered in scratches, her clothes and her hair tangled with goose grass and spikelets. She talks to herself, mumbling words, talking in turn to her mother, her father, her husband, as though they were in the room, recounts stories about saints, about curses, about the pigsty and the voracious sow; a long, rambling, unintelligible prattle. One winter afternoon, while Éléonore is peeling vegetables at the kitchen table and the widow is sitting next to her, she hears her say:

'... course I know he's not dead... told me he was badly maimed but that he'd be back... she's happier that way, like the rest of them... better a cripple than a corpse... he'll not set foot in my house again, let me tell you! Never!'

Éléonore sets the knife down on the cutting bard. She remembers Marcel's mother, his brother whose features she recognized and who was driving the cart, the two women talking in hushed tones, the widow going back into the house and picking up her sewing, the needle clicking against the thimble. *Got himself killed just like all the rest. I warned you. Maybe now you'll stop pining for him.*

'What did you say?' she asks.

The widow turns her bony face towards her daughter. She seems to recognize her.

'What did you just say?' Éléonore asks again.

The old woman shakes her head slowly, uncertainly, then says:

'She devoured him... That animal devoured him, she didn't leave a thing... Not a crumb...'

178

The pain gives Marcel only rare moments of respite. At best it fades to a dull ache that quietly throbs to the rhythm of his pulse somewhere in his devastated nerve endings. Even in his sleep he feels it lodged within him like a separate organism, a parasite, sometimes at the back of his patched-up jaw, sometimes deep in the empty eye socket, sometimes in his cervical vertebrae, patiently sinking its jaws into his bones, his tendons, his marrow, to feast on them. When it subsides, the absence leaves a void, an aura as fearsome as the recurrence it heralds. He remains alert to this queasy lack of pain, and to the first signs announcing the new wave of pain that will engulf him. It seems to be not in the nerves, but a boring pain in the bones, a sort of caries that is eating away at the maxilla, the zygoma. He refuses to give ground, he battles against this pain that would see him infirm, helpless. By sheer strength of will he pushes the boundaries of his tolerance, he digs, he hoes, he reaps, as though with each swing he is dealing a blow to his pain, and though a brusque movement, a sudden jolt, may make it worse, he will never submit, never surrender. Sometimes, in the solitude of the fields or the shadows of the lean-to, he falls to his knees and takes his head in his hands, feeling as though it might explode. He presses the head of his hammer or the blade of the scythe against his temple in the hope that the cold metal might bring a moment's relief. His salivary glands work overtime, as they did when the wounds were still raw. At such times he has to swallow litres of saliva, or spit constantly and sleep with a basin next to him. With his tongue, he feels the redefined shape of his gums, the swellings, the protuberances where the bone and periosteum taken from his tibia were grafted to rebuild his jaw. Smoking slightly dulls his mucus membranes; some days he smokes three

exchange sterile phrases. She consoles herself, deludes herself that they know each other too well to still have need of words. She believes that her devotion brings her closer to him when in fact she is keeping him at a distance, indeed repelling him with her attentions, her servile eagerness. He despises what she has become. When they work together in the fields and he looks at her, even briefly, he feels a flash of anger directed at her, a blind, instant hostility towards her gestures, her ragged clothes, her peasant manner, her flat figure, her stubbornness, her deference, everything that shapes and animates her; then there are moments when he is aware of his own apathy, as though pain in the body leaves no room in the heart and the soul for anything but indifference, as though it is an acid patiently eating away at every emotion that is not anger or bitterness. He has touched only one woman and he has forgotten her. A blonde Alsatian prostitute, barely of age, whom the soldiers passed around and he in turn entwined in a hayloft stinking of rats' urine on a small farm so badly gutted by a German shell that, amid the shards of stone, the splintered roof beams and broken, upturned furniture, there remains only the barn where the soldiers slept, attested by the blackened circle of a small campfire ringed by stones. When it comes his turn, he climbs the ladder of worm-eaten wood, rusted nails and broken rungs he must step over to reach the loft through a pair of shutters that rattle in the cold wind, onto the powdery wooden boards set on joists rotting from the damp. At first he stands motionless, head tilted over his right shoulder because the roof is too low for him to stand upright, his hair tangled in cobwebs, while the girl lies down on a bed of straw laid out for others before him. She hitches her dress up over the farm girl legs covered with

downy hair, up over the pale veined thighs dotted with
bruises spanning the spectrum of every possible colour
which she may have got knocking against the corner of
a tavern table, the shafts of a dog cart or the buckles of
soldiers' belts, up over her pubis, where the bushy hair
fringing the lips meets at the centre to form tufts like the
dry wheat on the hillsides quivering in the breeze, ash
blonde, in the sombre dawn or at close of day. She reveals her heavy breasts, the nipples purple, almost blue,
the skin completely pimpled with gooseflesh and, keeping her thick woollen socks pulled up over her ankles,
flaunts herself, then beckons for him to join her. He lies
down next to her on the bed of musty straw, allows her
to undo the buttons of his trousers, to pull them down
over his woven, grubby, stinking undershorts, over his
thighs bitten by parasites, then she blows into her cold
hands to warm them before grasping his timid penis
and kneading it, all the while silently looking into his
eyes. He sees his reflection in her black pupils, the still-
undamaged face of a frightened youth, cornered by the
violence of men, while on the breeze comes the sounds
of a dog barking, the voices of soldiers on sentry duty in
the neighbouring hamlet, and the distant crack of gunfire. Bored, the girl straddles him and slips his half-limp
penis inside her. She thrusts against his groin. Their
mingled breath mists on their lips. She does not trouble
to simulate pleasure. She applies herself to making him
come quickly and silently; to exciting this grimy body
worn down by long marches, by combat, by unforgiv-
ing nights; to bringing pleasure to this life that no longer
even hangs by a thread, and whose survival is now a
matter of probability. He comes inside her, a shameful,
involuntary ejaculation. She climbs off him, freeing
his glistening penis which immediately falls against his

thigh, and wipes away the useless semen with a handful of straw, before quickly dressing, *because it's cold as a
witch's tit*. Marcel arches his shoulders, lifts his buttocks
and pulls up his trousers, his whole body trembling
now, his teeth chattering, for this is what he has done,
lost his virginity in the bitterest cold he has ever experienced. Yes, he has only ever been with one woman, then
he forgot the urges that sometimes thrilled through him
before the war, the seed he spilled onto his belly, under
the sheet, in the glow of the little fire.

Fear, pain and shame have snuffed out desire. The sight
of gaping bodies on the battlefield. How could anyone desire them, knowing what is contained inside?
Everywhere, Marcel sees ambulatory sacks of skin
filled with steaming blue, yellow, green entrails, with excreta, sludge and biological fluids. The nurse who bends
over him to bandage his face, her breasts constrained in
her white blouse, and sometimes presses herself against
his shoulder. The revulsion inspired in him by the
thought of the heart beating, the spasmodic convulsions
beneath her ribs. The revulsion inspired in him by the
sight of his own face when the surgeon hands him the
mirror and he contemplates his deformed reflection.
And yet he is one of the *least worst, the most handsome* of
those in this gallery of monsters who still seem human,
unlike the droolers, those of whom all that remains are
wounds that gape even though they have scarred, chasms
and rifts that will never close in the centre of their faces, open to reveal exposed glottises, throats that twitch
like sphincters, the honeycomb of sinuses. Desperate
attempts are made to cover these grotesque masks with
malleable prostheses which the patients must learn to
shape with their own hands so that each day they can

refashion a counterfeit face, but the prostheses melt or bleach in the sun and the rain, and within days the feel of the paste and the glue quickly becomes intolerable. He can 'consider himself lucky', says the surgeon who took the bone and periosteum from his tibia to rebuild his lower jaw. The doctor removed the ruptured eyeball from the left socket and, from deep inside the cavity, picked out a sliver of bone. This had probably came from another soldier. Not one of those 'blown to kingdom come', those whose limbs were reassembled and their remains patched together so they could be stuffed into a coffin with a new uniform sacrificed for the occasion, and shipped back to their families. (Though there are no confirmed incidents, it is not impossible that such soldiers might end up with an arm, a leg, even the head of another.) Instead it had probably come from one of the soldiers who were blown to smithereens and scattered all around, pieces of their bones piercing the bodies of other men like shrapnel.

And yet he sees her hovering around him, seeking out his company, the proximity of his body. At first he does not understand what it is she wants, her constant touch, her consideration, her habit of suddenly shaking off her rustic manner to become languid, sighing and allowing her blouse to fall open over the sharp angle of her shoulder, her collarbone, her flat chest. At the height of summer, she mops her brow, revealing a dark, odoriferous armpit. She ties her hair into a chignon at the nape of her neck. She hitches her skirt up over her purple, calloused knees. As he is bathing one morning in the tub he has installed in the barn, out of sight, he feels a presence at the back of his neck. It is Éléonore, watching him through the gap in the door. Marcel turns his head and sees her shadow take flight. He remembers an evening before the war, on the feast of Saint-Jean; the bonfire they lit at the top of a fallow hill near the village. Surely, in that moment, he saw in her something more than a little girl, more than the cousin he was fond of, who kept him company? If it is not simply pity, her attraction seems to him to conceal some perversity – what can she still want from him, from this mutilated body? – but from this point he beings to feel the sexual tension, the nervousness that underpins their conversations. He looks at her with fresh eyes; he now sees her sex.

One morning in early November, he is digging out potatoes and Jerusalem artichokes from the claggy earth in the kitchen garden. Éléonore crosses the farmyard and goes into the still-empty sty, where the chickens sometimes lay their eggs. She shoots him a furtive glance before disappearing inside. Marcel drops his hoe and stands upright. He moves quickly, taking long strides, rubbing his black hands on his trousers. He follows her into the sty. Éléonore is waiting for him, sitting on the mildewed straw, beside a nest built and then abandoned by a hen, in which lie two warm eggs, their shells dirty. They stare at each other for a moment, then Marcel steps towards Éléonore, who lies back. He helps her hike up her skirt and take off her stockings. He tries to unbutton the collar of her blouse. His numbed fingers become tangled in the buttonholes and he pulls on the fabric until it rips. The buttons roll away in the straw bedding. She makes to caress him, but he grabs her wrist and pushes her away. For a moment, he breathes in the smell of her breasts, then, raising his head, sees that she is looking at him. He grabs her hips and forces her to turn over. She can feel his cold hands on her thighs, his sex as it

186

hesitantly pokes against the lips of hers. He spits in his hand to lubricate himself and enters her so roughly that it elicits a cry. He rucks up her blouse, grabs her hips, her sides, her shoulders, the back of her neck. She feels the rough fabric of his jacket chafe at the small of her back. She claws at the ground, dislodging a nail on the hard-packed earth beneath the thin bed of straw. With a loud grunt, Marcel shudders inside her and collapses onto her back, forcing her to bend under his weight, his ravaged cheek, whose bulge she feels for the first time, resting against her own. She is now breathing his breath. She sees a patch of the yard appear and disappear through the slowly swinging gate of the sty. There is a faint, insipid smell of eggs and dry chicken droppings from the abandoned nest beside her face. On the low ceiling, the cobwebs quiver from their conjoined breath and the heat radiated by their bodies. Marcel gets back onto his knees. He sees the crimson blood on his pale sex. He tucks the tail of his shirt into his trousers, buttons his flies, adjusts the hat he has not taken off, leaves the sty and heads back to the vegetable garden. Left to herself, Éléonore slips a hand between her thighs. With some difficulty, she straightens her clothes, then picks up the two eggs. She kneels for a moment, one hand resting on her groin, before leaning against the wall and wincing as she gets to her feet. As she leaves the sty, she sees Marcel smoking next to the kitchen garden. He gives a little wave. She waves back and heads towards the farmhouse. She brings the eggs up to her nose and inhales.

Marcel is settling the new pearl-grey heifer in the byre when she comes to find him and stands in the doorway, watching him scatter fodder at the foot of the ruminating animal.

'Well, come on,' he says, seeing her wringing the apron between her fingers. 'Out with it... what's the matter with you?'

From his nervousness, she suspects he has already guessed what she is about to say.

'I think I might be pregnant. There, I said it.'

He sets down the pitchfork, turns and, for a moment, observes her from the shadow of his broad-brimmed hat. When he steps forward and takes her hands in his, she stifles a fearful flinch. Marcel says:

'Well, then, we'll have to marry.'

Then he asks:

'Why are you trembling?'

'Because it's cold,' Éléonore lies.

He marries her in the spring, on a day of blazing sunshine, whirling with dust from the hot, strong Autan wind. She finds the dress that the widow wore for her wedding and carefully wrapped and stowed in a box so the clothes moths would not destroy it. Making the most of Marcel's absence, she takes out one of the mirrors and, setting it on a chair, tries the dress on while the widow watches. There is not enough space for her to step back and she contemplates her fragmented reflection: the face covered by the veil, the bodice and the cuffs of yellowed lace, the folds of the dress. She spins around in front of the widow, who is chewing at her top gums.

'I'm getting married,' she says.

'Oh, I can see that, I can see that,' the widow replies, nodding reproachfully, before pointing at her swollen belly and adding:

'Poor thing, given your misfortune, I hope that at least it'll be a boy.'

A fleeting burst of happiness trills through her as they step out into the churchyard. The villagers are loitering on their doorsteps or have found some excuse to be nearby, affronted not to have been invited to the wedding as custom would dictate, and when Marcel helps Éléonore into the cart – the same cart that carried her parents to their wedding, and carried the remains of the father to his final resting place – drawn by the heifer, whose collar she has strung with ribbons, and next to her the widow, who seems to think she is reliving her own wedding since she is smiling and waving at everyone, and looks happier than anyone has ever seen her, the inhabitants, resentful and unsettled, mutter in low voices as the cortège rattles down the road towards the Plains, with no other clamour but the clip-clop of the heifer's hooves and the screech of the wheels. Priggishly, they comment on this dubious union between blood relatives; on the pregnancy she thought she could hide beneath that old wedding dress; on their tightfistedness – why were they not invited if not to spare the expense of a wedding reception? On the drive back to the farm, Éléonore looks at the road, at the fields cloaked in a shifting down of absinthe green, at Marcel's profile, from which one could believe his face was still whole, and, beneath the brim of the hat he clutches from time to time against a gust of wind, there is something uncompromising in the eye that is staring straight ahead, as though nothing now can hurt him, or deflect him from the goal he has set himself, about which she knows almost nothing. With every jolt, she feels the shoulder of the widow, who is humming next to her, and the shoulder of Marcel. Behind them, the scattered guests are talking. A child runs in front of them. Her joy has vanished with the soar of red kites whirling above, carried on the updraughts.

190

They move the widow into the old scullery where Marcel has been living. They take over the box-bed, formerly the conjugal bed, later the father's death bed, and put away the child's bed on which Éléonore was still sleeping, her legs tucked up, the night before her wedding. They find themselves lying next to one another beneath the eiderdown, aware of their breathing, of the warmth of their bodies, thinking of all the nights to come. Soon she will be able to touch his body, though only by accident, during the brief couplings, and she will feel the scar on his stiff leg. Even an attempt at a caress seems to upset him. On several occasions, he brushes away the hand she tries to lay on him. One night, she is woken by groaning. Tortured by pain or tormented by nightmares, Marcel moans in his sleep. She tries to lay a hand on his forehead to calm him, but he wakes with a start, grabs her by the wrist and pins her against the pillow.

'It's me, it's me!' she tells him.

He stares at her with his mad eye, panting like an animal cornered by hunters, then lets her go. The following day, seeing her rub her bruised wrist, he asks:

'How did you get that?'

She tugs at her sleeve and evades the question.

'I don't know. I probably knocked it against something. It's nothing serious.'

Ever since, she has been on the alert for his starts, his wails, not daring to do a thing, confined to the far side of the bed, careful to leave as much space as possible between them. He sleeps for only a few hours, then pushes open the door of the box-bed and sits on the edge of the mattress holding his head in his hands, sometimes pounding it with his fists, then he gets up, dresses, and leaves the house. His aches tell him what the weather will be like. Without setting foot outdoors, he can simply run his fingers along his jaw and predict that it will rain. As Éléonore's pregnancy progresses, he worries about the child that is to be born. In his dreams he sees her giving birth to a tiny creature with a disfigured face, an avatar whose mouth is a gaping wound that opens onto the inside of a soft, pitted skull, a creature that inspires in him a nameless terror.

Like the pain, the images and impressions persist. When he closes his eyes, he sees himself marching in a column of men along a country road dressed in their dashing red trousers, their fine blue coats, already sweating in the summer sun. There is something unreal, something intoxicating about marching together under the awed gaze of onlookers waving handkerchiefs as they pass. The sky is a tranquil blue. The birds on the branches are singing at the tops of their lungs. In this light, the war towards which they are marching as one man seems impossible. Their hobnailed boots beat the ground in time, raising an immense cloud of dust that coats their noses and their throats. They exude a smell of new leather, of cobblers' shops and cattle. The weight of their rifles is already beginning to cut into their shoulders. They march as though they will never stop, straight ahead, even if they do not know where they are going. They leave behind the towns, the villages of an unfamiliar countryside, and cross endless fields, trampling cabbages and beets. They pass other regiments, telegraph poles lying across the road like trees felled by a storm. Men, already exhausted now that the exhilaration of the farewells has drained away, are resting in the shade of tall walnut trees. Soon, they will see the fleeing carts coming towards them, drawn by horses, their coats dark with sweat. The carts are filled with furniture, mattresses,

stink of gunpowder. A huge farmhouse blazes ceaseless-
ly, setting the night aglow. The black roof beams are still
holding out against the flames. The soldiers shiver in
their uniforms, wet and stiff with cold. They smoke to
warm themselves, but their tobacco pouches are damp
and the cigarettes sputter. They sip broth, its surface
floating with gobs of grease and lardons. A soldier greedily sucks marrow from a bone; his lips glisten obscenely.
Dysentery spares no-one; they drop their pants and,
with no regard for modesty, hunker down and shit next
to each other, staring at each other, then get up without
wiping their arses. When on furlough, the men go off to
meet up with a son, a wife, a mother. As he is about to
board the train, Marcel stands motionless on the platform and looks at the engine panting like an asthmatic
draught horse. The next image hurls him into the front
lines: he is digging the earth as fast as he can, clawing the
wall of the trench with his bare hands to make a hole in
which to shelter. He is shivering and his teeth are chattering so hard that he spits a gobbet of his cheek into his
hand. Other men have already dug themselves in, hugging their knees tightly, adopting a foetal position, like
bulbs that someone has planted. A chaplain is wandering
through the labyrinthine trenches, his face smeared with
mud and other, unspeakable things. Hands stretched out
before him, blinded by the smoke that has burned his
eyes, he gropes his way along, droning an unintelligible
prayer. He crashes into the mud walls, causing them to
collapse, trips over the body of a solider, then collapses
and blacks out or falls asleep – either way, he does not
move. All around are the corpses of men, of horses, of
mules, twined and tangled, the corpses of centaurs half-
swallowed by the earth. Infantrymen crawl through
the mud beneath a sky that now looks nothing like a

sky, streaked with clouds of unearthly shapes and colours, behind which the sun broods, like the eye of some drowsy beast, or the very heart of hell. In the evenings, to cheer themselves a little, they play cards by the light of an acetylene lamp and pick lice from each other's hair. One soldier has managed to tame a rat, now cleaning its whiskers while perched on his shoulder, and hiding the crumbs of stale bread the men give it in his collar. Bright plumes of smoke soar into the sky, then suddenly clods of earth rain down around them. One morning, during an advance, Marcel's detachment happens on a little clearing that seems to have been spared the madness of war. The grass is green and lush; there are even flowers. A stream snakes through it. The men stop, spellbound by this preternatural beauty. Are they dead? Is this the enchanted garden offered them despite their bloody hands? No: the strangeness of the place is in the colour of the brook, which is crimson, because upstream, hidden by a copse, the bodies of dead German soldiers have been tossed into the river and are slowly bleeding out. As the men approach, a horde of birds rises from the corpses, causing their hearts to stutter. They laugh quietly, a little embarrassed. While they are billeted on a farm, Marcel detects an acrid smell. He follows the trail and finds a pile of mouldering hutches in which the rabbits have died of thirst and starvation. Their silken fur is moulded to their bones. Some of the wounded are prescribed morphine to dull the pain from their deep wounds. Carried off in ambulances, they whimper in an artificial sleep from which they hope never to wake. A corporal's leg is eaten away by gangrene and vermin: he plugged a gash in his thigh with a fistful of mud. Marcel thinks about the farm sometimes. He remembers his native soil. In spite of his club foot, Albert Brisard enlisted.

just as the ducks the widow used to decapitate would run towards the little pond full of feathers and droppings at the back of the farm. When a German soldier raises his head above the trench opposite, Marcel trains the rifle on him. He is thinking, *It's like an animal, he's nothing more than an animal, an animal.* Then he fires. He is trembling so hard that the barrel swerves. The bullet hits the Boche in the neck. He is still alive when Marcel crawls over. Bright-red blood spurts between the fingers clutching his throat. Marcel would swear that the soldier is no more than seventeen. His eyes are a deep blue, ringed with dark-purple circles. He has a wispy adolescent moustache, and his cheeks are pale and beardless. The skin of his hands looks soft. Marcel thinks, *He's obviously a city boy.* The little Boche looks at Marcel; he tries to say something. His lips part to reveal a mouth filled with blood. Is he apologizing for this sad spectacle, for his incompetence as a soldier, or for the memory that the Frenchman will henceforth have to live with? He reaches out to Marcel with the hand that was compressing the wound, but Marcel's hand hangs limply by his side, unable to grasp it. He watches the boy bleed out, still murmuring something, then his eyes mist over and gutter out.

On a July afternoon in 1921, Éléonore gives birth to a healthy boy that, in honour of the dead father, they decide to name Henri. Marcel stares at the newborn, his umbilical cord tied off by the midwife, lying on the belly of his mother. When the nurse hands him the child so that she can wash Éléonore, and he walks off with the baby in his arm, a tear traces a furrow down his cheek: the child's face is intact. The widow is led in by the midwife to sit beside her daughter, whom she seems to recognize. She looks at Henri, then at Éléonore, and she reaches out a trembling, twisted hand and strokes the baby's cheek. In a short space of time, she has rapidly declined. She confuses names, faces, times, day and night. She has difficulty speaking in sentences, her voice grows hoarse and trails off. They no longer try to understand what she is saying and ask only questions, to which she sometimes answers yes, sometimes no. She eats only small mouthfuls of food which have to be mashed to a puree and fed to her because she chokes when she tries to swallow. She is shrinking, stooping forward, drawn by the earth. She soils herself; her clothes reek of urine. Éléonore feeds and changes her as she does the baby; she is a mother twice over.

Éléonore quickly realizes that she will have to intervene between father and child. One night, because the pain is tormenting him, and Henri has been crying incessantly, Marcel asks her several times to pacify him.

'I'm begging you, keep him quiet.'

She paces the room with the baby on her shoulder, patting his buttocks. She massages his belly, runs a finger over his gums, gives him a carrot to suck, but nothing calms him. Sitting at the table with a glass of hooch, Marcel takes his head in his hands, digging his thumbs into his ears. The baby's wail bores into his eardrums, sets his teeth on edge like the sound of nails scratching a blackboard. As Éléonore tries to put Henri in his cot, the child howls even louder. Marcel gets to his feet, strides over to the crib, deals three loud blows to the side of the box-bed, bellowing:

'SHUT-THAT-FUCKING-BRAT-UP!'

Éléonore bends over Henri. She stands motionless, shielding him with her body. When she looks up, Marcel has retreated several steps. He stares at the splintered side of the box-bed, looks from the congested face of his son in his crib to the ashen face of Éléonore. He walks away, grabs his jacket and leaves the house. Much later, in the early hours, he watches them through the window, not daring to cross the threshold: Éléonore has dozed off on the bed, the child is lying next to her, and Marcel goes off to sleep in the hayloft.

One night the following winter, the widow leaves her room and passes close to them, a spectral presence in her nightgown, whose soiled fabric clings to her scrawny thighs, but they are asleep and do not see her pause and look at them for a long moment. Images, fragments surface and are superimposed over her ruined consciousness. She sees Éléonore and Marcel in the box-bed and thinks she sees herself lying next to the father. She leans over the Moses basket in which Henri is sleeping and it is Éléonore that she sees. But things are not as they should be. The room has changed, the opening into the byre no longer exists, the arrangement of the furniture is completely wrong. The widow goes out into the yard and stares at the farm, strange and blue in the moonlight. The cold cuts straight through her, and she wraps her thin arms around her shoulders. Taking small steps, she walks barefoot over the frozen ground to the well and leans against the coping stone. She suddenly hears a breathy sound from inside the well. The rushing wind sounds like a voice calling to her. Trembling, she leans over, and sees her face appear on the surface of the still, black water. She recognizes it: it is the father calling to her from the far end of the tunnel, it is the father speaking to her from his long exile, across time and space, inviting her to join him. She breaks her neck in her fall, striking the stone wall. When her body hits the water, a faint splash drifts up to the yard and is immediately whipped away by the wind. The rippled surface is soon still again and the moon is reflected there once more.

They realize that the grandmother is missing at first light. Since her recent escapades, her physical health has markedly deteriorated and they are surprised that she could make it beyond the farmyard. They search everywhere for her, but she cannot be found. Marcel knocks at the doors of the neighbouring farms. Since he is loath to go into the village, Éléonore leaves him to look after Henri and goes to talk to the inhabitants of Puy-Larroque. No-one has seen the old woman. They begin to worry that she might be roaming the countryside wearing only her nightdress. How could she survive the bitter cold for more than a few hours? By late morning, a search party has been organized. With the help of a group of villagers, they scour the surrounding fields, search the henhouses, the byres, thinking that the widow might have sought shelter there. After nightfall, when they need lanterns, they abandon the search. At home with Henri, Éléonore paces frantically, holding her child in her arms. She already knows that it is too late to hope that they might find her, but when Marcel appears in the doorway, takes off his hat and shakes his head, she chokes back an anguished sob. In the days that follow, they continue to search the countryside with the help of the local policeman, expecting only to find the widow dead, frozen in a ditch or behind a hedge. She seems to have vanished. By the end of the week, they begin to lose heart and the searches become less frequent. There is farm work to be done. There is fitting and now clings to the body bloated like a sponge filled with water. Éléonore quickly takes Henri away to spare him the sight of this ruin. They bury the remains of the widow two days later, after the policeman concludes it was an accidental death; two days of bitter cold during which the corpse, encased in a pine coffin, froze solid in the church presbytery. They have to abandon the idea of dressing the body, but before the lid of the coffin is nailed down, Éléonore asks that the mourning dress the widow loved be laid on top of her remains, that a rosary be placed in her hands and the missal with the battered cover be placed next to her. The gravedigger reopens the tomb in which lie the jumbled remains of the father. He collects together the bones he finds and discreetly covers them with a layer of earth. Excited by the affair, and forgetting the contempt the widow felt for them, the villagers throng outside the church doors, eager to attend the funeral. When Father Benoît asks Éléonore to read a passage from the First Epistle of Saint Paul to the Corinthians, she remains seated in the pew, head bowed, unable to get to her feet, despite Marcel elbowing her in the ribs, and a murmur ripples through the congregation before the priest himself begins to read:

'But some man will say, How are the dead raised up? and with what body do they come? Thou fool, that which thou sowest is not quickened, except it die: and that which thou sowest, thou sowest not that body that shall be, but bare grain, it may chance of wheat, or of some other grain: but God giveth it a body as it hath pleased him, and to every seed his own body. All flesh is not the same flesh: but there is one kind of flesh of men, another flesh of beasts, another of fishes, and another of birds. There are also celestial bodies, and bodies terrestrial: but the glory of the celestial is one, and the glory of

202

the terrestrial is another. There is one glory of the sun, and another glory of the moon, and another glory of the stars: for one star differeth from another star in glory. So also is the resurrection of the dead. It is sown in corruption; it is raised in incorruption...'

Thawed by the heat of the candles and warmth of the flock, the coffin, its timber still beaded with holy water from the aspergillum, drips onto the catafalque and all the way down the aisle when Marcel and three men from the village lift it onto their shoulders, bear it from the church and place it on the cart standing in the churchyard. Éléonore holds Henri in her arms and, as the funeral cortège sets off for the cemetery, where the gravedigger is smoking, leaning on his shovel as he contemplates his handiwork, Marcel lays a hand on her back, encouraging her to walk next to him behind the coffin. The villagers who left the church before them join the procession. As they cross the village square, Éléonore hears someone mutter as she passes:

'Well, she'll not have a clear conscience, let me tell you...'

She recognizes the voice of Marie Contis, the same woman who, two years earlier, kicked her as she was being dragged along the ground on this same square and muttered threats against the widow. She grits her teeth, holds her sleeping son against her breast and, for a moment, she carries on walking. Then she turns to Marcel, presses the child into his arms and pushes her way back through the cortège. She finds her at the back, with Jeanne Cadours and some other gorgons. Marie Contis seems surprised to see Éléonore striding towards her and glances back at the church, thinking that perhaps she has forgotten something, but Éléonore walks straight up to her and deals her a vicious slap that knocks

203

her against Jeanne Cadours' shoulder. Voices are raised, a circle quickly forms. Blood from Marie Contis' nose trickles over her lips and drips onto her dress.

'She hit me! She hit me!' she splutters, trembling and holding out her crimson hands before the eyes of the witnesses.

'You dirty viper,' Éléonore replies. 'You think I didn't hear you? You think I don't know the lies you peddle about me, you bitch?'

She looks at the men and women around her and points to them one by one.

'Let this be a warning: the first one of you who dares spread your poison about me, my family or the memory of my mother will also wind up dead at the bottom of a well.'

Marie Contis whimpers and falls to her knees, supported by two women who press their handkerchiefs to her face. No-one dares move until someone takes Éléonore by the shoulder. It is Marcel, who has come to find her. He looks at Marie Contis, at the face of his wife and at the dumbstruck onlookers, and says:

'Let's go.'

Together, they return to the head of the procession and the cortège sets off once more. The mortal remains of the widow are lowered into the cold earth of Puy-Larroque and laid atop the debris, boards and bones of the father, who is crushed by the weight of the coffin. As the congregation disperses, Éléonore stands for a long time watching the gravedigger toss shovelfuls of earth into the pit until it is once more filled and he need only tamp down the earth with the flat of his shovel.

A few days after the funeral, they empty the wardrobe that contained the widow's belongings. Éléonore

204

discovers that the clothes are covered with a fine layer of sawdust. They shine a lamp into the wardrobe and see the holes bored into the timber by furniture beetles. Marcel takes the doors off their hinges.

'It'll need to be taken apart, sanded down, treated and repolished,' he says.

As they remove the shelves, they discover that one of the rear panels is loose, and was held in place only by the bracket of the shelf they have just removed. Éléonore tilts the board to reveal a dark recess in the wall where a brick has been removed, and in it, a rusted metal sugar tin. For a moment they stare at it without saying a word, then Éléonore reaches out her hand and grasps the box, whose contents jingle as she pulls it towards her. She sits on one of the chairs, sets the box on her lap, opens the lid and gazes at the few gold and silver coins and the handfuls of copper coins neatly stacked and tied up with raffia; the savings patiently collected by the widow over almost forty years from the sale of products from the farm in anticipation of rainy days, famine, penury, apocalypse, or perhaps for the simple satisfaction of saving, since, even during the war, she could never bring herself to dip into her nest egg. They lay the money on the table.

'Bloody hell,' Marcel breathes, causing the cigarette dangling from the corner of his lips to glow.

The following day, he goes in search of the owner of the farm, a docile, blind old man whom he persuades, in return for a derisory life annuity, to sell him the farm buildings and the seven hectares of land they farm. Soon, the fields are once more filled with livestock. They purchase a Mérens gelding that has been broken to harness, a few geese from Toulouse. While wandering through the pig market in Miélan, he sees a huge boar,

You little devil! What have you been playing at, to get yourself covered in mud like that? Come here so I can hose you down. Take off the T-shirt, hold out your arms, tilt your head. Where have you been? What have you been doing, you filthy little animal, you devil? Don't you think things are bad enough as it is? Can't you see what's going on outside? The end that's coming, that's already here? Why do you have to get involved in all this? Couldn't you keep yourself to yourself, hide out in one of those holes you're so fond of? Come here and let me dry you off, and wipe that savage little face of yours. You look like you've got older. Not like you've grown up, just like you're suddenly older, like an old man trapped in a child's body. That happened to me too, I ended up growing old overnight, a long lock of white hair across my forehead appeared just like that. But I thought they'd spare you. I couldn't be certain, but I thought it was possible that you'd avoid it, escape all this madness. Don't they say "Happy are the simple-minded?" But no, not you, you're different. You don't fool me, you know. You never did fool me. I've had all the time in the world to watch you, to see you in action. Obviously, there's a screw loose in that little head of yours, and God alone knows what goes on in there, but it's not empty. It might be the opposite, maybe it's full to bursting, full of coils and strange things, things we couldn't begin to imagine.

Go on, sit down – sit down I said – what else do you want to do? There's nothing for you or me to do here but sit down and wait. Someone will show up eventually… All this smoke, all this screaming, all the chaos will eventually alert the outside world. Then they'll come and they'll see. I can't tell you what will happen after that. I'm far too tired to try and work out what will happen. All I know right now is that we have to wait here, sitting opposite each other, on this chair and this sofa; you, the child, facing the grandmother I've become, with no dreams, with no hope, none of the things that usually keep a human being alive, but with a heart that goes on beating, in spite of me, let me tell you, because I'd rather have seen nothing and known nothing about all this... And yet there's no doubt about it, here I am to witness it, here alone, with you, still standing in the middle of this hell realizing what we've done, seeing with my own two eyes what we've been reduced to. This is my penance: to have seen it coming, powerless, useless, the time of this baleful harvest. Not that I'm surprised. You won't see astonishment on my face. Or what you might see as astonishment is nothing more than fear. The fear of a fragile, pitiful old woman, the fear of old Éléonore, unable to defend herself against anything, unable even to defend herself against her own family. It's something I've known for so long that I might have known it forever but, from time to time, I've forgotten, because, with habit, every-thing, even the most subtle and familiar threats come to seem less frightening. And yet when it's revealed, this veiled threat, this violence you think you have tamed, you recognize it as an old enemy you thought had become a confidant. It leaps at you, instantly breaking free of the chains you've spent a lifetime crafting to shackle its manifold, monstrous paws, the muzzles carefully placed over the countless jaws bristling with fangs, and everything explodes, even the leaden silence that seemed thicker than the thickest lead. Fear, oh yes, there is terrible fear, but no surprise, because deep inside I have always known that a person cannot sow so much discord, so much grief, so many secrets, so much hatred and go unpunished... I just thought I wouldn't live to see this bitter harvest, that I would be long dead, tossed into a pit with what remains of our lineage, buried deep in the earth of Puy-Larroque.

I clung on, in the teeth of everything, despite myself and my desire to die young, because I soon realized that there was nothing left for me but a life sentence surrounded by my cats, surrounded by all of you, though at a distance, in the old skin of an old woman you feed and care for out of a sense of duty, all the while hoping that the end will come to spare us the spectacle of her infirmity. Oh yes, I survived for all this time without really knowing why – another thing I've done out of habit – the comforting reduplication of hours, through moments when time felt unspeakably long, begging death to come and take me in my sleep, for there to be no tomorrow, only to wake with the feeling that one more day would not be so terrible, might even be desirable... Until now. Until this moment that sees me sitting here with you, my great-grandson, uncertain as to what is really going on beyond these walls, but not needing to know to realize that things – and when I say things, I don't just mean the years, the events, but every action, every detail, every word, every gesture, all those trifling moments of which no-one has the slightest memory – have begotten what they were bound to beget, have led our family to its ruin, have led farming and the world around it to the brink of collapse.

Nor am I surprised that this toxic legacy has converged in you, the last of the herd, the just-like-his-uncle, a mute bastard, filthy and uncontrollable; that the countless poisonous rivulets that course through the veins of each generation of our family now course through your slender, delicate veins, perhaps even more poisonous and more lethal. Pushing you to do what cannot be undone, that thing that you have committed with the hands of a child that are no longer those of a child, and indeed never were, for there is nothing innocent about them, they have been forever tainted. And how can I reproach you, how can I blame you, when I am right here in front of you, the eldest of the guilty? The one who brought about the catastrophe. We need to scrabble in the mud of memory, the silt of this family tree, to drag into the light of day the roots I'm telling you about, roots as difficult to rip out as broom – and what does it matter now whether the blame lies with me or with others who came before us? I am the one who is here today prepared to explain, to answer for our actions. Not that I am expecting absolution, not that I expect your forgiveness or even your compassion, but

212

simply because it is the least I can do: to try, always assuming it is possible, to piece together the story, our story, and therefore yours, for you, who has not asked anything and yet whose life and whose actions are guided by some invisible hand – why not call it fate, since everything had been decided for you – to try to reconstruct that collective memory, instilled in each of us and yet elusive and illusory.

And what matter if I don't know whether you will understand; I believe that to say these words, to say them out loud in front of you, will offer you some semblance of justice. All you have to do is sit there and listen to me just as you have done for days on end, over all these years, when you came and sat in that exact spot and we did not talk, in some sense foreshadowing what we assumed was bound to happen one day, you questioning me with your perpetual silence and me entrenched in mine, yet knowing that I should speak, on my own behalf, but not only, to speak for the others, for so many others, saving my voice, firmly convinced that the day would come when you would knock at my door as you did today, signalling that the moment had come for me to speak, to give vent to these words that will surely leave me for dead, or drained of the very last of my strength.

I don't know whether it is possible to survive such a thing, a confession that is not a confession but rather a purge, an emetic. Let me say again that I don't expect anything from you, no forgiveness, no blessing; I have only the vague hope that my words might ease your conscience rather than mine, for which it is much too late. I'm not even sure that I am equal to the task. Obviously I am capable of speaking, though it will pain me because, long ago, when I realized the ineffectuality to which I was reduced in the age of male domination, the futility of my attempting to influence the course of our family's fate, the fate that is finally fulfilled in you, I chose to save my breath, and with time it has waned, my voice has become tremulous and broken, a querulous old woman's voice that reaches my lips as

213

though buried beneath an avalanche of stones.

Yes, I will be able to speak, even if it means forever losing this voice and being once more reduced to silence. But how do I go about it? How do I reconstruct this story, so simple, so commonplace that it is almost banal, yet simultaneously complex and nebulous? How to depict what needs to be perceived so it can be understood at a glance, not horizontally, like the line of the story that I am about to tell you for want of any other, but simultaneously, like a point? It needs to be possible to take in all the moments it comprises at a single glance. Perhaps all of this will radiate some truth about what we are, about what you are, though I cannot swear as much, and it may prove impossible, because I have only my voice and my timeworn memory, treacherous and full of holes, and the time unfolding before us.

So, in a sense, everything I will tell you, this whole enterprise, is doomed to failure. I can only do my best and hope that something of it reaches you and eases a little of the weight that rests on your frail shoulders without your even knowing, for you came into this world and have grown up bearing this terrible legacy, but if we can experience, you and I, a little respite, a little peace, even for a brief moment, I suppose I can consider myself satisfied. I will at least feel that I have done something with my sad existence.

In the darkness traversed by a sliver of moon, coiled in the hollow of a coomb on the slopes of a valley, on the edge of a rustling oak grove, the farm buildings are just visible by the line of the roofs, the reflection of the tiles, the russet of the façades. The windows are black holes in which curtains of grey cotton hang, frozen. Thick earthenware plates are piled in the sink. Flies doze on the spattered oilcloth spread over the table. On the main building of the pigsty, sheets of fibre cement quiver like murky water. Quartz from the flat stones half-buried in

214

the black earth glitter faintly. Shards of flint cut through the humus on the edge of the woods, while woodlice and snails glide through the moss and the peat. A fox slinks between roots and brambles, its chops red with the spittle-slick hare it is gripping in its jaws. It stops, sniffs the east wind. Its eyes are two bronze orbs. Fur trembles on its flanks, and it disappears beneath a blackened stump. The raw-boned shadow of a dog crosses the farmyard. An owl hoots in the topmost branches of a tree, then silently takes wing. Inside the pig shed, where the opalescent night does not penetrate, the pigs lie on a grating. The sows are crowded next to each other in stalls, their hips, flanks and hocks smeared with their own faeces. The wind whistles between the sheets of fibre cement. A few boars doze in their pen. Under the infrared lamps, piglets squeal and suckle the teats of the nursing sows held in place by straps and metal bars. The sows are stupefied by exhaustion; their eyes roll beneath thick-lashed lids. Gestating sows lie sleeping on their taut, swollen bellies, twitching to the kicks of litters yet unborn. Their dreams are haunted by the shadows of men.

Jérôme wakes from a dream of mythological snakes, pits filled with dark water from which he flushes out insects with hairy, threadlike limbs that he picks up only for them to scratch his face, of roaring animals, shifting chimeras. He pushes off the sheet, sits on the edge of the bed, feet dangling above the floor, in the darkness of the bedroom. The twins, his cousins, are fast asleep; Thomas with the wheezing, laboured breathing brought on by his asthma and his permanently blocked nose, Pierre curled up beneath the eiderdown he takes with him everywhere. From this shapeless, grey rag, which is like a physical part of him, as though he trails an appendage, an unsightly prolapsed intestine around the farm, he pulls at the hollow shafts of the goose feathers poking through the fabric, using them to tickle his nose and upper lip as he drifts off.

Jérôme lies motionless, the only member of the family awake, his body suspended on the mattress, surrounded by the chirring of insects and the croaking of toads. He looks at the sleeping twins. They used to cry as babies when Jérôme stroked their soft skulls, their bulging, fluffy foreheads, and their mother would take them from him and press them to her breast. Now when they sleep next to him, once the light has been turned out and Gabrielle has kissed those same foreheads, now smooth and warm, Thomas talks to himself, muttering under the folds of a sheet stiff with snot, and Pierre waves his little hands full of goose feathers. The twins fill Jérôme's unending silence with their whispered words.

He is alert to the sounds made by the house. It shows its true face only at night, pitching its framework like an old-fashioned ship, its hundred-year-old worm-eaten skeleton, expanding its cold rooms, stretching its cracked roof beams, turning its hallways into a tapestry of shadows. Beneath the heartbeat pulsing in his eardrums, Jérôme can make out the breath of a gentle breeze in the loose tiles, the crack of the tarpaulin stretched over the roof, the scampering of a stone marten across the beams, the squeaking of a litter of baby rats in the hollow cob wall, the mother in her nest carefully fashioned from stolen boar bristles, fibreglass and wisps of straw, lying like the sows, offering her teats to ten pink pups, whose translucent skin reveals their purple veins and bellies gorged with milk.

The child slips out of the bed and the soles of his feet touch the grimy floor covered with dust, with the specks of clay, gravel and straw they traipse into the house on their socks, between their toes, under their unclipped nails, in the tangles of their hair and the cuffs of their trousers, trailing it into the bedrooms and even onto the sheets, which they impatiently brush every night before they climb in. He picks up the clothes strewn around the bed, pulls on his green corduroy shorts and the thick woollen jumper he has stretched out of shape, tugging at the sleeves to make them longer as his arms grow. For some time now, his body has been growing in a fitful, disharmonious way, his limbs thrusting him higher. Something inside him is stirring, insidiously reshaping his organs, his bones and his cartilage. Often, faced with his naked body reflected in the washhouse trough or the pond, he catches a glimpse of the barely perceptible change in his appearance.

He knows the creaky boards in the floor, where to place his feet to move soundlessly; he knows, without having to look, the location of the hole caused by damp, over which a board has been nailed for safety. Jérôme walks over to the window, opens it and inhales the scents of the night and the mustiness of the animals. A cool breeze caresses the bare skin of his legs, his arms, his neck. He runs his palms over his scrawny thighs, feels each tiny hair bend, slips his hand under his vest and runs his fingertips over his smooth belly, the depression in the ribcage near the solar plexus. Having shaken off sleep, the dreams now float above him, somewhere between the ceiling and the crown of his head. Jérôme rediscovers the familiar strangeness of his waking body. The open window casts out a rectangle of shadows onto the wall, whose flower-patterned paper is tattered

217

and peeling. Crane-flies flutter in and wheel above the beds, around the room, brushing Jérôme's cheek and his eyelashes.

He walks to the door. His eyes fall on Pierre. The little boy is awake and the two stare at each other for a moment without blinking. The child's eyes are puffy with sleep. A feather is stuck to his cheek with a thread of spittle. Jérôme reaches out, lays a hand on the boy's damp forehead and the fine hair plastered to his temples in kiss-curls. A smell reaches him of night sweats and the filthy eiderdown, the breath heavy with the night and the bowl of milk the boys drink before they go to bed. He remembers the depression of the fontanelle beneath his fingers, takes the feather from the boy's cheek, then runs a hand down his back to feel the damp sheet and the mattress cover.

Every day, pairs of sheets laundered by Julie-Marie or Gabrielle are hung out on the washing line behind the farm. In summer, when they play out in the meadows, they suck the tiny florets of clover, carefully plucking them from the capitulum. Jérôme will hold a buttercup beneath the chins of Pierre and Thomas. The reflection colours their smooth pale skin, letting him know that they are not going to stop wetting the bed any time soon. His elder sister will have to carry on washing their sheets and hanging them out beneath his bedroom window, and he will still be able to watch her, bare-shouldered and in a loose blouse in the hazy morning light, adjusting the clothes pegs on the nylon washing line. He pulls off the sheet and takes off Pierre's pyjama trousers – heavy and drowsy, the boy allows himself to be manoeuvred before instantly drifting back to sleep – then covers him with the eiderdown, turns and leaves the room.

218

He walks along the corridor and stops in front of Julie-Marie's bedroom. He brings his face close and smells the wood of the doorframe. He presses his cheek to the door, straining to catch a breath, a rustle, the cloying smell of the unmade bed, but everything is silent. Jérôme could go in, as the twins sometimes do in the early morning; as he used to do once, before the grandfather forbade him, slide in next to Julie-Marie's warm body so she would wrap her pale, heavy arm around his shoulders and kiss the back of his neck. He would feel the firm curve of her breasts and her belly against his shoulder blades, against the small of his back.

The kitchen is a huge space off the living room, furnished with a gas cooker, a solid wood table and a formica dresser. A layer of cooking grease, ash and dust covers the extractor hood and the walls of indeterminate colour. The room smells of cooking, small livestock and wet dog hair. The nights are still cold and the farmhouse poorly insulated; a fire glows in the stove set into the old fireplace.

If, every evening when they get back from the pig shed, the father and the uncle undress in the bathroom with its clawfoot bathtub and its cracked porcelain washbasin; if they exposed their nakedness to their indifferent phlegmatic gazes, revealing the startling contrast between their bodies – the one colossal and broken, the other broad and heavyset – then take turns soaping and shampooing themselves behind the white plastic curtain as they did as children, when their father told them to, taking on the role of their dead mother; if they splash their necks from the same bottle of aftershave, it is no longer in an attempt to mask the smell of mildewed cereal and skatole, but as though they are performing and perpetuating a ritual whose meaning has long since been forgotten. From the twins to their grandmother, they all carry on them, in them, this stench that smells like vomit, that they no longer smell since it is theirs, embedded in their clothes, their sinuses, their hair, impregnating their skin and their sour flesh. Over the generations, they have acquired this ability to produce and exude the smell of pigs, to naturally smell of pig.

Jérôme scoops up a ladle of cold stock and greasy clots from the surface of a large stewpot on the gas stove, brings it to his lips and slurps. He stuffs crusts of stale bread into his pockets. He slips his bare feet into rubber boots, then carefully depresses the handle of the back door. Jérôme crosses the yard and goes into the kennel next to the barn. The dogs are sleeping, curled into balls. Some open their eyes as the boy approaches. He offers each a piece of bread, which the pointers grip with their teeth and chew.

All along the dirt road rutted with two-wheel tracks, thickets of brambles and rushes create shadowy masses and lines. Jérôme breathes in the scent of grasses bowed by the dew, of the ditches in which the croaking of copulating frogs suddenly stops as he approaches, such that it seems as though he is accompanied by a block of silence or by an aura that reduces the vibrations of vocal sacs and the quivering of wing casings to silence, moving with him and around him in the dense, deep space, preceded by an explosive concert of nocturnal animals. Jérôme has no fear of the dark, of the creatures and the mysteries it hides. On the contrary, he feels assured, concealed from the eyes of his own kind, aware of the tension of every muscle as he walks, of the movement of his body as it is propelled through the deafening landscape.

A whiff of slurry carried on the breeze reaches him. The distant purring of an engine reminds him of nights spent spreading manure, sitting next to the uncle, the father or the grandfather, on the back of machines whose mechanical bellies he can feel growling, proud to be among the men, permitted to stay up with them in the cramped cab pervaded by the smell of diesel, and of the fertilizer being spread on the tilled fields. The windows are misted by their sweat, their breath, the smoke from their cigarettes.

The path dips and runs along the fields of soft wheat. Field mice scamper as he walks, while the dew pearls on the stalks of the plants, on the silvered fur of rodents and on Jérôme's skin. The silent forms of bats flit to and fro before his face. In a few months, glow-worms will glisten in the hedgerows, lighting up small patches of darkness, and Jérôme thinks about his sister, about her pale, immaculate skin, on which he would like to place these glorious glimmers, and the fleshy curve of her belly, beneath which there is now a dark, bushy growth that Julie-Marie hides from him.

He senses, knows without being able to name it, that she is inexorably evolving into another state, leaving the world of childhood; this world into which they threw themselves, reigning over the farm, over nature and the animals. He walks instinctively. The black, dilated pupils devour the irises of his eyes, giving his face the wild air of an animal in heat. He cuts through a fallow field, up a hillside towards a copse of aspens and black elders.

Here, created by his comings and goings, a path, almost a tunnel, runs through the thick, impenetrable

221

brambles besieging the trees, forming a rampart, an almost impenetrable wall, behind which, held up by the creeping ivy and boxwood, are the ruins of an ancient chapel which even the oldest of the locals have long since forgotten. For obscure reasons of inheritance, or divisions in the land registry, the fallow land Jérôme crosses no longer belongs to anyone, and children of his own age have long since stopped following him on his peregrinations, weary of his silence, of the games he plays that they do not understand, of his stench, like an invisible finger pressing on their windpipe, of his habit of ferreting around under every little stone, every piece of corrugated iron, every mossy, rotting tree trunk in search of animals that they find disgusting, and which the Idiot – sometimes, they mockingly call him the Happy Fool – immediately shoves into one of his jam-jars.

Jérôme stops for a moment to catch his breath. Stretched out before him, the landscape seems unreal, a succession of small valleys and dark hollows, frozen, pale and indistinct in the moonlight, from which rises a scent of crops that have gorged on water and manure, the musty tang of dungheaps behind farms. The child stands, motionless, a young lord, panting for breath, inhaling the scents of his lands, then disappears into the undergrowth.

—

At dawn one April morning, it is a rolling verdant valley through which a departmental motorway snakes like a slow worm through moss. Day is only just breaking, radiating a mauve spring sky speckled with sparse clouds. In the distance, the smoke from a late fire rises

222

vertically from a rooftop, and thin wisps of fog still linger here and there in the branches of the trees.

Henri wakes to the mansard ceiling of the room. His eyes follow the line of the joists, the ridge of the pig shed is visible through the mullioned window. He watches a couple of rooks who have perched there, their raucous croaking deepening the baleful feeling he had on waking.

For several weeks, the fever has not abated. At first fluctuating and bearable, it now burns day and night. His dreams no longer have any form, but are simply a tangle of hallucinatory visions, a scansion of enigmatic words, places and faces. His T-shirt and his pyjama trousers are drenched with the night sweats that leave him parched.

He runs a hand over the cold, damp mattress, then shivers. He gropes on the bedside table for the boxes of ibuprofen, aspirin and paracetamol he alternately takes to ease the crippling headaches. The back of his hand knocks against the framed black-and-white photograph, from which Élise, the dead wife, stares out at him, as though haloed by the yellowing paper.

Sitting on a bench beneath the velvet-leaved walnut tree that grew not far from here, she is wearing a dress blackened by the years. The tree casts shadows on her bare arms. Serge, their eldest son, runs past, a grey blur behind her. Élise's hands – Henri remembers her close-cropped fingernails – are resting on her swollen pregnant belly. He believes he remembers a moment of tranquillity in midsummer, even the weight of the camera in his hands, the pressure of the leather strap against his neck, his clammy skin.

It is the last image of her that he possesses, and one of the only ones he took with the Artoflex he had just bought, suddenly eager to create and record a family history. Through the viewfinder, things seemed more beautiful – the kitchen, with light bathing the sink against which she was leaning, the mane of her flaming hair in the blazing sun. The light and shadows seemed more real, life seemed innocuous. He remembers her amused indulgence, her embarrassment faced with this device intended to immortalize her through a face, a body, an expression. The following autumn, when Élise died giving birth to Joël, their second son, Henri set aside the camera, and the thought that all that would remain of her were a handful of 6x6 snapshots seemed unbearable, just as the urgency he had earlier felt to leave some trace of the past, of them living that past, suddenly seemed pathetic. He destroyed the camera, closed the lens cap, pulled the last roll of film out into the light, thereby destroying the last shots of Élise, of whom there remain only a few photographic negatives buried in mouldering boxes consigned to oblivion, and the enlarged print in the little frame that Henri picks up this morning and brings to his face.

He has no photographs of his two sons. Their shared family history is no more than a series of fleeting instants left to their fragile, uncertain memories. Of his own father, Henri has not a single image. Only Éléonore still preserves one of the retouched portraits in a trunk, in which he is captured in three-quarter profile so that his ruined face melts into the shadows. Henri runs a finger over Élise's face. In fact, the eyes staring out at him seem troubled by a disquiet he does not recognize, of which he has no memory, and the figure of Serge, in short trousers, has imperceptibly reached the edge of the

224

frame, trailing a shadow that stretches out to touch his mother's cheek. Henri is sixty years old, Élise will forever be twenty-eight; can he say that he still knows her, can he say that he ever knew her? He lives with a memory that is scarcely even that now, yet it haunts him, as might the memory of another man. He turns the frame and lays it on the bedside table.

He sits on the edge of the bed, presses two fingers to his carotid artery and assesses the beating of his heart. He massages a painless swollen gland that has appeared beneath his chin overnight, checks the size of those that run from groin to mid-thigh. He breathes slowly to dispel the panic gripping him. The wardrobe mirror returns the reflection of his hulking, half-naked body. He sees the salt-and-pepper beard that covers his cheeks, his arms, still brawny, though the triceps are slack, his legs, now hairless, the potbelly that rests on his legs. There are scratch marks on his legs, his buttocks, his forearms. Hands resting on the mattress, head bowed, back arched, Henri is attentive to the cawing of the rook, the creaking of the roof beams, and the silence of his long solitude.

He gets up, glances into the children's room, the door left open so that the twins can fall asleep to the glow from the lights in the hall. They are sleeping soundly, tangled in their blankets.

Jérôme's bed is empty, the sheet twisted. God alone knows where the boy can have gone prowling. Perhaps he should consider double-locking the doors. The boy is not disobedient, but simply indifferent to authority. He shuns the presence of adults, though he does not seem to prefer the company of other children. Henri has never felt any affection for his grandson, only mistrust and antipathy. He thinks the boy is malicious, sly, calculating, as children are wont to be. He feels that his mutism marks them out, accuses them. Jérôme can barely tolerate his cousins, the twins, and he can be seen trailing behind his sister like a shadow or a barely tamed animal, the only person whose contact and affection he constantly seeks out. Henri closes the door and walks away without a sound.

When he steps into the kitchen, Serge is already up and about. Henri sees him finish filling a metal hip-flask with whisky and slipping it into the pocket before quickly putting the bottle back into a cupboard. Father and son do not acknowledge each other. Serge already has a stovetop coffee pot standing on the gas cooker. He strikes a match and lights the burner before sitting at the kitchen table.

Soon, Joël appears. He takes a cup from the draining rack, cuts a slice of bread from the loaf sitting on the countertop and sits down. The men wait in silence while a wisp of steam rises from the coffee maker. Outside, a cock crows. Joël stares at the oilcloth, collecting crumbs of bread on his fingertip. When the cafetière begins to whistle, Henri turns off the gas, fills his cup, sits at one end of the table and sets the coffee maker down in front of him. He feels exhausted, wiped out by the night, electrified by his fever, but is determined to let nothing show, and if the two brothers notice his pallor, his eyes ringed with dark circles, the slight trembling of his hands, they do not dare say anything.

When Henri wipes his mouth on his sleeve and puts his bowl in the sink, the sons, as one man, immediately get to their feet.

In the hall, they pull on their parkas, put on their shoes. Their bodies stir, close and indifferent. Henri opens the door and steps out onto the porch, followed by his sons. The pack of dogs, a dozen Gascony Braque pointers, bark and jump up at the mesh fence of their kennel.

Joël is holding a pail filled with scraps and dry dog food. He crosses the yard, opens the gate to the kennel. Accustomed to parrying shouts and blows, the pointers usually keep their distance from Henri and Serge. They dart around nervously, heads bowed, yapping and slavering excitedly on Joël's shoes as he pats their heads, scratches their necks and their thin flanks. Outside hunting season, the dogs languish on the concrete kennel floor filthy with their excreta, or wander around the farmyard.

Joël steps into the kennels and pours the contents of the bucket into the old stone troughs once used to feed pigs. The pointers greedily pounce on the food. Joël takes a crumpled cigarette from his pocket and smokes, watching as Henri and Serge walk side by side across the yard to the pig shed, their shoulders hunched, their hands buried in their pockets. Their manner is so similar that, sometimes, and increasingly convincingly, Joël sees the figure of his father in his brother, in a gesture, a facial expression, the inflection of his voice. Both men have a forbidding, muscular physique, born of labouring on the farm.

Joël can just make out the figure of Gaby behind the lighted kitchen window. For an instant their eyes meet, then he looks up towards Catherine's bedroom. The shutters are still closed today. Gabrielle turns away.

Those who have eaten their fill slip between Joël's legs and out of the kennels, lap water from a basin left under a drainpipe, piss against the derelict cars and the tyres of

227

the tractor parked in the hangar.

Joël notices that one of the bitches has dragged a blanket into the shadow of the tractor, and is suckling a litter of newborn pups. He goes over and kneels down. He looks at the bitch, her coat sticky with sump oil, and the dog stares back at him, her head lowered. The animal wags her bony, balding tail, beating the dirt floor. Joël leans against the tractor wheel and, grimacing, stretches out his hand. He feels the still-viscid mass of pups, counting them with his fingertips. The bitch licks feverishly at his hand. The man remains hunkered next to her, arms folded over his knees, and finishes his cigarette as he watches the animal lick her pups clean.

'You'd do well to be discreet,' he says.

He spits on the ground, stubs the cigarette butt out in the spittle, gets up, and herds the dogs back into the kennel, closing the gate on them. Far ahead, downhill from the farm, his brother and his father are walking along the path deeply rutted by farm machinery.

—

Joël catches up with Henri and Serge. As every morning, they pause for a time beneath the overhang of the corrugated-iron roof of one of the rectangular buildings below the pig shed, fish packs of cigarettes from their pockets and smoke without looking at each other, watching night fade over the fields and the dense crops.

There is nothing to suggest the presence of the pigs, nor the tumult to come. Each of them stares at a fixed point on the ground, or into the indiscernible distance, but always in different directions. They might seem engrossed in some profound reflection were their eyes not fixed, empty of all thought, all volition. Then Henri

228

says, 'Come on,' and the sons instantly toss their cigarette butts and crush them under the soles of their boots.

In the changing-room next to the building, under the
fluorescent lights, they take off their boots and undress.
They put on blue coveralls, pulling the zips up to their
chins with no other sound than the rustle of fabric, the
clearing of throats, the hiss of breath and the squeak
of rubber boots on the cement floor. The father walks
ahead of his sons, unbolting the door that leads into the
pig shed. Joël and Serge drag metal trolleys under the
feed hoppers. The grain rumbles down the pipes and
pours out, instantly triggering a chorus of squeals, the
shrill, discordant grunt of a single voice, that of the
mythological beast the rumbling silos have woken from
centuries of sleep.

Henri pushes open the sliding doors in a gust of acid,
steamy condensation. Pale light spills from the sputter-
ing ceiling lights onto the pigs as they press against the
bars of their stalls, clamber onto the feed troughs, climb
over each other, scratching their backs and their flanks,
using their heads as battering rams, hunger foaming
on their snouts. Pushing the feed trolleys filled with
grain in front of them, the brothers set off down the two
aisles of the pig shed, plunging into the stench, breathing through their mouths, shallow gulps of ammoniacal
emanations; a smell of urine and faecal matter, animal
sweat, grain liquefied by salivary juices, bitter as the bile
spewed by the pig shed into the pale dawn.

They move along the aisles, through the liquid manure leaking from the stalls, from which they must
extricate their boots at every step. Then, in a series of
mechanical gestures, they dip pails into the trolley and
throw the feed over the stall barriers into the troughs
to the ravening pigs. Before long, the air in the pig shed

is thick with a cloud of grain dust, which settles on the sweaty faces of the men, the hairs on their forearms, enters their sinuses, their throats, their bronchial tubes, and powders the bodies of the animals.

As they move down the aisles, squeals give way to grunts of satisfaction and mastication, but still the noise is deafening. The men fall silent, since they cannot hear their own voices above the guttural growl that bores into their eardrums, whose phantom echo sometimes wakes them in the middle of the night.

Only the voice of Henri, standing in the doorway of the building, manages to carry above the squeals of the pigs. His watches his sons as they work, fumbles nervously in his pockets for his pack of cigarettes, then, feeling suddenly dizzy, leans against the wall of the barn, out of sight. The fever makes his eyeballs throb. He presses his damp hands to his eyelids. The shriek of the pigs is becoming increasingly unbearable to him. He feels an itch again, in his thighs this time, and frantically tries to scratch himself through the thick coveralls.

He decides not to smoke, and steps into the pig shed.

'Straw down, now,' he shouts to one or other of the brothers.

As one, Serge and Joël push open the two doors at the end of the aisles, at the far end of the building, stoop so they can pass through, and emerge into a concrete yard behind the pig shed.

They stand motionless some ten metres apart, their silhouettes framed against the light. They press their fingers to each of their nostrils in turn and expel jets of grey snot, then take deep lungfuls of air. Serge takes out his hipflask and drinks. In front of them steam rises from the slurry pit, static, toxic, black, its surface floating with clots of excrement. Oblivious to each other, Serge and Joël walk along the building to the next hangar in which the bales of straw are stored. They load barrows, then plunge back into the pig shed, which is stifling from the heat of the pigs. Into each stall they toss armfuls of straw, which the animals immediately trample and rootle. Henri heads down one of the aisles, checking each of the stalls. Joël sees him stop in front of one, climb over the barrier, bend over a group of sows, then stand up and furiously beckon him over.

When the son draws near, separated only by the gate of the stall, already resigned and servile, head bowed, hands balled into fists at his thighs, Henri says:

'Would you like to explain to me what this boar is doing here with the gilts?'

Joël glances at the pig, standing as far from the men as the space within the stall allows, amid a group of young females, moving with them as they hurl themselves against the planks of the pen in a desperate attempt at escape. He does not know how the young boar, which should be in one of the pens in the boar enclosure, has managed to end up here, in the feedlot, but it would be futile to try to apologize and any attempt at justification will simply stoke the father's anger, so he remains silent.

'How can you be so bloody careless...? It's like you don't give a tinker's curse about anything, or maybe you're just incompetent... It's not exactly brain surgery, what I'm asking, is it? Is it...? A little care and attention, that's all... Fuck sake, even your brother can manage it... That's what it means to do a good job, do you understand? No, of course you don't fucking understand... I'm the idiot here! I've told you time and again. But no, you're happy being mediocre, even though you know there's no place for that on my farm. Not here, Joël, you know that... Go on, shift your arse, get that fucking animal out of here...'

Henri's face turns purple. He looks as though he is trying to dislodge something stuck in his throat, and his lips twist into a rictus. A sinuous vein pulses in his temple and his neck.

You stick the knife in here, cut cleanly, keeping your knee on the pig's shoulder.

As Henri clambers back over the barrier, projecting his thickset frame, Joël takes a step back and waits until the father has left the barn before going back to work. His heart is hammering against his ribs, just as it is in the gilts and the young boar.

—

From the kitchen, Gabrielle sees Joël feeding the dogs in the kennel and, as always when her eyes linger on him, he seems taller, thinner, swimming in his baggy trousers. She imagines the gangling, quiet teenager he probably was, reduced to silence by the coalition between father and elder brother, always trailing in their shadow, trapped in this body that is strangely youthful yet already ravaged, which he drags through the muddy farm with his long, loping strides. Joël lifts his bony, freckled face towards Catherine's bedroom. His forehead is marked by two deep furrows near the scar that extends from his right temple to his eyebrow, and his pale, grave eyes are sunken by dark purple circles. Then Gaby leaves the kitchen.

Upstairs, she goes into the children's room, runs a hand over the tousled heads peeking from beneath the blankets. Thomas wakes and looks at his mother with sleepy eyes.

232

'Do you know where Jérôme's gone?' she asks, touching the boy's cold mattress.

The twins shake their heads. A few of the grandmother's cats have curled up at the boys' feet, or between their legs, purring in their sleep.

Gabrielle leaves the room, heads down the corridor and knocks on the door of Julie-Marie's bedroom. She waits for a moment, knocks again, then walks away as she hears the teenager stirring. She lays a hand on the handle of Catherine's door, takes a breath before stepping inside, walks over to the window and opens it, pushing the shutters, which thud against the outside wall, allowing a gust of salutary air into the room.

In the bed behind her, her elder sister moans and buries herself beneath the sheet and the blankets. Gabrielle looks around the room. The floor is strewn with clothes, dirty sheets and dust. The bar of the electric heater at the foot of the bed glows red, making a regular clicking sound.

'It's like a furnace in here,' she says, turning off the convection heater.

In the bathroom next door, she flushes the toilet filled with stagnant urine, turns on the light and turns on the hot water tap for the bath. She rubs the back of her neck, then goes back into the bedroom and sets about clearing the floor of the dirty clothes that Catherine sheds like old skin, often unable to bear the touch of them, and which she pushes under the bed.

Gaby sits on the edge of the mattress and pulls back the sheet to reveal the emaciated face of her sister, who tries to bury it in the bolster. She gets to her feet, folds the sheet and the blankets at the end of the bed, leaving Catherine naked, curled up on the mattress, her face covered by her hands, then she grabs her sister's legs, drags her to the edge of the bed, sits down beside her, slips an arm around her shoulder and sits her up next to her.

They are now sitting pressed against each other, Catherine shivering in her arms as her sister strokes her back, her left arm, but each stroke of her palm is painful and the face pressed into the sororal neck is twisted into a rictus of terrible weariness, the lips curled back over pale gums.

'Calm down,' Gabrielle says. 'Take it easy, everything's going to be fine...'

She slips an arm beneath the damp, hairy fold of her sister's armpit, presses one hand against her side, presses the other against the mattress for support and stands up, heaving Catherine to her feet as she whimpers and almost collapses. Together they take small steps across the room to the bathroom, where Gabrielle sits her on the edge of the tub, then dips a hand into the water to check the temperature before turning off the taps.

'I'm going to need you to help me a bit.'

Cathy shivers and shakes her head, utterly drained.

'I can't,' she says. 'I just want to be left alone.'

Her speech is slow and difficult. She opens her mouth, stretching her numbed jaw.

'Do you know what day it is?' Gabrielle asks, and, getting no response, says, 'It's Monday. It's a beautiful day.'

She lifts Catherine's legs, pivots and holds her as she sinks into the warm water, her eyes closed. Gaby gets to her feet, rubs her aching back and looks at her sister, her pale, limp body against the enamel of the hip-bath, her small breasts with their purple areolae, her long mane of brown hair streaked here and there with white. She

234

sits on the edge of the tub, soaks a washcloth and press-es it against Catherine's collarbones, her shoulders, her neck.

'Jérôme did a disappearing act again last night.'

Cathy does not respond; she allows herself to be man-handled, staring at the limescale-encrusted tap dripping at her feet.

'I worry about him, he's left to his own devices. He won't listen to me, he spends all his time off somewhere. I just can't cope, what with the twins, and the work... It's a lot for me to handle by myself, you understand?'

She wets her sister's hair as Catherine looks up at her, her eyes misty.

'What do you expect me to do about it?' Catherine says.

Gabrielle sets down the washcloth and nods.

'Nothing. Don't worry. You need to get some rest, that's all.'

She gently soaps her sister's arms, her armpits, her chest, shampoos her hair, massages her scalp. She reach-es for the shower head, flicks the diverter and rinses Catherine off, then she sits down on the floor and leans back against the tub. The two women are motionless and silent, the only sound the regular drip of the tap.

'I'll go fetch a towel,' Gabrielle says.

In the bedroom, she takes boxes of pills from the chest of drawers and sets them on the dressing table. She opens them, inspects the blister packs of Tercian, Teralithe 400 and Anafranil, and pushes the capsules, which burst through the protective aluminium film and drop into her hand. From another drawer she takes a clean bath towel, then she goes to the window and closes it.

She presses her forehead against the cool glass and

closes her eyes for a moment, until the dogs are quiet, then she goes back to the bathroom. Cathy is dozing in the steaming water, the back of her head resting against the tiled wall. Gaby plunges her hand into the water and jerks the chain attached to the rubber plug. She helps her sister out of the tub, supports her as they walk back into the bedroom and sits her on a chair while she changes the sheets.

No sooner has the bed been made than she hears Julie-Marie's door open and she leaves Catherine's room. In the corridor, Gabrielle runs a hand over her face, her forehead, her eyes.

'Could you take over? Help her get dressed and put her back to bed? I need to get the kids ready for school.'

The teenager nods, goes into her mother's bedroom and closes the door behind her.

—

Julie-Marie looks at Catherine, sitting askew on the chair next to the bed, shivering, the towel draped over her shoulders. A first ray of light bursts over the roof of the hangar, bathing the yard and the southern aspect of the farm, painting a patch of daylight, a luminous enclave on the bedroom floor, where motes of dust stirred up by Gabrielle's agitation still whirl and fall, tracing a line along Catherine's knee, above her pale, motionless leg. Julie-Marie steps forward, runs a hand over her mother's head, untangling the knots in her damp hair, then lays the hollow of her palm against the twisted, warm, clammy neck.

Every day, before she leaves the house to catch the bus that takes her to school, before she passes the gates and leaves behind the closed world of the farm for the hostile world beyond – this is what they all call it, marking it out as a dangerous, inhospitable terrain whose borders, like those of the farm, may be uncertain, but nonetheless exist and are vital, since they offer protection from the world beyond, from the people outside, from *them*, from *the others* – Julie-Marie comes into this bedroom to witness the benefits or the ravages night has wrought on her mother's body.

Daybreak sweeps through the room, storming the bed, the wall and Catherine's face. Her eyes are closed, her brow furrowed; her daughter cannot tell whether she is enjoying the light and the quiet of the room, or whether they are simply one more trial in her long ordeal.

'We need to get you dressed,' she says.

Catherine opens her eyes again, turns and looks up at her daughter. Her gaze expresses nothing, reveals nothing; she looks at her as at a perfect stranger.

'A nightdress,' Cathy says in a slurred voice fettered by medications, with a barely perceptible gesture towards the chest of drawers.

Julie-Marie looks at this face, which is no more than a pale imitation of what once was her mother's face, just as in her childhood dreams she would sometimes see pale imitations of people she loved, whose unsettling strangeness revealed slyness, deception, menace.

She walks over to the chest of drawers, grabs a threadbare cotton nightdress printed with a faded pattern, rolls it up and slips the collar around her mother's neck, guides the blind hands searching for the armholes, pulls the dress down over breasts that are still firm. And Julie-Marie wonders whether this is what her own smaller, paler breasts will one day look like, and what their mother infected them with when she and Jérôme suckled on unwholesome milk.

She recognizes her own features in Catherine's; she can see their obvious resemblance and, beyond that, the treacherous possibilities, the genealogical ramifications, the role of chance and fate or logic that has led mother and daughter to this point, the daughter caring for her mother, dressing her, combing her hair, tolerating the sight of the hairy vulva from which she emerged fourteen years earlier and which now sits on the rush seat of the chair, pressed against it, moulded to it, so that the labia, like the thighs and buttocks, will bear a purplish imprint of the woven rushes when she gets up to lay her miserable body on the bedsheet.

The mother has no modesty in front of the daughter: she does not attempt to pull down her nightdress if it rucks over the belly banded with stretch marks like mineral strata, the sediment of pregnancies that have strikingly altered the radiant body Julie-Marie still distantly remembers. It sometimes seems as though she revels in these lewd poses born of her illness, in displaying the depredations to which time, gravity and manic depression inexorably lead, the beginning and the ending that is the sex; the imprint of their passing on this body which already seems old, as though it is a warning, a threat levelled at the appalling youth of the daughter.

Julie-Marie helps her sit on the edge of the bed, to pull on a pair of pants. From the bathroom, she fetches a pair of stainless-steel scissors with short, curved blades, crouches down and sets about meticulously cutting her toenails, collecting the disgusting translucent slivers clipped from the mother's body in the hollow of her hand. When the tide ebbs, when exhaustion recedes, the mother recovers her charm, one that is commonplace and subdued – despite herself, she is still the same countrywoman, with her brusque gestures, her narrow ambitions, her plainness – yet marked by a natural gentleness that catches the eye because it suggests both fragility and rebelliousness. It is this palpable fault line, these relentless forces at work in some dark corner of her soul – telluric, sovereign, magnetic – that flicker on the surface, unnamed, and that once upon a time attracted the attention of local men, their looks, their lust, their dubious remarks, even if she were simply walking past the café terrace on the village square, holding her daughter's hand; their lechery whispered in chauvinist asides.

Sometimes, Julie-Marie has memories of the mother, radiant, in the years before the birth of Jérôme, shapes that dissolve as soon as she tries to trace their contours, fleeting, perhaps false impressions (was she not already prey to terrible bouts of sadness that heralded the breakdowns that would come later?), and so they are not hours of innocence, nor even of equanimity – it was surely written from the start that they would be denied such things – but the remaining hours of enchantment with the world. In these memories she cannot tell what is the echo, in those first years of life, of Catherine's happiness, or of her own by contamination.

Julie-Marie contemplates the shards of nail parings in her hand and they suddenly seem extremely precious, poignant in their banality, then, a moment later, repellent for what they actually are: the funereal debris of a body that bows, capitulates in the face of illness, allows itself to be swept away by the wave and is swallowed, slowly and inexorably, into those depths their voices can no longer reach. How long has it been now? Julie-Marie drops the nail parings onto the bedside table. A few cling to her palm. She flicks them off with her index finger, then makes a little pile on the pink marble slab ringed with cherrywood, a small, solemn, silent ossuary for some passing insect that will take the nail from the big toe back to its nest to cut its teeth. Julie-Marie supports her mother's head as she lays her on the bed, drapes a sheet over her and tucks her in. A cloud has appeared and the bright patch scudded across the courtyard, through the bedroom, sought refuge in the angle of the wall, in the ceiling, and faded into the damp plaster.

Catherine dozes off with Julie-Marie sitting next to her on the edge of the mattress, her elbows on her knees, her hands clasped, her face turned towards the window. Eyes fixed on the grey of the sky, she is not fourteen years of age, she is the age of children exiled from childhood, banished even before they were born; an age with no age and no history.

—

The village first announces itself at a curve in the valley as the ancient walls appear, ringed with plum trees, from which, in June, impatient children pick green fruits with pale, bitter stones that they bite into and spit out with a grimace.

Next comes the soaring steeple, its shadow at this hour extending only as far as the foot of the church steps. Finally, the village square is revealed, planted with grass and chestnut trees whose bare branches thrust towards the sky beautiful, deep mahogany buds, glossy and sticky with sap, fed by the flesh of Jacques Beyries, Albert Brisard, Armand Cazaux, Claude Fourcade, Georges Frejefond, Maurice Grandjean, Jocelyn Lagarde, Paul Lasserre, Jean-Philippe Montegut,

240

Roland Pellefigue, Jonathan Pujol, Patrice Roujas and Raymond Taupiac, who died for their country during the first and second wars, and whose bodies lie, shoulder to shoulder, in their disintegrating uniforms beneath the war memorial, a grey stone stela surmounted by a white marble plaque.

A few steps from the soldiers, from their remains which have crawled here from the cemetery and are now pierced by the roots of the chestnut trees and crowned by molehills, the old men of the village sit on a bench of weathered stone. Chins leaning on canes, or berets pulled down over their foreheads, they spend all day keeping an eye on the comings and goings in the square and the working order of the world. When Jérôme passes, the old men say: 'well, well', 'there he goes', 'where's he off to now', 'poor lad', 'not right in the head', 'you said it', or they say nothing at all but simply watch him pass without troubling to offer a greeting that, in any case, Jérôme would not return any more than he seems to notice their comments.

He takes the path past the old village washhouse, between the half-timbered houses, under whose roof tiles flocks of swallows will soon be nesting. Jérôme grips the wrought-iron handrail and carefully descends the steep, slippery steps used by hundreds of the village dead, passing the archway of the old fortifications of Puy-Larroque castle, towards the path below.

He is thinking about the body of little Émilie Seilhan that lies in the mud at the bottom of the huge washhouse trough, wearing a dress now green from the algae that, for decades, have embroidered the seams and hemmed her lashes and her hair with blue-green fringes. Her lips are mute, the pale eyes staring up at the surface have long since been blinded with watery lenses. Jérôme sees the washhouse trough into which fishermen have released some carp and tench to keep the water clean, even though the washhouse has been boarded over ever since the drowning, long ago, of little Émilie, who shoos algae from her bluish face with a languid gesture, or dreamily removes a crayfish from between her lips. Jérôme descends towards the view of the fields blazing in the spring morning, and walks on to the ivy-covered walls of the cemetery.

A simple chain and a broken padlock are all that secures the gate from which hangs a warped and mildewed twelve-page list of those interred here, and a statement from the mayor of Puy-Larroque inviting 'those family members with funeral concessions to clean and refurbish the graves such that they are not prejudicial to the safety of the cemetery, failing which the village council will be unable to reopen it'. But the 'family members' thus addressed are doubtless already buried, if not here in Puy-Larroque, then in some other country cemetery, in a crude, rough-and-ready coffin, since the names and the dates have long since worn away from these gravestones that are scarred with age and overgrown with moss, or have collapsed under their own weight and are being swallowed by the earth as the tombs beneath them cave in.

Jérôme removes the chain, and opens the gate whose hinges have been oiled by the municipal maintenance worker. He steps inside, closes the gate behind him, then surveys the cemetery bisected by a broad set of concrete steps. Beyond the wall, he sees hillocks of earth, hovering buzzards that, from time to time, let out a cry. He hears the distant barking of hunting dogs kept in the kennel of some farm and he savours the smell of the dew-damp fields the spring sun will quickly warm.

Ancient cypresses flank concrete slabs of steps cracked by landslips triggered by the restless village dead who can find no peace in the earth of Puy-Larroque and turn in their cramped coffins, plumb the darkness with empty sockets into which their eyes have shrivelled and fallen. The cypresses give off a dry smell of incense and turpentine. The ground is strewn with blue-grey cones that shatter underfoot or dry out on marble tombs sticky with resin.

Jérôme walks along the flight of steps, crouches down to examine the cracks in the concrete, made wider by the harsh frost. He slips his fingers into the sough slits, feels the cement dust, the grey earth and the flaking lichen in the crevices, beneath the watchful eye of unnailed Christs, held in place by a single, inverted hand on the cross, or fallen between two graves among the faded remnants of funeral wreaths and cypress cones. Wall lizards with banded flanks that have been lounging in the sun scuttle away and disappear beneath the tomb-stones. Many of them have only regenerated tails, the result of former captures they escaped only by virtue of their autotomy; but today, Jérôme ignores them, and when his fingertips brushes against a clutch of eggs in a damp hollow in the peat, he lifts up the shard of con-crete and rolls one of the chalky oblong eggs between his fingers, holds it between thumb and forefinger and lifts it towards the sun, closes his left eye and squints as he studies the veiny matrix, then puts it back and replaces the protective fragment of concrete.

Jérôme gets up and walks slowly around the cemetery walls. He lifts up discarded tiles, shards of terracotta pots. He rummages in the rubbish tip in the southern corner of the cemetery among the flowers, some rotting, others of faded plastic, with black stalks, with spongy corollas that give off an acid perfume.

Clouds of drosophilae rise up, forficulae and scolopendrae scuttle through brown liquid that oozes from the withered funeral wreaths, the overturned pots of brown peat, and eventually Jérôme looks away. He walks between the tombstones beneath which some of his kin lie among the dead: the first of the fathers, the woman whose framed photograph he has seen on Henri's nightstand, who smiles and waves to him when, in the grandfather's absence, he creeps into the lonely room, sits on the edge of the conjugal bed and gazes at her. None of the men ever speak of her. She watches the world of the living through the small screen of the frame, thrilled when Jérôme sets her down, turning the frame so that the sunlight streaming through the window can once more warm her face.

And yet he knows the name Élise because he has read it, carved and gilded on the marble (1924–1952), next to the name the grandfather (1921–) has had engraved on the family vault destined to receive those among them whom the undertakers will lay out and lower into the belly of Puy-Larroque.

When the rain comes down in torrents, overflowing the drainpipes, the streams and the gutters in the village, spilling down the steep slippery steps beneath the archway of the old castle and the levelled concrete slabs of the cemetery steps, the water seeps into the rich earth between the planks of the coffins and the dead shiver. Their bones clatter, they cloak themselves in strips of silk lining ripped out with their toothless jaws, press their blanched faces into the padded coffin lids then give up, allowing themselves to sink like stones.

Turned towards the cemetery gate, a cast-iron Virgin bows her face eaten by rust as though by smallpox and spreads her hands to welcome the deceased villagers to their final resting place.

We have been what you are and you will one day be what we are.

The rubiginous folds of her robe smell of small change. By the plinth of the statue, from among the thistles that have grown up through the cracks, Jérôme picks up the shed skin of a snake that has been softened by the dew. He delicately removes from it fragments of leaves, thorny twigs and quartz gravel, then uncoils it between his fingers and lays it on the coping stones surrounding the pock-marked Virgin at whose feet troops of ants march, busying themselves at clever tasks. He takes care not to tear the fragile, translucent sheath still marked by the imprint of scales, then he stands up and studies it.

The skin is that of a grass snake almost two metres long. He has placed a stone at the head and one at the tail and measured, placing the toe of one shoe against the heel of the other. Jérôme sits down on one of the steps. The sun on his face is pleasantly warm.

At this hour, the father and the uncle will have finished feeding the pigs. Jérôme likes going into the pig shed and walking past the stalls, looking at the animals and helping the men at their work. He holds a hand, palm open, towards their snouts and the pigs nuzzle it, sniffing his scent, sometimes licking his hand, then he runs his hand over their foreheads, their white bristles, their ciliated eyes. At this point they are silent and stand motionless as he strokes them. He brings strange tastes to them from the world outside: handfuls of fresh grass, acorns, chestnuts, an earthworm, a piece of carrion.

245

Sometimes, in spite of the fathers' warnings, he slips into the farrowing house. He walks soundlessly past the gestation crates where the sows lie on their flanks, confined by metal bars, suckling their litters. He takes some of the bodies of piglets unable to avoid being crushed by the painful convulsions of the sow in labour; those too weak to fight for a teat, those deformed and unlikely to survive that the fathers coldly pick up by their hind legs, raise above their heads and slam against the bars of the stall, or against the floor, leaving long bright red trails on the concrete floor, and slam again just to be sure, shattering their fragile skulls. Some of the piglets literally explode under the force of the blows. They then toss the swollen carcasses into buckets or into a barrow, where some spasm and eventually bleed to death while others, already dead, spill forth the tiny delicate ribbons of their entrails.

'There's always spoilage, it's like any form of production.'

When the fathers' backs are turned, Jérôme takes one or two little bodies from the barrow and slips them into his backpack or into the pockets of his trousers.

'This sow's producing too much spoilage, she's worthless, transfer her to the feedlot.'

Rather than incinerate them, Henri often feeds them to the dogs. He tosses the piglets into the air and they fall back to the sound of snapping jaws.

'It's good for their hunting instinct.'

Jérôme, for his part, takes them to the old chapel.

—

Serge leans the pitchfork against the wall, lights a cigarette and smokes, staring vacantly at the pigs he no

246

longer sees and who now make little noise besides the occasional satisfied grunt, the rustle of skin as they sprawl against each other in the cramped stalls and a few squeals of protest. He slips a hand into the pocket of his coveralls and strokes the metal hipflask.

For some years now, he can only bear to work in the pig shed when inebriated with alcohol; a mild intoxication but constant, necessary, a threshold he must maintain, and he can get to sleep only when half-drunk. The strip lights crackle, their glow dulled by the dusty webs of tegenaria spiders.

As silence returns to the building, the rats emerge from their shelters and scurry between the pigs, over the metal bars, along the beams until they come to the feed troughs where they pick off and nibble the pre-chewed remains of food.

Often, one of their number is lost, venturing too close to the men, who crush them underfoot, or hack them with the blade of a shovel, then grab them by the tail and toss them onto the manure heap; but, by sheer force of numbers, the rats reign in the hidden world of the pig shed that is revealed only when the doors of the barn are closed and the ciliated eye of the pigs is plunged into darkness. If from time to time the men kill one of them, it is only for the sake of form, perhaps out of instinct, since they have long since accepted their tacit defeat. The rats grow bolder, appearing from shadowy corners, taunting them by scurrying away under their very noses – their fur grey, their bellies white, their tails proud. The pig shed is no longer the territory of men, nor even of pigs: it is theirs. They rats have overcome their resistance, prevailed over their sovereignty.

Serge no longer sees the rats, any more than he sees the pigs. He turns away, leaves the shed, grabs one end of a coiled hose mounted on the wall, heaves it onto his shoulder and pulls it as far as the aisle where Joël, gripping a beater, is climbing into the stall enclosing the young boar. Serge lays the hose on the ground, grabs a restraint board and walks towards him.

'Wasn't fucking me that put him in there,' Joël says.

'Yeah, and I'm not the one you should be telling,' Serge replies, lifting the latch on the stall.

The pigs scatter, eyes wide, and huddle together in a corner. Joël hits them on the back to separate the boar from the sows, backs him against the railings and shoos him towards the stall gate. The young boar bounds towards the aisle, slamming into the board that Serge is holding, trying to butt it out of his way. Joël leaves the stall, closes it behind him, and, with shouts and lashings, the two brothers goad the animal to a stall where they can isolate it.

'I'll go take care of the farrowing house and the boar pens,' Serge says.

Left alone, Joël watches the breathless boar press against the metal bars, watching him with a feverish eye. He puts a hand through the bars, lays his palm against the boar's back and breathes with the animal until it is calm. Then he goes back to the far end of the aisle and grabs the Kärcher hose. The high-pressure jet gets rid of the excrement encrusted on the gratings, the concrete floors of the stalls and the aisles, the dropping in the corners, on the walls and on the bars.

The pigs piss and shit all day in stalls so cramped they can only just move, forcing them to relieve themselves, to wade through their excreta, to lie in it, wallow in it, until the urine that noisily splashes from the vulvas and the sheaths liquefies the clumps of turds, the droppings they expel, creating a mire in which they wade and instinctively dip their frantic, useless snouts. This slurry spills out, seeping through the smallest chinks, the narrowest cracks, trickles over the slightly sloping floor, pools into thick, black puddles in crevices and hollows.

The men are engaged in a constant battle with shit every day. At the beginning of every week, using pressure hoses, hard-bristle brushes and scrapers, they repel the faecal tide created by the pigs, soaking the concrete floor which swells, blisters and explodes under the pressure of the Kärcher, breaks off into small islands that hurtle downstream on the black torrent and disappear into the slurry pit outside. The liquid manure gradually eats away at the piggery buildings, and they would probably collapse if the men did not constantly plug the holes like an ancient ship that is taking in water through the hull and has to be bailed out by the crew.

To counter the shit, cement mixers churn and pour out cement into the *anus mundi* that is the pig shed, but it is a waste of time since, every night, the shed secretes what the men have managed to wash away by day, and by morning, the same pestilence awaits, the same unspeakable mire laps at their boots, spatters their bare hands and faces, spills into their dreams; a deluge of shit sweeping them away, drowning them, spurting from their stomachs, their arses, their cocks, spewing or oozing from every orifice, as though it has a life of its own whose only goal is to spread over them, beyond them, filling their nights with mudslides, waking them with a start, their hands clutching at the sheets, holding on lest they fall into a bottomless pit of slurry, their throats prickling with the familiar taste, their foreheads drenched with sweat and their ears ringing with the phantom squeal of pigs.

249

Henri's voice echoes in Joël's mind: *We manufacture meat here, not shit*, and he brushes, sweeps, scours, pushes the black tide into the drains, tips barrowloads of manure into the slurry pit, the never-sated belly of the pig shed that calmly waits for the next purge, while black continents, faecal nebulae, drift slowly over its fathomless surface. It is an ordinary day.

—

Henri steps into the cramped room next to the pig shed that serves as an office. Originally conceived as a junk room, it has no windows. A fluorescent light casts a bluish glow over the formica desk, the shelves filled with box files, their spines carefully marked, the livestock planner on the wall: the esoteric heart of the piggery. Henri closes the door, breathes in the familiar smell of stale cigarette ash, dust and grain. For a long time, he alone was allowed in here, forbidding his sons to set foot in the room. He opened the door to them only after Serge came of age, deciding that the time had come to induct him into the family business and the responsibilities of breeding.

'You do realize that what I'm doing for you, I wouldn't do for your brother, not anytime soon. That's proof of my trust. The trust I'm placing in you, you get me? Up to now, you've proved yourself worthy of that trust. I hope you won't disappoint me.'

As he pushes the initialled contract across the shellacked desk to Serge, and sits back in his chair, steepling his fingers in front of his face, he pretends not to notice his son's palpable unease, the curiously clumsy signature he scrawls at the bottom of the last page.

He believes that he brought up his sons in a manner

that is firm but fair, refusing to tolerate weakness or cow-ardice, two unforgivable defects in a man. He is secretly proud of having raised his two boys single-handed, even if Joël has never quite lived up to his expectations. After Élise's death, Éléonore supported him, but it was he and he alone who moulded his sons.

Henri steps around the desk, sits in the chair and lights a cigarette. And yet, can he truly count on their devo-tion, their loyalty, their ambition? Now that his sons are adults, can he congratulate himself on having succeeded in passing on to them more than just a farm: this con-viction, this faith in the land? He would like to believe in Serge, the more solid and dependable of the two. For a long time, the boy has followed in his footsteps, hung on his every word, looked at him with that mixture of admiration and respect, that desire to one day equal the imagined power and respectability of the father; then, as a teenager, he had treated him with a manly, unspoken respect. Yes, he believed in Serge; at least until Catherine burst into their disciplined, well-ordered, conventional lives, prompting the long-heralded but, from that point, definitive estrangement between the two brothers.

What has he managed to pass on to his sons? He feels as though he could count on the fingers of one hand the moments that sum up, if not their story, at least their relationship. When he used to run the boys' bath and the steam condensed on the mirror above the washba-sin, when he undressed them and put them in the water, then stayed to watch them play, taking toy figures and galloping them along the edge of the bath, walking them across the water, or having them dive into the depths be-tween their legs. Had he not wondered at the time how to preserve the memory of his love for his sons, of their perfect, radiant bodies in the grey, muddy bathwater, of the misted mirror and the water sporadically trickling down the shower curtain blotted with mould? Or had he felt nothing at all, but simply imagined how Élise would have felt had she still been alive? Had he ever mentally formulated the promise not to fail in what she would have wanted for them, to find the right words, the right gestures, but also to protect them for as long as possible, unable to imagine that it would be from himself that he would need to protect them?

On that rainy spring day in 1952, when even the sky and the fields seem sad and dirty, he walks behind the hearse carrying the remains of Élise, holding Serge's hand. The boy is not yet three. Dressed in a little grey mourning suit, he constantly tugs at the collar of the shirt that is pinching his neck. A few paces behind, Éléonore is carrying Joël in her arms, wrapped in a blanket the mother crocheted before she died giving birth to the son. Élise's family are walking behind them, coughing from the exhaust fumes of the hearse. The weeping mother-in-law, whom he will never see again except by chance, and who will always shoot him the same bitter look, is being supported by the eldest of her sons, the one who, when he heard about his sister's death, showed up in the farmyard drunk, reeling and screaming up at the windows:

'You're going to pay for this, you fucking bastard! You knew she couldn't survive it! You killed her! You fucking killed her! Come down here you son of a bitch! Come out and fight if you've got the balls!'

Henri walked him back to his car, the barrel of a rifle pressed into his flabby belly.

'Get back in your car and don't you ever set foot on my land again, or I swear on her grave I'll kill you.'

When he turned, having lingered for a moment to see the car disappear around the corner of the road leading to the farm, his elder son was watching him from the kitchen window.

Henri also remembers the pig shed, the working practices drilled into them, those instilled in him by his own father. The work ethic he instilled in them. The day when Serge, face a rictus of pain, teeth clenched so as not to cry, showed him his hands covered in blisters, the skin peeling away, and the father said, 'You're finally getting the hang of it,' and jerked his chin towards another stall to be shovelled out. He has come to believe that the pigs are a bulwark between them and the outside world, that it is simultaneously a rite of passage – though one that can only lead back to the piggery in a vicious cycle – and a last resort. Of course he would have wanted something else for them, but what? And who could tell what their lives might have been if Élise had not died?

Time was, he could easily call her to mind, remember her gestures, the way she moved, the tone and tessitura of her voice, refashion snatches of conversation, whispered words, brief scenes. Then her voice had grown fainter before disappearing altogether, diluted in time. Since then, it is in his own voice – muted, externalized, in fact inaudible – that her words come back to him. For there must surely have been a day when she confided that she was pregnant again. He can recall no date, no place, not even a quality of light, a time of day. Did they rejoice, did they make a pact, deciding to allow the child to live regardless of the price, or did they simply say nothing? There remains only a single instant, when the photograph was taken, one afternoon by the walnut tree, and Élise captured, an insect trapped in a droplet of amber. Henri has never spoken of it to the sons, but before the body of their mother was taken away to the hospital morgue, he took a lock of her hair, cut it with his pocket knife and slipped it into the pocket of his shirt. He placed it in the only jewellery box he possessed and never opened it again, superstitious about what alchemy might be wrought by the passage of time, what the box might now contain – a nest of vipers, a pile of dust, a tiny, funeral effigy of Élise?

The telephone ringing makes him start.

'Henri? Paul Vidal here. I'm calling because I've got the results of your most recent tests. Could you come see me? I think we might need to do a little more exploring.'

Henri pats his pockets for his pack of cigarettes. He knows the doctor, watched him grow up. A spineless, sententious man who used to attend the local school, was in the same class as Serge, and now speaks to him in a tone dripping with feigned condescension.

'OK, thanks for calling back, but I don't really have time for that right now.'

He glances at the unopened envelope he received from the medical laboratory lying on the desk, then he opens one of the drawers, slides it under a pile of papers and closes the drawer. Henri hears the little cough the doctor muffles with his fist.

'The thing is... I'd rather not have to talk to you about this over the phone, but the results seem to confirm my fears. I am going to have to order a biopsy of one of the swollen glands and...'

Henri lights another cigarette and, for a moment, loses the thread of the conversation from the receiver. His gaze moves over the shelves, the line of box files. A different colour for each year, blue, green, yellow, black, red, and how many hundreds of thousands of pig lives recorded therein.

Seven million piglets, that's what a sow and her issue would be able to produce within a lifetime.

'No,' he hears himself say, coughing a cloud of smoke towards the strip light. 'No, there'll be no biopsy. Seems to me I told you that the last time the subject came up.'

When, plagued by exhaustion, pruritus and fever, he had made an appointment and visited the doctor's surgery in the village rather than having him come to the farm so that the sons would not know – they have never seen him ill, and on those rare occasions when flu or some other virus should have laid him low, he carried on working, even more fiercely, more determinedly – he had sat in the waiting room, suffering the sidelong glances of other patients, their smug *bonjour-au-revoir-messieurs-dames*, he had vacantly leafed through stupid magazines for housewives, unable to decipher a single word, until the doctor appeared in the doorway, gestured for him to extricate himself from his chair, to follow him into the consulting room, to take a seat, to enumerate his symptoms, nodding sagely from time to time, then asked him to undress (he who has not been naked in front of anyone, not even a woman, for years, now compelled to take off his clothes in front of a man, to sit in his underpants on the soft, cold leather of the examination table, to show, to entrust his body to the doctor's hands that are also soft and cold; and the disgust he had felt at his own shudder as the doctor placed the bell of the stethoscope on his chest), then to remove his underpants so that he could palpate the swollen glands, roll his testicles between his fingers with a suspicious air of concern.

'I'm a little worried that I might not be making myself clear... If it did turn out to be lymphoma, which, to be completely honest, I fear it might, we would need to

255

discuss a treatment plan.'

Henri draws on his cigarette and ponders the irony that he will not die of lung cancer, as he might reasonably have expected.

'There'll be no biopsy, no treatment.'

The doctor is silent for a moment.

'Listen. At least come in and see me, if only so we can talk it through. These are decisions not to be taken lightly, and I need to be sure that you fully understand what...'

'I completely understand what we're dealing with. I'll drop in when I get a chance. In the meantime, please don't call me. Oh, Paul, it goes without saying that this information is nobody's business but mine, and should on no account reach the ears of my sons.'

Henri hangs up without giving the doctor time to reply, then finishes his cigarette and stubs it out in the ashtray overflowing with butts before taking another from one of the many packs that litter the desk.

He thinks about Élise, he thinks about the sons. He remembers everything, or almost everything, every past moment, every day gone by. They all telescope, merge, they can no longer be broken apart. Is that all there is to a life? he thinks contemptuously. So little and yet so much. But mostly so little. And what is there to show for it, at the end? Surely a man is supposed to have gained some wisdom, some understanding of things, if only partial and fragmentary? The truth is, Henri no longer knows anything with certainty.

—

Every evening, when the men finish feeding the pigs and close the doors of the pig shed, by unchanging ritual, they pay a visit to Éléonore. They sit around the table in the kitchen of the former barn, long since converted into independent lodgings. What they talk about, Catherine and Gabrielle do not know; the grandmother is taciturn, the men speak little, accustomed to their solitude, their elective isolation; they have grown accustomed to silence and have learned to read each other's minds. No doubt, as they sip the beer or the coffee that Éléonore serves them, they offer some thoughts about the pig rearing, the sows about to farrow, those that need to be serviced again, the next delivery to the abattoir, the knacker who is coming to take away two or three moribund animals which they plan to slaughter here. The grandmother listens, she says nothing; sometimes, an expression or a word from Henri or Serge will reawaken memories of Marcel, long dormant now and painless. She remembers the moment when she capitulated, when she realized that she would never be able to shield the boy from the violence of the father, the fits of temper, the hours he went missing which at first seemed incomprehensible until they found him dead drunk, slumped at the foot of a tree or a cow, in the orchard or the byre. What she does remember is that, one day, Marcel declared that, from now on, the boy would help with the farm work, since he was clearly old enough. She remembers the dread that shuddered in her belly, the feeling of being dispossessed, powerless; Henri, who was taken from her, whom she could not bind to herself. The following day, at dawn, she watched the father take their son with him, their conjoined silhouettes disappearing through the fog that lay over the fields.

—

257

To Jérôme, Éléonore has always been old and fragile, exuding a smell of cold ash and cats. Countless cats lie, dozing on every surface that is soft and near the hearth: the corners of a deep green velvet sofa, the crocheted cushion covers, the carpets whose patterns disappear beneath a tangle of matted hair of every colour. Though the fathers vainly try to get rid of the tomcats, one invariably escapes and impregnates a female who gives birth in some corner of the barn or the hayloft. Kept at bay by the men and the dogs, the cats live in the grandmother's lap, reigning over a stinking world of three rooms they survey through their gummy eyes like small ataraxic gods.

The massacres of the tomcats by the fathers and lack of new blood have given rise to a family of incestuous, consanguineous cats. Jérôme loves the kittens' misshapen faces, he likes their deformities. One day, one of the cats gave birth to a white two-headed kitten, each mimicking the other as they took turns suckling, but the aberration with the immaculate fur was not viable, and Jérôme buried its remains beneath a terracotta pot, near an anthill, and every day he checked the progress of the hardworking ants. Then he removed the skull with its four eye sockets and keeps it among the relics in his sanctuary, wrapped in a linen shroud.

Early in the morning, after Gabrielle has set down the breakfast tray on the table in the hall and taken the twins to school, after Julie-Marie has headed off to school, when the fathers are already at work in the pig shed, Jérôme pushes open Éléonore's door and sits in the rocking chair facing her, rocking as she sips a *café au lait*. Jérôme looks at the skin of her arms, beneath which veins which seem to have a life of their own, wind around tendons and woody bones. The cats mewl for a little butter, and Éléonore sometimes allows them to lick her *tartine* and they rub against her elbows, arching their backs. The twins are reluctant to visit Éléonore because they re-emerge from her room with their arms and legs covered with insect bites.

Every year, during the hot weather, hordes of parasites rise from the wooden floorboards where larvae have been patiently hibernating all through the winter; the fathers fumigate the rooms, chasing the grandmother and her cats out of the house. Éléonore spends long hours sitting on the wrought iron bench that replaced the small worm-eaten, hobnailed bench with the warped seat on which her father used to sit from the first evening in spring to the last vigils of autumn and which may now be buried in the earth beneath her, the pathetic relic of an ancient civilization long since forgotten.

For reasons unknown to Jérôme, even back in the days when she could still get out of bed, his mother never visited Éléonore. Gabrielle simply pops her head around the door and leaves trays of food, while Julie-Marie pays her no more attention than her great-grandmother pays her. The women shun the company of the grandmother who still reigns over the farm in counterpoint to the business run by the men simply by virtue of her mysteriousness, for though she says little, she always seems to have an opinion.

Jérôme loves the cats, the rustle of the bead curtain leading into the farmyard that quivers like a downpour when Éléonore pushes it aside with a hand stiff with osteoarthritis, the rickety wooden shelves filled with piles of grey porcelain trinkets, with shapeless, crocheted oddities, the wallpaper blackened by smoke from the hearth... Éléonore never beleaguers him with hugs and caresses likes the old women he sometimes meets in the village, any more than Jérôme seeks out the contact of her feeble, frumpish body. He simply likes to sit awhile with her, with her cats, knowing that he is bound to her by some tenuous genealogy whose implications are beyond him, one to which he suspects she holds the secrets, he glimpses when in her presence.

—

Three or four boars are sufficient to impregnate the breeding sows. One of them, the one they have nicknamed the Beast, is the result of years of selection and clever interbreeding. Never before have the men managed to breed such a specimen. The Beast weighs four hundred and seventy kilos, stands one metre forty hoof to shoulder, and measures four metres long. When they parade him past the stalls to check whether the sows are in their heat, the huge testicles swinging from left to right in his scrotum are like a sneer at the men's impotence, while urine trickles from the vulvas of the sows as they smell his sour breath. Aware of his physical superiority, frustrated by the proximity of sows, his confinement and the competition from other boars, the Beast can be volatile. He has already managed to corner Henri in one of the aisles of the pig shed, pinning him against the bars of a stall, and would have ripped off the hand he was about to bite had Serge not intervened and beaten him viciously. Yet the Beast is the father's pride and joy. Henri believed in him from the beginning. When he emerged from the womb of his mother, a first-class breeder, he was twice as heavy as the other piglets in the litter, four of which were so puny that the men had no choice but to destroy them.

'We'll not be castrating this one,' Henri said, pointing to the boar.

When the truck came to take the sow to the abattoir, he took the restraint board from Joël, making it a point of honour to escort the sow aboard. When she finally agreed to get in, he got into the truck with her and laid a hand on the sow's recalcitrant back, whispering in a low voice. The son watched in silence, thinking perhaps he was promising it an easy death, thanking it for being consistent, reliable, efficient, an excellent meat machine, for having given birth to the Beast, a boar like no other, one that might easily win them first prize in several categories at the next agricultural show. But Henri has always despised agricultural shows, refusing to perform like a circus animal, talking about 'exposing himself' to entertain those from the outside world for whom his hatred and contempt never ceases to grow, as though he himself would be dragged into a pen, exposed, groped, judged.

With this exceptional boar, he vows to revitalize the sales of breeding stock to Germany, Spain and Italy which have declined and affected the overall profitability of livestock ever since the pig rearing business began to slip out of their control, slowly, as a river reshapes a landscape with a movement that is barely noticeable when measured against the span of a human life, but only when measured against generations, where memory is lost, such that no-one remembers and no-one can say when it began to change its course.

—

When he finished whispering in its ear, the sow that gave birth to the Beast and countless other piglets is caged with animals it does not know, as frightened as it is at having been taken from their stalls, herded though the sorting pen into the dazzling light outside, then driven up into the truck before the ramp is taken up. As the motorways, the *routes nationales*, flicker past, the pigs see the russet, red and ochre earth, the grasslands, sights and smells that reach them through the gaps in the planks. Unloaded at the rear of a squat, silent grey building, they are herded through a narrow chute where already they smell the stench of blood and death. Some struggle to escape, but it is impossible for them to turn around because of the cramped confines of the passageway and the horde of pigs behind, trampling them, scrabbling over them, biting their croups while the men shout and beat them. Others, bewildered by the journey and the blows, uncomprehendingly move forward towards the waiting men in protective coveralls wielding captive bolt guns. Still others drop dead, brought down by a heart attack, and must be carried out of the passageway to the conveyor belt that will devour them. When it comes to the turn of the sow which birthed the Beast and dozens and dozens of other piglets, the slaughterman presses the captive bolt gun to her temple. It takes several attempts, three shots to obliterate her brain, before the sow falls to her knees. She is then stuck through the thigh with a hook, hoisted up and bled out. The slaughterman turns to his co-workers, shaking his head: 'She wouldn't fucking die, the bitch!'

—

In early May, as Serge is heading back into the pig shed looking for the pack of cigarettes he left in his coveralls in the changing room, he sees a glow on the control

262

panel indicating that the lights in the boar pen have been left on. He sets off to check the circuit breaker, lacing his boots, cutting through the farrowing house and entering the building reserved for the boars. He finds Henri in front of the boar pen, his arms on the top bar. The father does not hear him come in, does not move. His head is bowed, he is staring at the boar lying in the straw. At first Serge does not dare move for fear that he is interrupting something, a moment of privacy, of confidence or contemplation. Then his father turns.

'Everything okay?' Serge says.

'Yeah,' Henri says in a low voice.

'I forgot my cigs,' the son says, jerking a thumb over his shoulder towards the changing room, 'and I noticed the lights were on in the boar pen.'

The father says nothing and turns back to the stall housing of the Beast.

Serge steps closer, hesitantly walking along the aisle. He stares at the boar which stares back, motionless, indifferent to their presence, then he glances at his father's profile, the grim face weathered like old leather. He says:

'Is there a problem?'

Henri slowly shakes his head. He accepts the cigarette his elder son proffers. The flame of the Zippo illuminates the folds of his face and, for a moment, the smell of petrol overwhelms the scent of the Beast. They smoke as they stare at the animal.

'Have you noticed that their pupils always reflect our face?' Henri says. 'If you look carefully. It's just a detail, but sometimes I think there's more to it than that. It jumps out at you. It's like looking in a two-way mirror or into the bottom of a well. You see yourself, but you see something else, something moving underneath like... It's as though you see yourself the way they see you with their dumb, animal eyes.'

Serge says nothing. Henri is not usually inclined to spouting this kind of nonsense. An animal is an animal, and a pig is not even that. This is what his father taught him, a fact confirmed in the pig shed every day. Let this boar they tend, feed, clean and masturbate look at them with that contemptuous air of an indolent, lecherous emperor; he will end in the abattoir like all the cull boars when one of his offspring takes his place and his balls dry up.

'The eye was in the tomb and stared at Cain,' said Henri.

Serge chuckles politely.

'I'm going to go, I'm freezing my balls off,' he says at length.

But he waits a moment longer in the hope that the father will follow him, and then leaves him alone with the Beast and goes back to the changing room.

Serge closes the door behind him, lights a cigarette. In the distance, the fields consume a patch of glowing, tawny sky. What is it with the old man and that boar? Serge walks away, trailing the breath of buildings, the acrid stench of pigs that, despite his coveralls, impregnates every fibre of his sweater, every strand of his hair. Sometimes, he forgets this smell. For long periods, it disappears. Then he rediscovers it, often in his dreams – it comes with the shriek, the wail of a body of animals, a single, convulsive, menacing mass, hidden from view, brooding in limbo, in the deep shadows – just as those who lose their sight late in life see primitive images in their dreams. When it appears in his dreams, he instantly recognizes it and it catches in his throat, this stench that rises from buried worlds as through a rip in

264

the earth, in memory, in time: a smell of mire, of silt, of Archaean lava, of fossil layers, the foul smell of sickly, putrid wombs.

When he is awake and catches a genuine whiff of the pigs – he barely notices if the smell is subdued, diluted, carried on the west wind, exuded by the jumper he is removing, lurking in the breath he is exhaling – it is superimposed by the dream, and he feels the same innate disgust, the same gnawing dread. Sometimes alcohol can offer him a respite, a night with no nightmares, and he suffers the painful hangovers of the morning after with good grace. Puddles of mud lap at his feet as he walks towards the farmhouse, a grey monolith framed by the darkness, a gravestone half-buried in the valley slopes, a foundered, capsized ship whose sails still flutter in the wind; but it is simply the tarpaulins that he and Joël put up last autumn to deal with the sagging roof, the slates dislodged by the first gust of wind that skitter towards the drainpipes and shatter on the flagstones of the farmyard.

As he walks, his face becomes expressionless, he stares at the ground, his back hunches under the weight of shame. Like the smell of the pigs, he is sometimes reminded of her; it only takes a small detail: the blue tarpaulins covering the roof, wrecked cars piled up among the weeds, the closed shutters of Cathy's bedroom.

The farmhouse has become dilapidated at the expense of the pig units which have mushroomed since the advent of the common agricultural policy, and must be continually renovated, modernized, maintained at prevailing standards. Previously, breeding meant a rudimentary pigsty with a field of at least two hectares on which twenty pigs could be raised outdoors. The loan Henri took out in order to construct the new pig units and shift to enclosed breeding were intended to guarantee improved animal husbandry. The pivotal period was to span only the first few years, when earnings from the sale of pigs were not sufficient for the breeding programme to turn a profit, despite the development of long distribution channels. But, over time, Henri has continued to hint that farming is a constant risk. The accounting costs fall to him alone, the sons are allowed no say in expenditure and investment. Besides, they never talk about money, except to tell him what they have spent on grain and water, in vet's fees, on animals, machinery and materials, repairs and engineers, fertilizers, pesticides and seeds. An expense is legitimate only if it is justified by a potential profit, even if indirect.

Serge massages his left hand, which often suffers twinges and sometimes trembles. The hipflask is already empty and he is beginning to feel thirsty. Just as the smell of pigs or the weight of his shame are suddenly palpable, so he sometimes has the sudden feeling that there is a disruption to the order of life and the world of the farm. Serge cannot put a name to this sense of deterioration, but what is the tipping point, the source? We would have to retrace the path of the word, of the law decreed by the father, rediscover the first word, long forgotten, but whose echo still secretly resonates within them. Ever since the death of Élise, all they have known has been the slow decline of the farm buildings, which have rotted and decayed even as the piggery seemed to prosper, constantly produced more, proportionally increasing their workload and their violence.

A pig is there to be slaughtered. Never forget to show them who's boss.

Serge believes all the fires of hell smoulder beneath

the pig breeding business, threatening to erupt like Vesuvius and bury them if they should ever stop purging or feeding it. The nature of the piggery is that its walls cannot contain what it needs to constantly assimilate and regurgitate. It is a universe unto itself, perpetually expanding, that they strive to master. As for the memory of how things were in the olden days, it is a fragile, crumbling skin; their sorry state has become familiar, ordinary.

Serge cannot help but think that the Beast, which the father thinks of as a sign of the success of the breeding business, is actually the stumbling block. Like the Beast, the pig business has become bigger than they are. Do they still control it? Henri, obsessed with the boar, is now talking about overhauling the breeding programme, reorganizing the pigs, creating new buildings, putting more animals on slatted floors, hiving off the management of the gestation unit, all this in order to make constant improvements in efficiency, productivity... Serge pauses and turns, and stares for a long time at the pig shed.

—

Once the men leave for the pig shed and the dogs stop barking, Catherine is left in the silence of the empty house. Maybe Jérôme will open the door to her room and slip under the sheet next to her, or maybe he will change his mind, and she will hear him hesitate at the door, shifting his weight from one foot to the other, lower the handle, toy with the key in the lock, before deciding to obey the orders given him by Serge or Gabrielle and go to his grandmother, who is responsible for looking after him when the adults are absent.

Catherine knows nothing of the bond between the boy and the grandmother, who reminds her of those spiders in shadowy haylofts that weave webs so cunning that it is impossible for the unfortunate prey caught in them ever to break free. They seem to be indestructible, they are still there a year, a decade, even a century later, the web a little dustier, a little thicker, a little more forbidding. This is probably why Éléonore resents Catherine, for displacing her at the centre of the funnel web from where, as the only representative of her sex, she kept a watchful eye on her men, for forcing her into exile in the old byre with all her belongings. But Catherine's warnings to Jérôme about this ancient harpy have been futile, he does exactly as he pleases. Éléonore seems to have existed since time immemorial, rotting in her house filled with hideous cats, and perhaps continues to reign as dowager queen over the farm. And to think that she is only seventy-eight, Good God, she might well live for another thirty years... And besides, what difference would it make? None. The grandmother could drop dead; nothing would change. The damage has long since been done, so long that it is as deeply rooted in them as it is in the soil of Puy-Larroque. Catherine tripped over those roots, she is trapped in this web, and the more she struggles, the more she is trapped. Often, she would rather not think about it, rather not remember: the mistakes, the dreams of long ago, the hopes she had for her life, she would rather stuff it all into a sack and bury it deep in the mud that is now her consciousness.

The sickness has been around for so long, since well before the first breakdown, that it sometimes feels as though she has been living with it forever. As far back as she can remember it was there, at first a white noise, as though

268

she were constantly trying to find the right frequency on a radio, to somehow calmly comprehend the world; but at the time, she still had the feeling that there were possibilities lying dormant beneath the surface, the belief that there existed a thousand possible lives, and the conviction that she had simply to want it in order to live them. She was born on these lands that she desperately wanted to leave; she will probably die here. She remembers 14 July 1967: the stage that was built on the village square of Puy-Larroque, the paper lanterns strung between the branches of the chestnut trees, suspended haloes, the refreshment stall set up near the war memorial, the casks of wine and beer, the huge sacks of coal the men tipped into metal barrels cut lengthways and mounted on legs that served as barbecues... The plumes of black, acrid smoke that rose whenever they poked the embers and hung in wisps around the church steeple.

At seventeen, all she wanted was to run away from home, from her wretchedly miserable parents, her father breaking his back lugging sacks of cement on building sites or working as a farm labourer, her mother staving off boredom in front of the television – a brand new Sonolor for which they had patiently saved, and of which they were so proud that, when it arrived, the whole family gathered and sat on the sofa while the father turned on the set and adjusted the screen – nodding vehemently during the commercial breaks.

Climb behind the wheel of a Renault 4CV, and you are instantly at ease. No car in the world is more feminine, more effortlessly driveable! Just look at how easily it handles! Feel the acceleration! Appreciate the safety!

That night, the two brothers were standing next to each other, propping up the makeshift bar, frantically glancing around as though wondering what they were doing there. Serge was dark haired, stocky; everyone knew he was mean, a brawler. Then there was Joël, a quiet lad, or perhaps simply insignificant, his shoulders hunched, his red hair slick with Brilliantine. Were their faces not tarnished by the light of swaying lanterns? They exchanged not a word, not a look, as though they had never met, had ended up here by chance, elbows pressed together, in the smell of barbecued meat, stale smoke and aftershave. From a distance, Catherine watched them. It was this that had first seduced her, she seems to remember: their dissimilarity, their strangeness, their defiance in the face of the world. Like them, she felt nothing but contempt for this village fête, this awkward, foolish jubilation; like them, she wanted only to be drunk. Bats fluttered between the branches of the chestnut trees, devouring the swarms of mayfly buzzing beneath the paper lanterns. Serge came over to her, and Catherine could smell his thick breath as he leaned over her shoulder to talk to her; his open shirt exuded the sour smell of sweat from a bronzed torso, like the body of an animal.

'I should have avoided you like the plague, you and your kin, it would have been the best decision I took in my life.'

Yes, she would have been better advised to flee, to abandon her glass, her friends, the band, the dangerously bucolic village of Puy-Larroque. But that night, she knew almost nothing about the bond between the two brothers, about the shadow of Henri, their shared history, the future that was already conspiring against them, and she wanted them, wanted them with a huge cannibalistic desire, she wanted both of them, because alcohol made it impossible for her to distinguish between them, because she had sensed Serge's brooding violence, which at the

270

time she mistook for desire, a desire to do battle with life that rivalled her own, and Joël's sullen, intense reserve.

She let herself be carried away, and the three of them wandered away from the village square, through the alleys and the crumbling walls of the château. Serge would grab Joël by the back of the neck, jostled him, punched him in the shoulder, and the teenager allowed himself to be manhandled without complaint, a vague smile playing on his slips. Propping each other up, they went down the steep slippery steps. The darkness as they moved through it was heavy, muggy, filled with the croak of frogs, and icy breezes. The water in the wash-house reservoir seemed stagnant and murky. On the far side of the cemetery wall, the gravestone crosses were barely visible against the blue, languid backcloth of the landscape. They followed the path leading to the old oak and lay down in hollows between the roots beneath the dark mass of leaves. Inebriated, they lay for a long moment without speaking, listening to the distant clamour of the fête, to the cry of some animal in a thicket, the unceasing rustle of the oak. When Serge leaned in to kiss her, Catherine let him. He slipped a hand under her shirt and cupped her breast, pinching the nipple between thumb and forefinger, then let the hand slide down her stomach, up her thigh, under her skirt to her crotch and the swelling of her sex.

'Kiss her,' he said to Joël, raising his head.

She reached out to his shoulder and pulled him towards her, bit his lower lip and let his tongue slide between her teeth, before Joël backed away, leaned against the trunk of the oak and got to his feet.

'I need to piss,' he said.

He walked over to the edge of a field, where Serge

quickly joined him. Though they spoke in low whispers, the brothers' voices reached her:

'What's your problem?'

'Nothing. I ain't got a problem.'

'Is she not your type? Don't you fancy her?

'Leave me to piss in peace.'

'Or maybe you're queer?'

'Go fuck yourself,' Joël said, buttoning his fly.

He shot a glance at Catherine before walking away and disappearing into the darkness.

Why had she stayed with Serge that night in the shadow of the ancient oak, why had she allowed him to come back to her, to lie down next to her, to take her in his arms, his trousers around his knees, gripping the roots of the tree to brutally thrust into her, to come inside her with a drunken groan? When he withdrew, she had lain there, motionless, her skirt rucked up over her stomach, her dark, glistening vulva like a beast's lair, staring up into the swaying branches of the oak, its bark like the hide of some fearsome animal in the darkness.

And why must the images keep flooding back? She would do better to sleep, though she cannot know they will not follow her into the depths of sleep, into the dreams where she is often plagued by the smell, the wail of the pigs, a stench that cannot be masked by that of flowers rotting in the mud, by the smell of Serge that first night, a miasma of alcohol fumes and cheap aftershave, a stench she has come to loathe but one that she can smell even with the windows and the shutters closed, the house double-locked, as though the pig shed is determined to seep into her room by any means. And these squeals that are sometimes carried in the wind, and which the walls do nothing to muffle, the shrill wails of a newborn or a soul in pain...

272

When she had no choice but to marry Serge and to move to the farm, she quickly realized that she would have to ruthlessly fight the piggery that was all but knocking at their back door, that the brothers and the father carried with them, talked about incessantly. She saw the men lead the cull sows into the truck, some suffering rectal prolapse, dragging a sac of entrails forced out through the anus from years of farrowing, others unable to walk, crippled by arthritis, by forced immobility, by their own weight which their legs can no longer support. They beat them with a stick, kick them to make them move, and the animals squeal in pain and fear, drag themselves across on the concrete, their flesh red raw, their eyes rolled back in their heads.

'How can you do that?'

'Do what? I don't understand,' Serge said, panting for breath, wiping his hands on his shirt.

Catherine jerked her chin at the animals. Serge shrugged.

'Oh. That's how it goes... Sometimes you have to put them out of their misery. You get used to it, you'll see.'

But she refused to see, or even to know. She stripped the house of everything that could remind her of pig rearing, even indirectly, packed the knick-knacks, the little pigs in porcelain and blown glass into boxes, the old cast metal piggybanks, the medals won at agricultural shows. Like her mother before her, she begins to dream of a mundane happiness, a little house in the suburbs, a little car, travelling during the school holidays; everything suddenly seemed preferable to the never-ending agony in this crumbling farmhouse, surrounded by the stench, the squealing pigs and the cruelty of men.

—

A few days later, they find the gate of the boar's stall wide open. Joël goes to find Henri and Serge, who are working in the feedlot.

'He broke out,' he yells from the doorway of the hangar. 'The Beast has broken out, the stall is wide open, and the door to the building. I can't find him anywhere!'

The father and the elder brother join him in the search. Henri leans over the gates, stops outside the boar's stall. With his foot, he lifts the bolt and the padlock that are half-buried in the manure flowing into the drain. Both sons follow him down the aisles until they reach the front door, then they emerge from the building and find the surrounding fence trampled, the chain-link fence ripped open. Serge runs a hand over the metal studs the Beast has bent, next to the sign that reads PRIVATE PROPERTY NO ENTRY. He lets out a short, astonished laugh, and quickly stifles it. Henri retraces his steps as far as the main door to the boar pens. He feels the weight of the chain, inspects it, then bends down and picks up the padlock and shows it to his sons before viciously hurling it at their feet. It was Joël who made sure to lock up the pig units the day before.

'I swear, I...' he stammers.

'Get the fuck out my way,' Henri cuts him off.

Joël steps aside and the brothers watch the father stalk off and head back towards the farmhouse. Standing back, Serge lights a cigarette, trying to control his trembling hands.

'You believe me, don't you?' Joël says, his voice ragged with emotion. 'Don't fuck around, Serge, you know I'd never have forgotten to lock up! How the fuck could he break out of his stall?'

Serge turns away, shrugs his shoulders, then jerks his head towards the trampled ground beyond the chain-link fence, the mark of cloven hooves on the soft earth. He fishes out his hipflask, takes a swig, then wipes his mouth on his shoulder.

'I'll tell you what I believe, I believe what I'm looking at with my own two eyes.'

They decide to leave the gates open and to set out buckets of grain near the pig units and the straw barn. When the new units were first built, it sometimes happened that an animal would escape while being moved from one building to another, and they know from experience that although the pigs find the primal sense of freedom exhilarating, they have only ever known captivity, their pigswill served at regular times. So the fugitive, quickly overcome by fear, by the cold of unfamiliar nights, by hunger, would end up coming back and the men would find it lying in the straw in the hangar, or standing nervously next to the doors behind which his life and those of his kind have been lived out.

'A boar that size is hardly going to stay invisible for long,' Joël says as the brothers leave the pig shed.

All around, the woodlands are bounded by tilled fields that offer scant hiding places. Hunters easily flush out game and the boar population in the *département* is strictly regulated. Henri and his sons are the only pig breeders for almost thirty kilometres. Most of the other farmers in the area grow cereals and have long since stopped rearing livestock. Some still keep a few animals, one or two pigs for fattening, but nothing remotely comparable to the Beast. With a single glance, they would immediately know where he had come from.

'Unless one of them fuckers has already killed it,' Serge says, biting down on the filter of his cigarette.

'Yeah. And what if there's an accident?' Joël says.

275

'Imagine he runs out onto the motorway in front of a car, and ends up injuring someone?'

'That's not going to happen. We'll catch him. We have to catch him.'

But the Beast is not tempted by the buckets of grain. For three weeks, until mid-June, Henri and the sons organize nightly patrols around the pig units, then beyond the fences, without happening on anything other than two wild boars, a fox and a few stray dogs. They follow the animal's tracks, starting from the field next to the pig sheds, but the trail quickly comes to a road and disappears.

'It's like the fucker deliberately trotted along the tarmac to put us off the scent,' Joël says.

They organize hunting drives, extending the perimeter of the search area every day, taking the hounds with them, but all they manage to flush out are some hares and a few young roebucks. As for those living in the neighbouring farms and houses, no-one has seen a half-tonne boar crossing their lands, destroying a crop field or even a vegetable garden. The night patrols and the drives prove futile, the weeks pass, and summer settles in.

The Beast seems to have vanished into thin air.

—

After closing the gate behind him and going down the flight of flagstone steps fractured by snaking tree roots and the convulsions of the village dead, Jérôme lies down, arms folded across his chest, at the foot of the statue, beneath the merciful gaze of the Virgin, whose lips, cheeks and nose have been eaten away by a plaque of rust. He waits. The lizards sent scurrying by his shadow listen intently to the renewed silence, and when the chirping of sparrows perched in the cypresses quickly begins again, they leave their shelter, their keen eyes darting in syncopation, and stretch out on the marble, eyes half-closed, their striped flanks swelled by short breaths. A crow flies over the graves; their shadows scud over Jérôme, a small, motionless form on the concrete slab. He allows the minutes and the hours to wash over him, sometimes half-opening his eyes to watch the confused ballet of the swallows, the treetops of the cypresses swaying gently in the breeze, the cones falling, bouncing and skittering over the steps. When his neck begins to ache, he sits up and lets the sunlight warm the back of his neck. As the sun reaches its zenith, the shadows of those crosses still standing over graves gradually wane and the shadow of the Virgin slowly withdraws to the plinth from which she watches over the eternal rest of the dead lying in the graveyard clay.

The sun now is beating down on the slabs of marble and concrete. The bark of the cypresses oozes amber sap. A few metres from where Jérôme lies is a pink, granite gravestone, a corner of which has sunk into the earth. From the hole exposed by the tilting slab, the broad, olive-coloured head of a grass snake emerges. Jérôme holds his breath, sits utterly still. From time to time, the black tongue of the snake, sleek and sinuous, darts out, probing the apparent tranquillity of the cemetery, then it slithers from the grave, tracing broad curves, revealing its verdigris colouring, and seems to flow like water between the stones, a gently hissing rivulet moving through the dry grass.

A shudder runs through Jérôme's neck, for this is the same snake he saw last summer swimming on the surface of the lake as Julie-Marie was paddling beneath the branches of willow trees that swayed and whispered in the breeze, brushing her shoulders, water rising to her bare, broad waist, moving through the shifting shadows and flashes of light that tumbled, whirling with yellow leaves, and settled on the watery surface, leaves and flashes of light that she crumpled and pushed away with her hands. She walked silently through the soft mud, through the algae, watching the splintered reflection moving ahead of her through the roots of the willows. Shoals of gudgeon brushed against her pale legs, warped by the distorting mirror of the lake, chasing away the pond-skaters and the tadpoles wriggling in the warm, turbid shallows. Blinded by the glare of the sun, the grass snake did not see her as it calmly swam towards Julie-Marie's pale breasts in graceful convolutions. The same snake is now slithering amid the gravestones, between the bones which the earth, sated and gorged with the village dead, now regurgitates: greenish molars, patinated vertebrae, porous coccyges. The snake pauses as a sparrowhawk glides over the cemetery, the shadow of the bird briefly flickering over its bulging pupils, then it resumes its delicate winding until it reaches a shapeless block of granite, the remains of an ancient tombstone that lies in a pool of light, where the snake curls up.

When he sees it for the first time on the surface of the pond, Jérôme grips a willow branch with his left hand to steady himself as he climbs down to the narrow, muddy shoreline. Without pausing to take off his trousers, he steps into the water and Julie-Marie turns and flashes him a smile, about to say something, and then she notices that her brother is not looking at her. Following his gaze, she sees the snake and lets out a shrill scream that bores into Jérôme's eardrums and echoes around the

278

countryside. Julie-Marie runs back to the bank, sends up huge jets of water, slipping in the mud, collapsing onto the roots, which she grips and uses to haul herself ashore, still shrieking. Meanwhile, alerted by the vibrations, the snake disappears underwater and reappears in the middle of the pond, then swims towards the tall grasses of the far bank. Sheepish, Jérôme now turns and paddles back to the shore. Water trickles down Julie-Marie's arm as she hugs her shoulders, hiding her breasts from him, not yet troubled that he can see her genitals. She sees that her brother cannot tear his eyes from the dark, downy hair of her groin. Letting go her shoulders, she lets her arms hang by her side, and defiantly, or playfully, her palms pressed against her thighs, stands there utterly naked before the boy, before bursting out laughing.

'Jesus, you gave me such a fright! Come on. You're not going to tell me you've never seen a naked woman, are you?'

Of course he has; he has seen their mother naked when she took baths with him, washed his hair, allowing him to stare at her vulva. Julie-Marie picks up her clothes, turns her back to reveal the curve of her pale buttocks and, glancing at Jérôme over her shoulder, slowly, unhurriedly, gets dressed.

The snake is now dozing on the tombstone in the mid-day sun, coiled and still, the head, with its yellow labial scales, emerging from the whorls of its body.

You know that way you've got of looking at your sister, well I don't like it one fucking bit.

Jérôme moves a foot. The gravel of the cemetery crunches under his shoe. His palms are sweaty, his mouth dry. The buried dead, happy for a moment's

279

entertainment, holding their breath as he does, pressing their ears to the padded lids of their coffins so they can tell where he is from the crunch of his steps. He is just about to pounce when the snake rears up, darts out its forked tongue, opens its mouth wide, puffing up its body, hissing at the predator that has it cornered. It tries to escape, but Jérôme hurls himself towards it, grips it behind the head, but falls against the broken gravestone, which gashes his shin, and he rolls over, hugging the snake to his chest to protect it from the weight of his body.

His head hits the cemetery wall and he finds himself sprawled on his back, his face covered with a mask of dirt, powdered bone and dust, gasping for breath, dazzled by the sun glaring at him and numbed by the shock. He holds the snake up to his face and it coils around his forearm. He can smell the scent secreted by the cloacal gland, the black liquid trickling onto his neck. He sits on the cemetery path, his heart hammering in his chest.

The snake contorts, twisting its mouth to reveal the pink throat, the glottis and the sheath of the tongue. For a moment, it winds around the boy's chest and the beating of the animal's heart and the beating of the child's heart meet in a single saraband. Then the snake finally concedes, admits defeat and relaxes its grip.

Jérôme gets to his feet. His shin aches and his sock is crimson, he is out of breath, his throat is sore. He holds the snake at eye level and stares into the fixed, round pupils, gazing at his own reflection. He opens his mouth, places the snake's head on his tongue and closes his lips around its neck, then opens his mouth again and removes the snake, which tastes of the cemetery and of the lake, of the shadows of stones, of graves, of the corrugated-iron under which it hides, of fields of sunflowers where, when night comes, it hunts for rats and rabbits, of the fur of the animals it squeezes and the burrows into which it slithers.

It's just like pigs, you get runts in the litter; the mother's obviously passed on her madness to him, these things are in the blood.

Jérôme relaxes his grip and the grass snake slides between his fingers. He pushes up his T-shirt and feels the warm, dry scales as the snake slithers across his stomach, his chest, dips under the neckline and reappears on his throat. For a long time he lies there in the now inverted shadow cast by the pockmarked Virgin. The snake twines around his neck, his wrists, continually darting out its tongue, tickling his skin. The wound in his shin dries and grows dark in the afternoon heat perfumed by the cypresses, while in their coffins the village dead swelter, and are weary once more. Jérôme finally sets the snake down at his feet, where it lies, unmoving, suspicious, then stirs a little, a vague attempt at escape and, realizing that the boy does not try to catch it, weaves away though the graves.

Jérôme gets to his feet. Eyes closed, he stretches and shivers in the sun, the Mute, the Happy Fool, the Idiot, the Bastard. The Runt.

—

Arriving back at the farm, Jérôme pauses on the threshold. He strokes the multicoloured plastic strips of curtain pinned over the kitchen doorway, their ends chewed away by generations of puppies. Jérôme loves the rubbery smell it gives off when warmed by the sun and stirred by a gentle breeze. He sometimes feels that things can be much bigger than they seem, that they can contain life itself: the smell of the plastic curtain or of the abandoned tyres filled with pools of stagnant rainwater, the little curly hairs at the back of Julie-Marie's neck, a muddy puddle fringed by serried ranks of tadpoles. He goes upstairs and opens the door to Catherine's room, plunged into darkness by the closed shutters. She is awake and waves him in. He creeps through the half-open door into the sickly, stale perfume of his mother's body and her breath as she lifts the sheet, and he slides in beside her, pressed against her listless flesh. Catherine roughly hugs him to her, presses her nose against the back of his head, breathing the smell of his hair, the nape of his neck.

'Where on earth have you been? You're filthy. And you smell funny.'

She feels his limbs, his dirty feet, as though checking that he is really here, alive and well. He whimpers when she touches the gash on his shin.

'What have you been doing now? You're covered in scabs and bruises. You need to cut your nails, you're scratching me. Do you take a bath when your sister tells you? Does she wash you properly? Let me have a look, I'll check to see if you've got lice.'

She draws him towards her and he feels her thighs press against his buttocks, feels her breath heavy with sleep brushing the back of his neck as she suddenly whispers feverishly:

'Maman will get better, you'll see. Honestly, I'm feeling much better... Don't you think I look better? I'll get up in a little while... I just need a bit more rest, just a bit. I'm sorry, Jesus, I'm so sorry, just have a little nap here with me, please, stay with me until I fall asleep again.'

He lies there motionless until Catherine drifts off. Usually, when he comes into the room, she disappears, like the lizards at the cemetery scurry away when he

282

tries to catch them. She buries herself under the sheet, shudders and moans when he touches her shoulder. So he simply sits on the bed, staring at the empty medicine boxes, the fetid water in the vase on the bedside table, the brownish brittle film like the skin on raw milk, the bouquet of flowers that Julie-Marie or Gabrielle stubbornly put there, withered for want of daylight.

'What do you expect me to do with these? I can't bear that scent, it gives me a blinding headache... or I can't smell anything except this house, which smells like a pig shed. What are they? Roses? Did you pick them from the climbing rose? Is this lilac? The smell makes me want to heave, and they wither in two seconds flat, there's something pathetic about them. It's depressing, it looks like a deathbed. But maybe that's what you all want, to be rid of me, to bury me? You're all plotting against me, aren't you? Whatever you do, don't listen to your grandmother, don't believe a word she says, she's worse than... Throw them out, for God's sake. Why are you always bringing me these disgusting flowers? Why can't you understand I hate them?'

She begs them to take the flowers away, toss them on the dungheap, throw them to the hens so they can peck at the buds, and then two days later she will decide to throw open the shutters overlooking the farmyard, take a deep lungful of air. She will come back to life, start to tidy and clean her bedroom, the children's rooms, the whole house, airing every room whether it's raining, snowing or blowing a gale. In the kitchen, she will decide that the cupboards are empty and take it into her head to go shopping, ecstatic about the bright, gleaming supermarket shelves, the infinite variety of products, the neatly arranged pyramids of tins she tosses into the shopping trolley. She will drag Jérôme along with her because, at such times, she cannot bear the thought of being parted from him for a second.

'You and I are the same, we're two peas in a pod, aren't we? You're my little boy. You're your mother's son, aren't you? You came out of me, to me, flesh of my flesh, blood of my blood. Go on, admit it, you're your mother's son, a little devil, just like me! Do you think maybe we should go away? Just you and me, we won't tell anyone. We don't need anyone or anything, we're fine, just the two of us.'

On the main street of the little town, she pauses in front of every window, goes into every shop, the grocer's, the electrical goods shop, the tobacconist, the souvenir shop. A steam iron, a china owl, a lampshade, an ashtray, sundry pairs of shoes, a doll for Julie-Marie, she stares in wonderment at everything, to her eyes every object seems ingenious, necessary, anticipating her every need, cravings she did not know she had a moment earlier are now like tiny, throbbing wounds that she must soothe immediately. By the time she gets home, she has already lost interest in what she has bought: boxes and plastic bags litter the kitchen table, the draining board, the chairs, they are strewn all over the floor. When Serge comes home, there are heated arguments, insults fly, the father reproaches her for pouring money she has done nothing to earn down the drain, she accuses him of being a cheapskate, a skinflint, railing at the meanness, the selfishness he gets from Henri.

'The apple doesn't fall far from the tree!' she says.

She gestures around the room with theatrical horror and amazement, knowing it will needle him: the wallpaper eaten by mildew, the plasterwork flaking and crumbling from saltpetre.

'It's a pigsty! It's disgusting! I'm ashamed to live here!

284

And what about all the money you throw away on booze, you fucking drunk, why don't we talk about that?'

She starts screaming until her voice begins to crack, throwing anything that comes to hand, tossing the bags of groceries, the gift-wrapped boxes out the window into the yard, setting the dogs yowling in their kennel and at the same time swearing that she will take it all back, that she will demand her money back, humiliate herself in front of everyone for the sake of a few hundred francs. Serge grabs her, she struggles, punches his shoulders, his face, while he effortlessly lifts her, carries her up to the bedroom, kicking the door open, throws her down and slams the door. Catherine lies there on the ground, curled into the foetal position, sobbing bitterly, whimpering like a wounded animal, and sometimes Jérôme will go upstairs to her, run his fingers through her hair, wipe the snot from her nose until she calms down.

The boy knows nothing about his mother's illness except for what his grandmother has confided to him on one of those days when, without warning, she chose to break her silence and disregard that of the boy: that the breakdowns became much more serious after his birth, that she has been sent 'to the madhouse' on a number of occasions, coming back to the farm after weeks or months, always more broken, more devastated, stepping out of the car and slowly crossing the yard, supported by Serge.

'People can say what they like about my lad, and I'm not saying they'd be wrong, but no-one can accuse him of not loving your mother... It's not your fault, of course, but the things she's put him through... Not that's she's entirely to blame, I suppose but... Well... He may have forgiven her, but I won't... not ever. And yes, I know

285

there's the illness, but she could never be content with what she had. She should have done – sometimes in this life you have to just make up your mind and be content...'

Jérôme remembers the doctor sitting in the kitchen, looking at the father, sighing, running his tongue over his lower lip, shaking his head, then writing out another prescription.

'Things can't go on like this. I can't just keep writing prescriptions for serious medications that she takes only when it suits her, Serge. She needs to be institutionalized, to be monitored by specialists.'

'Out of the question. Anyway, she hardly leaves the house these days, that's all behind us. You know what happened last time, the bullshit they put into her head, the state she was in when I saw her. I'm telling you, she's much better off here. You just write the prescription – that's what I'm paying you for, isn't it?'

The doctor pushed back his chair, got to his feet, looked at Jérôme and then ruffled his hair.

'What about you, what do you think? Still determined to say nothing?'

Then, to Serge:

'Whatever you want, but if things get worse, it'll be your fault. And don't kid yourself, she'll get worse.'

—

During the day, the pig units become like furnaces, and they barely cool down at night. Pigs are unable to sweat and have difficulty regulating their body temperature. Since they cannot wallow in mud, they sprawl listlessly in their own excrement, panting in distress. The men get up at daybreak, refill the drinking troughs, hose down the animals. They throw open the doors of the pig sheds

286

in the hope that a through breeze might drive away the humidity and the stench, but this means they have to deal with the blowflies and horseflies that swarm in and hover in clouds over the stalls, clustering around every orifice of the pigs. Long before the sun has fully risen, they are forced to close the doors again.

The sons rake droppings from under the slatted floors and push the slurry into the drainage channels. The pig sheds are two thousand square metres, and the stalls are two metres by three, each containing between five to seven pigs shitting and wallowing in their excreta.

Sows about to give birth are housed on slats in cramped farrowing crates, firmly restrained to limit their movements and prevent them from crushing their litter. Some farrow standing up, dropping their young like turds onto the ground; others, convulsed by spasms, manage to kneel or to lie down, with only their hindquarters sticking out for the sake of hygiene.

This is where everything goes to shit, never forget that, This is where pig breeding gets fucked up, the urogenital system.

The sows evacuate piles of black, foul-smelling waste into the walkways and the drainage channels, which the men have to clear away as quickly as possible so the animals do no fall into them and catch an infection, and the piglets are not born in their mother's faeces, since a painstaking selective breeding process means that they are born with no natural immunity, Specific Pathogen Free, modified in other words – Henri prefers *optimized* – so as not to carry the bacteria naturally found in pigs, but which in the concentration camps of the pig sheds would likely cause an epidemic.

Joël has already seen piglets drag themselves along the ground, their bellies or their skulls half-eaten by the larvae that hatch from the eggs the flies are constantly laying. And so he and Serge shovel shit into barrows as fast as they can and tip it into the ravenous maw of the slurry pit, and they wash down the sows with high-pressure hoses and disinfectant before they farrow their young, to kill off the germs continuously contaminating them, contaminating their teats and, in turn, their piglets.

Because everything in the closed, stinking world of pig rearing is simply one vast infection, constantly contained and controlled by men, even the carcasses churned out by abattoirs to stock the supermarkets, even when they have been washed with bleach, cut into pink slices and packed in cellophane into pristine white polystyrene trays, they bear the invisible taint of the pig shed, minute traces of shit, germs and bacteria, against which the men fight a losing battle with their puny weapons: high-pressure hoses, Cresyl, disinfectants for the sows, disinfectant for wounds, worming pellets, vaccines for swine flu, vaccines for parvovirus, vaccines for Porcine Reproductive & Respiratory Syndromé, vaccines against porcine circovirus, iron injections, antibiotic injections, vitamin injections, mineral injections, growth hormone injections, food supplements – all this in order to compensate for deficiencies deliberately created by man.

They have modified pigs according to their whim, manufactured unhealthy animals that maximize growth and produce monstrous carcasses that are all muscle with almost no fat. They have created hulking beasts that are also sickly, animals that have no life beyond the hundred and eighty-two days spent vegetating in the half-light of a pig unit, with hearts and lungs that beat and oxygenate the blood only to constantly produce more lean meat for consumption.

Joël lifts the barrow and tips the slurry into the pit. Thousands of litres of slurry flow through the drainage system into the tank to be mixed. Joël wipes his sweaty forehead and steps back so as not to inhale the toxic fumes from the black sludge, the gases produced as the slurry decomposes: hydrogen sulphide, ammonia, carbon dioxide, methane.

'You're never to come here unless I'm with you,' Henri told them when mechanical diggers first began excavating the pit behind the brand-new pig shed.

Then, a few weeks later, as slurry began to pour in and fill the tank:

'All it takes is for you to breathe in the fumes, and you could pass out. It attacks the nervous system. Screws you up inside. So you pass out, you fall in, you drown. You sink to the bottom. And I'm not going to fucking empty it to fish you out, so get that through your thick skulls.'

Serge and Joël used to dream – still dream – of drowning, of this pit ready to engulf them, of sinking into the shadowy, all-consuming depths of the slurry, as deadly as the quicksand in adventure stories or the currents around the Bermuda Triangle. They reach out towards the surface they cannot see, their eyes are open but see only thick darkness. They try to scream for help but their mouths and lungs fill with putrid mud and they wake up with a start, clutching the bedsheets, that eternal taste of shit on their tongue.

When he is near the pit, Joël always has a sense of vertigo, a vague feeling that he might jump in, that someone might suddenly appear (but who – Henri? Serge?) and push him in, even when he is alone in the pig units, as he is now, so he takes a step back before lighting a cigarette. Then he once more plunges into the miasma of the pig shed. He sees his black fingers as he brings the cigarette to his lips. He is accustomed to the filth, to the slurry that covers him, spattering his blue coveralls, the skin on his hands, his wrists. As far back as he can remember, he has never felt disgusted by it. He can bury his hands into pig shit, into sows' vaginas, into the ripped bellies of carcasses. This is how Henri brought up the sons, weighing their character and their masculinity by their capacity to endure the suffering of animals, so that such things now provoke nothing in Joël, except perhaps indifference, a numbness that has gradually extended to everything else, an acid steadily eroding his nerve endings.

One of his first memories of Henri is seeing him hurl kittens against the wall of the pig shed and watching the shattered, broken remains fall at his feet on the bare concrete, seeing the haloes left on the brickwork, veering from red to brown to black as the days pass. Dogs and cats are the animals they are most reluctant to kill, but in the world of the farm, females give birth until they are worn out, and it is for the men to decide which of their offspring should survive. Serge tears puppies from their mothers' teats, rips them from kennels, grips their furry bodies in his left hand and, with his right, twists their heads until he hears the soft vertebrae crack and sometimes a brief whimper, then he tosses the remains in the soot-blackened steel barrel in a corner of the farmyard, which sometimes burns and smoulders for days, belching oily smoke, reeking of glowing scrap iron, melted plastic, burnt garbage. When the elder boy was no more than ten years old and Joël barely seven, Henri taught them to slit the throats of piglets. He would press into the childish hands the Laguiole knife he is never without and regularly sharpens on a gun barrel, leaning over

290

the kitchen sink, and close his own hand over theirs. He would lean his chest against their backs, forcing them to arch their necks, rest his chin with its stiff, black beard against the backs of their skulls. He would guide the hand holding the blade, show them how to thrust it into the throat of the hog-tied animal, then slice through the carotid artery:

'You stick the knife in here, cut cleanly, keeping your knee on the pig's shoulder. There, just like that. You just need to find the vein and work with a fluid motion.'

The scarlet blood would spurt onto a hand that was no longer theirs but merely an extension of the knife fused to the father's thick, hairy forearm, the bulging biceps, the dry, merciless palm to which they have no choice but to submit. One day Joël misses the artery and, fearing the father's reaction, plunges the blade twice more into the neck of the pig as it continues to squeal and struggle. Henri grabs his shoulder, pulling him so roughly that the boy ends up on the ground. Lying on the flagstones, the pig twitches and convulses as it bleeds out.

'Take a good look. It's your fault that he's in pain.'

Lying at their feet, the knife spins on its handle like a top. Henri picks it up and finishes off the animal, before bending down to pick up the son, lifting him much higher than is necessary, perhaps to demonstrate that he is weightless, worthless, leaving his bloody handprint on the boy's wrist.

Joël's eyes fill with tears and he cannot choke back a sob.

'Stop that right now or I'll belt you one! That'll give you something to cry about.'

Years later, when Henri happens on Joël standing in front of the bathroom mirror, face covered in shaving cream, he takes the razor from his son's hand and slides the blade over the beardless cheeks and downy shadow of his lower lip. The boy's reflection shoots Henri an anxious look as he lifts the chin with one finger and runs the blade over the throat where the Adam's apple is not yet visible. He rinses the razor in the half-filled washbasin on which float small islands of shaving foam, and says:

'Hey, kid, you know I'd never hurt you, don't you?'

This coldness, this hard-won indifference to the animals, has never quite managed to stifle in Joël a confused loathing that cannot be put into words, the impression – and, as he grew, the conviction – that there is a glitch: one in which pig rearing is at the heart of some much greater disturbance beyond his comprehension, like some machine that is unpredictable, out of kilter, by its nature uncontrollable, whose misaligned cogs are crushing them, spilling out into their lives, beyond their borders; the piggery as the cradle of their barbarism and that of the whole world.

—

Long before the new pig units were built, he had begun to feel a similar loathing for their relationship with the pigs (first Henri's relationship, but quickly their own), and, inextricably, for their oddness as a family, the long-kept silence about Élise's absence, the neglected family tomb with its pots of withered chrysanthemums that is from a bygone era, yet still threatens by the empty space waiting to be filled by the body of the father, who has already had his name engraved (1921–) next to that of his late wife, or the bodies of the sons Henri might one

292

day have to fish from the slurry pit should they happen to drown in it.

Before the two boys were sent to school and became aware of other kinds of childhood, they were unable to judge the peculiarity, the strangeness of their family. For almost twenty years, until Catherine arrived, Henri refused to buy a television. The world reached them only through the crackling of the transistor radio he turned on from time to time, glimpsed in the headlines in the window of the newsagents, distant, unreal and hostile.

Please fill out the form. Father's first name, surname, occupation. Mother's first name, surname, occupation.

Their relationship to Éléonore has long been shrouded in mystery. She was a mother to them, but she was also Henri's mother, working in the shadow of her son without managing to compensate for his power and authority by the brusque, awkward affection she felt for them. As children, the brothers never questioned the father's solitude, nor the presence of the portrait with the hazel tree on his nightstand, until one day Henri surprised Serge sitting on the edge of his bed, staring down at the photograph.

'That's her. That's your mother.'

Serge jumped to his feet so quickly that the picture slipped from his hands and fell on the wooden floor. He looks up towards the father, whose bulk completely fills the doorframe. Henri moves towards the bed, bends down to pick up the frame, then sits on the mattress and pats the sheet next to him.

'Come over here.'

Together, they gaze at the little photograph. Henri points to the boy in shorts running behind the bench.

'See there, that's you... And that's her. Maybe you remember her. She died giving birth to your brother.

I'm just telling you this so that you know, you shouldn't blame him. Joël, I mean. These things happen, kid. That's life; a huge tank of shit constantly being poured on your head. Might as well get used to it. If the day comes when you have to blame someone for something, blame me, no-one else. Got it?'

From his hoarse, strangled voice Serge can tell how painful it is for him to speak. He nods shyly.

'Now get out of this room. And don't let me catch you in here again.'

Later, the two brothers are walking through the countryside, collecting large branches to build a hut in the shape of a tepee, where they could shelter during a downpour. Serge spits on the ground, then stirs the foamy little gob of spittle with a twig.

'You know, we used to have a mum, but you killed her. She's the lady in the photograph. She died because of you, giving birth to you.'

'You're lying!' Joël says uncertainly.

'Am not! I'm not lying. You just ask him. He's the one that told me. I think that's why he doesn't love you as much. Can't blame him... I wish you were dead and she was still alive too.'

The brothers sit in silence until the cleansed sky clears again, illuminating the landscape with glistening light.

'C'mon,' Serge says, grabbing Joël by the hand. 'I'll show you!'

They wait until Henri leaves the farmhouse, then Serge leads his brother upstairs, pressing a finger to his lips. They tiptoe into the bedroom so as not to be heard by Éléonore, and go over to the wardrobe containing the relics of the mother. When they open the doors, a few

294

chalky clothes moths flutter into the room, wafting the smell of the mildewed dresses suspended on their hangers. The boys are dumbstruck by the sight of these pitiful shrouds. To the right of the wardrobe, on the top shelf, Serge picks up a dead butterfly that instantly crumbles to dust between his fingers.

'See?' he says, turning to his brother.

On a different afternoon, some ten years after Joël's birth, while rummaging in the attic, the two boys find a rectangular cherrywood box, simple, with no gilding, no carved arabesques, not even a tarnished silver latch to keep it shut. A commonplace box to hide a commonplace treasure.

They are sitting cross-legged in the dust and the sunbeams that slip between the roof tiles. Serge opens the box to reveal a garnet velvet pad, on which lie two gold rings, both slightly bent, one set with a small gemstone, a bracelet with a broken clasp and three pairs of earrings. Laid on top of them, carefully coiled, is a long tress of silken hair, which the brothers stare at for a long time, daring to pick it up and bring it to their faces. In the half-light of the attic, the lock of hair seems almost luminous, faded by time, by darkness and oblivion, even whiter than Éléonore's hair has been for a long time now.

As soon as Élise died, Henri began to neglect the grave; he has never gone to lay flowers there, has never taken his sons. From this day, however, the boys, who have always been aware of the family grave and careful to keep their distance, begin to weed the grave, uproot the woody plants surrounding the headstone, scrape away the lichen that has had long years to conquer the memorial. They never speak of this with Henri, just as they have never spoken of the dresses in the wardrobe, or the simple jewellery box.

In the years they spent behind their desks at the local primary school, it was not uncommon for Henri, on the pretext of running into the village, to come and spy on them in the playground, standing motionless, his fingers hooked through the chain-link fence.

'Friends will never be any use to you, family are the only people you can count on.'

Since their earliest childhood, he has always been open about his mistrust of the world. Being a misanthrope, he shuns all ideology, and has nothing but contempt for political causes, ideas, thoughts. He has always been as sceptical of state education as he has of popular education, of the very notions of education and socialization. He believes in nothing except in himself and in the value of work. Yet he did not care about the sons' academic successes, believing such things to be the prerogative of a woman, a mother, that to be able to read, write and count was more than sufficient. And so, when the sons turned sixteen, he took them out of school so they could devote themselves full-time to working on the farm.

'At least here, as long as you pull your weight, you're your own boss, you can take pride in a job well done, and you're not greasing someone else's palm. And besides, we're a family. A clan.'

—

One morning in July, having left Joël in the pig shed, while Henri is off surveying the Plains, as they call the lands they farm, Serge goes back to the house, takes off his shoes and goes into the kitchen. He opens a cupboard, grabs the bottle of Johnnie Walker, opens it and takes

296

a long swig before taking out his hipflask and filling it over the sink. A drop trickles over the edge; he laps it up and is putting the whisky bottle back in the cupboard just as Gabrielle comes into the room. He can immediately sense her hostile presence, fraught with fear and with reproach as he washes his hands in the sink.

'Are you not going to ask me how she is?'

Serge turns his back and scrubs his nails with an old toothbrush. Grey soapy water swirls at the bottom of the sink and disappears down the drain. He does not respond to his sister-in-law's question and, for a moment, she is silent. Serge turns off the tap, grabs a dishcloth and meticulously wipes his hands.

'She's going to need to be hospitalized again,' Gabrielle says.

'You know what I think about that. You know what she thinks.'

'She's in no fit state to think anything. I have to drag her out of bed, she's completely stupefied by all the pills she takes.'

Serge sets down the dishtowel and turns to his sister-in-law. He can feel the alcohol warming his throat, his stomach. Gabrielle nervously grabs a packet of ground coffee and sets about preparing a cafetière.

'I thought things were clear, Gaby. When the twins' father pissed off and you came to live here, it was on condition that you take care of her and look after the children. That was the deal, and it suited everyone, you most of all. I'm not feeding and putting a roof over your head out of the goodness of my heart. I've got enough on my plate with the pig units. I thought we agreed.'

'I don't depend on you, and neither do my sons. I make money with my cleaning jobs.'

'Just don't take me for a fool, that's all I ask. Cathy is

not going back into hospital.'

'She needs to see somebody...'

'She already sees a doctor, for God's sake! If you don't want to take care of her, fine, we'll manage without you, but in that case, you take your belongings, you take your sons, and you fuck off.'

Gabrielle is speechless, pale and trembling. The tea-spoon clinks against the side of the cafetière and the ground coffee spills onto the countertop. She is afraid of him, he knows that. She sweeps the coffee into her palm and he looks at her pale profile. Sometimes she reminds him of Catherine before she fell ill, the young Catherine, sensual and wild. Serge steps forward and lays his hands on Gabrielle's shoulders, presses his chest against her back. She quivers, suddenly short of breath. He says:

'Look, don't worry so much. You know what these breakdowns are like; she'll come through this one like she came through all the others. All we can do is wait, and do our best. We all need to pull together.'

Serge closes his eyes, buries his face in the nape of his sister-in-law's neck and inhales, hoping to smell Catherine, not as she is today, a sickly, medicinal smell, but the Catherine of old, fragrant and intoxicating. He slides his hands down her arms, cups her bosom, press-ing his palms against her breasts.

With a quick twist of her shoulder, Gabrielle extri-cates herself, then steps around the table so that it is now between them.

'You reek of booze... If she could see you...'

'So what? You think she was some sort of saint, do you?'

'Shut up, please. Just shut up.'

He can see the disgust in her face; the same disgust he inspires in Catherine. He nods, feeling a wave of anger wash over him, and he leaves the house as quickly as he can.

Serge walks towards the gates, opens the padlock and tugs at the chain, then, feeling the chain resist, lashes out with a violent kick. He walks along the dirt road, turns onto the main road, past rolling fields in the midst of which are clacking irrigation sprinklers that look like fantastical prehistoric beasts. From here, the only part of the piggery visible is the sudden flash of a grey concrete building that seems bogged down in the earth, pierced by narrow windows like arrow slits, which let in only a faint murky glow since they are partially obstructed by the overhang of the roof, and caked in dust and grease. The muscles in Serge's jaw spasm convulsively. His heartbeat propels the rage secreted by some hidden, sovereign gland, constricting his throat, and courses, quivering, through his elbows and his fingers.

He stops for a moment, opens the hipflask and drinks eagerly. He slaps himself in the face, then hits himself again, this time with a closed fist. He mumbles aloud, fragments of sentences. Perched on high-voltage cables, silent magpies watch as he passes. A solitary buzzard glides over the crop fields, its shadow skimming them like a caress. Soon, the Plains appear in shimmering heat haze, vast expanses of ripe wheat, fragrant and copper-coloured, and maize, pale green with silken inflorescences. From the distance comes the rumble of a combine harvester. A cloud of yellow dust drifts across their fields. In a few days, they too will have to bring in the harvest, and ensilage the grain.

Serge thinks of Catherine. The children are now the only bond between them. Julie-Marie, the little girl who once adored him, now a diaphanous, elusive teenager;

and Jérôme, whom it has taken him time to learn to love as a son, although, despite his best efforts, the boy still stirs in him the same feeling of shame as when he is suddenly conscious of the stench of the pigs, a feeling he has been battling with for more than ten years.

If given the opportunity, Jérôme seeks out the company of animals rather than that of the father. He trails after him, watching his movements, leaning over the stalls to pat the flanks and the snouts of the pigs, immured in his permanent silence. When he is alone with the boy, Serge feels no awkwardness, no embarrassment. He enjoys the furtive presence of the boy, who is attentive to the work they are doing together. He is not troubled by his silence, in fact he sees it as respectable, as an act of resistance, of defiance. The doctors they took him to see in the early years never diagnosed any physical disability, any deformity that might explain his aphasia, and eventually ascribed the boy's mutism to a form of autism. After four years of preschool classes at Puy-Larroque Municipal School, faced with the teachers' helplessness and Jérôme's increased distress, Serge and Catherine, on Henri's advice, decided to take him out of school. Since then, the boy has grown up in a parallel dimension to theirs, joining their reality only now and then.

He is touched by his son's strangeness, the manner he has of baulking at orders, of only accepting suggestions. Serge will hold out a bucket of grain for him to pour into the feed trough, and Jérôme will look at the father's face, at the proffered bucket, and may take it or may turn away. He is the only one never to tremble in front of him, never to submit to his authority, or even the supreme authority of Henri, but to meet it with unvarying apathy. When Serge and Jérôme are alone in the pig shed together, the father feels as though he has rediscovered the original link that bound him to the child as a babe in arms. But such moments are rare and, despite himself, whenever Henri is in the vicinity, Serge feels the unspeakable prickle of shame, which destroys the complicity he believed he had established with the boy. He is suddenly impatient again, his tone curt, he imagines and anticipates Henri's irritation, the shadow that looms over them by virtue of his mere presence, one that the brothers have learned to fear, to forestall, to avoid; suddenly he finds him bombarding Jérôme with reprimands, with unnecessary warnings, *don't touch that, shift your arse, move out of there, get out of my way*, and finally shoos him away, not so much to be rid of the boy as to appease the imagined irritation of the patriarch.

Henri shows no consideration, no affection for his grandson, any more than he shows any empathy for Catherine. To him, illness of whatever kind is a weakness, an indulgence, and Jérôme's strangeness is a defect. Though he does not openly accuse his daughter-in-law of conspiring against them, does not criticize his son's decision to let his wife shut herself away behind a bedroom door she has long since closed to him, forcing him to sleep on the sofa, his silence says much about his contempt, his disapproval and his determination to singlehandedly keep up the struggle to manage the farm.

When I think I've spent my whole fucking life slaving away, bleeding myself white for that ungrateful shower of brats.

Serge would like to tell the father that he does not give a damn about his opinion, that he has no right to criticize Catherine, Jérôme, his choices or Joël's, but he says nothing; even if he dared challenge the patriarch's authority, he would be lying, since nothing matters more to him than the father's approval, since he would not know how to free himself from the yoke that he and the sweat streaming down his neck. He follows the father as he moves between the furrows. Henri lifts an uprooted ear of maize, then crouches down and lays his broad ruddy hands, his fingers splayed, on the warm, damp earth next to a hoof-print.

'It's him,' he says again, his voice tremulous, and he gets to his feet.

When Henri turns, Serge can see excitement spread over his sombre face, one pupil curiously dilated.

'He can't be far. Take a couple of dogs with you and go let your brother know what's going on.'

'Are you sure you're alright?' Serge says.

'What the fuck kind of question is that?' Henri says, spitting out the cigarette stub dangling from the corner of his mouth and wiping his face with his hand. 'I'm fine, it's just this bloody heat... Now shift your arse, we've no time to waste. I'll catch you up.'

Behind the pig units, Joël stubs his cigarette out in one of the sand-filled barrels that serve as ashtrays. Despite the ventilation system, the heat inside the pig shed is already unbearable. He drinks from the standpipe and ducks his head and face under the water before going back inside to clean the stalls.

Occasionally Joël wonders whether it was the piggery that made monsters of them, or their monstrousness that infected the farm. Joël has never really liked the pork they have eaten all their lives, more for the sake of thrift than for the taste; the pork that fills their freezers to overflowing – *you're not leaving this table until you clean your plate, here, let me give you another ladleful, you need to eat if you want to grow up to be a man, rather than the weedy runt you are now* – whereas Serge has always made it a point of honour to wolf it down, licking his plate, gnawing on the bones, sopping up the gravy and asking for second helpings just to please their father. This is probably the moment in their childhood when their difference was established: the determination of one son to consume the flesh of the pigs, to literally conflate their existence and that of the piggery, and the reluctance of the other son, that primal, visceral revulsion at the idea of being merely a masticating cogwheel, accepting the flesh tipped by the pig units into their proud, grateful, sated, gaping mouths, then chewing, digesting, shitting that flesh so it can once more fertilize the lush meadows of the Plains (with the sludge carefully transformed by the local sewage treatment plant, mixed with the slurry from the animals, contaminated by the products they feed to them, inject into them, and which they ingest with the meat) to serve as fertilizer for the grain they grow to provide fodder for the pigs, thereby creating a virtuous or a vicious circle in which shit and meat can no

306

longer be dissociated.

Joël pushes the wheelbarrow in the farrowing house, where the nursing sows lie on slatted floors, held in place by straps, restraints and steel bars. Squealing piglets press against their teats or doze piled up on each other, shivering in a corner of the stall. Although the sows are isolated to prevent them crushing their litters, it is also to save space, since large, roomy stalls would be needed for them to safely suckle their litters. The nursing sows form lines of flesh, red from the glow of the heat lamps, crushed by the steel bars, unable to turn over, reduced to merely standing up and lying down to offer their teats to the piglets, to eating, defecating and sleeping.

What do they dream of? Fluorescent lights, scalpels, sticks beating, voices shouting?

Joël sets to cleaning the walkways, scraping the shit away with the blade of the shovel, loading it into the barrow, scrubbing the concrete with a brush, but his movements are automatic, he is no longer in the barn, he is riding his Caballero TX 96 through the countryside, leaving the farm far behind. The tattered late-afternoon sky blazes and creates large bright enclaves in the valleys. Joël has his helmet hooked over the crook of his elbow, and as he cleaves the air, it draws tears from his eyes and drags them across his temples. Small insects get caught in his thick red beard. He feels the thrill, the fear gripping his belly, making his mouth water, Under the denim of his jeans, his testicles are cramped, almost painful, crushed against the leather of the seat, ready to retract into his abdomen, as they do when he castrates piglets – *you make a quick incision with the scalpel, two to three centimetres, no more, you squeeze the testicle out and grab it, keep your finger hooked, yeah, like that, you hook the testicular cord and pull it out* – feeling that dread course through his body that the blade might slip, fall from his hand and plant itself in his own balls.

Then you cut the cord, and do the same with the other testicle.

He no longer knows whether he is predator or prey, he can no longer distinguish between the fear and the excitement which meld into a single feeling that numbs his mind and leaves him panting for breath, his heart hammering, just as the boars pant for breath, their hearts hammering when they are led into the sows' pen to see which ones are in heat, snuffling at the vulvas of the sows, forcing their snouts inside, biting their croups (meanwhile, the men palpate the sows, assess the colour of the vulva, checking it against the sort of swatch card you might use to pick out wallpaper, then lean all their weight on the sows to ensure they remain still, ready to be serviced), then, when the boar mounts them, in a stall or in the walkway, Joël, Henri and Serge heave the male onto the sow's huge body, half-lying across her back so they can reach out one hand and grab the already ejaculating penis and guide it into the sow, as though it is they who are coupling with the animal instead of the boar, at the same time as – *there's nothing more disgusting than mating, soon we'll be able to shove a syringe full of cum into them and there'll be no need to get it all over our fingers* – the boar, and the stench, the nauseating smell of the mating animals, clings onto their hands long after they have been soaped and scrubbed, that smell of animal sexual organs they come to think might be their own, their own pricks thrusting into the warm, hairy, shit-smeared flesh, the acrid smell of spilled secretions...

It is a thought that flares from time to time, one that Joël dispels, sickened, as the rolling ribbon of motorway and the green-grey ditches seem to dissolve as he speeds by. He dutifully carries on filling the barrow in the farrowing house. Because he is not riding his Caballero, he cannot feel the rain on his face, the tears being dragged across his temples, the tingle of excitement and fear that sometimes makes his hands shake. He is in one of the pig units, surrounded by livestock, scraping shit from concrete, and it does not matter that he would rather be anywhere but here. It is to the pig shed that he belongs, not to the strangers who lay their hands on him behind bus shelters graffitied with illiterate tags and with terrible, heartbreaking poetry, or in the toilets of motorway service stations, it is to the pigs that he comes home, to their pale skin, to their eyes faded from the half-light.

They look like huge troglodytes, like gigantic, hairless moles moving through the silt at the bottom of a cave. Sows give birth three months, three weeks and three days after the mounting which has been carefully noted in the breeding record (date – sire # – dam # – number of services: one, two, three, four, five, six – total of live births, stillbirths), then, as soon as the piglets have been expelled from the womb, the men take away the placentas so that flies cannot lay their eggs, so germs cannot breed that might contaminate the livestock. The extreme prolificacy of sows achieved by careful selection and crossbreeding also produces 'parchment' or mummified foetuses. Having died in utero, they become desiccated and hard and are born fibrous as scraps of leather. At farrowing time, the men lubricate their forearms and insert them into the sow's vulva and rummage around to make sure that a dead piglet is not obstructing the birth canal. Then there are the 'false stillbirths', the piglets that do not 'meet required standards', which they dispatch, wringing their necks or smashing them against

309

the concrete floor because they are sickly or deformed.

In two seconds the whole place can be crawling with worms, it's a breeding ground for infections, you need to keep in mind that any slippage in hygiene standards has an immediate impact on productivity.

Henri has talked to them until they are sick and tired of hearing about hygiene, sanitation, fear and disease, about the countless looming epidemics whose shadow hangs over the livestock like the sword of Damocles, about the microbes and the bacteria ready to fall upon them like the plagues of Egypt...

Of course, they will never succeed in making the pig shed – *it's a fucking biosphere, a self-contained ecosystem, the slightest thing could screw it up* – a sterile environment, but they need to keep it below an invisible threshold that can only be measured by the fertility of the sows.

What would the father say if he knew that Joël goes out roaming the countryside in search of men, their caresses, their unfamiliar breath, their familiar pricks, not caring whether the sunset is dismal or blazing, beneath steel-grey skies, and always after a day's work, trying to purge himself of this desire to which the father has denied him the right, to shake off some of the apathy that pig rearing creates in him, to feel alive, if only for a brief, hollow moment? What would the father say if he could see Joël wandering amid the nervous, predatory shadows of strangers watching, sizing each other up, groping each other in the stench of public toilets?

Would he feel disgust? Would he, like his son, feel fear coursing through every fibre of his being? Would he feel an excitement unfamiliar to him? Would he warn Joël about viruses, as he does about the countless viruses that threaten the farrowing house? Would he worry that the 'urogenital region' of his youngest child might also be tainted by some germ, some venereal disease, some purulent pox, or would he simply disown him, walk him to the farm gates, to the boundary of their lands on the Plains, and warn him never again to step across that line? The constant dread of hearing the contempt in the father's voice, of feeling like a little boy who has shat his trousers, the constant humiliation of being relegated to the position of a son, an illegitimate son; never the feeling that Henri is speaking to him man to man...

Three months, three weeks and three days.

The sows farrow, and their litters are left with them for thirty days before being taken away to be weaned.

Nine piglets per sow and per litter, and at least two point five litters a year, that's what you need for the farm to be profitable. You wait and see, in ten, fifteen years, sows will be averaging fifteen piglets a litter.

The female is moved to a pen with a group of unfamiliar sows. Food and water are reduced and they are fed only erratically in order to exacerbate the anxiety caused by being separated from their litters and confined in the pen. The bewildered sows strive to create a hierarchy. They fight, they jostle and bite each other. Their flanks and rumps are quickly covered with wounds, bruises and scratches. Eventually, their stress levels rise so much that it triggers a rush of hormones, putting them prematurely in heat again. The men then lead them back to be serviced, then to gestation and the farrowing house, a cycle that is repeated five or six times before they are sent to the slaughterhouse, or to the knacker's yard in the case of those that are drained by successive litters, those suffering from oedema, purulent mastitis, prolapse, or those that have broken a leg between the bars of their stall.

—

Serge climbs into the Lada Niva, keys the ignition and reverses the car towards the pig shed, weaving between the rusty skeletons of cars and the boneless engines, the washing machines with wonky drums, the children's bicycles buried under weeds and the rotting wheelbarrows. The dogs bound when they see the four-wheel drive approaching. Serge fumbles in his pockets for his hipflask, throws his head back to drain the dregs, then tosses it on the passenger seat.

He is thinking about the Plains, the hoof-print in the dirt, although he can no longer picture it, he can remember only the father's hand laid flat on the soil, that broad hand with those long, blackened nails, as though the father is determined to keep some crumbs of nourishing earth with him at all times, some proof of his labours as a reminder to the sons – *when I think of all the sacrifices...* – that same hand, with its stubby fingers, its fleshy, grey knuckles, its liver spots, that completely enveloped their own hands, as children, when he was training them at farm work.

Take a good look. It's your fault that he's in pain.

And yet, did he not pass on to them everything necessary for a man's honour, for his survival: courage, strength of character, determination, discipline? Obviously, he was not always fair, but what parent is, what father, what mother, what adult could possibly embody justice to a child and never fail? Serge himself has failed. Serge has variously proved himself cowardly, inconsistent, dishonest and shameful towards Julie-Marie, towards Jérôme; what right, then, has he to blame Henri (but is this not what he is doing right now, focusing his memory on Henri's failings, on the most appalling

312

moments, *Stop that right now or I'll belt you one! That'll give you something to cry about*, as though there was nothing else worth remembering?), and what right has he to criticize Henri for failing to live up to the expectations that he put on a father condemned to loneliness, to raising his sons single-handed?

Can he even be truly sure that he ever experienced that moment outside the old pigsty? Is he absolutely convinced that he saw Joël trembling under the father's threats, his eyes welling with tears, his hand smeared with the blood of a piglet the father had forced him to slaughter? What evidence is there today that might constitute irrefutable proof that this incident ever took place, or any other incident for that matter, other than these memories, scattered, fragile, ready to shatter and doubtless distorted by time? There is no proof that he experienced any of these things. He should draw a line under his childhood, wipe it off the map, and yet here it is re-entering the fray, determined to do battle, reappearing when he least expects it, like the Beast on the Plains...

Serge gets out of the car, slams the door, goes around to the back of the Lada and opens the boot. He goes over to the kennel and inspects the dogs, chooses two, herds them into the back of the four-by-four, and leaves the boot open. He is crossing the yard towards the farmhouse when Julie-Marie steps out onto the porch. She no longer wears a bra under her white T-shirt and the slight sway of her breasts is visible through the neckline.

'Where are you off to?' Serge says spitefully.

'Just going for a walk...'

'At this hour of the morning? What's with this new

obsession of yours for spending the whole day wandering around?'

'There's nothing for me to do here...'

'What d'you mean, nothing for you to do? Have you been in to take care of your mother?'

An exasperated expression flickers over her face. Serge is a mean drunk, easily riled, and he knows it, but for some time now Julie-Marie has been treating him with a barely disguised hostility that he cannot simply put down to adolescence. She used to be a secretive, melancholy child, but she constantly showed her affection, mingled with fear and adulation. Is this rebuke he now sees in her dark eyes, under which there is a shadow of eyeliner she has failed to remove?

Should he let her know that he is not duped by her deviousness, rather than allowing her to accuse him, even tacitly, of being to blame for Catherine's illness, or at least of being unable to help her, of unloading the burden of care onto her or Gabrielle, of having fallen into disgrace, of having been banished by his wife – rightly or wrongly – and of meekly accepting his banishment without protest? Perhaps Gaby has turned his daughter against him, accused him behind his back of letting Catherine waste away and refusing to let her go to hospital for fear she might escape him, or because he is trying to control all of them?

He sometimes thinks about telling Julie-Marie about the clinic where her mother languished, slumped in a chair, surrounded by headcases, lunatics, pariahs, the sort of people who never recover, about how he had to take her out of there, how Catherine herself begged him; about her pitiful hand gripping his arm, her pained, strangely serious voice, the flecks of spittle at the corners of her mouth, the plastic bracelet marked with her

314

name and patient number, like a body in a morgue, or the identity tag of a stray dog.

'How do you think she's doing at the moment?' he asks.

'I dunno... same as always... not any better, I mean.'

'Oh,' Serge says. 'Try not to worry too much. You know how these things go... I'm sure she'll get better soon.'

She turns her face away when he speaks and Serge realizes she is avoiding the stink of alcohol on his breath, just as she avoids his eyes, staring fixedly at the patch of ground under her feet, digging at the dusty yard with the tip of her battered flip-flops. In that moment, he is devastated by the knowledge of his failure, his utter futility. Julie-Marie is being torn from him by some higher force, carried so far, so fast into the space that lies between them, those few scant metres that expand to become an infinity, the farmyard as an expanding universe, carrying her away without giving him the time to do something to hold her back. She briefly looks up to him as a petition for him to let her go now.

'Okay, well,' Serge stammers, 'be careful... I don't like... I don't like to think of you wandering around...'

Julie-Marie immediately walks away, a little too quickly, and he sees her reach the gates before he steps into the house. He goes into the kitchen and quickly takes down the whisky bottle, also empty, tosses it into the sink, thumps the countertop and swears. He searches the other cupboards, pushing aside the bottles of cooking oil and vinegar, the cartons of UHT milk, until he finds a bottle of pastis. He has never seen his father touch a drop of alcohol, on the pretext that his own father, a complete bastard, apparently, was handy with his fists... Something to do with terrible war wounds, from what

Serge understands, though Henri and Éléonore have always avoided the subject, and said little about their shared past, their history, as though to say anything was to twist the knife in the gaping wound of their memory. Serge grabs a glass, pours pastis until it is three-quarters full, barely diluting it with a trickle of water from the kitchen tap, then downs it in one gulp. He stares through the window for a moment at the farmyard, white-hot in the blistering sun. He listens to the silence of the house, senses the spectral presence of Catherine upstairs. Is she asleep? Is she too watching his every movement? Did she hear the words he and Julie-Marie exchanged on the threshold? Surely he should at least try knocking on her door, try to get her to talk to him, to acknowledge his existence? Like this house, their marriage – if they ever truly had one – is a ruin. And yet Serge has borne it all: the outbursts, the complaints, the unfounded accusations, the petty tricks, even the unforgiveable betrayals. A sudden creak on the stairs makes him turn sharply. One hand on the banister, Jérôme is standing at the foot of the stairs, watching him. Neither father nor son move an inch. Jérôme and his unbearable stare, his smooth, pale face, framed by a shock of hair as red as wildfire, Jérôme and his deafening silence. How Serge wishes he could have spared him all this... He stumbles towards his son, his steps lumbering and uncertain, he seems about to say something, then sighs, turns away and plunges back into the sweltering farmyard.

—

Joël is checking the pens of the gestating females when, in the midst of a group, he notices the remains of misshapen piglets on the floor and the sows snuffling them anxiously. It sometimes happens that a gilt will miscarry, as a reaction to stress or to a particular vaccine. In such circumstances, the men are told to remove the bodies and write up the incident. But in sows that have farrowed before, like the ones Joël is inspecting, miscarriage is a rare occurrence.

A sow miscarrying is a symptom of a dysfunction, a cog in the system gone awry, there's always a reason, you've just got to know where to look.

Joël shoots back the bolt and steps into the pen. The pigs scurry towards the far railing, leaving one sow that struggles to its feet, then goes over to blend into the herd. A purulent whitish discharge trickles from her vulva, down her hocks, forming a pool on the concrete floor in which the aborted foetuses lie, small sacs of pink, blood-smeared skin with undeveloped limbs, some still encased in the placenta like – *half-hard dicks in latex condoms* – formless things, neither human nor animal.

With his bare hands, Joël picks up the piglets, their bones still soft, as limp and warm as entrails, tosses them into the bucket and leaves the pen. In the next stall, the sows also seem anxious: they can probably sense that one of their number has miscarried.

He is thinking: what if Henri did banish him from the farm, from the family, wouldn't that be the best possible outcome, a deliverance? Has he not spent all these years doing everything in his power to show his father he has no interest in pig rearing? Not that he did so deliberately... he simply could do nothing else. The moment he sets out for the pig units, he is overwhelmed by a wave of apathy. Perhaps the father's contempt for him is merited; Joël has never proved himself to be good at anything and would never have been able to make a life for himself beyond his supervision.

317

Joël moves to the third pen and pulls back the bolt. Here, too, a sow has lost a litter. He retraces his steps, takes a notebook from his coat pocket and jots down the numbers of the pens and the number of dead piglets, seven in the first stall, nine in the last. He fetches a thermometer from the medicine chest and a handful of cotton wool he soaks in rubbing alcohol. He finds the sow in the first pen, isolates her, using a restraint board to press her against one wall, and slides the thermometer into the animal's rectum. To calm her, he whispers to her in a gentle voice, but she seems resigned, and makes no attempt to struggle as he pushes the restraint board against her flank.

Her temperature is 38.5°C. Normal for a pig. He grabs the sow's ear and checks again, then sterilizes the thermometer and goes to the third pen.

As Serge enters the pig shed, Joël is just picking up the last foetus.

'The old man sent me to get you,' the elder son says.

Joël closes the stall behind him and sets the bucket down at his feet.

'What the fuck happened?' Serge asks, looking at the miscarried foetuses.

'I don't know...' Joël says, wiping his forehead with his sleeve. 'Two sows have miscarried. One of the gilts in the first pen, and a sow on her second farrowing in the third pen.'

'Are they running a temperature?'

'No, I checked both.'

'In that case, it must be a coincidence.'

'We have to tell him, though, don't we?'

'Absolutely not, not right now. I don't think it's anything serious,' Serge says, staring at the bucket. 'One of the crop fields on the Plains has been destroyed.'

318

'What are you talking about?'

'It's been ploughed up. Looks like it's been trampled by a fucking herd of wild boar. We found a hoof-print. It could be the Beast. At least the old man seems pretty convinced.'

'You're shitting me?'

'I came back to fetch a couple of dogs. He wants you to come with us.'

'And what am I supposed to do with this?' Joël says, lifting up the bucket.

The sows snuffle the puddle of amniotic fluid, and the pile of pink flesh in the bucket.

'Burn the lot and keep your fucking mouth shut. This is really not the time, take my word for it... We're heading off in twenty minutes. Go get ready.'

They will say nothing to Henri. Why give him another reason to worry? It is not as though an epidemic is going to decimate the herd in the next couple of hours... For a while now – a few weeks? months? – the father has not simply been volatile in a way Serge has learned to anticipate, as he might the outbursts of an old, cantankerous animal. He has been much more unpredictable, so the reappearance of the Beast – assuming it is real – is not a good thing. How is it possible that the damn animal could prowl around the farm unnoticed for months? Serge would have sworn the Beast was gone for good, that they would never find it.

After the boar escaped, Serge and Joël meekly carried out Henri's orders, made the rounds of the farm, lighting their way with flashlights, a dog running on ahead, never for a moment believing they would encounter the Beast. Serge cannot say that this animal is possessed of intelligence – the very thought that pigs possess anything more than instinct is something he finds repugnant – but to be able to elude the packs of hounds, the hunters, the pilgrims walking the route to Santiago de Compostela to say nothing of the locals, at the very least the animal must have solid instincts... Maybe they have been too hasty in coming to their conclusions. Surely Serge should have studied the hoof-prints more carefully, instead of allowing himself to be swayed by the father's assertion? Yes, he had seen the track mark in the soil, but it had been Henri's hand, that terrible, obdurate hand, that had held his gaze far more than the hoof-print. And what did it really prove, in any case? A track mark in a patch of sodden earth, one that might seem bigger, broader because a foot slipped. It has been barely half an hour since he saw the damage to the field, and what proof has he that the print they saw is that of a farm-reared pig, a Large White, and not simply that of a fair-sized wild boar? Serge has seen wild boar that would almost tip the scales at two hundred kilos. Henri is claiming that all the damage was caused by a single animal, but they did not take the time to check for other hoof-prints.

But no, Serge had immediately nodded, as always, accepted the father's sacred pronouncement and rushed back to the farm to pile a couple of dogs into the pick-up, without taking a moment to consider the situation, without even walking to the edge of the Plains looking for other track marks, for damage or animal droppings. He had meekly followed the father as he marched, like a man possessed, his boots sinking into the soft, cold mud, 'It's him,' picked up a clod of earth, 'It's him,' pointed to a freshly dug hole, excitedly saying over and over:

'It's him!'

—

By the time Henri arrives in the farmyard, the dogs have been loaded into the back of the pickup and are lying on an old blanket, panting. There is no sign of Serge. He has probably gone looking for his brother in the pig units. The other hounds, eager to be part of the hunt, are yapping, and leaping up at the chain-link fence of the kennel.

'Down!' Henri roars, and the dogs scurry away as he strides off.

He too can feel the excitement that has stirred up the hounds. The adrenaline coursing through his veins. Unless perhaps this is another symptom of his illness? It hardly matters, at least it allays the terrible dread that now wakes him in the night, has him whispering, 'I don't want to die I don't want to die I don't want to die,' because in a dream he could feel something swoop on him, something too dark to be a shadow, perhaps a bird of prey come to perch on his shoulder, a vulture come to tear him to pieces, or the thing that lurks behind closed doors in every nightmare, a thing so fearful, so terrifying, we do not want to find out what it is...

At other times, the knowledge of his own mortality leaves him indifferent. When he stands on the border of the Plains at five o'clock in the morning, and night yields to day, it does not pale, but founders, cracks like a piece of royal blue enamel, behind which swell the veins of clouds the colour of wild roses; at such moments, death seems less fearsome, as though it simply means becoming one with this forever, the versicolour lands, the light pouring out to form great, hot pools, the timorous song of the birds, the warm breeze scented with the smell of the fields.

If only it would appear here, now, cut me down with its scythe, I would crumple to my knees, fall to one side or face down into the dirt, and all would be well.

But in the silence and solitude of night, when everything is blue, ominous and cold, when the shadows of spectres move in the darkness, nothing seems to him more terrifying than dying. Or is it simply the prospect of the suffering, the agony, that is to come? The thought of shitting himself, desperately clutching the rails of a hospital bed, just like a cull sow, like one of the half-dead beasts they have to dispatch with a captive bolt gun? The thought of having to have his arse wiped by his own sons, of being fitted with an incontinence pad by some compassionate nurse practitioner? Because obviously they would force him to accept treatment, would suddenly see him as an old man, a dying man on whom they have a duty to lavish their care, their compassion, would take over decisions as to what is best for him. *Better to die like a dog.* Better to load a cartridge into the breech, put the barrel into his mouth and get it over with.

But he lacks the courage. This man who has spent his whole life striving to appear proud and strong in the eyes of his kith and kin lacks the courage... He is paralyzed by fear. The fear of a lonely, frail, vulnerable child. The same fear that would grip him when his own father, drunk and mad with grief, would come home and wreck the living room, forcing him to cower in a corner in Éléonore's arms, convinced that his father would one day kill them in a fit of fury. And he finds his fear all the more humiliating because Élise died right before his eyes, without a whimper, without a protest, not even clutching at the sheet to try to cling to this world, as though, in the end, dying were merely a detail, a minor formality, but one that did not require an ounce of courage from her, while he tosses and turns in the night, choking and groaning, unable to breathe, leaps out of bed like a jack-in-the-box, hurtles down the stairs and goes out into the farmyard, barefoot and dressed only in pyjamas. He stands there, trying to catch his breath, grunting like a worn-out animal, like a boar being herded into the ab-attoir truck. Not knowing where to go, he runs towards the pig shed, thumping his chest, stepping in the muddy puddles, staining his pyjama bottoms. In his mind, he sees his father's remains as they were, laid out in a wood-en coffin over which he leans, the face carefully draped in an immaculate white sheet; he remembers extending his hand to stroke the cheek through the fabric, then balling it into a fist and, angrily, viciously, bringing it down on the stiff chest; he remembers the body echoing hollowly, like a tribal drum beating a funeral march. Is it not the same grave, hollow sound he hears when he thumps his own chest? In the moonlight, he looks like a disarticulated puppet, like a lunatic escaped from an asylum, like a man already dead, a cursed soul vainly, blindly groping its way through limbo, on the banks of the river Styx, constantly colliding with shadows.

True, there are moments when the thought of dying seems bearable, even comforting, but only for a fleeting instant, before he resumes his bargaining with Death, addressing him as a confidant, an old and fearsome friend with whom he has spent his whole life coming to terms and whom he now asks to take him a little later, when he has had a chance to talk to the sons, when he has had time to settle the matter of his estate – of course he will include Joël, though he needs to make sure that the sons will not tear each other apart, destroy his life's work – when the harvest has been gathered in... When they have brought the Beast back to the boar pen.

This, now, seems more important to him than anything else. The reappearance of the boar must surely be a sign of Providence, an unexpected opportunity to finally put things in order, to restore balance, to get to the root of the problem? Maybe when these things have been settled, Henri might find a little peace; maybe the thought of *what comes next* will seem less terrifying.

He heads towards the pig shed. All around, the bleak, grey stubble fields suddenly seem ominous, funereal.

Your test results confirm that you're suffering from lymphoma, a cancer of the lymphatic system... We have very little information on the subject right now, but some recently published studies indicate a possibility that the use of agricultural pesticides may be a contributing factor to...

Of course, he knows. Of course, he has thought about it. Although men in these parts are loath to talk about illness, Henri knows others who have been plagued by the same disease for years: those forced to take on a labourer in order to help out, only to have to hand the reins over to him; a man he has known all his life, built like a brick shithouse, who can now be seen shuffling across the village square, his muscle melted away, sapped by cancer or chemotherapy, his face waxen, still raising his glass in his trembling hand, still propping up the bar, though his heart is no longer in it, and then suddenly gone...

They have long suspected that the things they have been sprinkling and spraying on the land over the years – DDT, Chlordane, PCBs – are poison; they see the warning symbols on the bottles, feel the burning in their eyes, their throats, the nights of itching after days spraying copper sulphate, machines belching hundreds of thousands of litres into the air and onto the land. But what doesn't kill you makes you stronger, they think, and over time they stop thinking about it at all. Their yields have grown exponentially, everything pushes them towards using pesticides: Europe, farming associations, common sense. They believe in progress, technology, science.

And besides, Henri thinks, maybe people are making too much of the whole thing. It might just as easily be the cigarettes after all... Or simply the work, the backbreaking work. And the stress, all these misfortunes big and small that mark out a life must surely end up lodging themselves somewhere and crystallizing, and then fucking everything up. Isn't it possible to simply die of loneliness, boredom, disappointment? Who knows...? But, yes, the backbreaking work, definitely. How long has he been telling them that he is working himself to death for them? They have broken him, the bastards. His own children. Henri shoots a vicious glance at the fields, the vast monochrome expanses where wheat, barley, corn or rye stretch out as far as the eye can see. Around the edges is a band of dead land ten metres wide, where nothing grows but brambles and nettles.

And all that shit you pump into the pigs, it has to go somewhere, doesn't it? What do you have to say to that, you old bastard?

The Lindane, which they spray the animals with to combat scabies, and which apparently makes meat unfit for human consumption for three years – *What the fuck are you on about, like someone is going to come round here to check! Chuck it into the next shipment* – the antibiotics to which pigs have become increasingly resistant, such that new strains have to be constantly developed. Then there are the injections and oral treatments, flukicides, deworming solutions, anticoccidials, neuroleptics, vaccines and hormones... Where does it all go if not into the slurry pit – the heavy metals: zinc, copper, arsenic, selenium, iron, manganese – only to be spread on the land? And what has it become, this land handed down to him by the father he so loved and hated, sometimes in the same instant? What has he made of it? Has his greed, his negligence, his blindness left the sons vulnerable? Has he sacrificed himself, and his family with him?

Jesus Christ, when will you learn to shut that big fucking gob of yours!

Is it possible that all these things that he has built with his bare hands, for himself, for the family, are an impossible lie, and that he, the father, the patriarch, is no more than a pathetic impostor?

When he reaches the pig shed, Henri goes into the office, closes the door and rummages in the desk drawers for his contacts book, leafing through it frantically to find the phone number for Dr Vidal. It takes him three attempts before he manages to dial the number on the rotary telephone. After several ringing tones, there is a click.

'How long?' Henri says bluntly.

'I beg your pardon?'

'I want the truth. How long have I got?'

'Henri, is that you? Look... that's not a question I can easily answer, certainly not over the phone... You can't just refuse to come in for a consultation and then demand that...'

'Tell me. Please. I have to know.'

Henri hears the doctor sigh and reposition the receiver.

'I can't say anything for certain. There are too many variables...'

326

'Give me an idea, an educated guess.'

'I would say... If you refuse treatment, I'd say two to six months.'

Henri lights a cigarette and takes a long drag. To give up smoking. Never to smoke again. To never again be able to light a single fucking cigarette.

'And don't overestimate your own strength,' the doctor says. 'Take it from me, it's all too easy to end up dying alone. Like a beast. With no-one. Even for you, Henri. So for once in your life, forget your pride. Obviously, you're free to refuse treatment, but there are ways we can alleviate the fever, the pain...'

To die like an animal, this is precisely what he would like: animals die quietly, with no drama, no fuss, they seek out a private place, embrace their solitude, and then perish.

'Thank you,' Henri says, and slowly replaces the handset in its cradle.

He gets up and goes over to the cabinet where they keep the hunting rifles, two sixteen-gauge shotguns and a twelve-gauge double-barrelled shotgun that belonged to his father, a gun Henri has always forbidden the sons to touch, the same gun that Marcel took with him forty-three years ago, on 3 September 1939, when, even before the broadcast of President Daladier's speech had finished, he pushed his chair back from the radio, got up without a word and left the farmhouse for the last time. Henri takes a rifle and lays it before him on the desk. The reappearance of the Beast no longer seems an opportunity to put things in order on the farm, but a threat, a backlash, a punishment. Is it the fever that is making him rave like this? He is becoming superstitious; everything seems so... intensified, quivering with hidden meaning.

327

He opens a drawer and takes out a box of paracetamol, bites his tongue to make himself salivate and swallows three tablets, which scrape his gullet as they make their way painfully to his stomach. Even the sound from the fluorescent light is unbearable. An insect drone, like a swarming anthill. Even when he puts his fingers in his ears, the drone persists as tinnitus. And this cold, ashen light... Mortuary light. He tries closing his eyes for a moment, then jumps to his feet, jabs the shotgun at the ceiling, using the barrel to shatter the aluminium grille and the two fluorescent tubes, which rain down in shards over him. The room is suddenly plunged into total darkness, but still ghostly fluorescent tubes float before his sightless eyes. Battered by overmedication, his heart begins to pound in his chest as blackness closes in on him, the fear of this darkness, a visceral fear – how do the pigs live in the harsh fluorescent glare they cannot avoid, he thinks, and what shadows do they languish in when they, the men, leave the pig shed, switch off the lights, and close the doors? – and he wails and lurches forward, arms outstretched, trampling the slivers of glass, knocking against the chair, the corner of the desk, feeling along the surface for the desk lamp, the flex, the switch. Light bursts forth once more.

In his haste, Henri has gashed his hand. Blood drips from his palm and trickles onto his shirt cuff. He leans against the wall, slides down onto the floor, taking his head in his hands and trying to regain his composure. He lights a cigarette and smokes, occasionally sucking on the wound, his eyes never leaving the shotgun. He will track down the Beast, no matter what it takes, no matter whether there is any sense to the idea; then he will put his affairs in order, the piggery, the inheritance. He will talk to Joël, give him his fifty per cent stake in the business, just as he gave the other fifty per cent to Serge. Then it will be time to decide, to put an end to this looming infirmity. Henri gets to his feet and picks up the shotgun, slides back the breechblock, checks the barrels, then loads two cartridges and cocks the gun. Short of breath, he mops the sweat from his face and sets the gun down on the ground. He is stubbing his cigarette out in an ashtray when Serge knocks on the door of the office. The son looks up the ceiling, where the aluminium grille is dangling, then looks at the father, at his bloodstained shirt sleeve.

'What the hell happened?'

'Nothing. One of the fluorescent tubes exploded. Here, take this,' Henri says, handing him the rifle.

Serge immediately realizes his intentions.

'I thought you wanted to bring him back alive for breeding.'

'This has gone on too long. Just take it!'

The elder son grabs the butt of the shotgun. He has come to despise this animal, has convinced himself that the Beast was the personification of the father's obsession with pig rearing and the overcrowding of the pig units, but as he watches Henri load the other rifles, the back of his black shirt stained with sweat, accidentally smearing blood across his temple, Serge feels an ominous dread twist his stomach. Even if Henri is not mistaken about the hoof-prints in the field of maize, are they really going to search the countryside again, armed this time, day and night?

'Where's your brother?' Henri says, turning to him.

'On his way.'

'Right, then, let's go.'

They leave the office and the father slams the door behind them.

After incinerating the piglets in a bucket around the back of the hangar, Joël leaves the pig units. Along the way he sees Henri and Serge, their figures quivering in the midday heat haze, one behind the other, the barrels of their shotguns resting on their shoulders. As he comes closer, Serge shoots him a long, meaningful look and shakes his head, to indicate that perhaps they should challenge the father, try to make him see sense. When they reach the farmyard, they put the shotguns in the pickup. In the boot, the dogs whine, heads bowed, overcome by heat and thirst. Joël fills a bucket with water and, while they are drinking, Henri leans his hands on the scorching body of the truck. He is deathly pale, his neck covered with red blotches and scratches. Serge and Joël look at him, and neither now is in any doubt that the father is dying, that he is lost, that Death has swooped right before their eyes, and they did not notice, did not do anything to save him. And although Joël has hated him with a passion, has dreamed a thousand times of the liberation that his father's death would one day bring, has imagined every possible situation, every conceivable death, he now feels his legs buckle under him.

The farm, the pigs, this world that he abhors, but that they built with their own hands, this world that is theirs in spite of everything, is the only one Joël knows: how can it possibly carry on without Henri, without the father, even if he is old, wiped out by his illness, haunted by his madness, able to stand on his own two feet only because he is swept along by his deep-seated rage, and his ingrained suffering, which in this moment are entirely focused on tracking down the Beast?

—

330

The uniform brown of the landscape soon gives way to myriad shades of green. Nocturnal animals fall silent and the song of the Lemures quavers and gives way to the chirrup of birds shaking themselves in the branches of the trees. An eagle owl gives a last hoot which is quickly answered by a rooster, the sated fox returns to its lair as a strip of sky purples then flames at the edge of the land, and the day finally breaks, scattering the last pockets of shadow, burning away the mist lying on the fields. Jérôme walks towards the lake. His knees and thighs scratched by brambles, blistered by nettles. He is in no hurry, and stops to inspect the ditches. All along the main road, he has found countless hedgehogs, weasels and martens, sometimes even a badger or a dog; three roebucks that have been hit by cars, which took every ounce of strength for him to drag to the old chapel. When he reaches the edge of the lake he waits, nibbling on some biscuits, a piece of bread, while the sun rises and warms the stones and willow fronds. Then he takes off his T-shirt, throws it against the trunk of a tree and steps into the warm lake water. He feels mud squelch between his toes as his feet sink, and he carefully lifts them out, arms stretched wide to keep his balance, so as not to stir up the mud. Long strands of algae caress his ankles and fingerlings dart from the calm pools where they shelter from carp and disappear into the depths. The quicksilver leaves of the willow rustle in the flickering light reflected from the lake, and roots bristle from the crumbling edge of the bank, where coypu shelter in the deep, cool hollows. The air is pervaded by the smell of parched ditches where brown rushes grow, and the milky sweet perfume secreted by the leaves and tender shoots of fig trees.

In the shadow of the roots, in the hollows of their

331

curves, beneath the fallen, buried branches, crayfish lie in wait for small prey, and all that is visible are their tapered pincers, their delicate antennae. In the decades following the excavation of the reservoir, long before Jérôme was born, it is possible that someone drowned here and has ever since been a prisoner of its cold, watery depths. Ever since he learned about the water tables and underground lakes that feed the country's water supply, Jérôme has imagined a vast network of rivers, streams and invisible channels through which little Émilie Seilhan, whose faded photograph he has seen on the gravestone dedicated to her memory in the cemetery, might come and go as she pleases, drifting in her moss-green dress, the winding algae of her hair trailing behind like a bridal train, watching the world from below, a bubble of air between her parted lips.

Gripping a supple branch, he moves forward, careful not to cast a shadow over the crayfish. From his pocket, he takes a piece of ham wrapped in tinfoil that he stole from the fridge. He cuts it into tiny pieces, which he drops on the surface of the water so that they sink to the bottom, mere centimetres from the frantic pincers of the crustaceans.

Jérôme waits for a crayfish to emerge from its hiding place, drawn by the bait, then, carefully aiming for the middle of its shell, he jabs with his branch and pins the crayfish into the mud, grasps it between thumb and forefinger, fishes it out of the water and deposits it in his net.

Last year, he took them to Éléonore and watched as the grandmother deveined the crayfish on a board on the kitchen table – the threadlike black intestines clinging to her fingernails – and cooked them in a sauce of tomatoes, shallots and white wine that perfumed the whole house and, for a brief moment, dispelled the smell of cat litter. This year, she does not want them, claiming that her fingers are not as agile as they were, nor her eyesight as keen. She no longer uses the gas cooker, which sits gathering dust, and Jérôme no longer smells the acrid sulphur matches or the gas burners, the onions sweating. Unbeknownst to the grandmother, he stole the electric gas lighter and took it to the ruined chapel, where, sometimes, in the dead of night, he lies in the ossuary and watches the blue arc illuminate his fingers like a minuscule lightning bolt.

He feels Éléonore's decision to stop cooking is a bad omen, because he has seen animals that are old and weak refuse to hunt or to fight for their food, watched their flanks grow thin, the gleam in their eyes slowly dwindle and fade, until they, like the grandmother, only leave the confines of their nest or their territory reluctantly, fearfully. Éléonore strokes her cats with her gnarled, veiny hand, the palm and fingers stiff, the hesitant caress with which the old stroke the back of a child or an animal.

Jérôme sits on a stone warmed by the sun and dries off as he watches the ripples on the surface of the water, the bubbles that rise from the depths where little Émilie Seilhan builds playhouses from roots, fallen branches and pieces of driftwood. He gets to his feet, pulls on his T-shirt again and wanders away from the reservoir, past towering sunflowers with their brown, perfumed centres. He studies the cobwebs, the burrows created by crickets, mentally recording their locations. Drunk on pollen, bees reel from flower to flower. Jérôme cuts across a fallow field, in the middle of which are a few old magnolia trees, whose flowers, as they decay, exude a sweet smell. He stretches out on the long grasses, creating a little burrow, and watches the gliding buzzards and the vanishing trails left by airplanes. Ants run across the downy hair on his bare legs. A green lizard with a blue throat basks in the sun on one of the walls of the old fortifications, and quickly vanishes when a red kite lands on top of a telephone pole, its shadow gliding across the wall.

Jérôme dozes in the muggy heat of the fragrant grasses, as he does in the bathtub, when the skin on his fingers is as pale and wrinkled as the skin on Éléonore's fingers, pinching his nostrils and allowing himself to slowly sink below the surface. Under the water, he can hear his heart beating, the muffled sounds of the plumbing, the clatter of dishes in the sink, indistinct mutterings from the television or the deep voices of the fathers. When he opens his eyes beneath the murky water, he sees the face of his mother bending over him, talking to him, but he cannot make out her words. Jérôme holds his breath and Catherine sits patiently on the edge of the bath until the boy's heart is pounding in his chest and he is forced back to the surface to catch a breath.

'You've been in there for more than an hour, the water's stone-cold,' she says, rippling the surface of the water with a fingertip.

Jérôme gazes at her beautiful face, the long mane of auburn hair she never combs but leaves tangled and pins at the back of her neck with a barrette or sometimes simply a pencil.

She picks up a bar of soap – one that smells of honeysuckle, which she bought especially for him – makes a lather in her soft, dry hands, and Jérôme gets up and stands in the tepid water while Catherine, or Gabrielle or Julie-Marie, soaps him, since care for his body falls to the mothers who blow his nose, scrub, wash, shampoo

334

and dry him, clean between his toes, drop his pants and wipe his arse, cut his nails and his hair when they decide they are too long, dust him with talcum powder, with nit powder, splash him with lavender that leaves his skin soft and fragrant, and lastly, smear him with sunscreen to protect his delicate skin.

Jérôme surrenders himself to the expert hands that for eleven years have cared for and cosseted him. His mother rubs the back of his head, the whorls of his ears, each hand mimicking the gestures of the other; she gazes at him with that same air of resignation and melancholy, without saying a word, a half-smile playing on her lips. She says:

'When you were little and I used to bathe you in the sink, you... You were so tiny... I'd hold your head in the palm of my hand... And you'd float, your whole body floating... and you'd curl up in the warm water and fall asleep... as though you were back in my belly... and you looked so happy... and I was paralyzed with fear... And so, sometimes... Sometimes I thought I could just let you go... Take my hand away... Leave the bathroom for a minute, close the door... That you would be better off that way... That you wouldn't even suffer, you'd just drift off to sleep... And I'd pull you out of the water so quickly you'd start wailing... So I'd wrap you in a towel and I'd sit there on the floor... holding you against me and sobbing with you.'

Hearing the sound of children's voices reach him, Jérôme gets to his feet. He walks to the edge of the clearing and stands, speechless, in the shade of a tree. A little way away, some boys from Puy-Larroque who look about twelve years old are playing football. They are stripped to the waist and Jérôme can make out their damp skin, their sunburned necks and shoulders, their sweaty foreheads, the locks of hair plastered to their temples. He watches their enigmatic game. He can sense their excitement from their shouts, the way they spit on the flattened grass, the loud backslaps and friendly thumps they exchange in their feigned masculine camaraderie.

Jérôme knows most of them; he was in nursery school with them before he was taken out. He remembers days that dissolved in the late-afternoon sunshine, the silence of the hallways before the bell rang, the muted voices of the pupils behind the doors of the three village school classes, the smell from the school canteen that permeated everything, the yellow light that slipped through the dusty fanlights of toilets that smelled of damp paper, stale urine and juvenile sweat, the metallic taste of water so cold it makes your teeth ache and seems to explode in your stomach.

To mark out the pitch, the boys have lined up their T-shirts along the ground. One of them, a blond, tough-looking boy who goes by the name Lucas Campello, goes back towards the goalposts when he spots Jérôme. He pauses, then turns to the other players and shouts something, hands cupped around his mouth, and points at Jérôme. In a single rush, the seven boys abandon the ball and follow after Lucas at top speed. Jérôme sees the band of half-naked children running straight at him. As they come closer, they do not swerve to avoid him. A dull thud knocks the breath out of him and he is pitched backwards, crushed beneath Lucas Campello, who leans all his weight on him, his crimson face framed by the blue of the sky. The boy pins Jérôme's arms above his head, pressing his wrists into the grass.

'Grab his feet,' Lucas says.

The other boys immediately grip Jérôme's ankles;

one grabs a fistful of his hair.

'What the fuck are you doing staring at us like that? Are you spying on us?'

With a look of disgust, he pretends to sniff Jérôme's face.

'Fucking hell, he stinks to high heaven!'

'It's because he's a redhead,' one of the boys says, and the rest of the gang laugh.

'Yeah,' Lucas says, 'and he lives with pigs. Maybe he is a pig; maybe his father fucked a pig! We should check and see if he's got a wiggly tail.'

The boys laugh raucously. Jérôme makes no attempt to struggle free. The boys' faces radiate sheer cruelty.

'He's soft in the head,' one of them says, trying to explain Jérôme's unresponsiveness.

'Just like his mother,' Lucas Campello says, then, turning to Jérôme, 'It's true, isn't it, your mother is crazy? Everybody in the village says so. My mother says she's *not right in the head*.'

Jérôme gazes at the blue eyes that are boring into him, inhales the sweet breath the boy blows into his face.

'Your whole family is crazy. Like your sister, always playing the whore. I heard she gives free blowjobs...'

The gang of boys all whoop.

'Really, really?' one of them asks, a boy with dark green eyes that Jérôme has always favoured.

Lucas nods:

'She'll fuck pretty much anyone and she doesn't even charge. My brother told me. Last month, at the village fair dance, he screwed her in the community centre car park. What have you got to say about that, Fuckwit?'

Jérôme lowers his eyes and looks at Lucas' puny torso, the boy's small oval breasts, the jutting ribs of his heaving chest. He can no longer feel his hands. The sun appears over the boy's shoulder, dazzling him. His brother is a red-faced teenager with chronic acne who drives around the district day and night at breakneck speed on a motorbike with the exhaust pipe sawn off. As Lucas presses his weight down, Jérôme feels his brother's body over Julie-Marie, his hands slipping under her dress, stroking her hips, her belly, her breasts. He pictures the boy jerking down his sister's pants, leaving them rucked over her pale thighs, then sticking his fingers or his acne-swollen face into Julie-Marie's willing vagina.

He pictures Julie-Marie kneeling in the dry, sun-scorched grass around the Puy-Larroque community centre, sees her pull down the teenager's fly, undo the single button of his boxer shorts, and later sees her get to her feet and smooth down her dress against the imprint left on her knees by the grass and pebbles. Jérôme feels a shudder in his groin and his penis harden against Lucas Campello's thigh.

'He doesn't even say anything, the dumb fuck. You call his sister a slut, and he doesn't say anything.'

'You're the dumb fuck. I just told you, he can't talk. He's mute.'

'What do you mean, he can't talk? Grab his arm.'

Lucas releases one of Jérôme's wrists and grabs his jaw, pushing his thumb into the boy's right cheek, pressing the other fingers into the left to force him to unclench his teeth.

'Fetch a stick,' he orders, as Jérôme resists.

One of the boys runs off and quickly returns with a broken hazel branch. Lucas takes it and shoves it between Jérôme's closed lips, gouging the gums as he forces it past his teeth. When Jérôme finally gives in, Lucas inserts the stick crossways like a bridle bit, then

338

leans down and examines the tongue covered with flecks of bark and bloody drool. He tosses the stick away and Jérôme runs his tongue over his swollen gums and swallows.

'Anyway, it's not his tongue he needs cut off, it's his balls. I mean, we can't have him fucking his sister, can we? What do you think, Fuckwit?'

From the back pocket of his shorts, Lucas takes out an old Opinel knife and carefully unfolds the blunt blade.

'Give me a hand getting his pants off, take care of it,' he says.

Jérôme remembers watching as the fathers simultaneously grabbed squealing piglets from suckling at a sow's teats, gripped them between their tensed thighs, made an incision in the scrotum with a scalpel, pressed the edges of the wound, squeezed out the tiny glands and severed the spermatic cord, then cut off the cartilaginous tail with a flick of the wrist as the piglets shrieked and vainly struggled, milk foaming around their mouths and gushing from their snouts. The fathers dabbed the wound with a wad of gauze soaked in hydrogen peroxide, gave the piglets an intramuscular iron injection before setting them down again, trembling and bewildered, next to their mother. Tiny testicles and scraps of tails littered the walkways of the pig shed, clung to the hairs on their hands and their arms, exploded beneath the soles of their boots.

'Just let him alone,' one of the boys in the gang says finally, a boy whose pale skin and dark, silken hair Jérôme has always loved.

'I'm out of here. C'mon, guys, let's get back to the game. Bet we beat you two–nil!'

Relieved, the other boys nod and release their grip on Jérôme's limbs. The blood rushes back. They get to their

339

feet and walk away, leaving only Lucas, who closes the blade of the Opinel with an affected expression of disappointment and slips it back into his pocket.

'Pity. The fun was just starting.'

He bends over, once more blotting out the pale sky, and allows a long thread of spittle to dangle from his mouth towards Jérôme's face, and just as it is about to touch his lips, Lucas noisily sucks it back into his mouth, wipes his lips with the back of his hand and jumps to his feet. Leaning his weight on his aching hands, Jérôme sits up, dazed, half-blinded by the blazing sun that makes him wince. Lucas Campello sniffles, clears his throat and hawks a gob of spit that catches on a dandelion, then turns away and runs back to join the other boys.

—

Jérôme rubs his wrists and gazes up at a distant hot air balloon drifting. By the time he gets to his feet, the boys are once more chasing their ball and pay no more heed to his presence. Jérôme turns and walks back towards the village.

'You know that way you've got of looking at your sister, well I don't like it one fucking bit,' Henri says, and sets down the last of the piglets he has just castrated and docked, and it staggers across the bare concrete, twitching, the tiny stump of the tail topped by a crimson droplet.

'You'd do well to watch your step, lad, or I'll do to you what I did to him,' Henri says, jerking the tip of his scalpel towards the piglet. Jérôme feels his scrotum shrink and his testicles retract into his abdomen.

He feels Julie-Marie's hands when she is the one to bathe him. She quickly learned to do as Gabrielle and

340

Catherine did, to take on the role of little mother in order to support her aunt. Jérôme gazes at her curly, silken hair, grasps a lock, winds it around his finger and smiles. He can smell her as she moves around the cramped bathroom beneath the fan from the small electric heater, the vanilla perfume she borrows from Gabrielle, spiced by that of her sweat as they mingle. Her attentions are still focused on him alone, and he has no doubt that Julie-Marie belongs only to him, that her love is his and his alone.

He brings her the animals he manages to flush out, hunt and capture, in the way the cats bring the remains of voles and field mice to the grandmother's doorstep. She never deviates from the ritual: Jérôme will bring her a creature – often a butterfly, because he knows that she loves them, sometimes a stick insect or a praying mantis – that he has placed in a jam jar, having perforated the lid with a corkscrew, and wrapped it in a kitchen towel. Every time, Julie-Marie lights up in amazement and exclaims:

'A surprise! I wonder what it could be?'

She sets the precious gift on her lap and, with infinite care, unties the knot in the dishtowel, simpering just to please him. Then, just as carefully, she lets her eyes grow wide and her mouth gape to signal that words fail her. Then she lifts the jar to eye level, gazes at the creature scrabbling or fluttering against the glass.

'It's magnificent.'

She holds it for a moment or two, sometimes claps it against her belly while she takes Jérôme's hand, pulls him to her and kisses his forehead or ruffles his hair, allowing him to nestle for an instant in her familiar, reassuring smell, then says:

'Why don't we let it go again, what do you think?'

And Jérôme takes her by the hand, leads her to the long grass behind the clothesline on a patch of ground the fathers no longer cultivate. Julie-Marie unscrews the lid of the jam jar and they both watch the butterfly flit away or some nameless insect gracelessly scurry into the bushes. As they pass the great oak, does Julie-Marie see, as Jérôme does, the body of the altar boy, Jean Roujas, swinging from the lowest branch, turning around and around as he has for decades, sometimes clockwise, until the rope becomes twisted, sometimes anticlockwise?

A baby rabbit is wandering through the grass by the side of the road. Jérôme goes over and crouches down. The animal sniffs him but makes no attempt to run away. It is blinded by myxomatosis, its eyelids glued shut by yellowish rheum. The young rabbit fitfully jerks its head, probing a world crushed by sweltering heat, dissolved by a light that, to its eyes burned by conjunctivitis, appears only as a dazzling, diffuse glow.

Jérôme reaches out and strokes the animal's twitching fur. He knows this man-made disease. He has seen countless rabbits dying in ditches, lying in the middle of fields or roads. He brought them back to the ruined chapel. Now, he looks around, sees a large half-buried rock and begins to dig it out, exposing the tunnels of an ant colony. Sterile worker ants flee indiscriminately, carrying eggs in their mandibles.

Jérôme hugs the stone to his body and carries it back to the rabbit, which seems to take advantage of the shadow he casts to lie quietly in the grass. The boy kneels next to the animal, raises the stone high, and brings it crashing down. The rabbit is killed instantly, its chest crushed, its pink tongue protruding from its mouth, a gaping wound in the fur of its belly, from which spill the

342

viscera in a whitish sac. One of its paws twitches.

She'll fuck pretty much anyone and she doesn't even charge.

Jérôme raises the rock and he brings it down again, and again, and again, and again, until the rabbit is an amorphous mass of bloody fur half-buried in the scutch grass, then Jérôme lets himself fall back onto the hot tarmac, staring at the pathetic remains.

What have you got to say about that, Fuckwit?

—

When he is finally calm again, he scrapes up the remains of the rabbit, takes off his T-shirt, lays it on the road, places the little body in it and wraps it up. The sun quickly begins to burn his back and his neck, but he pays no heed and keeps walking down the middle of the road, the T-shirt crumpled into a ball against his stomach.

Reaching the shade of a fig tree, he takes a stick and digs a narrow trench. Here he buries the remains of the rabbit wrapped in its makeshift shroud, then replaces the disturbed earth and covers the burial mound with small stones he finds among the tree roots. For a long time he remains motionless, haggard, staring at the little grave. His gums are still sore. His saliva tastes like iron.

We have to give them the injections to prevent anaemia, see? They're born with weak blood, bad blood, pigs these days, they grow too fast and the sows don't have enough iron in their milk, so we have to help out.

Sometimes the injection site becomes infected despite the hydrogen peroxide swab, sometimes the piglet has an allergic reaction and dies from anaphylactic shock. In such cases, the fathers register the animal's number in a log.

Perhaps the rabbit lying now motionless beneath the

clay is waiting for Jérôme to leave before it returns to its former shape and digs a burrow that will lead it to moles, as blind as it is, who can guide it? Or perhaps, in its burrowing, it might find its way to the old wash-house, to the pool in whose depths lies the body of little Émilie Seilhan, and she might try to tame him and the days might not seem so long?

Jérôme gets up and heads back towards the farm.

Julie-Marie no longer watches over his games or those of the twins as she once did, when she was happy in their company, happy to follow them on their walks and join in the babbling conversations of Pierre and Thomas. Now she seems more distant, as though preoccupied, offering only vague responses to his invitations, and usually to decline them. She continues to help Gabrielle out with the daily chores, but she is more sluggish, more lethargic. She still hangs out the laundry every morning. Jérôme gets up so he can watch her from his bedroom window; the sheets dripping onto the tall grass, the red admirals alighting to drink, probing the fabric with their feverish probosces, the dogs that often scamper around and jump up at her as she calls them by name, throws sticks that they bring back and lay at her feet, and Jérôme confusedly feels that the fragile equilibrium of the world depends on the recurrence of this moment, these repeated actions, now that all the others have begun to fade, now that she no longer opens her door to him at dawn so he can lie down next to her, *come on, you're a big boy now, it's not right*, now that she hides her nudity from him, the strange sex she used to show him as a little girl, lying in the grass and hiking up her dress, then parting the lips to reveal... – he hesitates, what he can see is both a flower with pale pink petals, like the pale pink petals of the magnolias in the fallow field, and

344

an animal lurking between her thighs, a terricolous animal – *no, we can't do it any more, we can't do it any more.*

'It's magnificent,' she says for the umpteenth time, staring at the insect in the glass jar, before enveloping Jérôme with her arms, her caresses, the kisses that leave the damp, cool feeling of her saliva on his neck, his forehead, but now she accepts his gifts with barely disguised lassitude, hurriedly unknotting the dishcloth, setting the jar down on the nearest piece of furniture with barely a smile (*another one, you shouldn't have, thanks, but you really should leave these poor little creatures in peace*), and immediately forgets the insect, no longer worrying about setting it free, and if her brother does not do so, finds it lying on its back, legs curled up, shrivelled at the bottom of the jar.

Jérôme pushes open the farm gate and goes into the yard, which is quiet at this time of the afternoon, when the dogs doze in the shade of the barn, in their kennels or in the rusted shells of old machinery, and the twins are taking their nap. On the days when Catherine returns from among the dead and sets about spring cleaning, the windows are thrown wide and sometimes left open so that the heat can dry the floors scrubbed down with bleach.

The whole house stinks like a pigsty – is it really too much to expect you to wash as soon as you get back from the pig sheds?

He inhales the scent that rises from the tiled floor, darker where the mop has just passed. There is nothing that Jérôme likes more than the silent, somnolent house at two o'clock in the afternoon; the empty rooms, their shutters closed, plunged into a darkness, cut through by a single beam of light that moves from wall to wall as the hours pass; the quiet, dusty rooms, suspended in time by a summer day, balmy with the scent of wallpaper and bedspreads warmed by the sun. He climbs the stairs and listens intently, resting a hand on the banister. He pushes open the door to the grandfather's room, crosses and sits on the bed. From the battered picture frame, the young woman gazes out at him; he knows they are related from the name carved on the marble stone of the family vault. The weather seems to have changed to stormy, because the photograph is darker, the branches of the hazel seem to sway in the wind. A patch of sky in the left corner lowers while the blurred figure of the boy forever running in the background seems to tilt his face with its indistinct features to watch the huge rolling clouds massing just beyond the confines of the photograph. Élise's eyes seem more anxious than usual, she is frowning slightly, her lips parted, as though about to speak, to give him a piece of advice, a warning, and, looking closely, it seems to Jérôme that she is pulling the fabric of her dress taut over her rounded belly.

—

She is indifferent to the bodies of boys. She takes them inside her, takes their virginity, milks their sperm like whey. Julie-Marie also takes what she demands, what they give her without demur: a couple of cigarettes, a little money, a dented silver bracelet, a bottle of perfume filched from a mother, a sister. The more vile, the more pitiful the object, the more it secretly pleases her. She displays her trophies on a shelf. She has sometimes envied Jérôme his freedom, but midsummer reminds her how tiresome are the days spent only in the company of her brother, the twins and the ghost of her mother. So whenever she manages to escape, she wanders the

346

byways, the village streets. When she meets the gang of teenage boys who meet near the bus shelter behind the village hall, next to the water tower, she dawdles, she flirts. Sometimes one of them peels away from the group and leads her away; sometimes, they wave for her to join them and they all head off together towards the edge of the woods, the shade of a hayloft, the back seat of a car.

I'll not have you wearing make-up like a slut when you're only fourteen, get back up them stairs, wash your face and change your clothes right this minute.

All this for a little eyeliner that Catherine had applied one morning, when she had allowed her daughter to do her make-up, opening up the lacquered wooden box, pretending that this was a sign that she would feel better tomorrow, and even better the following day... and Julie-Marie said nothing, but trudged back upstairs, went into the bathroom, washed her face and stared at her dripping reflection... The little-girl face that is no longer that of a little girl who no longer has to meekly obey, to allow herself to be treated like a child, a girl who Serge expects to assume the role of a mother and look after Jérôme and take care of Catherine.

'I really need you, you understand, the pigs take up all my time, so in a sense you're the head of the family.'

She finds her father pitiful, with his blue coveralls stained with engine grease and things so foul she prefers not to think about them. Pitiful, with his breath that reeks of cigarettes and the booze he drinks in secret, thinking no-one knows.

'Oh, he always drank, boys around these parts have always been partial to a drink or two, they want to enjoy life, though I have to say he didn't drink quite so much before your brother was born... And then when your mother really got sick, it was a bitter blow.'

Pitiful, for the preposterous authoritarianism he vainly tries to wield to hide his weakness – it's Henri's fault, it's Jérôme's fault, it's Catherine's fault; not that he would ever say such things aloud, but it's clear from everything about him that this is what he means – and lastly, the pathetic way he shirks his responsibilities and simply turns a blind eye, tends to the pigs and goes out to bars to get drunk. Then there are the flashes of violence, of fury, of cruelty he no longer knows how to channel or towards whom...

The grandfather, the father, the uncle continue to impose unjustifiable rules that no-one is allowed to challenge, even though Julie-Marie would rather not have to bathe her brother, or dress her mother any more, but would rather go out, like any other teenager, aimlessly riding a moped along country roads, chatting and smoking joints behind the bus shelter, even if it means coming home, as agreed, by eleven o'clock at the latest.

Her father is contemptible, coming home with his face covered in bruises – fewer now, but increasingly frequently as he gets older – turning away, ashamed that he cannot hide the fact that, for the umpteenth time, he has been brawling outside some bar at closing time and probably ended up, as usual, with his face pressed into the pavement and a mouth full of blood because he is no longer as light on his feet as he was, and besides his heart is no longer in it (the men, the nightly violence, politics as an excuse, the arguments over a wrong word, a look, the brawls, even the booze), though he feels that it is better to get himself beaten up than one day beat one of his own children.

He has never laid a hand on them, despite all the anger she knows he is holding inside, the fury that sometimes wells up and bursts. He has probably made a deal with himself, and Julie-Marie sometimes finds him asleep in his car, the windows misted over, parked in the farmyard when she is on her way to school, and she is convinced that on certain nights, when he does not go to bed, it is not because he passed out from exhaustion and whisky as soon as he came through the gate and turned off the engine, and it is not because Catherine's bedroom door is closed and she has barred him from entering, but because he is terrified of what he might be capable of. He is terrified of himself.

Perhaps the punches he takes from some other drunk are enough to rid him of his hatred, his blind resentment for a time, to absolve him and leave him lying peacefully on the pavement or lapping water from a gutter, or perhaps the reason he still gets into fights is simply habit, routine, reflex, nostalgia. Maybe even boredom, who knows? Julie-Marie no longer cares, this girl who used to trace his bruised, swollen face with her fingertips as he winced; this girl who felt that Serge was taking on the hostile world outside, keeping the barbarians at the gate, who would feel her father's biceps when he used to flex them for her, to prove his incontestable strength, while Catherine looked on, disappointed.

It's as though you're my little wife now.

She who was never supposed to grow up, never supposed to betray the love of father and brother, never have desires other than those that farm and family could meet and even forestall. And yet she does; she has desires, fierce longings, and they are no longer those she once had, they can no longer be sated by nature, by the animals Jérôme took her to see, by the trees oozing sap, by the reservoir pervaded by the perfume of thickets of broom and ripe wheat, nor even by the little girl's body, naked and still undeveloped, that Jérôme would stare at,

349

filled with desire and dread.

She can no longer be satisfied by the pure love of a little boy to whom she offered herself, graciously, knowing that she was doing nothing wrong, but simply responding to the burgeoning excitement, the extraordinary unsated ardour within them, that anything could allay for a short while: the goosebumps from the chilly waters of the reservoir, the fur of animals, their lewdness and their couplings, the sweltering summer nights and the straw fires along the roads, their clammy hands and their secret embraces in the bluish bramble thickets; everything that could see, feel, touch, everything that poured into them without ever filling, ever sating them, as though together, the two of them could encompass the whole universe of the farm and countryside beyond. Julie-Marie grew bored of it. What she wants now, what seems to her more interesting that anything else, is the violence of the world outside.

Julie-Marie has always envied other children, their frivolousness, their laziness and their savagery, but without ever truly being one of them, one of the groups that form fortuitously. She would stand outside, unable to find the slightest crack through which she might become part of their gang, penetrate their inner circle. In the playground, she learned to pretend to be having fun, because obvious boredom or stasis seems suspicious to schoolchildren, who are attentive to every slight deviation. For years, she played vaguely in their vicinity, attempted to blend in, copying their gestures, following them as they raced around, chanting their incomprehensible catcalls. Their games are so different from those she and Jérôme shared in the world of the farm...

A long time ago, a sow died during farrowing. Julie-Marie still does not know why her uncle attempted to save one of the piglets, not by placing it with another sow's litter, but among a litter of puppies in an isolated kennel. Obscured by the smell of the pups, the piglet suckled and grew up like another little dog, sleeping with them, playing with them, running after balls, even learning to growl like them, perhaps believing it was one of them. Then, suddenly, it disappeared. One morning, Julie-Marie and Jérôme, who loved the little piglet, could not find it in the pen reserved for nursing bitches, or anywhere in the yard. Now that the pups were weaned and the bitch's maternal instinct dulled, she had spotted him, and seeing among her litter one of the little pigs that the grandfather sometimes threw to the dogs as food, she had killed it and shared the carcass with her real pups.

The other children learned to tolerate the satellite, commensal presence of Julie-Marie, and sometimes allowed her to join them; accepted her for the space of a game, a breaktime, an alliance or a scheme. Then they lost interest in her and instinctively sent her back into orbit. They are the same age, speak the same language, but they are separated from her, distanced by a fundamental difference, one perhaps inculcated by their parents. At first, as they grew up, they became indifferent to her. They no longer noticed her, she floated among them, attaching herself to those who were prepared to accept her colourless presence for a moment, only to drift towards other groups of children when they made their annoyance or their irritation clear, rejected with scant ceremony.

So when her classmates started to insult her, it seemed to Julie-Marie as though they finally expected something of her, that they were offering her a way of existing

in their eyes, nor did she mind that it was the polar opposite of what Serge, Jérôme and even Catherine expected
of her. What had suddenly, inexplicably prompted the
children's interest in her as the focus of their savagery?
They had never accepted her as one of their own, at least
not until she willingly accepted the role they seemed to
discover in this girl they used to mock: the loose woman,
the village bicycle, the slut; until she agreed to kiss them,
feed on their mouths, to eat and drink down their spittle,
caress their hairless skin, open herself to their clumsy
bodies.

—

In the days that follow the discovery of the hoof-prints,
the men do not find the Beast. Until mid-August, they
continue to make their rounds under Henri's command,
alternately taking a few hours off. But the boar is not to
be found and the track marks at the edge of the Plains
quickly disappear. Work on the harvest is delayed and
the father has no choice but to allow the sons to go back
to the fields and the pig shed to deal with the harvest and
the silage even as his fixation sets him steadily adrift,
taking him far from the farm work, whose management
he leaves to them.

Over the summer, there are other miscarriages, although initially they are sufficiently infrequent that
Serge and Joël simply record the fact without becoming alarmed. Then one morning in the first week of
September, when the brothers are inspecting groups
of pregnant sows, they discover numerous stillbirths.
Working in separate pens, they glance at each other over
the railings.

'There's something seriously fucked up going on

here,' Serge says.

He scribbles the number of miscarried piglets in his notepad.

'How many have you got?'

'Seven in that one, nine in that one. Another nine in that pen. Eleven in this one,' Joël says.

'This is not good. Not good at all. We need to search all the pens, make sure we haven't missed any... You deal with that, I'll be right back, I just need to check something.'

Serge strides to the door of the pig shed and goes straight to Henri's office. He pauses for a second, pats his pockets in search of his keys, and slots the spare key into the lock. He pushes open the door; the cramped room is musty and smells of stale cigarette smoke. He flicks the light switch several times before realizing that Henri has not replaced the fluorescent bulbs. Serge walks over and turns on the desk lamp, broken glass cracking under his boots. The aluminium grille is still dangling over the battered leather office chair and there are drops of dried, black blood on the corner of the desk. Pinned to the wall is the livestock planner that once reminded him of the Kabbalah, of a mandala whose esoteric interpretation was known only to the father. The planner determines the day-to-day running of the farm according to the cycles of the sows, matings, farrowings; it presides over the life and death of the pigs. Serge is comparing the information he has jotted in his notepad with the predictions on the planner when Joël appears in the doorway.

'Maybe it's time we sorted out this shit-tip,' he says.

Serge simply glances over his shoulder at his brother.

'We're looking at about thirty per cent stillborn mortality on the early farrows when in normal circumstances it shouldn't be more than five per cent. We've never had anything like this...'

'We need to talk to him,' Joël says.

Serge lights a cigarette and for a long time he is si-lent, nervously tapping his foot as he studies the arcane mysteries of the planner, as though waiting for them to reveal something.

'No,' he says, turning to his brother. 'We don't tell him anything just yet. We check the feeding troughs and take the sows' temperatures morning and night.'

'What about the thirty animals due to go to slaughter tomorrow?'

'We ship them as normal. Besides, the feedlot hasn't been affected. Call the abattoir and confirm.'

They leave the office and go back to the pig shed.

'I have a bad feeling about this,' Joël says, walking next to Serge. 'If the old man finds out we've been hiding things from him...'

'You want to go look for him? Go ahead. I don't even know where the fuck he is! Can't you see we can't rely on him any more? He wouldn't be able to deal with some-thing like this, and in the end he'll blame us as usual.'

Joël says nothing as they disinfect their boots before going back into the farrowing house.

'Listen,' Serge says, 'between the two of us, we can deal with the situation. Let's start by clearing away all this shit and systematically isolating any sows that pres-ent with symptoms... We clean our boots before we enter every pen, and put on new boots when we go to another unit...'

Joël nods and the two men set about picking up the bloody remains of piglets and the placental sacs, then wash away the pools of amniotic fluid with a pressure hose. When they fill the troughs with grain, only two of

354

the sows do not come to eat. They stand off to one side, apathetic.

'This one is running a fever. Forty-one degrees,' Joël says, taking the mercury thermometer from the animal's rectum. 'We need to contact the vet and ask him to run some tests.'

'Yeah, yeah, we'll do that, yes... In the meantime, hose them down with cold water before isolating them,' answers Serge.

In the days that follow, they disinfect the farrowing house from top to bottom. Joël isolates all the ailing sows in a single pen away from the other pigs. Serge eventually agrees to contact Leroy, the vet, but he carefully erases a number of the matings and miscarriages that have occurred in the past two months from the livestock planner. Early the next morning, just as the brothers are getting ready to leave the house, Michel Leroy pulls into the farmyard.

'I'll deal with this,' Serge says. 'Where's the old man?'

'No idea. Still asleep, I think,' replies Joël, 'The pickup is still parked outside and I thought I heard him come in late last night.'

'You stay here. If he wakes up and asks what's going on, tell him it's just a routine visit.'

Serge dons his parka and goes out. Joël watches as he goes over to Leroy, and from the way he is walking he can tell that Serge is still drunk from his bar crawl the night before. Leroy is a tall, skinny guy with thinning hair, wearing a raincoat that is much too big. The two men shake hands, exchange a few words, then head towards the pig shed.

'How is your father?' the vet asks.

'Tired. He's coming down with something. We don't

know what. That's why I'd rather we keep this just between the two of us. We don't want to worry him,' Serge
says.

'Tell me everything. You were pretty cagey on the
phone...'

'We've noticed some problems in the farrowing
house. Sows that are lethargic, feverish... Loss of appetite... We've also had a number of miscarriages in the
first litters...'

'When did you first notice the symptoms?'

'The first thing we noticed were the miscarriages. A
few weeks ago? A month at most...'

Having reached the pig shed, they put on protective
coveralls and boots, and go into the building. Leroy examines four of the sick sows, asking questions to which
Serge barely replies, as though stubborn or distracted,
staring at the backs of the animals. Then they inspect
the rest of the pens.

'Well,' the vet says finally, shrugging, 'all things considered, I don't think you have much to worry about. I'd
say we start by trying a broad-spectrum antibiotic...'

'We already test a large number of the breeders every year to screen for infections, and we treat the rest of
them with antibiotics as prophylaxis.'

'That's why I'm not too worried. Still, we'll take
some samples and run some tests. If there are any more
miscarriages, send everything to the lab, the stillborn
animals, placenta, everything. You'll also need to check
their food. I've seen a case where ergot in the wheat
affected sows in pig. At first it didn't occur to us, but
then the pigs became crazy, and the sows repeatedly
miscarried...'

'Got it,' says Serge.

The two men talk for a little while as they move along

the walkways before Leroy takes his leave. Once he is gone, Serge, feeling nauseous, goes out to the back of the farrowing house to get some fresh air. He paces around the huge flagstone beneath which the drains seething with black water from the pig shed flow towards the slurry pit. He takes a swig of whisky from his hipflask and it trickles over his chin, onto his neck bristling with a three-day beard peppered with grey hairs, then he suddenly falls to his knees and spews alcohol and bile onto the concrete. For a long time he stays on all fours, racked by convulsions, hands pressed against the ground, long after he has nothing left to vomit, belching air and groaning with each spasm of his diaphragm. When, finally, he manages to regain his composure, he rolls onto his side, then onto his back, drained of all strength, all thought, eyes filled with tears, gazing at the tattered sky. Hearing a door slam behind him, Serge struggles to his feet. Joël walks towards him.

'Give me a cigarette,' the older brother says.

Joël takes a pack from his pocket and grimaces, glancing at the yellowish puddle of bile.

'Jesus, you really look like shit...'

'Thanks,' Serge says, cupping the lighter to shelter it from the wind.

'I talked to Leroy as he was leaving. Why didn't you tell him?'

'Tell him what?'

'The truth. About the sows. About everything.'

'For fuck's sake, I've told you, I've got everything under control! I hope you didn't snitch.'

Joël shakes his head and says nothing for a moment.

'I don't understand why you tried to play down the symptoms...'

Serge sighs and once more begins pacing the flagstones, sucking greedily on his cigarette.

'If Leroy has all the relevant information, he could probably tailor a treatment plan...'

'There's already a treatment plan, you know that as well as I do. All the sows are on antibiotics – what more do you want?'

'I don't know. Run some tests, run an antibiogram, talk to the old man, put our heads together. Doing something rather than sit on our arses, turning a blind eye, waiting for things to sort themselves out.'

Serge sneers.

'You don't think we're struggling enough as it is? Go on, then, go find him! Go! He's spent the past two months combing the fucking countryside for miles around. Have you seen the state of him? He's scrawny, filthy, he's talking to himself. He's gone completely mad!'

'We should call the doctor.'

Serge says nothing for a moment, but stands swaying and smoking next to the slurry pit.

'There's something I need to tell you... It was me who went back to the barn that night... It was me who left the door of the boar pen open and the bolt on the stall drawn back... I don't know what the fuck was going through my head... I wasn't sure... I knew the Beast could do it, but I didn't think he'd smash his way out or that he'd be able to get past the fence...'

Joël says nothing.

'I just couldn't stand seeing the old man so obsessed with that fucking animal, you know? It was all he talked about... His plans for the pig units, extending the breeding programme, increasing the livestock, when everything is already fucking falling apart...'

'I'll go and sort out the farrowing house, then I'll look in on the gestating sows, then I'll move on to the rest,'

Joël says.

Serge steps forward and takes his brother's face in his broad hands. He looks up at the scar that snakes across Joël's forehead and his temple, then traces the ridge with the tip of his thumb.

No-one has forgotten the day when the elder son burst into the feedlot where Joël was finishing feeding the pigs. Seeing him barrelling down the aisle towards him, Joël set down the feed trolley and raised one hand as a sign of appeasement before Serge punched him in the face, sending him slamming against the bars of one of the stalls. Joël had no time to get to his feet before Serge rushed at him, grabbing the bars with both hands, taking a run-up and kicking him in the stomach. Joël scrabbled through the pigshit, trying to escape, but Serge was relentless, lashing out viciously at his hips, his thighs, his testicles, at a body strangely numb to the rain of blows. Far away and yet so close, the terrified pigs were squealing. A protruding nail gashed Joël's forehead and blood streamed into his eye, over his shit-smeared cheek and into his mouth. Joël tried to breathe but could only moan. Then the blows ceased. Joël painfully rolled onto his back, spitting blood and shit. Overhead, he watched the strip lights whirl, merge and explode. He tried to get to his feet, to lever himself off the ground, but slipped in the pig shit and once again found himself sprawled in the aisle. Serge had stalked away but, turning his head, Joël saw him marching back with a shovel raised above his shoulder. Instinctively, Joël curled into a ball and put his head between his knees. He squeezed his eyes closed, waiting for a blow that never came. In the endless seconds, he thinks about the games they played as children whenever they managed to escape the father, roaming the fields, building tree-houses, shooting birds with

359

catapults, forcing frogs to smoke. Warily, he opened one eye and saw Henri grab Serge by the throat and slam him against one of the stalls. The father had wrested the shovel from him and it lay at his feet. Finally, Joël could breathe. He sat up, crawled across the concrete floor and propped himself against the feed trolley...

Now, almost twelve years later, Joël is staring at his pale face, his bushy beard, the whites of his eyes yellow from alcohol. He can smell the sour breath, feel Serge's hands tremble against his cheeks. He fears the worst. He grabs Serge's wrist.

'I let him blame you,' the elder son says. 'But what if it was my fault that all this happened... What if I'm the one who hasn't lived up to his expectations, the one who failed him?'

'You're completely pissed. You need to go sleep it off. Let me handle things today. Now, let me go.'

Serge nods repeatedly, still stroking his brother's forehead insistently, as though trying to erase the scar.

'Yeah, you're right... You're probably right...'

He pulls his brother's face towards him, plants a loud, wet kiss at the corner of his mouth, then lets him go, pats him on the shoulder and walks away clutching his belly.

—

The dogs are barking and Catherine cannot manage to sleep. How many times has she thought about throwing open the kennel doors and the farm gates? Maybe the dogs are not as servile, as domesticated as she is, maybe they would run, abandoning the farmyard to silence and leaving her to stew in her servile, animal resignation. Or maybe she would run too, take off with the dogs, run from the farm as fast as she could and never look back...

360

She has to stay, for the children. To stay for the children. Hah! Now that is a pathetic charade. Who is she trying to convince? How can she try to justify herself in other people's eyes when Jérôme has learned to live with a mother who can vanish overnight, who barricades herself in her room and who no longer offers the slightest display of affection, of interest – to say nothing of protection, love, those things a mother is supposed to provide for her child?

Perhaps after all she should take the advice of Gabrielle, who, for years now, has been suggesting that they run away together? Take the twins, Jérôme and Julie-Marie, fling some clothes into suitcases and simply disappear, leaving the men and the pigs far behind. But then what reserves of energy she would need to draw on simply to get out of bed first... And even if she were able to, after the breakdown, even if she recovered her senses, she would simply think she was being melodramatic, that things were not so terrible after all, certainly better than being hospitalized again; and besides, where would they go, with their brood...?

And then again, Catherine cannot be sure that Jérôme is actually unhappy. He seems beyond reach; what right has she to tear him from the only world he has ever known?

Just take away my hand, leave the...

Sometimes she would threaten to end it all, to throw herself out the window, swallow all the pills she has and down the bottle of whisky that Serge thinks no-one knows about in one of the kitchen cabinets. Serge promptly burst into her room with a hammer to nail the window shut, and she simply lay there, stunned and speechless he would use such force, shattering nails, smashing a pane of glass, and then swing a sledgehammer at the whole window, sending glass raining down into the farmyard, then turning back to her, his face trembling, his eyes puffy and bloodshot from too many drunken binges, too many sleepless nights on the decrepit sofa, as Gabrielle and Joël raced into the room to stop him.

'If I stay alive, it's for the children.'

She addressed him with this grandiloquent heroism, this brazen cheek, and Serge dropped the hammer on the ground before his brother could grab his wrist, and he said:

'Just look at yourself. You're incapable of looking after them. Whether you're alive or dead makes no fucking difference.'

He left the room, head bowed, utterly drained. When he came back late that night (that night, and a hundred more), wreathed in an alcoholic, animal smell, it was to try to get into the bed, and crush her with all his weight, to kiss her lips and grope her body. He covered her chin with spittle and tears, spluttering drunkenly:

'I'm so sorry, I'm so sorry, I didn't mean what I said, I can't bear the thought of you leaving me, I don't want to be alone.'

She managed to break free of his grip and push him off the bed. She cowered against the wall, pulled a blanket over her, while he stood at the foot of the bed like a castigated child, moaning *please* and then turned on his heel and left the room to spend the night slumped on one of the sofas, without even bothering to take off his trousers.

And yet there are times when she remembers old sensations, and, seen through that prism, everything does not seem so black, so tainted in advance. She remembers the birth of Julie-Marie, for example, remembers being alone with the newborn baby in a bright hospital room. She did not want this – how could she *want* to be a mother at the age of seventeen? – but as she holds the baby in her hands, this naked creature fashioned by her own flesh, so vulnerable, so dependent on her, she has a realization, a sudden internal flash, that the baby gives her a reason to live, ensures a future, if not a destiny. She will grow accustomed to this presence next to her, she will manage to make a decision, she will give up on Joël and finally choose Serge.

Or perhaps the mere existence of this child will transform her own and there will be nothing to choose, nothing to give up, events will conform to logic rather than simply to her free will, she will be relieved of all this anxiety, all these doubts, all the regrets she feels for those things (she cannot say exactly which) that she has not experienced or will never experience. The vast immensity of desires, of possibilities, now seems insignificant compared with the existence of the child, all the things the child will give her, those things that, until now, Catherine has despised: a relationship, a family, being a parent, watching television, doing homework, the school, the supermarket, a respectable life.

But this feeling, this immense reassurance, lasts no more than a few days, and is reduced, in fleeting time, to no more than an instant, a vague epiphany, before she even leaves the clinic and moves into the farmhouse, with her mother in the back seat sobbing all the way, blowing her nose into a handkerchief on which she has probably embroidered her initials, not because she is sorry to see her eldest daughter leave home so soon, condemned to take on the same role she did at that age, but at the thought of being alone, of being thrust onto the gentle slope of old age; after all, Gabrielle too will leave, such is life, and she will be left with nothing but the presence of their father and tedious afternoons spent daydreaming in front of the television, brooding over her life, over the dim past, or cleaning the house to prevent it turning into a mausoleum.

Then came the mundane years devoted to Julie-Marie, thinks Catherine, a life shut away with three men, having to suffer their snubs, their mistrust, albeit unintentional, and the arrogant silence of the grandmother, who watched her slightest gesture and only ever spoke to her when compelled.

It was like landing in the middle of a pack of wolves.

The monotonous routine, the days spent caring for the baby, vacantly wondering what can have happened for her to end up alone in this huge ramshackle house that she loathes, how there came to be such a yawning gap between her dreams and her reality. How can it be that Serge falls asleep next to her every night, and how can the child sleeping in the Moses basket at the foot of the bed be theirs?

During those early years, she struggles to take part, to make sense of this life. At her insistence, and only after protracted machinations to get Henri to allow Serge time away from the farm, they occasionally go on holiday. They go to Mimizan-Plage, not even to Cap Ferret, where they rent a two-room self-catering unit in an aparthotel. They do what they feel they are supposed to do: they eat in cheap restaurants along the seafront, they go to the fun fair to see the merry-go-rounds and the flashing lights and eat candyfloss. In a souvenir shop, they buy a postcard to send to Catherine's parents, a few sea shells and dried seahorses for Julie-Marie's bedroom, which they are planning to decorate...

But as they are walking along the beach one windy morning, with Serge striding ahead, Catherine stares at his back, his neck which is nearly as thick as his head. He is indifferent to the sea, to the waves flecked with white caps crashing onto the shore. He smokes silently, sullenly (suddenly he has gone from smoking not five or ten cigarettes a day, but a whole pack, and then two packets, like his father), and he seems to have momentarily forgotten Catherine with Julie-Marie sleeping on her shoulder. If she were to stop now, he would probably carry on walking, never looking back, until he reached the far end of the beach, and she would see him gradually vanish into the sea spray. Or she could walk towards the ocean, paddle into the water with the child in her arms and be swept away by the waves without him noticing.

The sheer vastness of the beach that stretches out before them seems like the years ahead. She has barely turned eighteen, Serge is twenty-one. How will they ever be able to fill the time, this breathtaking boredom? And what came next, what happened after this memory of the day at the beach? Everything is so tangled and confused: the months, the seasons, the years, the routine. Time no longer exists. Past, present and future have been obliterated.

Then, the first breakdown comes. They are all gathered around the table for dinner one evening and Catherine suddenly has the feeling of being swallowed up into herself, the way sometimes tectonic activity will create up a breach in the bed of a lake and drain it of its water. Sounds and images still reach her, but she perceives them with a body that is not her own. At first, she thinks it is just a dizzy spell, and under the table she jabs the tines of the fork into the skin of her wrist. The pain spreads through her arm, or rather the impression of pain, coursing along faltering synapses. She feels panic rising in her belly, she is overwhelmed, in freefall. Can she instruct her body to stand up? She knocks over the chair and rushes out into the yard and begins to pace in broad circles, carrying with her this bottomless abyss that threatens to engulf her. Serge comes outside, but she waves him away.

'It's nothing, I'll be fine, I just need some fresh air.'

The voice that comes from her mouth is unfamiliar to her. She thinks she sees Éléonore watching from the living room window. How did she manage to say these words without even thinking them? She paces for a long time, until the feeling slowly subsides, leaving her exhausted. Serge takes her hand and leads her back to the house. In the kitchen, Joël and Henri are still sitting at the table, dumbfounded; they watch her walk past, as pale as death. Serge takes her up to the room and puts her to bed. She sleeps for more than fifteen hours. When she wakes, she no longer really remembers what happened. Didn't she think she was dying, or that something worse was about to happen? How can she describe this feeling of dying, of being annihilated? And yet, in time, she forgets. For a time, life reasserts itself. The solitude of the men, their strangeness, the crumbling farmhouse all come to seem familiar. The barking of the dogs no longer wakes her in the dead of night. It slips into her dreams; she imagines packs of rabid animals chasing her, she cannot say whether they are pigs or dogs, but they are close behind, their jaws flecked with spittle, snapping at her.

—

Henri comes back to the house only now and then, filthy, sullen and unkempt, his eyes blazing with the fire that is consuming him. He seems to haunt the farm and the surrounding lands. He spends his days and nights driving along the byroads at a snail's pace, the rifle lying on the passenger seat. He no longer goes to bed and sleeps only when overcome by exhaustion. More than once, he almost kills himself when he loses control of the pickup. At such times he quickly parks by the road and slumps over the steering wheel.

The Beast appears in his every dream. Lurking in the shadows, it leaps out and charges. In a recurring nightmare, he finally collapses from his illness in one of the pig sheds. Back when hungry pigs used to roam the countryside and the villages, they would sometimes eat a child. He remembers his father's warnings: never crouch down or play on the ground if there's a pig nearby. In his dream, he is sprawled on the ground, lying in liquid manure that trickles into his mouth, his nose. He cannot move an inch. All around, animals are moving beyond the circle of light that illuminates him. He remembers that he has been neglecting them, has forgotten to feed them for so long that they are probably feral and emaciated. At first he cannot see them, but he can sense them in the shadows, twitching, at first fearful, then driven by hunger. Gradually, they become bolder, they move towards him and snuffle. He can feel their warm breath on his cheek, their snouts pressed against his neck, his hands. He tries to call to the sons, but no sound comes. Then one pig, more daring than the others, bites his face. Though Henri feels no pain, he can sense the hunk of flesh that the animal has ripped away with a powerful jerk of its head, gradually arousing the instincts of the other pigs, and they too begin to gnaw at his face, devouring the nose, the lips, their molars grinding through cartilage. Through their massed bodies, he glimpses a figure standing in the doorway of the pig shed, a silhouette that looks on impassively. It is his father, hiding his own mutilated face in the shadows, shaking his head almost imperceptibly and saying:

You can't say I didn't warn you. You know how this is going to end.

He wakes up howling, opens the door of the pickup, falls into the ditch, gets up and stumbles aimlessly through the fields before he comes to his senses. The drugs can no longer alleviate the fever that is making him delirious. Soon, nightmarish figures begin to encroach upon reality. He sees Marcel in the distance, standing at the far end of the road on which he is driving, shimmering like a mirage he can never reach; he sees him on the edge of a coppice of trees or standing in the middle of a field, always frozen, impassive.

He recalls impressions he believed had vanished forever: his mother's protection, even if sporadic, the sense of her presence, her firm, enveloping body, and the cold, mysterious authority of the father. These are his first memories walking the fields next to that sturdy, imperious body. Marcel sometimes lays a hand on his head, gripping the whole skull between his fingers. Henri can smell the stale tobacco smoke that stained the tips of his middle and index fingers yellow, mingled with that of soil, of the metal tools, of the breath and the droppings of the animals.

He is accustomed to his father's monstrousness; he sees it only through the prism of others, those they encounter in the village or at the market, through their eyes as they linger or turn away, pitying or patronizing, or the eyes of children as they widen in terror. For the first time he feels the sting of shame as he walks among them, his hand in the intractable grip of the father. He learns to prefer their comparative solitude, which shields them from strangers, from *those in the outside world*. He applies himself to demonstrating to Marcel his obedience, his devotion, in counterpoint to the savagery of the world.

'See that line of oaks, way over there? Right up to that line. One day you will own all of it.'

Marcel took him to the edge of the Plains, laid a hand on his frail shoulder and with a sweeping gesture takes in all the fields that Henri will gradually buy as the piggery expands, sometimes at the cost of acrimonious negotiations, striving to recreate the precise territory designated by the father that day as the ultimate accomplishment in his life, even buying this useless plot, purchased by bribing a family in Puy-Larroque, this strip of land tainted by the blood of the patriarch, spilled like a curse upon the Plains.

He goes back to the pickup to find the door still open, the hazard warning lights still blinking. He presses the dashboard lighter, takes a cigarette from a crumpled pack and chews on the filter. The first puff heaves his heart into his mouth, then he slumps back in his seat, closes his eyes and tries to drive out the voices, the figures, the impressions. Cars honk their horns as they overtake him.

His condition is inexorably deteriorating. Before long, his face is covered with a shaggy beard. Whenever he goes home and encounters one of the sons, the grandchildren or Gabrielle, he finds some excuse to avoid them. He can see his reflection in their silence, in the worry and the pity they can no longer hide, the reflection he cannot bring himself to look at in the bathroom mirror or in the rearview mirror. When even he cannot bear his own stench, he resolves to take a shower. Looking down at the jutting ribs of his chest, at the

369

bruises covering his stomach and his thighs, he surveys the state of his ravaged body. He has lost some fifteen kilos over the course of the summer. The scalding water pulsing from the showerhead onto his skin is soothing, and for a long time he sits, exhausted, in the bathtub, eyes closed, hugging his calloused knees, dozing. Then he wakes and clutches the edge of the bath. The Beast or Marcel have once again appeared in a wisp of dream, reminding him of his quest. He manages to extricate himself from the bath with great difficulty, dries his scalded back, drapes a rough towel around his bony shoulders, his knobbly vertebrae.

He no longer takes a dog with him. He spends some nights sleeping under a blanket in the back of the Lada Niva, parked on some dirt track near the Plains. One day in mid-September, as he painfully clambers out of the truck, Henri discovers another field of maize destroyed, the earth ploughed up in broad furrows as before. He walks over and kneels down. The animal's hooves have left deep marks in the damp soil.

'I was right!' Henri whispers as he gets to his feet.

A stabbing pain in his chest doubles him over. He groans, brings his hand to his heart and stumbles into the field beneath a sky in which a few faint stars are still holding out.

'I was right!' he roars, before being overcome by a coughing fit which sends him sprawling and puts a flock of pheasants to flight.

The field extends over a coomb. Farther off, on the other side of the valley, framed against the bourgeoning light, stands the shadow of Marcel, ringed by a purple halo.

'What d'you have to say to that, you old fucker?'

Henri shouts, jabbing a finger at the father's ghost.

He stares at him for a moment.

'Say something! What do you want? What are you waiting for, you rotting bastard?'

The only response is silence. Henri coughs again, a harsh, painful cough, then hawks a gob of spit and a thread of blood-streaked saliva trickles down his chin and into his beard. The pain eventually subsides and he manages to stand up. He lights a cigarette, smokes, scans the horizon, then heads back to the car, muttering to himself, swearing and panting for breath. When he reaches the pickup, he leans for a moment on the bonnet, wincing. The fever has left his lips chapped and split. His mouth and his throat are burning. The rash that has spread over his belly is now a single raw wound, a constant burning with little variation. His heart begins to beat irregularly. He feels it spasm beneath his ribs like something with its own life, something barely hatched. The sun rises over the fields and the sky is now pure blue, almost white. He no longer sees Marcel in the distance, simply a gnarled dead tree covered with ivy and tinder fungus.

—

The torpid silence of the house is troubled only by muted mumbling from the television in front of which the twins are sitting, bare-arsed on the carpet. Near the grandfather's bed, on the nightstand, the still-warm sun of early autumn is no longer able to comfort the woman in the photograph. Standing in the doorway of Julie-Marie's bedroom, Jérôme breathes in his sister's smell, the fragrance of the incense paper she burns in the saucer on the shelf that is filled with the remains of the

371

perforated cut strips that have been reduced to ashes and crumbled to dust which rises in whorls if he breathes on it or makes a sudden movement close by – *I know that you've been in my room again* – but also the plastic smell of the hands and faces of the dolls, their bodies stuffed with rags, that lie abandoned in a corner of the room, relics lined up on top of a wicker trunk in serried ranks, shoulder to shoulder, like the soldiers who lie beneath the war memorial, when they go to sleep at night, exhausted at having spent all day crawling through the tunnels they have bored beneath the village square.

The dolls are still intact, their hair coarse from being brushed too often. Their eyelids, rimmed with lashes like the eyelids of the pigs, are open and reveal eyes of glass, porcelain or plastic, which can close when the doll is tilted, and the mechanism makes a rattling sound inside their heads, *click-click-click-click*. Jérôme loves their sweet smell, the soft fabric bodies that once were white and are now grey, sometimes brown, stained with the carefully cooked mud pies that they pointedly refused to swallow.

'You're a naughty little girl! Take that! And that! I'll teach you to behave!'

Are they bored sitting on the trunk, their eyes somewhat opaque since a veil of dust has settled on them like the cat's cataracts or the rabbit's myxomatosis? Jérôme liked to watch Julie-Marie playing with her dolls, sitting them around a stone transformed into a table, with a handkerchief or a dishtowel as a tablecloth, bathing them the way she bathed him.

Then, suddenly, nothing; a brutal indifference that nothing and nobody could have predicted; at first the dolls lay, forgotten, on the bedroom floor or amid the grass in the yard, left out in the rain, torn limb from limb by the dogs, their cloth bodies eaten by mildew – that one there has no hands, simply a mess of mangled plastic, that one's face was melted by the sun into a terrifying mask – until finally Julie-Marie gathered them all up again, out of loyalty or nostalgia, and created a small pointless shrine to their former glory or to their memory. But they are crude and ugly now, with their faded features, the dresses that were knitted for them by the grandmother or the mother with poor-quality wool, back when they knitted, knitted, knitted as though their lives depended on the number of woollen articles they could produce, and the whole family walked around in sweaters, scarves, socks, hats, while the needles endlessly clicked on...

These days, Jérôme needs to tug on his sleeves so that they grow with him, unless Catherine decides to burst from her room in an attempt to restore order to their lives and the whole farmhouse, and takes him – as she usually does – to the flea market in the village to kit him out from head to toe in mismatched clothes that belonged to other people and smell of unfamiliar washing powders, other wardrobes, other bodies than theirs.

'Look at this! Five francs! It's a bargain! Do you like it? No? You don't think it's cool? Oh, you can be such a difficult boy. We'll take it anyway.'

Jérôme goes into the room and closes the door behind him. What has happened? Where has the Julie-Marie he knew gone? Why does she not let him follow her around as she used to, when they roamed the country roads. He would pick blackberries from the brambles and bring them to her, and she would wait, sitting under the magnolia tree in the fallow field, whose flowers, when they rot, give off a sickly fragrance, and soon Julie-Marie's fingers and her lips would be purple with the juice of

373

soft, ripe blackberries.

Why does she push him away now when he tries to hug her, *you're a big boy now, we can't do that any more,* and why will she not release the moth from inside his head the way she did when he wanted to listen to the hum of a hawkmoth caught in the heady perfume of a privet hedge? He captured it in one of the baby food jars Gabrielle uses to feed the twins, but when he brought it to his ear, the moth, desperate to escape, flew inside his head. There was a sudden roar, a shooting pain, and he could feel his eardrum thrum with the butterfly's wings; Jérôme had screamed at the top of his lungs, rolled on the floor, beating his head against the wall until Julie-Marie managed to calm him, to get him to lie down with his head on her lap, and she removed the hawkmoth from his ear canal with a pair of tweezers, but only in stages, because the cornered insect was tenacious, refusing to come out, and now avoided the tweezers, and seemed ready to burst into Jérôme's skull, where it would be impossible to reach, and would flutter against the roof of his skull until the end of time.

There's nothing in the lad's head, it's an empty shell; his mother's gone and passed on her madness.

Meanwhile, Julie-Marie, using a flashlight to work, blindly shredded the wings, the legs, the thorax of the moth, until she could finally remove the remains of the insect, the thorax, head, the tip of a wing, and then: silence was restored, Julie-Marie stroked his hair to soothe him, her fingertips caked in the dust of the hawkmoth's wings, her jeans wet with snot and tears...

Perhaps he should listen to other butterflies, allow them to flutter into his head, maybe then his sister might come back to him, never mind the pain, which she will eventually take away with a pair of tweezers. But the

374

bedroom is empty, gloomy in the yellow light and...

She'll fuck pretty much anyone, she doesn't even charge. My brother told me.

... Julie-Marie is gone, passing him over for other boys that she covers in kisses and caresses, whom she allows to cover her in kisses and caresses, insensible to the pain that Jérôme feels in his belly, in his throat at the very thought of her forbidden, naked body being offered up to hands, to eyes, to lips other than his.

He goes over to the shelves laden with objects he does not recognize, frivolous things alien to the world of the farm, and, suddenly, he sweeps everything from the shelf with the back of his hand. The saucer crashes to the floor and shatters, reducing the perforated strips of charred incense paper to dust. From the wall, he rips a jigsaw puzzle in which white horses, yellow with age, have forever been running across a beach without reaching the end, then tears down the posters pinned over wallpaper peppered with holes over the years.

Jérôme stamps on the slot-in record player until the red plastic shell cracks and shatters from the kicks. He takes Julie-Marie's few vinyl records from their cardboard sleeves, grips them with both hands and snaps them over his knee. One by one, he grabs the dolls and rips off their arms, leaving gaping wounds in their torsos. Then Jérôme spots the schoolbag that has been tossed under the bed for the summer holidays. He sits down on the carpet and catches his breath. He crouches down, reaches in, grabs a strap and pulls the bag towards him. He opens it and pulls out the exercise books filled with careful cursive handwriting. He shreds the pages one by one, takes out the pencil case from the bag and opens the zip. A rain of little notes falls over his lap. Dozens of scraps of paper torn from the squared pages of exercise books and neatly folded. Jérôme unfolds them and lays them on the carpet in rows, the same letters, the same words, written by different hands, clumsy scrawls he manages to decipher with difficulty –

SLUT
DIRTY PIG
WHORE

– while the dolls pour onto the floor a bloodbath of stuffing.

—

Henri rummages in the car for a bottle of water and drains it in one gulp. When he turns back towards the old oak, he catches a faint glimpse of the animal, standing motionless on the boundary of their lands where the figure of the father stood. Henri closes his eyes, runs a hand over his face, but when he opens them again, the boar is still there, in plain sight. A light breeze is blowing in the opposite direction and the Beast has probably not sensed his presence. Henri reaches his hand through the rolled-down window, gropes along the seat, never taking his eye off the animal, he feels his fingers close around the barrel of the rifle and pulls it towards him. He glances back towards the road. He has no time to warn the sons; it would mean letting the boar escape again.

Henri walks perhaps a hundred metres along the edge of the maize field. From the road, he is now looking down over the coomb over which the crop field extends. The ears will soon be harvested, and right now are almost two metres tall. They sway gently in a light breeze, obstructing Henri's view as he struggles to gauge his distance from the boar. To reach the animal, he must either skirt around the field or walk through it. Either way, the dense barrier formed by the maize means that he will lose sight of it. The brambles on the edge of the crop fields would hamper his progress and make it difficult to get close, so he decides to cut across the field. If he heads due east, he should come to the spot where the boar is standing. Henri sets off through the maize, pushing the heavy ears aside with the back of his hand. Although he leans on the rifle butt for support, every step requires a considerable effort. He moves silently along the furrow, staring at the dry, cracked earth beneath his feet. At this hour, the damp twilight still hovers over the field, exuding the sweet smell of maize mingled with that of the soil. From time to time, Henri looks up. As the sun bursts over the horizon, he is forced to close his eyes – the pupils abnormally dilated by his fever – against the blinding glare. On his closed eyelids, he sees an afterimage of the blazing sun and the moving shadow of the Beast.

He advances painfully. The field seems to become more impenetrable as he progresses, the ears of maize standing stiffly as though to block his path. The chalky leaves slap against his arms, his face. Feeling himself suffocating, Henri pauses, hunkers down and lays one hand on the ground. All around, the field is rustling softly, a gentle hiss like a sea swell, and it feels as though the earth itself is beginning to sway, as though he can suddenly sense its perpetual motion. He feels drained by an exhaustion that is age-old, as old as the earth and its forlorn rotation. Henri lays the rifle on the ground, curls up like a hunting dog, and whimpers, his teeth chattering, and eventually he dozes off.

He wakes to see a golden ground beetle, its shimmering wing-cases a metallic green, scuttle across his hand, drop to the ground and disappear between the tangled, adventitious roots. Henri gazes up at the sky towards which the ears of maize are pointing. He does not know whether he has been asleep, in a dreamless, formless sleep, or whether he passed out. He grabs the rifle and hauls himself to his feet using the butt. Many hours have clearly passed, because the sun is now high in the sky. Henri no longer knows which direction to take. He looks around to find his own footprints on the tamped, dusty ground and then continues his groping progress through the reddish ears of maize, pushing them aside with the rifle barrel before quickly moving forward, slashing at the stalks, which bend and break under the weight of the ripe ears.

Suddenly, he finds himself on the edge of the field, by a stony path. He glances around, struggling to catch his breath. He does not recognize anything, not even the field from which he has just emerged, which now seems to be a meadow of wild grasses, or the surrounding hills, which are melting from the light and his blurred vision. Henri does not recognize the topography, the crop rotation, or even a single tree that might confirm that he is still somewhere on the Plains. A flock of ducks passes overhead and he looks up, shielding his eyes with his hand, watching them fly away, expecting to see them suddenly disappear. He takes a few steps along the path, stumbling over the stones. Surely that is the boar he can suddenly see straight ahead of him? It looks to him as though the animal has raised its head. Is it possible that the Beast has been waiting for him all this time, while he was wandering lost in the field of maize? Henri dares not move, and the animal casually trots off along the stone path, stopping now and then and turning its head towards Henri, as though gauging the distance that separates them, making sure that the man is definitely following.

Henri hesitates, glances around, feels his feverish forehead, then follows the animal, skirting copses and thickets. With an astonishingly agile bound, the Beast leaps over the ditch that separates the path from a field ground that looks like tillage, an expanse of fallow land covered with tall grasses through which the boar lurches, leaving a large breach in its wake. Henri in turn steps over the narrow ditch and takes a route that runs parallel to that of the boar, making sure to stay at least ten metres behind and to make no sudden movements. Henri kneels, opens the rifle breech, gripping it tightly to muffle the *click*, loads the chambers and gets to his feet again. He raises the barrel and attempts to get the animal in his sights, but his hands are trembling too much to hold it steady, and the sweat streaming from his forehead into his eyes blinds him.

The Beast begins to move off again, changing its course, and Henri walks on, closing on the animal obliquely. Slowly, they reach the peak of the valley, from which they dominate the strangely tranquil countryside. Henri takes a few steps and surveys the landscape. From here, he should be able to see the Lada Niva, the scattering of farm buildings that circumscribe the Plains, the main road, the village of Puy-Larroque... But whichever way he turns, he sees only a vast expanse of wilderness that looks as though it has been stripped of the presence of men, given up to the ebb and flow of autumn light, vast wooded plains and grasslands on which there is not a single house or village, only the tops of ancient trees. Henri bites the inside of his cheek to make sure that he is not dreaming; a metallic taste washes over his palate.

The Beast has stopped some twenty metres in front of him. Henri is not sure he recognizes the animal. The boar is thinner, sleeker. Its body is covered with a bushy coat. Its bristles are claggy with earth, leaf mould and dry grass. Curved, yellow tusks protrude from either side of the snout, and on its flanks are the white scars left by the chain-link fence. Henri raises the rifle, rests the trembling butt against his shoulder, and takes aim.

Suddenly he recognizes what is in front of him, directly in his sights, the patch of worthless land in the middle of the Plains, this accursed strip of land where the father took his own life the day after general mobilization was declared. And now it is not the Beast but Marcel that he sees; Marcel who walked all this way, carrying this same shotgun; Marcel who unlaced the heavy leather boots he waterproofed with lard, took them off and carefully set them next to each other, tucking his heavy woollen socks inside; Marcel who, bare feet planted in the earth, placed the rifle barrel under his chin and pressed the trigger with a toe slipped through the trigger guard, without a flicker of hesitation, spraying half of his skull into the warm air of a late afternoon, forty-three years ago.

The first thing the sons find is the pickup truck, doors open, hazard lights blinking. They search for the father, they call out to him. The dog they brought with them eventually picks up his scent and, yapping, dashes off down one of the furrows of a field of maize, closely followed by the men. They find Henri, half-conscious, sprawled on his side next to his rifle amid the ears of corn. The sons wraps the father's arms around their shoulders and easily lift him to his feet. This man who

380

for so long they thought of as a colossus, heavy-set, imperious, is almost weightless now, and he lets himself be dragged back to the Lada Niva and laid on the back seat. When they get back to the farmhouse, Gabrielle rushes out to help them get him out of the truck, into the house and up the stairs. While Joël telephones the doctor, Serge and Gabrielle set about undressing Henri, whose trousers are stained with earth and urine, and whose shirt is drenched with sweat. Only then do they see his chest, his stomach, covered with black scabs, red patches, and yellowing bruises caused by his constant scratching.

'Jesus fucking Christ,' Serge whispers.

They manage to sit him up and pull on a T-shirt. Henri watches them, his eyes half-closed; he looks like one of the pathetic, shrivelled, worn-out old men in hospices who it is impossible to imagine were ever anything other than these pale imitations of human beings.

An hour later, when he leaves Henri's bedside after his examination, the doctor joins them in the kitchen and sets his briefcase on the table. Gabrielle pours him a cup of coffee, but he waves it away.

'You should have called an ambulance straightaway,' he says. 'We need to get him to hospital.'

'Have you seen the marks on his body?' Serge says. 'What's wrong with him?'

'Lymphoma. Your father has cancer, it's very advanced. He didn't tell you about it?'

The brothers glance at each other and say nothing.

'He came to me a number of months ago complaining of fever, swollen glands...'

'So what did you prescribe?'

'Nothing. We did tests, but he refused treatment. He

381

forbade me from saying anything to any of you. It's not for want of trying, on several occasions. I warned him of the risks he was running... But he refused everything: no treatment, no additional tests, he wouldn't even come to see me at the surgery... You know your father.'

'So, if he goes into hospital now, is there anything that can be done? Is there a chance he might go into remission?' Joël asks.

The doctor shakes his head.

'I don't think you understand. There is no chance of remission. At this stage, treatment is not even an option. The fact that he has survived this long without treatment is a miracle. All anyone can do now is try to alleviate his suffering.'

When the paramedics carry him out of the house, Éléonore, who saw the ambulance drive into the farmyard, opens her door and steps out onto her porch. Joël goes over to her, takes her elbow and leads her to the stretcher. The grandmother looks at her son. She brushes his cheek with her dry palm, runs her fingers through his grey beard. She clasps Henri's hand in gnarled fingers with raddled veins and tendons sharp as blades. She has not seen him for weeks, perhaps months; she barely recognizes him. Henri brings her hand up to his chest, squeezes it briefly, then lets go. The paramedics carry the stretcher across the yard and carefully load it into the ambulance, and the clan gathered in the farmyard watches as it drives away, taking the patriarch with it. For a long time, Éléonore stands there, swaying in the light, leaning on Joël's arm. She says:

'Help me,' and he walks her back to her home and settles her in her chair in the living room.

'He's very sick,' he says. 'He didn't say a word to us.

We didn't know... I'm sorry.'

The grandmother looks at him with her pale, stern eyes.

'For a mother, even one as old as I am, even one who knows she'll soon be dead, to see her son die, it should be... I'm the one who is sorry... Sorry for losing him ... I lost him so long ago now that I feel nothing.'

She beats her narrow chest with the flat of her hand, then beats it again.

'Don't you understand? I don't feel anything. I don't even feel grief any more.'

—

Serge steps away from the farm, losing himself in the local bars. Now he rarely gets up before mid-afternoon and spends hours slumped on the sofa with the television on in the background, chain-smoking, drinking endless coffees and bottles of Johnnie Walker that quickly strew the floor, before disappearing again until dawn the following morning. Soon, Joël is the only one to take the path to the pig sheds. One morning, he finds that the infection has spread to all the pig units. He sends a first set of samples to the laboratory, but the test results that come a week later are all negative. When he gets them, Joël walks back to the house, goes into the kitchen and tosses the papers on the table, where Serge is sitting.

'Look at them. There's nothing. Absolutely fucking nothing! No sign of pathogens in the blood samples, nothing in the miscarried foetuses. No bacteria, no antigens. They found small amounts of mycotoxins in the feed, but not enough to explain the miscarriages.'

Serge stares vacantly at the papers.

'Well, that's good,' he says.

Joël suddenly spreads the papers in front of him.

'This morning, I found two more dying sows... We're getting more and more deaths in the feedlot, sick sows in the farrowing house and there's no end to the miscarriages... None of it makes sense...'

Serge lights a cigarette. His hands now tremble visibly, the large purple circles under his eyes eat into his cheek. He says nothing, but takes a deep drag on his cigarette, stifling a spasm of pleasure or disgust.

'If you could see him,' he says, blowing a plume of smoke, 'if you could see him in his hospital gown, with his arse hanging out... He's completely pathetic... I sat next to him for hours, waiting for him to wake up, you know... And when he opened his eyes and he saw me sitting by his bedside, he waved me closer... I could tell it took him every ounce of strength just to wave me over... So I got up from the chair and I leaned over to listen... and d'you know what he said? He told me to leave... Yep, told me to get out of his sight... So I wouldn't have to see him in that state, reduced to... Told me to let him die alone, with dignity... What kind of son would do that? What kind of son would leave his father to die alone... I didn't move, I wasn't sure I had heard him right, or maybe I wanted to reason with him... He grabbed me by the shirt and yelled at me to get out... He managed to scream at me to get out... He spat in my face like he never wanted to see me again... and jerked his finger towards the door so roughly he pulled out the IV drip and started bleeding all over the sheet and he didn't even notice... Me – after everything I've done for him, after I sacrificed my whole fucking life for the man... that's how... that's how he treats me ... And d'you want to know what I did? I said nothing, Joël... I didn't say a fucking word... I did what I've been doing ever since I was born... I obeyed, I put my head down, gave up and left the hospital room...'

He stubs the cigarette out in the bottom of his coffee cup. At first, Joël is silent, then he gets to his feet and says:

'We'll take things in hand. I've told Leroy to come take another set of samples from the sows. We'll have more tests done. Sooner or later, they'll find out what's going on. I counted more than thirty miscarriages in the past month. You have to help me, Serge, otherwise the animals are going to die in droves.'

'You really don't get it, do you? All this... The units... the pigs... We're not up to it, you and me, it's... We're never going to solve anything, fix anything...'

Serge grabs the bottle of Johnnie Walker and is about to pour another glass, but Joël snatches it and hurls it against the wall, where it shatters.

'You're as much to blame as me, you get that? As much as me, and as much as the old man.'

Serge shrugs.

'Yeah, sure, fine. So what?'

Joël jabs an accusing finger at Serge, then gives up and storms out of the house, slamming the door so hard he splits the frame.

—

Jérôme looks at the dolls. He and Julie-Marie went on holiday with them countless times. Whenever she decided, it was holiday time; then she would haphazardly stuff a few things into a suitcase, a pair of shorts, a few T-shirts, some underwear and socks, and she would lead Jérôme to the rusty carcass of the Renault 4CV propped up on breeze blocks in the long grass at the back of the farmhouse.

385

Julie-Marie would settle him next to the dolls in the back seat and tell him to keep an eye on his sisters and not to bother them, because it only takes a second for an accident to happen, a momentary distraction and, *bam crash wallop*, you've got a tragedy on your hands, you end up in a ditch or wrapped around a tree, your body broken and tangled with the arms and legs, the hollow heads of the dolls... She would slam the creaking door, whose windows had long since turned green, and, for the time it took her to walk around the car, she would leave Jérôme alone inside the car that smelled of rust and hot metal, of rotting foam seats soaked with the piss of the cats who took shelter here, crawling in through one of the many gaps made in the bodywork by time, rust and humidity.

Then Julie-Marie would settle into the driver's seat, facing the missing steering wheel – the fathers stripped the wrecked cars and sold the pieces for spare parts – adjusted the rearview mirror on which the silvering is pitted, made sure that the imaginary siblings were sitting quietly; then she would announce their destination – which was never anything other than 'the sea' or 'the mountains', the only places they knew existed in the outside world – before slotting the invisible key into the ignition, cursing when the missing engine coughed and spluttered, and then finally sat back in her seat with a satisfied air, arms outstretched in the empty space, when she heard it purr into life.

They would drive off, leaving behind the farm, Puy-Larroque, the familiar fields, and Jérôme would listen as Julie-Marie described the landscapes they were passing through, harbouring curious treasures, troglodyte villages, volcanoes that belched clouds of ash and spilled glowing lava down their slopes, lakes from whose still, shimmering surface leapt flying fish with metallic scales, vast grey cities which rose up into the sky, fashioned by the hands of men, while steep granite cliffs crumbled into the roiling seas as they drove past, risking their lives along the winding ribbon of road. Jérôme would listen, staring at the overgrown garden through the green windows of the Renault 4CV, seeing nothing but the wrecks of cars, vans, washing machines, and his head would begin to nod and he would doze off. He would wake up a moment later: Julie-Marie was no longer in the car, the door was open. When the sun blazed, the battered car was like a furnace. Sometimes it was one of the fathers, sometimes Catherine or Gabrielle who would call to him from the yard and wake him, sweating, from his daydreams. At such moments he truly had the impression of having travelled through space and time, through infinite dimensions and other universes.

When Julie-Marie was driving, Jérôme would sometimes grab the dolls, pull their hair, bang them against the windows or the seats, or twist their arms and legs, while Julie-Marie scolded and threatened that if they carried on misbehaving she would pull over on the side of the road, get in the back and give them a good thrashing, something she would promptly do, suddenly jerking the invisible steering wheel, braking as hard as possible, getting out of the car and throwing open the rear door. She would climb into the back or order Jérôme to take down his trousers and underpants and get over her knee so she could give him a spanking, muttering *you're-a-very-naughty-boy* in the same tone she used to scold the dolls when they refused to eat the mud porridge she gave them, and Jérôme would wriggle voluptuously as she slapped his bare buttocks, pressed against Julie-Marie's thighs, able to feel all the prickly, translucent little hairs

like the dolls lying dead on the carpet, become super-
fluous, redundant, like all the things Julie-Marie now
seems ashamed of and dismisses as childish? Toys fit for
a baby or a little girl, while she now prefers the boys from
the outside world... Does she put on shows for them, perform sexy dances? Has she played *make believe* or *only
pretend* the way she used to with him, when she would
make him kiss her closed fist, squeezing her fingers tight
and pressing her hand to his mouth?

'You stick out your tongue and twirl it around, keep
your eyes closed. Close your eyes, I said!'

And Jérôme would practise on his own fist, and later
on a hole in the bark of a tree, a hollow in a misshapen
stone, the mouth of one of the dogs, which would joyful-
ly lick his face with its pink, soft tongue.

'What are you doing, you filthy little pig?'

Julie-Marie had popped her head around the door of
one of the kennels where Jérôme used to go, back when
he was still small enough to crawl inside and lie down
entirely on the straw and smelly old blankets. He looks
at her without even thinking about taking his hand from
the sheath of the dog he is masturbating for the very
good reason that the dog enjoys it. Julie-Marie shakes
her finger under her nose and frowns. She scolds him
now, and drags him from the kennel by his feet.

How can he know what is good and what's bad? The
dog likes it, doesn't he? Is it really more wicked than
sticking a tongue into his fist, or even between the silken
thighs of Julie-Marie when she lies down in a makeshift
bed in the middle of a wheat field and pushes her knick-
ers down to her knees covered with scabs and grazes?

*We're not supposed to do it any more, we're not supposed to
do it any more.*

Why is it not wrong to hit the animals, to rip away

hunks of flesh, to smash their heads against a wall or drown them in a bucket, and why is it wrong to give pleasure to the animals or to Julie-Marie? Even Gabrielle lectures him when she catches him playing with his own penis or those of the twins.

'Stop tugging on it or it'll fall off. Don't do that in front of other people. And leave the twins in peace.'

Jérôme sees Henri set the piglet down on the duck-board and point the scalpel in his direction; one of the testicles he has just cut is still stuck to the side of his hand.

'You know that way you've got of looking at your sister, well I don't like it one fucking bit.'

Don't the fathers masturbate the boars to multiply the pigs 'like the loaves and fishes'? His body is not distinct from those of animals, of plants, of stones. He desires them all equally.

What can he do to hold on to Julie-Marie, to make sure things do not change and disappear? Little Émilie Seilhan, who drowned in the washhouse pond she had been forbidden from playing near, has never changed. The cameo photograph set into the marble headstone has simply faded with time, the glass has been covered by greenish moss, but she is still the same little girl with the same faraway stare, the same pale skin, wearing her dress with crocheted collar and cuffs; she will never tire of the games Jérôme plays with her, she will always be waiting at the bottom of the old washhouse pool, ready to listen to the stories he makes up, to follow his snake hunts, to swim beneath him amid the shadows and the algae. Does she play, or does she simply remember, making vague, weary gestures out of habit, mere memories of games? It hardly matters, since she will forever be little Émilie Seilhan, his one and only friend, frozen in the memory of Puy-Larroque when she drowned in the washhouse pool – around which the villagers erected stakes and a chain-link fence that has quickly rusted – and who is mentioned in warning to children, *don't you go playing near the old washhouse or you'll end up like little Émilie*, or *like the little Seilhan girl*, though most of them are not sure she ever truly existed.

This is what it would take to keep Julie-Marie: for her to sink to the bottom of the washhouse pool, or the bottom of the lake. She would probably go willingly if she was aware of the insidious changes taking place in them, of the discord, the tensions caused by her. And if Catherine or the fathers should forget, Jérôme will always be there to remember his sister as she was, as she should always be.

He could bring her back to life whenever he wanted, as he does little Émilie Seilhan, and she would spend the rest of her time partly in the alluvial mud of the lake, partly in the earth of Puy-Larroque cemetery. To make sure that she did not find the time too long, he would slip the dolls into Julie-Marie's coffin, having persuaded Gabrielle to refill and sew up their bellies. He would line them up around the sides, pressed against the pleated silk padding, and Julie-Marie would wear her tutu in pale pink tulle so she could pirouette at the bottom of the lake and teach little Émilie Seilhan to do *pas de chats* and *sauts de biches*.

Or, after he drowned Julie-Marie in the lake, Jérôme would carry her body to the old ruined chapel and lay it on the altar sometimes dappled with coloured light from the last stained-glass window. She would remain perfectly unscathed, like a photograph beneath a glass cameo set into a gravestone, like the princesses in the fairytales she used to read, who lie in castles buried in dark forests or in glass coffins.

—

Has she been asleep for days, for weeks, for months? She feels as though she has woken from an unfathomable bottomless night where time has been abolished, from a narcotic limbo in which images and voices were projected onto the vortex of her ruined consciousness without her being certain that she could distinguish between them.

She sits on the edge of the bed. A dull blue line behind the curtains, through the gap between the shutters. Catherine gets up and walks to the window and opens it. She pushes back the shutters and they bang against the outside wall. Dawn is diluting the darkness of the farmyard. She breathes in the scents of autumn, the smell of the brimming earth, the rotting trunks, the layers of leaf mould. She surveys the chiaroscuro of the bedroom. The things, the objects appear to her exactly as they are, static and pathetic: the limescale-streaked vase next to the bed, the picture Julie-Marie drew long ago on the bare plaster, the dressing table whose mirror traps the diaphanous reflection of the room and her dried-up body in her nightdress.

When Jérôme was born, her mother, knowing nothing of the cancer growing in her own breast, spent all day sitting in the plastic hospital chair next to her. This is what Catherine remembers, this, and the impression of a determinism she can never escape: she will one day be forced to sit by a hospital bed, to sit by her own daughter, and though old and disillusioned, she will be forced to rejoice at the birth of this child, this grandchild, to see

392

the lineage, even if corrupt, carried on, or perhaps, satisfied that there is a place in the world for this child, that there is meaning and legitimacy to this new life, to this continuation, that there is truth and beauty in all this.

Catherine takes off her nightdress, folds it and sets it on the rush seat of the chair. She feels a chill course through her and runs a hand over her arm, her breast, her side. The sensation is no longer one of pain; she feels the presence of this body that had become alien to her, that she once more incarnates, as though she has breathed new life into herself. She observes with a new acuity its gestures, its feelings, its contours, the downstrokes and the upstrokes. She walks over to the dresser, opens a drawer and randomly chooses the clothes she will put on. Did she not wake up one morning after Jérôme was born, crushed by a baleful sense, a vast shadow, that left her for dead, as though expelled from herself, unable to care for the child, unable even to care about him?

A bright spring day, when the feathery buds of the magnolia in the fallow field split open to reveal soft, white petals and the body of her mother, ravaged by chemotherapy and by surgeries, is laid to rest, she cannot even get out of the car unaided. Gabrielle and Serge have to support her every step of the way as she moves through the small cemetery following the funeral procession, so deathly pale that it seems that it is she they are about to bury. The daylight sears her retinas, and the cawing of crows that keep their distance, perching on the tombstones, bores into her eardrums. In fact, she feels no grief, nor even sympathy for her father, lost among all the people, all this ritual, glancing around for his daughters' approval – am I sitting in the right place? Am I behaving appropriately? Am I saying the right words? Am I going

393

in the right direction? Catherine would like to hide him from her view, to blot out the light and the voices, the feeling of Serge's hand on her arm, the black hole of the grave, the sympathetic mourners and the cawing of the crows. As soon as the ceremony is ended, she begs Serge to drive her home. The death of her mother, the solitude of the father she sees less and less, her own divagation, punctuated by periods of remission in which she finds the children changed, grown up, more distant and more alien, before she is once again engulfed by her private shadows; this is the story of the next eleven years, until this damp, chill autumn morning at daybreak when she makes her preparations, knowing nothing of the plight of the pig farm, of the long-supressed violence now unleashed and about to swoop on them. In the silence, she dresses, filled with a sudden realization: there is nothing now to keep her prisoner. Not these walls, nor the men. Not even the children, whose presence she somehow senses beyond the walls. What has she ever had to offer them?

She takes nothing with her. She leaves the room and walks along the corridor. As she passes the sepulchral bedroom of the patriarch, she sees the door has been left ajar, and she stares at the bare mattress, at the elastic straps of the mattress protector hugging the corners. On the nightstand, the photograph frame lies in shadows. The photograph looks as though it has been blackened with a magnifying glass, as though the storm brewing in the background has reached the branches of the hazel tree, has reached Élise, engulfing her completely. All that remains is the figure of a child, still running, never reaching the edge of the frame, who now seems to be fleeing the ominous darkness pursuing him. Catherine goes down the stairs as quietly as possible. As she heads for the front door, she sees Serge slumped on the sofa in the living room that reeks of smoke, stale sweat and the alcohol fumes he exhales as he sleeps. She goes over, stares at him for a long time, before bending down and laying a hand to his forehead. He whimpers in his sleep and then falls silent; Catherine turns away. She opens the front door and leaves the farm. She walks past the dark ditches, sometimes running jerkily for a short distance, and with each step she breaks the invisible ties that bind her. The scutch grass on the verge crunches beneath her shoes. Further off, towards the Plains, as the sun rises, migratory birds take wing from the powerlines and the trees where they perched for the night, forming vast ink blots in the sky. When Catherine eventually glances back over her shoulder, the farm is no longer visible, a huge sleeping beast, mired beyond the valleys of the Plains.

—

Joël works like a man possessed, alone among the pigs, breathing the putrid miasma of the pig sheds. His muscles are sapped, his arms ache with tendinitis. Every day, the ritual is the same. In addition to the daily maintenance, he inspects the stalls, tosses the stillborn piglets and the placentas into buckets, washes down the animal pens with a pressure hose and tirelessly scrapes the concrete.

The acrid stench of Cresyl and slurry attacks his bronchia, burns his sinuses and his throat. Sometimes, he still believes that he might manage to contain the epidemic, that he might find favour in the eyes of Henri, perhaps even of Serge. He will prove his worth to them.

Perhaps he might even bring the news to his dying father in his hospital bed, explain to him how he saved
the piggery. A moment later, the very notion seems stu-
pefying. Why should he break his back to save the pig
units everyone has abandoned? Is he not the one who
has dreamed that the family business, the farm, the
clan would collapse? But does he not owe it to Serge, to
Catherine? And, after all, to Jérôme?

He tries to push back the tide of the excrement produced
by the pigs, and the slurry pit relentlessly continues to
fill, but it is an impossible task, one that would require
two or three men. The phone in the office rings all day
long, but he never has the time or the energy to answer.
Because the shit continues to collect in corners, quickly
forming stinking, infectious little mounds where flies
come to lay their eggs, the same flies that swarm around
the pigs, clustering around their eyes, the snouts, around
every orifice. Soon, pale larvae begin to hatch, millions
of them slithering through the mud that overflows from
the drainage channels and over the walkways as slowly
and inexorably as a lava flow.

By the end of September, the contagion has spread to
every building in the piggery. Joël begins to dread that
he too could be infected. Does he, too, not breathe in this
miasma? Does he not spend all day handling the pigs?
When he showers, he washes himself with bleach, and
the smell soon begins to trail after him, though he never
quite gets rid of the stench of the pigs. Before long, su-
perficial burns cover his eyelids, his lips, his genitals. He
rubs his skin with surgical spirit, whimpering in pain.
    He continues to tip the waste behind the pig units,
but all too quickly there are the bodies of the stillborn

396

piglets, then the gilts, then the fattening pigs to be loaded onto the barrow and removed from the units. Almost
all the sows are now suffering from purulent metritis.
Thick, blood-streaked pus flows off their vulvas and
collects in large pinkish pools that mingle with the shit
on the floor of the pens. Joël tries to help them to stand.
He pushes at their rumps, desperately beats them with a
stick. They try to stand in order to get away from him,
but collapse under their own weight. They shriek, and
he begins to shriek with them.

Joël loses all track of time. An hour spent in the pig units
feels like an eternity. After a time, he no longer leaves.
He sleeps in the father's office, on a bench in the changing room, or sometimes on the floor. He eats the grain
intended for the pigs. He pisses and shits like them in the
middle of the walkways. Behind the bars of the stalls, the
dying animals crawl through a sea of slurry. He decides
to slaughter them, with all his strength, with a pickaxe
buried in their skulls. Seeing him kill one of their own,
the sows no longer have the strength to try to flee; they
crumple and wait for their turn to come.
  The lighter carcasses he manages to pile up on the
flagstone over the pit, then he douses them in petrol and
sets them ablaze. Columns of oily smoke rise in the stagnant air. The stench of the contaminated crimson flesh
makes him puke his guts up so he decides to simply toss
the bodies into the slurry pit, where they float, swell with
the gases released during putrefaction, and eventually
explode.

Because he can no longer find the strength, Joël stops
feeding the animals. Starving and sick, the pigs become
aggressive. They begin to attack each other. When one

suffers a prolapse, the others sometimes eat the organs, leaving the pig disembowelled and half-dead. The rats no longer hide. Hundreds of them swarm into the pens, swimming through the faecal sludge Joël can no longer contain, leaping from one dead body to another, feasting on the bodies, devouring the cartilage first, the ears, the snouts, before starting on the thick layers of fat. As he is trying to haul the carcass of a young boar from one of the pig sheds, Joël hears a cracking sound in his back and crumples to the ground, felled by the pain. He has to crawl over to the railings of the stall to pull himself to his feet. Ever since, he simply leaves the bodies to rot.

One morning, he is woken from sluggish sleep by the telephone ringing. He finally answers.

'Jesus Christ, I've been trying to get in touch with you for over a week!'

'I'm sorry – who is this?' Joël says, hoarse from his constant shouting and from the acid of the pig sheds.

'It's Leroy. That you, Serge? How are things there?'

'It's Joël... Things are... well... it's pretty complicated, here... Is there any news?'

'Yeah. I had the lab run more exhaustive tests on the last round of samples. Something about the haematologic profiles didn't add up, so I wanted to double-check. The leukocyte count was off. The count had been fine up until now, that's what misled me and cost us valuable time. The samples show an increase in monocytes and...'

'Can you be more clear?' interrupted Joël.

'It's a sign that the pigs' immune system is out of whack, that there's a chronic infection in the livestock. I asked for more tests from a specialized laboratory. Turns out that twenty-two of twenty-five sows and five of the six stillborn piglets tested positive to brucellosis...'

'It's not possible,' Joël says.

'I grant you it's pretty rare, especially with enclosed breeding. The usual cause is contamination by a wild boar, or sometimes through contact with carrion...'

'With carrion?'

'From small animals, for example... Though it's not impossible that a carrier was brought in with the last batch of gilts.'

Joël says nothing for a moment but stares at the livestock planner on the wall opposite.

'How do we deal with it?' he says at length.

'There's only one way, I'm afraid: all the animals will have to be destroyed. An abattoir will be requisitioned by the Veterinary Services Directorate, sealed trucks will come and collect the animals from the farm. They'll be counted in and counted out to make sure that there are no escaped animals. Listen... there's something else I need to tell you... This type of epidemic is considered to be the responsibility of the breeder... There is no question of there being any compensation.'

After he hangs up, Joël wanders, dazed, among the pens. The pigs behind the barriers are no longer squealing. A strange silence hovers over the piggery. From time to time, a cloud of flies, disturbed by a rat or the convulsions of a dying pig, rise to reveal a carcass, and the air is filled with buzzing, then they settle again, drape the carcass with a quivering metallic shroud. Here and there, a healthy half-starved boar or gilt can be seen wading through the putrid sludge of a pen, avoiding the half-buried carcasses. Their pale skin covered by layers of excrement makes their eyes, wide with terror and hunger, seem clearer, more penetrating. They see the man pacing the walkways, taking small steps, gripping the planks and railings of the enclosures so he can extricate his boots from the slurry. His face, his neck, his hands, his arms are also spattered with shit and pus. His eyes move sightless from one pig to the next. He draws back the bolts, raises the latches, opens the pens. Some of the pigs burst from the stalls into the walkways, looking around wildly. Joël pushes open the great sliding doors, allowing sunlight and fresh air to sweep the pestilence from the buildings.

He goes out to the back of the pig units, followed by young, blinded animals, weaving their way across the large flagstone, not knowing which way to run. One of them runs into the boundary fence and falls into the slurry pit. Stock-still, his arms hanging limp, the man watches as it floats among the corpses for a moment before it sinks, disappearing in viscid swirls. Joël goes around the pig units to the storeroom where Henri stores the jerrycans of petrol, loads them onto a barrow which he pushes to the hay barn. He unscrews the cap of one of the canisters and pours half of it over the ricks and the bales. He then goes into each of the pig units, moving down the walkways, holding a jerrycan high above the pens and stalls, splashing the wooden partitions, the piles of carcasses, the feed trolleys filled with grain. Swarms of rats escape across the roof beams. The healthy pigs bolt as he approaches, letting out an endless wail. Others, half-dead, lie on their flanks, and from their open mouths there comes only a deep groan as Joël douses them with petrol.

—

Jérôme wakes on a bed of springy twigs and russet leaves. He returns from among the dead, from a sleep without dreams, without consciousness that, at first, he struggles to shake off, engulfed by nothingness. Through half-closed eyes, the daylight catches on his lashes in explosions of colour and quivering lines. Majestic nebulae of shadows merge and sunder. He feels nothing, neither the weight of his body resting on the vegetal bed, nor the shadow of the ruins. He has no recollection of the preceding hours, nor of a previous existence; he is filled only by a feeling of deep, deafening peace. Then, the diffuse, impalpable world re-emerges as the child returns to his own surfaces. He feels his aching muscles, the envelope of his body. He opens his eyes and sees the treetops, the branches between which the pale sky crumbles and falls, then, leaning one hand on the ground, he sits up.

The child recognizes his temple, the ruins of walls buried beneath thick ivy, the flagstones displaced by roots, between which grow saxifrage and dry stalks of foxgloves, the powdery remains of timbers and gravel. His pale eyes move over the scene, and then he gets to his feet, reeling a little before finding his balance. Where the choir once stood, the child finds an ossuary, antlers green with moss supported on stones, scattered furs and strips of leather that hang from huge, dry branches like delicate, softly hissing fruits, skeletal remains piled up to create animist ossuaries, where the pale skulls of rodents are cleverly dovetailed with those of small carnivores, greyish skeletons with delicate ribcages, the tusks of wild boars, vertebrae of every kind strung on slender cords, wisps of brindle fur, red or brown, the tails of squirrels, of foxes, of badgers, the remains of toads and hedgehogs squashed on the roads. Against the apse, blurred shapes give up their mysteries in streams of blackish fluid.

The child bursts from between the thickets of

brambles, stumbles between the trees. Arms stretched out before him, he walks like a blind man, bumps into tree trunks, trips over stones, plunges down ditches and falls into the dry riverbeds of brooks and streams. When he finally reaches the edge of the wood, he rushes into the light and walks down the middle of the road, a drunken urchin dressed in rags, scratched by thorns, arms hanging limp, besmirched with mud from the lake, his face hidden beneath a brown mask, from which wild eyes stare out. He moves like an animal, his body shaken by spasms and shudders, his limbs twitching with sudden jerky movements as hoarse, uncontrollable sounds emerge from his throat. He walks past the cemetery, where the gravestones exude the smell of sepulchres and sweet stone. The dead who lie beneath the earth and the marble tombstones nostalgically recall the sun of each day dipping behind the valleys of Puy-Larroque, leaving a sky so crimson and spectacular that it brought a pang of emotion to even the oldest among them to their dying day.

When he reaches the farm, Jérôme stops in the middle of the yard. Pigs are wailing close by, wild-eyed piglets scurry between the broken cars, the rusted remains of agricultural machinery and washing machines, the gutted sofas on which chickens perch and squawk. An acrid smoke rises from behind the house, a black tombstone against the cloudless morning sky. In the kennels, the dogs are barking frantically, charging the chain-link fence which bends under the weight of the pack. Spittle sprays from their mouths and gets caught in the mesh of the fence. The child watches as the column of smoke sucks up hot embers that glow and whirl and disappear. The crackling blaze grows louder. A gilt hurtles around a corner of the building, letting out a long, shrill wail.

She stumbles across the yard, flanks smeared with soot, bristles charred, flesh raw, trailing a smell of burnt pork rind. Suddenly, a few metres from Jérôme, she slows, then crumples, falling onto her flank, her restless trotters twitching. Her eyes blink as she stares up at the sky. The child crouches down and lays a hand on the gilt's head. The lashes of her dark, wide eyes tickle the palm of his hand.

The child walks towards the house, pauses when he comes to the door, then walks on towards the old barn in the west wing of the farmhouse. He taps on the window. The door quickly opens and the old woman appears. She stares at him through eyes reddened by years of sitting by the hearth, and for the first time, the look, which has always seemed to him to be stern, unyielding, is simply that of an old woman who is distraught or perhaps a little mad. The cats dart between her legs and she makes no move to stop them; they race across the farmyard, disappearing under broken engines and piles of scrap iron. Then she sees him, beneath the mud mask, the last of the herd, the boy-so-like-his-uncle, the filthy, mute, unruly bastard. He holds out his hands and she looks down at the open hands and palms the child is showing her, caked in mud like the rest of him. She grabs him by the wrists, flexing her scrawny arms with their pale, translucent skin. The child feels the gentle pressure of her fingers. She gently pulls him towards her and he steps into the dark room. Still gripping the boy's arm, the old woman closes the door. She leads him into the kitchen, to the sink. She lifts up his T-shirt and takes it off, revealing his pale belly, his skinny torso. The child makes no protest. The walls muffle the cries of the dogs and the pigs; they cannot yet hear the distant wail of the fire truck speeding towards the farm. In the eyes of the old woman, the boy sees a profound weariness, and he realizes that she might have lived for a thousand years before he was born. In her pale eyes, he also sees something else, something to which he cannot put a name. She recognizes him for what he is. She realizes that every second of her life has been leading to this moment, in which she steers the child, one hand on the nape of his neck, bends him over the sink, runs clear water into the hollow of her hands and washes his face.

The Beast is wide awake, unsettled by the proximity of sows in heat, whose smell reaches him through the porous partition walls of the building dedicated to gestation. With his snout, he pushes against the gate of his stall. The latch is slightly loose – it rattles and jiggles every time he hits the metal bars. He headbutts the gate, grips one of the railings in his jaws, pushes, pulls it towards him, then pushes again, and gradually the screws come loose from their sockets. After hours of patient manipulation, the bolt and the latch clatter onto the bare concrete walkway, the gate swings open and the boar charges, ready to face the wall of men massed against him. He trots past other stalls, he smells four other breeders that wake as he passes, and, beyond the porous walls, the whiff of nervous gilts, of pregnant sows and piglets. His hulking mass moves silently through the darkness.

He is guided by another smell, one more urgent than that of sows in heat; it is the faint scent of the night, filtering through the chinks and cracks of the building. The Beast trots back along the walkway to the main door. He presses his snout into the gap, and with a fierce jerk of his head, slides the door back on its track. He steps out onto the huge concrete slab, looks up and takes a breath. The countryside is dark and still. A shudder of excitement trills through the massive body of the boar. For a moment, he glances at the doors of the farrowing house, where the fertile sows have sensed his presence from his pheromones and his heavy breath, then the Beast turns away and trots towards the chain-link fence that bounds the piggery. Beyond, the countryside rolls away, shimmering and fragrant with the scent of grasses and tubers, of unfamiliar animals and small prey, of damp bushes and ancient orchards that are blue in the moonlight. The boar bites and twists and without much difficulty rips the chain-link fence, creating a hole through which he can slip his head, then he rests all his weight on the mesh, bowing the fence and bending the stakes set into concrete. The opening becomes large enough for him to push his forelegs through. The rump, the hands of men grabbing at his ear and twisting, dumping feed into the trough, the hands that make water flow, their hands that guide him towards the motionless sow, grasp his penis, grope and guide him. Finally, the fearsome oval face of men leaning over the railings of the stalls, controlling day and night.

He feeds on acorns, berries, roots, snails, bulbs and chestnuts, sometimes a carcass abandoned by a fox. He grazes on soft grasses, on red alfalfa. His comings and goings create paths through the undergrowth. His bristles grow as the winter cold sets in. His tusks reshape his jaw; the tips raising his upper lip and emerging from the mouth. One day at dusk, he is drawn from his wallow by the barking of a pack of dogs. He bounds from his nest, snuffling the cold air: he can smell the dogs, smell the men moving towards him. He makes his escape, taking one of the paths that lead to the reservoir, where he tries to hide among the withered rushes. Already the dogs are bounding from the woods, where they scented his lair, and are hurtling downhill, cutting through the crop fields, towards the reservoir. The boar moves along the still, black surface, but the dogs continue to race, and they quickly catch him up. They leap down from the bank onto the lake shore, one falls sprawling into the silt and bounds to its feet again. The pig stops, turns to face them. He can see them now; there are three of them, barking and circling around him. Are they surprised not to find a wild boar? None of them attack. They stand at a respectable distance, yapping. Threads of drool trickle from their chops. They breathe great plumes of vapour. The boar scans the lake shore, studies the positions of the dogs, but he would have to run through them to reach the bank, which is too high at this point of the shore for him to scale. From the edge of the woods come the booming sounds of men's voices. The dogs turn and bark in response; then the boar retreats into the mud and feels the icy lap at his belly, his throat, leaving him breathless. The dogs bark louder, but do not dare to come closer. The boar runs into the waters of the lake. Suddenly, he loses *his footing and disappears beneath the surface. Instinctively, he thrashes his legs and manages to resurface. His vast bulk no longer seems to weigh anything. He swims away quickly, trailing a broad wake. Back on the lake shore, the dogs howl. They consider running to the other side of the lake, but the bank is blocked by the building that houses the pumping station, and two huge metal pipes run down to the lake shore and disappear under the water. One of the dogs dives in, swims a few metres, only to turn back and scramble out, shaking itself dry. It has no layers of fat to protect it from the icy water. When they reach the reservoir, the hunters find the dogs running in circles, yapping incessantly, hindquarters low, wagging their tails. There is still a slight swell in the middle of the lake. The gathering darkness is thicker now. One of the men sweeps a flashlight along the shore. Cornered by the pack, the pig took to the water, so the hunter can see no hoof-prints. He thinks perhaps there were some coypu that escaped, then he kneels, grabs the dogs by their collars and, one by one, pulls them back up onto the bank.*

The boar runs through a ploughed field, trips over the hard, frozen furrows, gets to his feet, reaches a thicket of trees and disappears inside. He is cold and shivering, wisps of steam rising from his wet bristles. The men and the dogs leave. He decides not to return to the oak forest, to abandon his nest. He cowers in this grey, withered thicket, which is too sparse to hide him in daylight. When the land is calm once more, he emerges from his refuge and wanders, disoriented, through fields and gloomy orchards. He comes to a wall of stone and mortar and aimlessly follows it. It is the outer wall of a small farmhouse, of which nothing remains but ruins overgrown with thick brambles. Here and there, the wall has crumbled. The boar moves some rubble to clear a path, then a tunnel through the brambles. He comes to a patch of beaten earth, strewn with wooden planks, old broken furniture, roof beams that have fallen and been reduced to powder by time and woodworm. The ceiling and the

Thanks

To the Centre National des Livres
To the dear friends who have accompanied the writing
of this book
To Claudine Fabre-Vassas and to Jean-Louis Le Tacon
for their illuminating works
To the Archives Départementales du Gers.

Co-funded by the
Creative Europe Programme
of the European Union

Co-funded by the Creative Europe Programme of the European Union.
The European Commission support for the production of this publication
does not constitute an endorsement of the contents which reflects the views
only of the authors, and the Commission cannot be held responsible for
any use which may be made of the information contained therein.

Fitzcarraldo Editions
8-12 Creekside
London, SE8 3DX
United Kingdom

ISBN 978-1-910695-57-9

Design by Ray O'Meara
Typeset in Fitzcarraldo
Printed and bound by TJ International

This book is supported by the Institut Français
(Royaume-Uni) as part of the Burgess Programme

fitzcarraldoeditions.com

Fitzcarraldo Editions